Emily Giffin is the internationally bestselling author of *Baby Proof*. She lives in Atlanta with her husband and three young children.

Visit her website at www.emilygiffin.com

LOVE THE ONE YOU'RE WITH

In the diner Leo doesn't see me at first, and that gives me a vague sense of power, which goes when his eyes find mine. He strides toward my table, and I am fearful that he will kiss my cheek. But that isn't his style — Andy kisses my cheek. He looks the same — perhaps bulkier. A stark contrast to Andy's fine features. Andy is easier on the eyes, I think. Andy is easier, *period*. The same way a walk on the beach is easy. A Sunday nap. A square peg in a square hole. 'Ellen Dempsey,' he finally says, staring into my eyes. I couldn't have scripted a better opening line. I stare back into his brown eyes. 'Ellen *Graham*,' I announce proudly.

Books by Emily Giffin
Published by The House of Ulverscroft:

BABY PROOF

EMILY GIFFIN

LOVE THE ONE YOU'RE WITH

Complete and Unabridged

CHARNWOOD
Leicester

First published in Great Britain in 2008 by
Orion Books
an imprint of The Orion Publishing Group Ltd.
London

First Charnwood Edition
published 2009
by arrangement with
The Orion Publishing Group Ltd.
An Hachette Livre UK Company
London

The moral right of the author has been asserted

All the characters in this book are fictitious, and any resemblance to actual persons living or dead is purely coincidental.

British Library CIP Data

Giffin, Emily
Love the one you're with.—Large print ed.—
Charnwood library series
1. Marriage—Fiction 2. Chick lit
3. Large type books
I. Title
813.6 [F]

ISBN 978–1–84782–533–9

Published by
F. A. Thorpe (Publishing)
Anstey, Leicestershire

Set by Words & Graphics Ltd.
Anstey, Leicestershire
Printed and bound in Great Britain by
T. J. International Ltd., Padstow, Cornwall

This book is printed on acid-free paper

For my sweet Harriet

Acknowledgements

Deepest gratitude to Mary Ann Elgin, Sarah Giffin, Nancy Mohler, Lisa Elgin, and Stephen Lee, who were with me from start to finish. I am so lucky to have you.

Heartfelt appreciation to my family and friends, especially Allyson Jacoutot, Jennifer New, Julie Portera, Brian Spainhour, Laryn Gardner, Michelle Fuller, Jim Konrad, Yvonne Boyd, and Carrie Minton.

Many thanks to my fabulous editor Sara O'Keeffe and everyone at Orion Books, and to my wonderful agents, Lorella Belli and Stephany Evans.

An abiding thank you to David 'Sarge' Tinga, my one-of-a-kind mentor and dear friend who will never be forgotten.

And finally, my thanks and love to Buddy, Edward, George, and Harriet.

1

It happened exactly one hundred days after I married Andy, almost to the minute of our half-past-three-o'clock ceremony. I know this fact not so much because I was an overeager newlywed keen on observing trivial relationship landmarks, but because I have a mild case of OCD that compels me to keep track of things. Typically, I count insignificant things, like the steps from my apartment to the nearest subway (341 in comfortable shoes, a dozen more in heels); the comically high occurrence of the phrase 'amazing connection' in any given episode of *The Bachelor* (always in the double digits); the guys I've kissed in my thirty-three years (nine). Or, as it was on that rainy, cold afternoon in January, the number of days I had been married before I saw him smack-dab in the middle of the crosswalk of Eleventh and Broadway.

From the outside, say if you were a cabdriver watching frantic jaywalkers scramble to cross the street in the final seconds before the light changed, it was only a mundane, urban snapshot: two seeming strangers, with little in common but their flimsy black umbrellas, passing in an intersection, making fleeting eye contact, and exchanging stiff but not unfriendly hellos before moving on their way.

But inside was a very different story. Inside, I

was reeling, churning, breathless as I made it onto the safety of the curb and into a virtually empty diner near Union Square. *Like seeing a ghost*, I thought, one of those expressions I've heard a thousand times but never fully registered until that moment. I closed my umbrella and unzipped my coat, my heart still pounding. As I watched a waitress wipe down a table with hard, expert strokes, I wondered why I was so startled by the encounter when there was something that seemed utterly inevitable about the moment. Not in any grand, destined sense; just in the quiet, stubborn way that unfinished business has of imposing its will on the unwilling.

After what seemed like a long time, the waitress noticed me standing behind the Please Wait to Be Seated sign and said, 'Oh. I didn't see you there. Should've taken that sign down after the lunch crowd. Go ahead and sit anywhere.'

Her expression struck me as so oddly empathetic that I wondered if she were a moonlighting clairvoyant, and actually considered confiding in her. Instead, I slid into a red vinyl booth in the back corner of the restaurant and vowed never to speak of it. To share my feelings with a friend would constitute an act of disloyalty to my husband. To tell my older and very cynical sister, Suzanne, might unleash a storm of caustic remarks about marriage and monogamy. To write of it in my journal would elevate its importance, something I was determined not to do. And to tell Andy would be some combination of stupid, self-destructive, and hurtful. I was bothered by the lie of

2

omission, a black mark on our fledging marriage, but decided it was for the best.

'What can I get you?' the waitress, whose name tag read *Annie*, asked me. She had curly red hair and a smattering of freckles, and I thought, *The sun will come out tomorrow.*

I only wanted a coffee, but as a former waitress, remembered how deflating it was when people only ordered a beverage, even in a lull between meals, so I asked for a coffee and a poppy seed bagel with cream cheese.

'Sure thing,' she said, giving me a pleasant nod.

I smiled and thanked her. Then, as she turned toward the kitchen, I exhaled and closed my eyes, focusing on one thing: how much I loved Andy. I loved everything about him, including the things that would have exasperated most girls. I found it endearing the way he had trouble remembering people's names (he routinely called my former boss Fred, instead of Frank) or the lyrics to even the most iconic songs ('Billie Jean is not my mother'). And I only shook my head and smiled when he gave the same bum in Bryant Park a dollar a day for nearly a year — a bum who was likely a Range Rover — driving con artist. I loved Andy's confidence and compassion. I loved his sunny personality that matched his boy-next-door, blond, blue-eyed good looks. I felt lucky to be with a man who, after six long years with me, still did the half-stand upon my return from the ladies' room and drew sloppy, asymmetrical hearts in the condensation of our bathroom mirror. Andy

3

loved *me*, and I'm not ashamed to say that this topped my reasons of why we were together, of why I loved him back.

'Did you want your bagel toasted?' Annie shouted from behind the counter.

'Sure,' I said, although I had no real preference.

I let my mind drift to the night of Andy's proposal in Vail, how he had pretended to drop his wallet so that he could, in what clearly had been a much-rehearsed maneuver, retrieve it and appear on bended knee. I remember sipping champagne, my ring sparkling in the firelight, as I thought, *This is it. This is the moment every girl dreams of. This is the moment I have been dreaming of and planning for and counting on.*

Annie brought my coffee, and I wrapped my hands around the hot, heavy mug. I raised it to my lips, took a long sip, and thought of our year-long engagement — a year of parties and showers and whirlwind wedding plans. Talk of tulle and tuxedos, of waltzes and white chocolate cake. All leading up to that magical night. I thought of our misty-eyed vows. Our first dance to 'What a Wonderful World.' The warm, witty toasts to us — speeches filled with cliché's that were actually true in our case: *perfect for each other . . . true love . . . meant to be.*

I remembered our flight to Hawaii the following morning, how Andy and I had held hands in our first-class seats, laughing at all the small things that had gone awry on our big day: *What part of 'blend into the background' didn't the videographer get? Could it have rained any*

4

harder on the way to the reception? *Had we ever seen his brother, James, so wasted?* I thought of our sunset honeymoon strolls, the candlelit dinners, and one particularly vivid morning that Andy and I had spent lounging on a secluded, half-moon beach called Lumahai on the north shore of Kauai. With soft white sand and dramatic lava rocks protruding from turquoise water, it was the most breath-taking piece of earth I had ever seen. At one point, as I was admiring the view, Andy rested his Stephen Ambrose book on our oversized beach towel, took both of my hands in his, and kissed me. I kissed him back, memorizing the moment. The sound of the waves crashing, the feel of the cool sea breeze on my face, the scent of lemons mixed with our coconut suntan lotion. When we separated, I told Andy that I had never been so happy. It was the truth.

But the best part came after the wedding, after the honeymoon, after our practical gifts were unpacked in our tiny apartment in Murray Hill — and the impractical, fancy ones were relegated to our downtown storage unit. It came as we settled into our husband-and-wife routine. Casual, easy, and real. It came every morning, as we sipped our coffee and talked as we got ready for work. It came when his name popped into my inbox every few hours. It came at night as we shuffled through our delivery menus, contemplating what to have for dinner and proclaiming that one day soon we'd actually use our stove. It came with every foot massage, every kiss, every time we undressed together in the dark. I trained

5

my mind on these details. All the details that comprised our first one hundred days together.

Yet by the time Annie brought my coffee, I was back in that intersection, my heart thudding again. I suddenly knew that in spite of how happy I was to be spending my life with Andy, I wouldn't soon forget that moment, that tightness in my throat as I saw his face again. Even though I desperately wanted to forget it. *Especially* because I wanted to.

I sheepishly glanced at my reflection in the mirrored wall beside my booth. I had no business worrying about my appearance, and even less business feeling triumphant upon the discovery that I was, against all odds on an afternoon of running errands in the rain, having an extraordinarily good hair day. I also had a rosy glow, but I told myself that it was only the cold that had flushed my cheeks. Nothing else.

And that's when my cell phone rang and I heard his voice. A voice I hadn't heard in eight years and sixteen days.

'Was that really you?' he asked me. His voice was even deeper than I remembered, but otherwise it was like stepping back in time. Like finishing a conversation only hours old.

'Yes,' I said.

'So,' he said. 'You still have the same cell number.'

Then, after a considerable silence, one I stubbornly refused to fill, he added, 'I guess some things don't change.'

'Yes,' I said again.

Because as much as I didn't want to admit it, he was sure right about that.

6

2

My favorite movie of all time is probably *When Harry Met Sally*. I love it for a lot of reasons — the good eighties feel to it, the quirky chemistry between Billy Crystal and Meg Ryan, the orgasm scene at Katz's Deli. But my favorite part is probably those little, old, twinkly-eyed couples, perched on the couch, telling their tales of how they met.

The very first time I saw the movie, I was fourteen years old, had never been kissed, and to use one of my sister Suzanne's favorite expressions, was in no hurry to get my panties in a wad over a boy. I had watched Suzanne fall hard for a number of boys, only to get her heart smashed in two, more often than I had my braces tightened, and there was nothing about the exercise that seemed like a particularly good time.

Still, I remember sitting in that over-air-conditioned theater, wondering where my future husband was at that moment in time — what he looked and sounded like. Was he on a first date, holding someone's hand with Jujubes and a large Sprite between them? Or was he much older, already in college and experienced in the ways of women and the world? Was he the star quarterback or the drummer in the marching band? Would I meet him on a flight to Paris? In a high-powered boardroom? Or the produce aisle

7

in the grocery store in my own hometown? I imagined us telling our story, over and over, our fingers laced together, just like those adoring couples on the big screen.

What I had yet to learn, though, is that things are seldom as neat and tidy as that starry-eyed anecdote you share documentary-style on a couch. What I figured out over time is that almost always, when you hear those stories from married couples, there is a little poetic license going on, a romantic spin, polished to a high shine over time. And unless you marry your high school sweetheart (and even sometimes then), there is usually a not-so-glorious back story. There are people and places and events that lead you to your final relationship, people and places and events you'd prefer to forget or at least gloss over. In the end, you can slap a pretty label on it — like serendipity or fate. Or you can believe that it's just the random way life unfolds.

But no matter what you call it, it seems that every couple has two stories — the edited one to be shared from the couch and the unabridged version, best left alone. Andy and I were no different. Andy and I had both.

Both stories, though, started the same way. They both started with a letter that arrived in the mail one stiflingly humid afternoon the summer after I graduated from high school — and just a few short weeks before I'd leave my hometown of Pittsburgh for Wake Forest University, the beautiful, brick school in North Carolina I had discovered in a college catalog and then selected after they offered me a generous scholarship. The letter contained all sorts of important details about curriculum, dorm living, and orientation. But, most important, it included my much-anticipated roommate assignment, typed neatly on a line of its own: Margaret 'Margot' Elizabeth Hollinger Graham. I studied her name, along with her address and phone number in Atlanta, Georgia, feeling both intimidated and impressed. All the kids at my public high school had common names like Kim and Jen and Amy. I didn't know anyone with a name like Margot (that silent *T* got to me the most), and I definitely didn't know anyone with two middle names. I was sure that Margot from Atlanta would be one of the beautiful girls featured in Wake Forest's glossy brochures, the ones wearing pearl earrings and Laura Ashley floral print sundresses to football games. (I had only ever worn jeans and hooded sweatshirts to sporting events.) I was certain that she had a serious boyfriend, and imagined her ruthlessly dumping him by semester's end, moving on to one of the lanky, barefooted boys sporting Greek letters and tossing a Frisbee on the quad in those same brochures.

I remember running inside with that letter to tell Suzanne the news. Suzanne was a rising junior at Penn State and well-versed in the ways of roommates. I found her in our room, applying a thick layer of metallic blue eye liner while listening to Bon Jovi's 'Wanted Dead or Alive' on her boom box.

I read Margot's full name aloud, and then shared my predictions in an accent right out of

Steel Magnolias, my best frame of reference for the South. I even cleverly worked in white pillars, Scarlett O'Hara, and servants aplenty. Mostly I was joking, but I also felt a surge of anxiety that I had picked the wrong school. I should have stuck to Pitt or Penn State like the rest of my friends. I was going to be a fish out of water, a Yankee misfit.

I watched Suzanne step away from her full-length mirror, propped at an angle to minimize the freshman-fifteen she hadn't been able to shed, and say, 'Your accents *suck*, Ellen. You sound like you're from England, not Atlanta . . . And jeez, how 'bout giving the girl a chance? What if she assumed that you were a steel-town girl with no fashion sense?' She laughed and said, 'Oh yeah . . . she'd actually be *right* about that!'

'Very funny,' I said, but couldn't help smiling. Ironically, my moody sister was at her most likable when she was ripping on me.

Suzanne kept laughing as she rewound her cassette and belted out, 'I walked these streets, a loaded six string on my back!' Then she stopped in mid-lyric and said, 'But, seriously, this girl could be, like, a farmer's daughter for all you know. And either way, you might *really* like her.'

'Do farmer's daughters typically have *four* names?' I quipped.

'You never know,' Suzanne said in her sage big-sister voice. 'You just *never* know.'

But my suspicions seemed confirmed when, a few days later, I received a letter from Margot written in perfect, adult handwriting on pale

10

pink stationery. Her engraved silver monogram was the elaborate cursive kind, where the *G* of her last name was larger and flanked by the *M* and *H*. I wondered which rich relative she had slighted by overthrowing the *E*. The tone was effusive (eight exclamation points in all) yet also strangely businesslike. She said she couldn't wait to meet me. She had tried to call me several times but hadn't been able to reach me (we didn't have call-waiting or an answering machine, a fact that embarrassed me). She said she would bring a small refrigerator and her stereo (which played CDs; I still hadn't graduated from cassettes). She was hoping we could buy matching comforters. She had found some cute pink and sage green ones by Ralph Lauren, and offered to pick up two for us if I thought this sounded nice. But if I wasn't a pink person, we could always go with yellow and lavender, 'a fine combination.' Or turquoise and coral, 'equally pleasing.' She just wasn't wild about primary colors in interior designing, but was open to my suggestions. She told me she 'truly' hoped that I would enjoy the rest of my summer and then signed the letter 'Warmly, Margot,' a closing that, oddly enough, seemed more cool and sophisticated than warm. I had only ever signed letters with 'Love' or 'Sincerely' but made a mental note to try 'Warmly' on for size. It would be the first of many things I'd copy from Margot.

I worked up the courage to phone her the next afternoon, clutching a pen and pad in my hand to be sure I didn't miss anything, such as a

11

suggestion that we coordinate our toiletries — keep *everything* in the pastel family.

The phone rang twice and then a male voice said hello. I assumed it was Margot's father, or perhaps it was the gardener in for a tall glass of freshly squeezed lemonade. In my most proper telephone voice, I asked to speak to Margot.

'She's over at the club, playing tennis,' he replied.

Club, I thought. *Bingo*. We belonged to a club, technically speaking, but it was really just the neighborhood pool, called a club, which comprised a small, rectangular pool flanked by a Fritos-serving snack bar on one end, a diving board on the other, all surrounded by a chain-link fence. I was fairly certain that Margot's club was a different sort altogether. I imagined the rows of clay tennis courts, the dainty sandwiches served on china plates, the rolling hills of the golf course spotted with weeping willows, or whatever tree was indigenous to Georgia.

'May I take a message?' he asked. His Southern accent was subtle, only revealing itself in his *I*.

I hesitated, stumbled slightly, and then shyly introduced myself as Margot's roommate-to-be.

'Oh, hey there! This is Andy. Margot's brother.'

And there it was.

Andy. My future husband's name — which I would later learn was short for Andrew Wallace Graham III.

Andy went on to say that he went to

12

Vanderbilt, but that his best friend from home was going to be a senior at Wake Forest, and he and his buddies would be sure to show us the ropes, share their insight about professors and sororities, keep us out of trouble, and 'all that good stuff.'

I thanked him, feeling myself ease somewhat.

'No problem,' Andy said. And then, 'So Margot's going to be excited to hear from you. I know she wanted to discuss bedspreads or curtains or something . . . I sure hope you like the color pink.'

I replied with an earnest, 'Oh. *Yes*. I *love* pink.'

It was a fib that would be recounted for years to come, even working its way into Andy's toast to me at our rehearsal dinner, much to the delight of Margot and our closest friends, all of whom knew that although I had my feminine side, I was far from a girly-girl.

'Well. *Aw*-right,' Andy said. 'A match made in pink heaven.'

I smiled and thought, no matter what else unfolded with Margot, she had a very nice brother.

As it turned out, I was right about both Andy *and* Margot. He *was* nice, and she was just about everything I wasn't. For starters we were physical opposites. She was a petite yet still curvy, fair-skinned, blue-eyed blonde. I had dark hair and hazel eyes, skin that looked tanned even in the dead of winter, and a tall, athletic frame. We were equally attractive, but Margot had a soft, whimsical look about her while my features were

13

more easily described as handsome.

Our backgrounds, too, couldn't be more different. Margot lived in a huge, beautiful home on several acres of gorgeous, tree-lined property in the wealthiest part of Atlanta — an estate by any measure. I grew up in a small ranch with Brady Bunch-orange kitchen counters in a blue-collar part of Pittsburgh. Margot's father was a prominent attorney who also served on the board of several companies. My dad was a salesman — selling unglamorous goods like those projectors for mind-numbingly boring filmstrips that lazy teachers made you watch in elementary school. Margot's mother was a former beauty queen from Charleston, with a Babe Paley-esque fashion sensibility and fine, elegant bones. Mine had been a no-nonsense junior-high pre-algebra teacher before she died of lung cancer, even though she had never smoked, the day before my thirteenth birthday.

Margot had two older brothers, both of whom adored her. Her family was the Southern WASP equivalent of the Kennedys, playing touch football on the beach at Sea Island, taking ski trips every winter, and spending occasional Christmases in Europe. My sister and I spent our vacations at the Jersey Shore with our grandparents. We didn't own passports, had never been out of the country, and had only been on an airplane once.

Margot was a cheerleader and former debutante, brimming with the brand of confidence that belongs to wealthy, well-traveled WASPs. I was reserved, slightly neurotic, and

14

despite my strong desire to belong, far more comfortable on the sidelines of things.

Yet despite our differences, we became best friends. And then, years later, in what would make a perfect documentary-style couch story, I fell in love with her brother. The one I just *knew* would be as cute as he was nice.

But a lot of things had to happen before I married Andy and after that letter from Margot arrived in the mail. A *lot* of things. And one of them was Leo. The one I would love before I loved Andy. The one I would grow to hate, but still love, long after we broke up. The one I would finally, *finally* get over. Then see again, years later, in a New York City crosswalk.

3

'Where are you now?' Leo asks.

I inhale sharply as I consider my answer. For one beat I think he means the question in a philosophical sense — *Where are you in life?* — and I nearly tell him about Andy. My friends and family. My career as a photographer. What a good, contented place I'm in. Answers that, until recently, I scripted in the shower and on the subway, hoping for this very opportunity. The chance to tell him that I had survived and gone on to much greater happiness.

But as I start to say some of this, I realize what Leo is actually asking me. He means *literally* where am I sitting or standing or walking? In what little corner of New York am I digesting and pondering what just transpired?

The question rattles me in the same way you feel rattled when someone asks you how much you weigh or how much money you make or any other personal, probing question you'd strongly prefer not to answer. But, in refusing to answer it outright, you're afraid you'll look defensive or rude. Later, of course, you replay the exchange and think of the perfect, politely evasive response. *Only my scale knows the truth . . . Never enough money, I'm afraid.* Or in this instance: *Out and about.*

But, there in the moment, I always clumsily blurt out the answer. My true weight. My salary

16

down to the dollar. Or, in this case, the name of the diner where I am having coffee on a cold, rainy day.

Oh well, I think, once it's off my tongue. After all, it is probably better to be straightforward. Being evasive could translate as an attempt to be flirtatious or coy: *Guess where I am. Come find me, why don't you.*

Still, Leo answers quickly, knowingly. 'Right,' he says, as if this diner had been a special hangout of ours. Or, worse, as if I were just *that* predictable. Then he asks if I'm alone.

None of your business, I want to say, but instead my mouth opens and I serve up a plain, simple, inviting yes. Like a single red checker sidling up to double-decker black ones, just waiting to be jumped.

Sure enough, Leo says, 'Good. I'm coming over. Don't move.' Then he hangs up before I can respond. I flip my phone shut and panic. My first instinct is to simply get up and walk out. But I command myself not to be a coward. I can handle seeing him again. I am a mature, stable, *happily wed* woman. So what is the big deal about seeing an ex-boyfriend, having a little polite conversation? Besides, if I were to flee, wouldn't I be playing a game that I have no business playing? A game that was lost a long time ago?

So instead I set about eating my bagel. It is tasteless — only texture — but I keep chewing and swallowing, remembering to sip my coffee along the way. I do not allow myself another glance in the mirror. I will not apply a fresh coat

17

of lip gloss or even check my teeth for food. Let there be a poppy seed wedged between my front teeth. I have nothing to prove to him. And nothing to prove to myself.

That is my last thought before I see his face through the rain-streaked door of the diner. My heart starts pounding again and my leg bounces up and down. I think how nice it would be to have one of Andy's beta blockers — harmless pills he takes before court appearances to keep his mouth from getting dry, his voice from shaking. He insists that he's not really nervous, but that somehow his physical symptoms indicate otherwise. I tell myself that I am not nervous either. My body is simply betraying my head and heart. It happens.

I watch Leo give his umbrella a quick shake as he glances around the dinner, past Annie who is mopping the floor underneath a booth. He doesn't see me at first, and for some reason, this gives me a vague sense of power.

But that is gone in an instant when his eyes find mine. He gives me a small, quick smile, then lowers his head and strides toward me. Seconds later, he is standing beside my table, shedding his black leather coat that I remember well. My stomach rises, falls, rises. I am fearful that he will bend down and kiss my cheek. But no, that is not his style. Andy kisses my cheek. Leo never did. True to his old form, he skips niceties and slides into the booth across from me, shaking his head, once, twice. He looks exactly as I remember, but a little older, and somehow bolder and more vivid — his hair darker, his build bulkier, his jaw stronger. A stark contrast to Andy's fine features, long limbs, light coloring. Andy is easier on the eyes, I think. Andy is easier *period*. The same way a walk on the beach is easy. A Sunday nap. A round peg in a round hole.

'Ellen Dempsey,' he finally says, looking into my eyes.

I couldn't have scripted a better opening line. I embrace it, staring back into his brown eyes, banded by black rims. 'Ellen *Graham*,' I announce proudly.

Leo furrows his brow, as if trying to place my new last name, which he should have been able to instantly trace to Margot, my roommate when we were together. But he can't seem to make the connection. This should not surprise me. Leo never cared to learn much about my friends — and never cared for Margot at all. The feeling was mutual. After my first big fight with Leo, one that reduced me to a sniveling, *Girl, Interrupted*-worthy mess, Margot took the only pictures I had of him at the time, a strip of black-and-white candids from a photo booth, and ripped them in a neat line, straight down a row of his foreheads, noses, lips, leaving my grinning faces unscathed.

'See how much better you look now?' Margot said. 'Without that asshole?'

That's a friend, I remember thinking, even as I located a roll of tape and carefully put Leo back together again. I thought the same thing about Margot again when Leo and I broke up for good and she bought me a congratulations card and a bottle of Dom Pérignon. I saved the cork,

wrapping the strip of photos around it with a
rubber band and stowing it in my jewelry box
— until Margot discovered it years later when
returning a pair of gold hoop earrings she had
borrowed from me.

'What's this all about?' she said, rolling the
cork between her fingers.

'Um . . . you got me that champagne,' I said,
chagrined. 'After Leo. Remember?'

'You saved the cork? And these pictures?'

I stammered that I viewed the cork as a token
of my friendship with her, nothing else
— although the truth was, I couldn't bear to part
with anything that had anything to do with Leo.

Margot raised her brows, but dropped the
subject, the way she dropped most controversial
things. It seemed to be the Southern way. Or at
least Margot's way.

In any event, I have just stated my married
name to Leo. A not-so-small triumph.

Leo raises his chin, pushes out his lower lip,
and says, 'Oh? Congratulations.'

'Thanks.' I am jubilant, buoyant — and then
slightly ashamed for feeling so victorious. *The
opposite of love is indifference*, I silently recite.

'So. Who's the lucky guy?' he asks.

'You remember Margot?'

'Sure, I do.'

'I married her brother. I think you met him?' I
say vaguely, even though I know for an absolute
fact that Leo and Andy met once, at a bar in the
East Village. At the time, it was only a brief,
meaningless encounter between my boyfriend
and my best friend's brother. An exchange of

20

How ya doin? . . . *Nice to meet you, man.* Maybe a handshake. Standard guy stuff. But years later, after Leo and I had long broken up, and Andy and I had begun to date, I would deconstruct that moment in exhausting detail, as any woman would.

A flicker of recognition crosses Leo's face now. '*That* guy? Really? The law student?'

I bristle at his *that* guy, his faint tone of derision, wondering what Leo is thinking now. Had he gleaned something from their brief meeting? Is he simply expressing his disdain for lawyers? Had I, at any point, discussed Andy in a way to give him ammunition now? No. That was impossible. There was — and *is* — nothing negative or controversial to say about Andy. Andy has no enemies. Everyone loves him.

I look back into Leo's eyes, telling myself not to get defensive — or react at all. Leo's opinion no longer matters. Instead I nod placidly, confidently. 'Yes. Margot's brother,' I repeat.

'Well. That worked out *perfectly*,' Leo says with what I am pretty sure is sarcasm.

'Yes,' I say, serving up a smug smile. 'It *sure* did.'

'One big happy family,' he says.

Now I am sure of his tone, and I feel myself tense, a familiar rage rising. A brand of rage that only Leo has ever inspired in me. I look down at my wallet with every intention of dropping a few bills on the table, standing and stalking off. But then I hear my name as a featherweight question and feel his hand covering mine, swallowing it whole. I had forgotten how large his hands were.

21

How hot they always were, even in the dead of winter. I fight to move my hand away from his, but can't. *At least he has my right one*, I think. My left hand is clenched under the table, still safe. I rub my wedding band with my thumb and catch my breath.

'I've missed you,' Leo says.

I look at him, shocked, speechless. He *misses* me? It can't be the truth — but then again, Leo isn't about lies. He's about the cold, hard truth. Like it or leave it.

He continues, 'I'm sorry, Ellen.'

'Sorry for what?' I ask, thinking that there are two kinds of *sorry*. There is the sorry imbued with regret. And a pure sorry. The kind that is merely asking for forgiveness, nothing more.

'Everything,' Leo says. *'Everything.'*

That about covers it, I think. I uncurl my left fingers and look down at my ring. There is a huge lump in my throat, and my voice comes out in a whisper. 'It's water under the bridge,' I say. And I mean it. It *is* water under the bridge.

'I know,' Leo says. 'But I'm still sorry.'

I blink and look away, but can't will myself to move my hand. 'Don't be,' I say. 'Everything is fine.'

Leo's thick eyebrows, so neatly shaped that I once teasingly accused him of plucking them, rise in tandem. 'Fine?'

I know what he is implying so I quickly say, 'More than fine. Everything is *great*. Exactly as it should be.'

His expression changes to playful, the way he used to look when I loved him the most and believed that things would work out between us. My heart twists in knots.

'So, Ellen *Graham*, in light of how *fine* everything has turned out to be, what do you say we give the friendship thing a try? Think we could do that?'

I tally all the reasons why not, all the ways it could hurt. Yet I watch myself shrug coolly and hear myself murmur, 'Why not?'

Then I slide my hand out from under his a moment too late.

4

I leave the diner in a daze, feeling some combination of melancholy, resentment, and anticipation. It is an odd and unsettling mix of emotions exacerbated by the rain, now coming down in icy, diagonal sheets. I briefly consider taking the long walk home, almost *wishing* to be cold and wet and miserable, but I think better of it. There is nothing to wallow in, no reason to be upset or even introspective.

So I head for the subway instead, striding along the slick sidewalks with purpose. Good, bad, and even a few mundane memories of Leo swirl around in my head, but I refuse to settle on any of them. *Ancient history*, I mutter aloud as I take the stairs underground at Union Station. Down on the platform, I sidestep puddles and cast about for distractions. I buy a pack of Butterscotch Life Savers at a newsstand, skim the tabloid headlines, eavesdrop on a contentious conversation about politics, and watch a rat scurry along the tracks below. Anything to avoid rewinding and replaying my exchange with Leo. If the flood-gates open, I will obsessively analyze all that was said, as well as the stubborn subtext that was always so much a part of our time together. *What did he mean by that? Why didn't he say this? Does he still have feelings for me? Is he married now, too? If so, why didn't he say so?* I tell myself that none of it matters now. It

24

hasn't mattered for a long time.

My train finally pulls into the station. It is rush hour so all the cars are packed, standing room only. I crush my way into one, beside a mother and her elementary-age daughter. At least I think it is her daughter — they have the same pointy nose and chin. The little girl is wearing a double-breasted navy coat with gold anchor buttons. They are discussing what to have for supper.

'Macaroni-and-cheese and garlic toast?' the daughter suggests, looking hopeful.

I wait for a 'We just had that last night' sort of parental objection, but the mother only smiles and says, 'Well, that sounds perfect for a rainy day.' Her voice is as warm and soothing as the carbohydrates they will share.

I think of my own mother as I do several times a day, often triggered by far less obvious stimuli than the mother-daughter pair beside me. My mind drifts to a recurrent motif — what would our adult relationship have felt like? Would I distrust her opinion when it came to matters of the heart, intentionally rebelling against what she wanted for me? Or would we have been as close as Margot and her mother, talking several times a day? I like to think that we would have been confidantes. Perhaps not sharing-clothing-and-shoes, giggly close (my mother was too no-nonsense for that), but emotionally connected enough to tell her about Leo and the diner. His hand on mine. The way I feel now.

I cobble together the things she might have said, reassuring tidbits like: *I'm so glad you found Andy. He is like the son I never had. I never cared much for that other boy.*

All too predictable, I think, digging deep for more. I close my eyes, picturing her *before* she got sick, something I haven't done lately. I can see her almond-shaped hazel eyes, similar to mine, but turning down slightly at the corners — bedroom eyes, my father always called them. I picture her broad, smooth forehead. Her thick, glossy hair, always cut in the same simple bob that transcended trends or era, just long enough to pull back in a squat ponytail when she did housework or gardening. The slight gap between her front teeth and the way she unconsciously covered it with her hand when she laughed really hard.

Then I conjure her stern but fair gaze — befitting a math teacher at a rough public school — and hear these words uttered in her heavy Pittsburgh dialect: *Listen here, Ellie. Don't go giving this encounter any crazy meaning like you did with him the first time around. It doesn't mean a thing. Not a thing. Sometimes, in life, there is no meaning at all.*

I want to listen to my mother now. I want to believe that she is giving me guidance from some faraway place, but I still feel myself caving, succumbing to the memory of that *first* chance encounter at the New York State Supreme Court on Centre Street when Leo and I were both summoned to jury duty on the same Tuesday in October. Prisoners trapped together in a windowless room with bad acoustics, metal folding chairs, and at least one fellow citizen who

26

had forgotten to apply deodorant. It was all so random, and as I foolishly believed for a long time, romantic *because* of the randomness.

I was only twenty-three years old, but felt much older due to the vague fear and disillusionment that comes with leaving the safety net of college and abruptly joining the real-world ranks, particularly when you have no focus or plan, money or mother. Margot and I had just moved to New York the summer before, right after we graduated, and she landed a plum marketing position at J.Crew's corporate office. I had an offer for an entry-level position at Mellon Bank in Pittsburgh, so had planned on moving back home to live with my father and his new wife, Sharon, a sweet-natured but slightly tacky woman with big boobs and frosted hair. But Margot convinced me to go to New York with her instead, giving me rousing speeches about the Big Apple and how if I could make it there, I'd make it anywhere. I reluctantly agreed because I couldn't stand the thought of separating from Margot any more than I could stand the thought of watching another woman take over my house — my *mother's* house.

So Margot's father hired movers to pack up our dorm room, bought us one-way tickets to New York, and helped us settle into an adorable two-bedroom apartment on Columbus and Seventy-ninth, she with a brand-new corporate wardrobe and crocodile briefcase; me with my useless philosophy major and stash of T-shirts and cut-off jean shorts. I had only $433 to my name and was in the habit of withdrawing five

27

dollars at a time from the ATM, an amount that, shockingly enough, couldn't score me a pastrami sandwich in the city. But Margot's trust fund, set up by her maternal grandparents, had just kicked in, and she assured me that what was hers was mine because, after all, weren't we more like sisters than friends?

'Please don't make me live in a hovel just so you can afford half the rent,' she'd say, joking, but also quite serious. Money was something that Margot not only didn't *have* to think about but didn't *want* to think about or discuss. So I learned to swallow my pride and ignore my prickly hot neck every time I'd have to borrow from her. I told myself that guilt was a wasted emotion, and that I'd make it up to her one day — if not monetarily, then somehow.

For almost a month during that first vivid summer in the city, I spiced up my résumé with exaggerations and fancy fonts and applied for every office job I could find. The more boring the description, the more legitimate the career seemed because at the time I equated adulthood with a certain measure of hosiery-wearing misery. I got a lot of callbacks, but must have been an abysmal interview, because I always came up empty-handed. So I finally settled for a waitressing job at L'Express, a café on Park Avenue South that described itself as a Lyonnaise *bouchon*. The hours were long — I often worked the late-night shift — and my feet hurt all the time, but it wasn't all bad. I made suprisingly good money (people tip better late at night), met some cool people, and learned

28

everything I ever wanted to know about charcuterie and cheese plates, port and pigs feet.

In the meantime, I took up photography. It started as a hobby, a way to fill my days and get to know the city. I wandered around various neighborhoods — the East Village, Alphabet City, SoHo, Chinatown, Tribeca — as I snapped photos with a 35-millimeter camera my father and Sharon had given me for graduation. But very quickly, taking photos became something more to me. It became something that I not only loved doing, but actually *needed* to do, much the way authors talk about their urge to get words down on paper or avid runners just *have* to go for their morning jog. Photography exhilarated me and filled me with purpose even when I was, literally, at my most aimless and lonesome. I was starting to miss my mother more than I ever had in college, and for the first time in my life, really craved a romantic relationship. Except for a wild, borderline-stalker crush I had on Matt Iannotti in the tenth grade, I had never been particularly focused on boys. I had dated a few guys here and there, and had sex with two college boyfriends, one serious, one not so much, but had never been anywhere close to being in love. Nor had I ever uttered — or written — those words to anyone outside of my family and Margot when we both had a lot to drink. Which was all okay with me until that first year in New York. I wasn't sure what had changed inside my head, but perhaps it was being a real grown-up — and being surrounded by millions of people, Margot included, who all seemed to have definite dreams and someone to love.

So I concentrated all my energy on photography. I spent every spare cent on film and every spare moment taking pictures or poring over books in the library and bookstores. I devoured both reference guides to technique and collections by great photographers. My favorite — which Margot bought me for my twenty-third birthday — was *The Americans* by Robert Frank, which comprised a series of photos he took in the 1950s while traveling across the country. I was mesmerized by his black-and-white images, each a complete story unto itself. I felt as if I knew the stocky man bent over a jukebox, the elegant woman gazing over her shoulder in an elevator, and the dark-skinned nanny cradling a creamy white baby. I decided that this sense of truly believing you knew a subject, more than anything else, was the mark of a great photograph. *If I could take pictures like that*, I thought, *I would be fulfilled, even without a boyfriend.*

Looking back it was perfectly clear what I should do next, but it took Margot to point out the obvious — one of the many things friends are for. She had just returned home from a business trip to Los Angeles, rolling in her suitcase and pausing at the kitchen table to pick up one of my freshly developed photographs. It was a color photo of a distraught teenaged girl sitting on a curb on Bedford Avenue in Brooklyn, the contents of her purse spilled onto the street around her. She had long, curly red hair and was beautiful in that adolescent, no-makeup way that

I didn't fully recognize at the time because I was so young, too. The girl was reaching out to retrieve a cracked mirror with one hand, the other was barely touching her forehead.

'Wow,' Margot said, holding the photo up close to her face. 'That's an *amazing* picture.'

'Thanks,' I said, feeling modest — but proud. It *was* an amazing picture.

'Why's she so sad?' Margot asked.

I shrugged, telling her I seldom talked to the people I photographed. Only if they caught me taking their picture and talked to me first.

'Maybe she lost her wallet,' Margot said.

'Maybe she just broke up with her boyfriend,' I said.

Or maybe her mother just died.

Margot kept studying the picture, commenting that the girl's bright red knee socks gave the photo an almost vintage feel. 'Although,' she added in her usual, fashion-obsessed way, 'knee socks *are* coming back in. Whether you like it or not.'

'Not,' I said. 'But duly noted.'

That's when she said to me, 'Your photos are pure genius, Ellen.' Her head bobbed earnestly as she wound her soft, honey-colored hair into a bun and fastened it with a mechanical pencil. It was a haphazardly cool technique I had tried to emulate a hundred times, but could never make look right. When it came to hair or fashion or makeup, everything I copied from Margot fell somehow short. She nodded once more and said, 'You should pursue photography professionally.'

'You think so?' I said offhandedly.

Oddly enough, it was something I had never

31

considered, although I'm not sure why. Perhaps I was worried that my enthusiasm would exceed my ability. I couldn't bear the thought of failing at something I cared so much about. But Margot's opinion meant a lot to me. And as insincere as she sometimes was with her Southern pleasantries and compliments, she was never that way with me. She always gave it to me straight — the sign of a *real* friendship.

'I *know* so,' she said. 'You should go for it. Do this thing for real.'

So I took Margot's advice and began to look for a new job in the photography field. I applied for every assistant's position I could find — including a few for cheesy wedding photographers on Long Island. But without any formal training, I was once again turned down by everyone and ended up taking a minimum-wage position as a film processor in a small, boutique-y photo lab with ancient equipment. I had to start somewhere, I told myself, as I took the bus to dreary lower Second Avenue on my first day and unpacked my peanut-butter-and-jelly sandwich in a drafty back room that smelled of cigarettes and bleach.

But, as it turned out, it was the ideal first job thanks to Quynh, the Vietnamese girl who was married to the owner's son. Quynh spoke little English, but was a pure genius with color and taught me more about custom printing than I could have learned in any class (and more than I eventually *did* learn when I finally went to photography school). Every day I watched Quynh's thin, nimble fingers feed the film and twist the knobs on the machines, adding a little more yellow, a little less blue to yield the most perfect prints, while I fell more in love with my fledgling chosen profession.

So that's where I was when I got that infamous jury summons. Although still quite poor, I was fulfilled, happy, and hopeful, and none too anxious to put my work (and pay) on hold for jury duty. Margot suggested that I ask Andy, who had just started his third year of law school at Columbia, for his advice on how to get excused. So I gave him a call, and he assured me it would be a cinch.

'You can't lie on voir dire,' he said as I listened, impressed with the Latin term. 'But you can exaggerate your bias. Just imply that you hate lawyers, don't trust cops, or resent the wealthy. Whatever it seems they're looking for.'

'Well,' I said. 'I *do* resent the wealthy.'

Andy chuckled. He could tell I was kidding, but he also must have known from Margot how broke I always was. He cleared his throat, and continued earnestly, 'Impetuous body language can do the trick, too. Look pissed off and put out to be there. Like you have more important things to be doing. Keep your arms crossed. Neither side wants an impatient juror.'

I said I would definitely take his advice. Anything to get back to my regularly scheduled life — and my much-needed paycheck.

But all of that changed in a flash when I saw Leo for the first time, a moment frozen in my mind forever.

It was still early morning, but I had exhausted

my stash of magazines in my tote bag, checked my watch a hundred times, and called Quynh from a pay phone to give her a status report, when I sat back in my chair, scanned the jury room, and spotted him sitting a few rows diagonally in front of me. He was reading the back page of the *New York Post* as he nodded to the beat of a song on his Discman, and I suddenly had a crazy urge to know what he was listening to. For some reason, I imagined that it was the Steve Miller Band or Crosby, Stills and Nash. Something manly and comfortable to go with his faded Levi's, a navy fleece pullover, and black, loosely tied Adidas sneakers. As he glanced up at the wall clock, I admired his profile. His distinctive nose (Margot would later dub it defiant), high cheekbones, and the way his wavy, dark hair curled against the smooth olive skin of his neck. He wasn't particularly big or tall, but he had a broad back and shoulders that looked so strong. I envisioned him jumping rope in a bare-bones, stripped-down gym or running up the courthouse steps, Rocky style, and decided that he was more sexy than handsome. As in, the 'I bet he'd be great in bed' definition of sexy. The thought took me by surprise as I wasn't accustomed to assessing strange men in such a strictly physical way. Like most women, I was about getting to know someone first — attraction based on personality. Moreover, I wasn't even that into sex. *Yet*.

As if reading my mind, Leo turned in his seat and shot me a wry, intelligent look that said, 'I busted you,' or maybe just, 'Jury duty sucks, doesn't it?' He had deep-set eyes (so deep set that I couldn't quite tell the color) that somehow managed to look mysterious under yellow fluorescent lights. I held his gaze for what felt like one dangerous beat before pretending to concentrate on the droning bureaucrat at the front of the room who was explaining what constituted a valid medical excuse for at least the fifth time.

Later Leo would tell me that I appeared flustered while I would vehemently deny it, insisting that I barely noticed him at all. Either way, we would agree that that was the moment jury duty no longer completely sucked.

For the next hour, I was acutely aware of Leo's every small move. I watched him stretch and yawn. I watched him fold his newspaper and stow it under his chair. I watched him saunter out of the room and return with a pack of peanut butter crackers which he ate openly despite the No Food or Drink signs posted around the room. He never once looked back at me, but I had the feeling that he was aware of me watching him and this fact gave me a strange thrill. I wasn't about to call it anything as crazy as love at first sight — I didn't believe in things like that — but I knew that I was intrigued in an inexplicable, unprecedented way.

And then my jury-duty fairy godmother granted my wish. Our names were called, in a list of other names, and we ended up side by side in a jury box, mere inches apart. There was nothing grand or gilded or movie-set worthy about the small courtroom, yet there was still a sense that something somber and important was about to unfold, a tension that made sitting so close to Leo feel wildly intimate. From the corner of my eye, I could see his sturdy forearm crisscrossed by blue veins and was taken aback by a fluttery longing that was reminiscent of that high school crush I had on Matt, and my euphoria when he sat next to me one morning in our musty auditorium during a lackluster assembly about all the ways doing drugs could destroy our lives. I remember basking in Matt's heavy application of Aramis cologne (which I can still sniff out in a crowd) and laughing at his wisecracks about all the ways that weed could actually *improve* your life. Come to think of it, Leo almost resembled an older-brother version of Matt, which made me wonder whether I actually *did* have a type, despite my protestations to Margot otherwise. If so, he was definitely it. And, with this observation, the DA directed his attention at Leo and said with false cheer, 'Juror Number Nine. Good morning.'

Leo gave an aloof but respectful nod back.

'Where do you live, sir?' the DA asked.

I sat up straight in my chair, hoping that his voice would live up to his looks. There is nothing worse than a high, thin voice on a man, followed closely by delicate wrists, sloping shoulders, and a weak handshake.

Of course, Leo did not disappoint. He cleared his throat and out came his deep, self-assured voice with a New York accent. 'Morningside Heights.'

'Did you grow up there?'

36

'No, I'm from Astoria,' Leo said. 'Born and raised.'

Yes! Queens! I thought, as I had already begun to fall in love with the outer boroughs. Perhaps because Brooklyn and the Bronx and Queens reminded me of home — blue collar and authentic. Perhaps because my photos away from the heart of New York's riches were always more compelling.

The DA continued, asking Leo what he did for a living, as I thought to myself that voir dire was better than a first date. Someone else asked the questions while you got to eavesdrop. And he had to tell the truth. *Perfect.*

'I'm a writer . . . A reporter,' Leo said. 'I cover a few beats for a small newspaper.'

Perfect, I thought again. I pictured him roaming the streets with a spiral notepad and chatting up old guys in dark bars in the middle of the afternoon for a feature about how the city is losing all of its character and toughness.

And so it continued over the next few minutes as I swooned over Leo's answers as much for the content as for his deadpan yet still colorful delivery. I learned that he went to college for three years and dropped out when he 'ran out of funds.' That he didn't know any lawyers — except a guy named Vern from elementary school 'who was now an ambulance chaser, but a pretty decent guy in spite of his line of work. No offense.' That his brothers and father were fire-fighters, but that he never found the family profession 'very compelling.' That he had never been married and had no children 'that he knew of.' That he had never been a victim of violent crime, 'unless you count being on the losing side of a couple fights.'

And with Leo's last quip, my desire to get dismissed completely dissipated. Instead, I embraced my civic duty with a newfound fervor. When it was my turn to answer questions, I did everything Andy advised me *not* to do. I was friendly and eager to please. I flashed both lawyers my best school-crossing-guard smile, showing them what an ideal, open-minded juror I would make. I fleetingly considered my job and how much Quynh needed me at work, but then high-mindedly concluded that our criminal justice system and the Constitution upon which it was built were worth a sacrifice.

So when, several rounds of questioning later, Leo and I were selected as Jurors Nine and Ten, I was elated, a state that I intermittently returned to over the next six days of testimony despite graphic details of a brutal box-cutter stabbing in Spanish Harlem. A twenty-year-old kid was dead and another on trial for murder, and there I was hoping the evidence would take a good long while to shake out. I couldn't help it. I craved more days beside Leo, the chance to talk to him. To know him in some small way. I needed to know whether my crush — although that term seemed to trivialize what I was feeling — was founded. All the while, Leo was friendly, but inaccessible. He kept his headphones on whenever possible, avoiding small talk in the hallway outside the courtroom where the rest of the jurors would chat about everything but the case, and he ate lunch alone every afternoon rather than joining us in the deli adjacent to the courthouse. His guardedness only made me like him more.

Then one morning, right before closing arguments, as we were settling in our jury-box seats, he turned and said to me, 'This is it.' Then he smiled a genuine, slow smile — almost as if we were in on a secret together. My heart fluttered. And then, as if foreshadowed by that moment, we actually *were* in on a secret together.

It started during deliberations when it became clear that Leo and I shared the same view of the testimony. In short, we were both in favor of an outright acquittal. The actual killing wasn't in issue — the defendant had confessed and the confession was unchallenged — so the sole debate was whether he had acted in self-defense. Leo and I thought he had. Or, to put it more accurately, we thought there was plenty of reasonable doubt that the defendant *hadn't* acted in self-defense — a subtle distinction that, scarily enough, at least a half-dozen of our fellow jurors didn't seem to grasp. We kept pointing to the fact that the defendant had no prior criminal record (a near miracle in his rough neighborhood), and that he was deathly afraid of the victim (who had been the toughest gang leader in Harlem and had been threatening the defendant for months — so much so that he had gone to the police for protection). And finally, that the defendant was carrying the box cutter in the normal course of his job with a moving company. All of which added up to our belief that the defendant had panicked when cornered by the victim and *three* of his gang-banger friends, and had lashed out in a state of panicked self-defense. It seemed like a plausible scenario — and definitely plausible enough to reach the benchmark of reasonable doubt.

After three long days of going around in aggravating circles, we were still in a gridlock with the rest of the panel, all of us miserably sequestered by night at a dreary Ramada Inn near JFK Airport. We were allowed to watch television — apparently the trial wasn't newsworthy — but we weren't allowed to make any outgoing phone calls, nor could we discuss the case with one another unless in the jury room during official deliberations.

So when my hotel room phone rang one night, I was startled, wondering who it could possibly be, and secretly hoping that it was Leo. Perhaps he had taken note of my room number on our way back from our bailiff-supervised group dinner earlier that evening. I fumbled for the phone and whispered hello into the receiver.

Leo returned his own hushed hello. Then he said, as if there had been any confusion, 'It's Juror Number Nine. Leo.'

'I know,' I said, feeling blood rush from my head to my limbs.

'Look,' he said (after three days of deliberations, I knew that he started his sentences with 'look,' a quirk I loved). 'I know I'm not supposed to be calling you . . . but I'm going crazy over here . . . '

I wasn't sure what he meant by this — going crazy from being sequestered or going crazy because he was so into me. I figured it had to be the former. The latter was too impossibly good to be true.

'Yeah. I know what you mean,' I said, trying to keep my voice even. 'I just can't stop thinking about the testimony. It's all so frustrating.'

Leo exhaled into the phone and after a long silence said, 'I mean, how bad would it suck to have a dozen morons deciding your fate?'

'A *dozen* morons?' I said, trying to be funny, cool. 'Speak for yourself, pal.'

Leo laughed as I lay in bed, buzzing with excitement.

Then he said, 'Okay. *Ten* morons. Or at least a good, solid eight.'

'Yeah,' I said. 'I know.'

'I mean, *seriously*,' he continued. 'Can you believe these people? Half of them don't have an open mind at all — the other half are wishy-washy half-wits that blow with whatever their lunch buddies think.'

'I know,' I said again, feeling lightheaded. I couldn't believe we were finally having a real conversation. And, while I lay in the dark, under the covers, no less. I closed my eyes, picturing him in his bed. I couldn't believe how much I wanted a virtual stranger.

'I never thought this before,' Leo said, 'but if I were on trial, I'd rather face a judge than a jury.'

I said I might have to agree with that.

'Hell. I'd rather have a *corrupt* judge taking

41

bribes from my enemies than this loser crew.'

I laughed as he proceeded to joke about the more outrageously off-point anecdotes that a few of our jurors had shared. He was right. It was one tangent after another in that claustrophobic room — a free-for-all of life experience with no relevance to the deliberations whatsoever.

'Some people just love to hear themselves talk,' I said. And then added, 'You don't seem to be one of them, Mr. Aloof.'

'I'm not aloof,' Leo said unconvincingly.

'Are too,' I said. 'Mr. Wear-Your-Headphones so you don't have to talk to anyone.'

'I'm talking now,' Leo said.

'It's about time,' I said, thinking that it was easy to be brave in the dark, on the phone.

A long stretch of silence followed which felt warm and forbidden. Then I stated the obvious — that we'd be in big trouble if Chester, our bailiff babysitter, busted us talking on the phone. And about the case, no less.

'Yes, we would,' Leo said. Then he added very slowly and deliberately, 'And I guess we'd be in even more hot water if I paid you a visit right now, huh?'

'What's that?' I said, even though I had heard him, loud and clear.

'Can I come see you?' he said again, his voice slightly suggestive.

I sat up abruptly, smoothing the sheets around me. 'What about Chester?' I said, feeling the good kind of weak.

'He went to bed. The halls are clear. I already checked.'

'Really?' I said. I could think of nothing else to say.

'Yes. *Really* . . . So?'

'So?' I echoed.

'So can I come see you? I just . . . want to talk. Face to face. Alone.'

I didn't really believe that was all he wanted — and a large measure of me hoped that it wasn't. I thought of how much trouble we'd be in if we got caught together in a jury-duty booty call, and that we owed it to the defendant to follow the rules — that our reckless behavior could result in a mistrial. I thought of how unsexy my Steelers T-shirt and cotton panties were and that I had nothing nicer in my hastily packed suitcase. I thought about the conventional girly wisdom that if I said yes — and then something *did* happen — that Leo might lose respect for me and we'd be over before we could begin.

So I opened my mouth, poised to protest, or at the very least, deflect. But instead, I breathed a helpless *yes* into the phone. It would be the first of many times I couldn't say no to Leo.

5

It is completely dark by the time I turn onto our quiet, tree-lined block in Murray Hill. Andy won't be home until much later, but for once, I don't mind the hours he's forced to bill at his white-shoe law firm. I will have time to shower, light a few candles, open a bottle of wine, and find the exact right soundtrack to purge the last traces of the past from my mind — something cheerful, with absolutely no Leo associations. 'Dancing Queen' would fit the bill, I think, smiling to myself. There is absolutely *nothing* about ABBA that conjures Leo. In any event, I want the evening to be all about Andy and me. About *us*.

As I step out of the cold rain into the brownstone, I breathe a sigh of relief. There is nothing lavish about our building, but I love it that way. I love the shabby lobby with its creaky herringbone floors and brass chandelier in dire need of a good polish. I love the jewel-toned Oriental rug that gives off a subtle scent of mothballs. I even love the lumbering, claustro-phobically small elevator that always seems on the brink of a breakdown. Most of all, I love that it is our first home together.

Tonight, I opt for the stairs, taking them two at a time while I imagine a day far into the future when Andy and I return to this spot with our yet-to-be-born children. Give them a grand tour of where 'Mommy and Daddy first lived.' Tell them, 'Yes, with Daddy's family money we could have afforded a plush Upper East Side doorman building, but he picked this one, in this quiet neighborhood, because it had more character . . . Just as he chose me over all those blue-eyed Southern belles.'

I reach the fourth floor, find my key, and upon turning it, discover that Andy has beaten me home. A virtual first. I feel something between sheepish and shamefaced as I push open the door, glance through our galley kitchen into the living room, and find my husband sprawled on the couch, his head resting on an orange chenille pillow. He has already banished his jacket and tie to the floor and his blue dress shirt is unbuttoned at the collar. At first I think he is asleep, but then I see one of his bare feet moving in time to Ani DiFranco's *As Is*. It is my CD — and so far afield from Andy's usual happy Top Forty tunes (or his sappy country music) that I assume our stereo is on random-play. Andy makes no apologies for his taste in music, and while I'm listening to my favorites, stuff like Elliott Smith or Marianne Faithfull, he will roll his eyes at the more turbulent lyrics and make cracks like, 'Excuse me while I go chug some poison under the sink.' But despite our different tastes, he never makes me turn my music off or down. Andy is the opposite of a control freak. A Manhattan litigator with a surfer boy, live-and-let-live, no worries mentality.

For a long moment, I watch Andy lying there in the soft amber glow of lamplight and am filled

45

with what can only be described as relief. Relief that I got to this place, that *this* is my life. As I take another few steps toward the couch, Andy's eyes snap open. He stretches, smiles and says, 'Hey, honey.'

'Hi,' I say, beaming back at him as I drop my bag on our round retro dinette table that we found at a flea market in Chelsea. Margot and her mother hate it almost as much as they hate the kitschy knickknacks that congregate on every free surface in our apartment. A coconut monkey wearing wire-rim glasses perches on our windowsill. Beads from a recent Mardi Gras hang from our computer monitor. A collection of salt-and-pepper figurines parade across our countertop. I am much more neat and organized than Andy, but we are both pack rats at heart — which Margot jokes is the only dangerous part of our being together.

Andy sighs as he sits, swinging his long legs onto the floor. Then he glances at his watch and says, 'You don't call. You don't write. Where've you been all day? I tried your cell a few times . . . '

His tone is easy — not at all accusatory — but I still feel a shiver of guilt as I say, 'Here and there. Running around in the rain. My phone was off.'

All true statements, I think. But I still know that I'm keeping something from my husband, and I fleetingly consider revising my vow of secrecy and telling him the rest. What *really* happened today. He would most certainly be annoyed — and probably a little hurt that I let

46

Leo come back to the diner to see me. The same way I would feel if Andy let an ex-girlfriend come share a coffee with him when he could have, nearly as easily, told her to kiss off. The truth might even start a small argument — our first *married* argument.

On the other hand, it's not like Andy feels threatened by Leo or feels hostile toward him. He simply disdains him in the typical, offhanded way that nearly everyone disdains their significant other's most-significant ex. With a mild mix of jealousy and competitiveness that recedes over time. In fact, Andy is so laidback that he probably wouldn't feel *either* of those things at all if I hadn't made the mistake of disclosing a little too much during one of our early-relationship, late-night conversations. Specifically, I had used the word *intense* to describe what Leo and I had shared. It didn't seem like that much of a revelation as I had assumed that Margot had told him a thing or two about Leo and me, but I immediately knew it was news to him when Andy rolled over in bed to face me, his blue eyes flashing in a way I'd never seen before.

'Intense?' he said with a wounded expression. 'What exactly do you mean by *intense?*'

'Oh, I don't know . . . ' I said.

'*Sexually* intense?'

'No,' I said quickly. 'Not like *that*.'

'Like you spent *all* your time together? Every night and every waking moment?'

'No,' I said again. My face grew hot with fresh shame as I recalled the night that Margot accused me of blowing her off for Leo. Of being

47

one of *those* girls who puts a man ahead of a friendship. *And an unreliable man with no marriage potential to boot*, she added, disgusted. Even then, somewhere deep down, I knew she was probably right, but despite my guilt and better judgment, I just couldn't stop myself. If Leo wanted to see me, I dropped everything — and everyone — else.

'So what then?' Andy pressed. 'You loved him to the heavens and back?' His voice dripped with playful sarcasm, but his hurt look remained.

'Not that kind of intense either,' I said, struggling to find a way to put a detached, nonpassionate spin on *intense*. Which is impossible to do. Sort of like inserting a joyful note into the word *grief* or a hopeful note in *doomed*.

I cast about for a few more seconds before I finally offered up a weak, 'I didn't mean intense . . . I take it back . . . It was a bad choice of words.'

It *was*, indeed, a bad choice of words. But only because it was true — intense was *precisely* what Leo and I had been together. Nearly every moment we shared felt intense, starting with that very first night in my dark hotel room when we sat cross-legged on my bed, our knees touching, my hands in his, while we talked until sunrise.

'Too late,' Andy said, smirking and shaking his head. 'No take-backs. You can't strike this one from the record, Dempsey.'

And so it *was* too late.

Fortunately, Andy wasn't one to beat a dead horse, so Leo's name seldom came up after that.

But for a long time, whenever someone used the word *intense*, Andy would shoot me a knowing look or make a wisecrack about my 'oh-so-smoldering, ever-passionate' ex-boyfriend.

I am not up for that kind of scrutiny now — joking or otherwise. Besides, I reason, as I peel off my jacket and hang it on our wobbly wooden coat rack, if the tables were turned, I'd rather not know about a chance run-in he had with Lucy, his most-beloved and long-time ex, who is now a third-grade teacher at a snooty private school in Atlanta. According to Margot, Lucy was as smart and wholesome as they come while still looking like she could be a body double for Salma Hayek. It was a direct quote I could have lived without.

With this rationalization, I decide once and for all that it is in everyone's best interest to keep my insignificant secret a secret. I plop down on the couch next to Andy and rest my hand on his leg. 'So why are you home so early, anyway?' I ask him.

'Because I missed you,' he says, smiling.

'C'mon,' I say, feeling torn. I like this answer, but almost hope there is more to it this time. 'You've *never* been home this early.'

'I *did* miss you,' he says, laughing. 'But my case settled, too.'

'That's awesome,' I say. I know how much he had been dreading the even longer hours that come with a full-blown trial. I had been dreading them, too.

'Yeah. Such a relief. I have sleep in my future now . . . So anyway, I was thinking we could get changed and go to dinner? Maybe somewhere nice? You up for that?'

I glance toward the window and say, 'Maybe a bit later . . . It's really coming down out there . . . I think I'd rather just stay in for a bit.' I give him a seductive smile as I kick off my boots and sidle onto his lap, facing him. I lean in and plant a kiss on his jaw, then another on his neck.

Andy smiles, closes his eyes, and whispers a bemused, 'What in the *world*?'

It is one of my favorite of his endearing expressions, but at this moment it strikes a small note of worry in my heart. Does my initiating foreplay really warrant a *What in the world?* Aren't we occasionally spontaneous when it comes to sex? My mind races to come up with some recent, juicy examples, but disappointingly, I can't think of the last time we had sex anywhere other than in bed, at bedtime. I reassure myself that this is perfectly normal for married couples — even *happily* married couples. Andy and I might not swing from the chandeliers and go nuts in every room of the house, but you don't have to be nailing each other willy-nilly on the kitchen counters and hardwood floors to have a solid physical connection. After all, sex on and against hard surfaces might look hot in the movies, but in real life it is uncomfortable, overrated, and contrived.

Of course there was that one time with Leo in his office . . .

I desperately try to push the memory out of my head by kissing Andy again, this time on his mouth. But as is the way when you're trying not to think of something, the scene only grows more vivid. And so, suddenly, I am doing the unthinkable. I am kissing my husband while picturing another man. Picturing *Leo*. I kiss Andy harder, desperate to erase Leo's face and lips. It doesn't work. I am only kissing Leo harder. I work at the buttons on Andy's shirt and slide my hands across his stomach and chest. I take my own sweater off. We hold each other, skin to skin. I say Andy's name out loud. Leo is still there. His body against mine.

'Hmm, Ellen,' Andy moans, his fingers stroking my back.

Leo's hot hands are digging into my back with crazy pressure, urgency.

I open my eyes and tell Andy to look at me. He does.

I look into them and say, 'I *love* you.'

'I love you, too,' he says, so sweetly. His expression is frank, sincere, earnest. His face is the face I love.

I squeeze my eyes shut, concentrating on the feel of Andy growing hard against my thigh. Our pants are still on, but I center myself over him, grinding back against him, saying his name again. My husband's name. *Andy*. There is no confusing who I am with right now. Who I love. This works for a while. And continues to work as Andy leads me to our bedroom where the all-or-nothing radiator is either dormant or sputtering steam everywhere. Right now, the room is downright tropical. We push away our goose down comforter, and slide against our soft sheets. We are completely undressed now. This bed is sacred. Leo is gone. He is nowhere.

And yet, moments later, when Andy is moving inside me, I am back in Leo's apartment on the night the not-guilty verdict finally came down. He is unshaven and his eyes are slightly glazed from our celebratory drinks. He hugs me fiercely and whispers in my ear, 'I'm not sure what it is about you, Ellen Dempsey, but I *have* to have you.'

It was the same night I gave myself to him completely, knowing that I would belong to him for as long as he wanted to keep me.

And, as it turned out, even longer than that.

6

Margot calls the next morning long before the sun is up — or, as Andy would say, before anyone in their right mind is up. Andy seldom gets agitated, but three things consistently set him off: people who cut in lines; bickering about politics in social settings; and his sister calling too early in the morning.

'What the *hell*?' he says after the second ring. His voice is scratchy, as it always is the morning after a few beers, which we ended up downing the night before at a Third Avenue bistro, along with burgers and the best shoestring fries in the neighborhood. We had a good time, laughing even more than usual, but our dinner didn't jettison Leo any more than sex had. He was stubbornly there with me all night, remarking on the crabby man at the table beside us and the Joni Mitchell background music. As I finished my third beer and listened to Andy talk about his work, I found myself drifting back to the morning Leo told me that my face was his favorite in the world. He said it just like that, utterly matter-of-factly and unsentimentally over coffee. I was wearing no makeup, my hair pulled back in a ponytail, sun from his living room window streaming in my eyes. But I believed him. I could tell he meant it.

'Thank you,' I said, blushing, thinking that his face was by far my favorite, too. I wondered if this, more than anything else, is a sign of true love.

Then he said, 'I will never get tired of looking at you . . . Never.'

And it is this memory, perhaps my top-ranking memory of Leo, that once again fills my head as the loud ringing continues in our bedroom. Andy groans as the caller finally gives up, waits a few seconds, and tries again.

'Let it go to voicemail,' I say, but Andy reaches across me and grabs the phone from my nightstand. To be sure of the culprit, he checks caller ID — which is completely unnecessary. Short of an outright emergency, it can only be Margot. Sure enough, her husband's name, Webb Buffington, lights up the screen, along with Atlanta, Georgia, where, much to my disappointment, they returned last year. I always knew the move was inevitable, particularly after she met Webb, who was also from Atlanta. As much as Margot loved New York and her career, she's a Southern girl at heart and desperately wanted all the traditional trimmings that come with a genteel life. Moreover, Webb was, in his words, 'So over the city.' He wanted to golf, wanted to drive, wanted space for all his fancy electronic toys.

As evidenced by this morning's call, Margot and I still talk daily, but I miss the face-to-face time with her. I miss having brunch on the weekends and drinks after work. I miss sharing the city — and some of the same friends. Andy misses her, too, except in intrusive moments like these, when his sleep is impacted.

He jams the talk button with his thumb and barks into the phone, 'Jesus, Margot. Do you know what time it is?'

I can hear her high voice say, 'I know. I know. I'm *really* sorry, Andy. But it's *legitimate* this time. I promise. Put Ellen on. Please?'

'It's not even seven o'clock,' he says. 'How many times do I have to ask you not to wake us up? That the only decent part of my job is the late start time? Would you do this if Ellen were married to someone else? And, if not, how about asking yourself if you shouldn't respect your own brother just a little bit more than some random guy?'

I smile at *some random guy*, thinking that the guy wouldn't be random if I were married to him. Then I think of Leo again and cringe, knowing that he will never only be some random guy to me. I get Andy's point, though, and I'm sure Margot does, too, but he doesn't give her a chance to respond. Instead, he thrusts the phone at me and dramatically buries his head under his pillow.

'Hey, Margot,' I say as quietly as possible.

She issues a perfunctory apology and then trills, 'I have *news*!'

They are the exact words, the same singsongy, confiding tone she used when she called me the night she and Webb got engaged. Or, as Webb is fond of saying in the retelling of their betrothal, before she could even muster a yes to him. He is exaggerating, of course, although she did call me first, even before her mother, which gratified me in a way I couldn't quite pinpoint. I think it had something to do with not having my own mother and the reassurance that friends might supplant family, even in the absence of death.

'Omigod, Margot,' I say now, fully alert and no longer concerned about disturbing Andy.

Andy uncovers his head and says with a contrite, almost worried, expression, 'Is she all right?'

I nod happily, reassuringly, but he continues to look fearful as he whispers, 'What is it?'

I hold up a finger. I want confirmation even though there is absolutely no doubt in my mind what her news is. That voice of hers is reserved for exactly two things — weddings and babies. She had at least three significant promotions at J.Crew and had been blasé about every one. It wasn't so much modesty as it was that she never cared all that much about her career, despite how good she was. Maybe because she knew it had a self-imposed expiration date. That at some point around thirty, she would voluntarily retire and begin the next phase of things, i.e., marry, move back to Atlanta, and start a family.

'*Are* you?' I ask, fast-forwarding to envision Margot, swollen-bellied, in a couture maternity gown.

'Is she what?' Andy mouths.

I look at him, wondering what else he thinks we could *possibly* be talking about. I feel a surge of affection for his boyish cluelessness. *Yes, Andy, she is making snickerdoodles this morning. Yes, Andy, she is in the market for a baby grand piano.*

'Uh-huh!' Margot squeals. 'I'm *pregnant*! I just took a test!'

'Wow,' I say, feeling overwhelmed even though I knew that they were trying, and that Margot nearly always gets what she wants — in part due to her dogged, Type-A personality. But more because she's just one of those charmed people for whom things just work out. Small things, big things, in-between things. I've known her for fifteen years and literally the only setback I've ever witnessed, the only time she genuinely struggled, was when her grandfather died during our senior year. And you really can't count a grandparent's death as a serious hardship. At least not once you've experienced the premature death of a parent.

I say all of this about Margot without resentment. Yes, my mother died at age forty-one, and yes, I grew up wearing hand-me-downs on class-picture day, but I still wouldn't say that I come from the school of hard knocks. And I've certainly had it pretty good in my adulthood, at least so far. I'm not unemployed or directionless or prone to depression. I'm not sick or alone. Besides, even if those things were all true, I'm simply not in a competition with my best friend. I've never understood those women, those troubled, complicated relationships, of which there seem to be plenty. Am I occasionally envious of Margot — particularly when I see her with her mother? Do I wish I had her fashion sense and confidence and passport stamps? Yes, of course. But that is not to say that I would ever take those things from her — or begrudge her happiness in any way. Besides, I'm in her family now. What's hers really *is* mine now.

So, despite the fact that this good news is far from unexpected, here I sit, stunned and giddy and overcome with joy. After all, there is a huge disparity between *planning* to have a baby, and actually getting that positive pregnancy test. Of knowing that in a matter of months you'll become somebody's mother — or in my case, somebody's aunt.

'Congratulations,' I say, feeling teary.

'She's *pregnant?*' Andy finally guesses, wide-eyed.

I nod and smile. 'Yeah . . . Are you still pissed off, Uncle Andy?'

He grins and says, 'Gimme the phone.'

I hand it over.

He says, 'Maggie Beth! You should have just said so!'

I can hear her say, 'You know I had to tell Ellen first.'

'Over your own flesh and blood?'

'Only one of you is happy to hear from me *any* time of day,' she says.

Andy ignores her playful dig and says, 'Damn, this is great news. I'm so glad we're coming down there next weekend. I can't wait to give you a big hug.'

I snatch the phone back and ask her if she's calculated the due date; does she think it's a boy or a girl; has she thought of names; should I give her a shower in the city or Atlanta?

She tells me September twenty-first; she thinks it's a girl; no names yet; and a shower would be lovely anywhere.

'What did Webb say?' I ask, remembering that

there is another party involved here.

'He's happy. Surprised. A little pale.' Margot laughs. 'Do you want to talk to him? He's right here.'

'Sure,' I say, even though I'm not in the mood to talk to him. In truth, I'm *never* really in the mood to talk to Webb — even though he has never been anything but friendly to me, which is more than I can say for some of the guys Margot dated before him. She's always been drawn to an arrogant type, and Webb, too, certainly has the makings to be arrogant. For one, he's an ultra-successful sports agent and former, semi-famous tennis pro — at least he's known in tennis circles, once defeating Agassi on the junior circuit. And on top of his success and wealth, he has swoon-worthy, classically handsome looks, with frighteningly good hair and teeth so straight and white that I think of an old 'Brush your breath with Dentyne' commercial every time he throws his head back in laughter. He has a big, loud voice and large presence — and is the kind of guy who knows how to give an eloquent speech that thrills the ladies and deliver a punch line to an off-color joke that makes the guys hoot and holler. So, by any measure, Webb *should* be intolerably smug. But he's not. Instead, he's humble, even-tempered, and thoughtful.

Yet, for some reason, I just don't feel comfortable around him — perhaps because we have almost nothing in common except Margot. Fortunately I never admitted this to her when they first started to date — probably because I suspected right away that he was 'the One.' It was the first time I had seen Margot totally, unabashedly smitten with anyone, the first time she liked someone as much as — or even *more* than — they liked her. I didn't broach the subject with Andy either, perhaps because he seemed to be such a huge Webb fan, perhaps because I wasn't exactly sure what I didn't like.

But I did confess my feelings to my sister once, right before Margot's wedding when I was back in Pittsburgh for a random weekend. We were having lunch at the Eat'n Park, our favorite hangout in high school, and still our sentimental pick whenever I go home. Every table has multiple memories, and we chose the one closest to the door that conjured her post — junior prom meal with a guy now doing time for something; my father's impromptu nosebleed one evening (that we all thought was ketchup at first); and the time I ate five chili dogs on a bet. As Suzanne and I decked our Big Boys with an array of condiments, she asked about Margot's wedding with what I detected as a bit of disdain that always seemed to be present when she discussed the Grahams — disdain that was, in my opinion, both unwarranted and a tad mean-spirited. But despite her tone, I could also tell that Suzanne was intrigued by Margot in the same shameless and superficial way we used to be intrigued by Luke and Laura on *General Hospital* and Bo and Hope on *Days of Our Lives*.

'This is *so* stupid,' Suzanne would always say as we watched the couples on our favorite soaps. She'd roll her eyes as she pointed out the improbabilities and inconsistencies of the

60

on-screen romances, but there she'd sit, riveted to the television, hungry for more.

Similarly, as we ate our burgers, Suzanne wanted all the details on Margot's upcoming nuptials, ferreting out any potential drama.

'That was a short engagement, wasn't it?' she asked, brows raised. 'Could she be knocked up?'

I laughed and shook my head.

'So what's the hurry?'

'They're in love,' I said, thinking that their entire courtship was storybook, including its brevity. Their engagement preceded mine, despite the fact that Andy and I were dating first.

'How big's the ring?' she asked, somewhat critically.

'Huge,' I said. 'Colorless, flawless.'

Suzanne digested this and said, 'What kind of a name is *Webb*?'

'Family name. Short for Webster.'

'Like the television show,' she said, laughing.

'Yeah,' I said.

'Do you like him?' she asked.

Given her mood, I considered lying and giving her an unequivocal yes, but I have never been able to lie to Suzanne. Instead, I told her the truth — that although he seemed to be the perfect guy, I wasn't all that psyched about Margot marrying him. I felt selfish and disloyal admitting it, and even more so when Suzanne probed, 'Why? Does she blow you off for him?'

'No. Never,' I said, which was the truth. 'She's not like that.'

'So what is it then? . . . Does he *intimidate* you?'

61

'No,' I said quickly, feeling myself becoming defensive. I loved my sister, but it was not an uncommon dynamic between us since I had moved to New York and she had stayed put in our hometown. She'd subtly attack, and I'd subtly defend. It was almost as if she resented me for leaving Pittsburgh for good. Or worse, she assumed that I felt superior — which was completely untrue. In all the important ways, I felt like the *exact* same person I had always been. I was just exposed to more. I had a layer of sophistication and worldliness that comes with living in a big city, and frankly, being around the Grahams. 'Intimidated by what?'

'I don't know. By his looks? His money? His whole slickster, tennis boy, agent bag?'

'He's not really a slickster,' I said, trying to remember what exactly I had told Suzanne about Webb in the past. She had an infallible memory — that she often used against me. 'He's actually pretty down-to-earth.'

'A down-to-earth multimillionaire, huh?' she said.

'Well, *yes*, actually,' I said, thinking that I had long since learned that you couldn't lump all people with money into one category. The wealthy were as varied as the downtrodden. Some were hardworking, some lazy. Some self-made, some born with a silver spoon. Some modest and understated, some ostentatious braggarts. But Suzanne's views had never evolved beyond our *Dallas* and *Dynasty* and *Love Boat* watching days (my sister and I watched a *lot* of television growing up, unlike

Andy and Margot who were limited to a half-hour per day). To Suzanne, every 'rich' person (a term she used derisively) was the same: soft, selfish, and likely 'a lying snake of a Republican.'

'Okay, then,' she said. 'So maybe you're just intimidated by the fact that he belongs in Margot's world, and you . . . don't.'

I thought it was a harsh and narrow-minded thing to say and told her as much. I went on to say that I was well beyond such adolescent insecurities, and that the intimidation factor ended in college sometime after sorority rush when Margot was swept up in a sea of blond, BMW-driving debutantes, and I had incorrectly feared that her going Greek would dilute our friendship. Moreover, I told my sister that I clearly *did* belong in Margot's world. She was my best friend and roommate. And I was likely going to marry her brother, for God's sake.

'Okay. Sorry,' Suzanne said, sounding not at all sorry. She shrugged as she took a bite of her burger. She chewed and swallowed slowly, took a long drink of Coke from her straw and said with annoyed sarcasm, 'It was just a theory. Please *forgive* me.'

I forgave her, as I could never stay mad at Suzanne — but I didn't soon forget it. In fact, the next time Andy and I went out to dinner with Webb and Margot, I fretted that my sister was right. Maybe I was the odd woman out. Maybe Margot would finally come to her senses about how different we were and Webb would steal her away for good. Maybe Webb really was an elitist snob, and he just hid it well.

But as the evening wore on, and I paid close attention to him and all his mannerisms, I decided that Suzanne truly was off the mark. There was nothing *not* to like about Webb. He was a genuinely good guy. It was just an inexplicable disconnect with another person. Webb gave me the same feeling I had as a kid when I slept over at a friend's house and discovered an odd smell in their basement or a foreign cereal selection in their cupboard. He didn't intimidate me; he didn't offend me; he didn't worry me with respect to Margot. He just made me feel vaguely . . . *homesick.* Homesick for what, I wasn't sure.

But despite this, I was determined to bond with Webb on some nonsuperficial level. Or, at the very least, get to the comfortable stage of things where we could be alone in a room together and I wouldn't be casting about, hoping for a third party's return.

So when Margot passes Webb the phone now, and he booms a confident 'Hey, there!' into the phone, I pump up my own volume to match his exuberance and give him an enthusiastic, 'Congratulations! I'm so happy for you!'

'We're pretty happy, too . . . for lo, these forty-five seconds! Your girl doesn't waste much time, does she?'

I laugh, wondering if he's annoyed or amused by our constant phone lifeline and our vow to visit one another at least once every other month, and then say, 'Look forward to seeing you guys next weekend. We'll have to celebrate.'

'Yeah, we'll have fun,' he says. 'And you, Andy, and I will just have to suck it up and drink for Margot, too.'

I force another chuckle and say, yes, we'll have to do just that. Then Webb passes the phone back to Margot, and she tells me she loves me. I tell her I love her, too. Andy tells me to tell her that he loves her. And we both say we love the baby on the way. Then I hang up and lie back down next to Andy. We are facing each other, our feet touching. His hand is resting on my hip, just under my oversized T-shirt. We smile at each other, but say nothing, both of us processing the big news. News that feels way bigger than, say, running into an ex-boyfriend on the street.

And so, for the first time since I left that intersection, I feel a sense of perspective wash over me. Perspective that wasn't ushered in by sex. Or a fun dinner out. Or a night sleeping next to my adorable husband and awaking every few hours to hear his reassuring, steady breathing. Leo has no place in this moment, I think. He has no part in Andy's family. *Our* family.

'You want one, too?' Andy says, his hand moving around me, and then massaging the small of my back.

'One what?' I say, even though I know what he's referring to.

'A baby,' he says. 'I know you and Margot like to do things together.'

I can't tell whether he's joking or propositioning me or speaking theoretically, so I just murmur, 'Someday.'

Andy's hand moves more slowly and gradually stills. Then he closes his eyes for a few more minutes of sleep while I watch his eyelids flutter and imagine someday, every day, with Andy.

7

Thoughts of Leo fade almost completely over the next week, which I credit to my contented life with Andy, Margot's exciting news, and maybe most of all, my work. It's amazing what a productive, satisfying week of work can do for your psyche, and I consider myself very lucky (or as Margot would say — *blessed* — a nice, spiritual spin on the source of good fortune) to have the kind of job I can get happily lost in. I read once that when the hours pass in a blur while you work, you know you have found your calling, and although every day isn't like this for me, I certainly am no stranger to that immersed feeling.

I now own my own one-woman photography business, working on a freelance basis. I have an agent who books assignments for me — anything from advertising shoots for hefty sums, sometimes as much as several thousand dollars for a couple days' work, to smaller, editorial assignments, which I actually prefer from a creative standpoint.

I love portraiture most of all — perhaps because I'm not a very outgoing person. I don't talk easily to strangers, although I wish I could, and taking someone's portrait allows me to make that inroad. I enjoy meeting someone for a leisurely afternoon, becoming acquainted over lunch or coffee, and then getting down to business. I love the trial and error of it all, tinkering with various positions and lighting until I get it just right. There is nothing more satisfying than capturing that one, perfect image. My interpretation of another soul. I also love the variety of the work. Shooting an entrepreneur for *Business Week*, for example, feels very different from taking photos for a piece in *The New York Times* Style section or a glossy spread for *Town & Country*, and the people I'm photographing vary as much as the publications. In the past few weeks alone, I've shot a bestselling author, the cast of an art-house film, a college basketball star and his legendary coach, and an up-and-coming pastry chef.

In short, I've come a long, *long* way since my days of processing film on Second Avenue, and my only lingering regret about my encounter with Leo — other than that it happened at all — is that I didn't have the chance to tell him about my career. Of course I would rather he know about Andy than my work; but ideally, I wish he knew about *both*. Then again, perhaps he knows more than he let on. Perhaps the reason that he didn't ask about my career is that he has already found my Web site or stumbled across one of my more prominent credits. After all, I've sheepishly poked about for his bylines, skimming his features with a bizarre combination of detachment and interest, pride and scorn. It's a matter of curiosity — and anyone who says they are utterly indifferent to what their significant exes are doing is, in my opinion, either lying or lacking a certain amount of emotional depth. I'm not saying it's healthy to be past-obsessed, ferreting out details of every ex. But it's simply human nature to have an occasional, fleeting interest in someone whom you once loved.

So assuming Leo *has* come across my Web site or work, I hope he goes on to surmise that our breakup was a catalyst in my life — a springboard for bigger and better things. In some ways, he would be right about this, although I don't believe you can fully blame anyone else for your own lack of ambition — which was certainly a trend during our relationship.

To this point, I cringe when I think back to how complacent I became on the career front when I was with Leo. My love for photography never waned completely, but I certainly loved it with far less urgency — just as everything in my life became secondary to our relationship. Leo was all I could think about, all I wanted to do. He filled me up so completely that I simply had no energy left to take photos. No time or motivation to even contemplate the next rung on my career ladder. I remember riding the bus to the photo lab every day, well after I had learned everything I could possibly learn from Quynh, and saying things to myself like, 'I don't need to look for another job. Money isn't important to me. I'm happy with a simple life.'

After work, I'd head straight for Leo's new place, back in Queens, ever available to him, only returning to my own apartment when he had other plans or when I needed a fresh supply of clothes. On the rare nights we were apart, I sometimes went out with Margot and our group of friends, but I preferred staying in, where I would day-dream about Leo or plan our next adventure together or compile cassette mixes of songs that seemed cool enough, smart enough, soulful enough for my cool, smart, soulful boyfriend. I wanted so much to please Leo, impress him, make sure that he needed and loved me as much as I needed and loved him.

At first, it seemed to work. Leo was just as smitten as I, only in the less sappy guy way. He never completely abandoned his work like I did, but he was also older, and further established in his career, with important assignments and hard deadlines. He did, however, include me in his professional life, letting me tag along to his interviews or bringing me into his office on the weekends where I'd organize his files or simply watch him while he typed up his stories (or seduced me on his desk). And he was just as willing as I was to blow off his friends and family, preferring our time together to be alone, just the two of us.

For months, things stayed that way, and it felt blissful, magical. We never tired of talking. Our good-byes, whether on the phone or in person, were always lingering, as if it might be the very last time we would ever speak. We sacrificed sleep for conversation, asking endless questions about each other and our respective pasts. No childhood detail was too trivial, which is always a sure sign that someone is in love — or at the very least obsessed. Leo even took a photo of my six-year-old front-toothless self from an album in my bedroom, declaring it 'the cutest thing ever' before tacking it up on a bulletin board in his kitchen.

I exposed every part of myself to him, keeping no secrets, no defense mechanism in place. I revealed all my insecurities, from insignificant but embarrassing things, like how I've always hated my knees, to deeper issues about how I sometimes felt inadequate around Margot and our other well-traveled, wealthy friends in the city. Most important, I told him all about my mother, including uncut details of her death that I had never discussed with anyone. How she looked so frail that it conjured images from the Holocaust. How I had watched my father clear out her throat with his hand one night when she literally couldn't breathe — an image that continues to haunt me now. How at one point I actually said a prayer for the end to just come — and not only so she'd be put out of her misery but so the hospice people and the smell of sickness would be purged from our house, and my father could stop worrying about her death, hiding his notebook of funeral arrangements whenever I came in the room. And then how horribly guilty I felt the moment it finally happened, almost as if I made her die sooner than she would have otherwise. I told Leo how I sometimes felt almost ashamed to be motherless, like no matter what else I did in life, I would always be marked and categorized and pitied for that one fact.

At every turn, Leo listened and consoled me and said all the right things — that although I had lost her at a young age, she had still formed the person I was today. That my memories of her would never fade and the good times would slowly supplant the end. That my descriptions and stories were so vivid, that he felt like he knew her.

Meanwhile, the confessions weren't one-sided. Leo shared his own secrets, too — mostly dysfunctional family tales about his passive, homemaker mother who had no self-esteem, and his mean-spirited, controlling father whose approval he could never quite win. He told me that he wished he had had the money to go to a better, bigger-named college and actually graduate, and that he, too, sometimes felt intimidated by the Manhattan rich-kid set with their fancy journalism school credentials. I felt it hard to believe that someone as amazing as Leo would have any insecurities, but his vulnerability only made me love him more.

And then, aside from everything else, and maybe more important than everything else, there was our chemistry. The physical connection. The mind-blowing, ridiculous sex which was the stuff of both poetry and porn — so unlike anything else I had ever experienced before. For the first time, I wasn't at all self-conscious or inhibited when it came to sex. There was nothing that felt off-limits. Nothing I wouldn't do for him, to him, with him. We kept saying that surely it couldn't get any better. But somehow it did, again and again.

In short, we were completely in sync, insatiable, and sickeningly, crazy in lust *and* love. So much so that it seemed too good to be true.

And so it shouldn't have surprised me to discover that it *was* too good to be true.

I can't say exactly when it happened, but about one year into our relationship, things began to change. There was nothing dramatic that happened — no rift based on a major life issue, no big fight with nasty, irretrievable words. Nobody cheated or lied or moved across the country or delivered an ultimatum about what should come next. Instead, there was just a shift I couldn't quite pinpoint, a quiet transfer of power. It was so subtle, in fact, that for a while I thought I was just being paranoid — a typical, needy girl, something I had always prided myself on *not* being, and something I never had to be with Leo. But after a while, I knew it wasn't in my head. Leo still loved me; he told me he did, and he would *never* say those words if he didn't mean them. But our feelings definitely became lopsided. Only slightly perhaps, but that's the thing about love — even slight differences are readily apparent, marked by small but irrefutable changes in behavior. Little things, like instead of calling me right back, he'd wait a few hours, sometimes even a full day. He started going out with the boys on a regular basis again, and joined an ice hockey intramural team that played on Saturday nights. We began to watch television at night rather than just talk, and sometimes he was too tired for sex, unfathomable in our early days when he'd often wake me up in the middle of the night, touching me everywhere. And when we did make love, there was all too often a feeling of remoteness afterward. A disconnect as he'd roll away from me or stare into space, lost in his own, private thoughts, another mysterious place.

'What are you thinking?' I'd ask, a question both of us once posed ad nauseam, the other answering with exacting detail. A question that now seemed to set him on edge.

'Nothing,' he'd snap.

'Nothing?' I'd say, thinking that such a thing is impossible. You're always thinking *something*.

'Yes, Ellen. *Nothing*,' he'd say as I frantically took note that he wasn't calling me by his usual pet form, Ellie. 'Sometimes I'm just thinking *nothing*.'

'Okay,' I'd say, determined to give him space or play it cool, all the while relentlessly, doggedly analyzing his every move, speculating about what was wrong. Did I get on his nerves? Was I too far from his ideal? Did he still have feelings for his ex-girlfriend, an Israeli artist six years his senior (which made her a *dozen* years more experienced than I)? Was I as good as she in bed? Did he love me as much as he once loved her — and more important, did he love me as much as he once loved *me*?

At first, these questions were all internal musings, but slowly they surfaced, sometimes in the middle of a heated argument, other times as I broke down in frustrated tears. I demanded assurances, fired off questions, painted him into corners, started arguments about everything and nothing. One night, when I was alone in his apartment, I even snooped through his drawers and read a few pages of his journal — the sacred book stuffed with cards and clippings, photos and musings. A book that he carried everywhere and made me feel a rush of love for him every time he cracked it open. It was a huge mistake — not because of what I found or didn't find, but because I was left with an awful, hollow ache afterward, an almost unwashed feeling. I was *that* kind of girl now; we were *that* kind of couple. I tried to put it out of my mind and move on, but just couldn't get past what I had done — what he had *made* me do. So, a few days later, I broke down and confessed, leading to an explosive fight in which I got him to admit that he didn't believe he could ever make a permanent commitment. To me. To anyone.

'Why not?' I said, filled with devastation and frustration.

'Marriage just isn't for me,' he said, shrugging nonchalantly.

'Why not?' I said, pressing him for more. Always for more.

He sighed and said marriage was essentially a contract between two people — and contracts are signed when people don't fully trust one another. 'Which clearly you don't,' he said, throwing all the blame my way.

I apologized and cried and told him that of course I trusted him and that I had no idea what had come over me and that I didn't care about marrying him, I just wanted to be with him, forever.

His expression became steely as he said, 'I'm twenty-nine. I don't want to talk about forever.'

'Okay,' I said, feeling the onset of groveling. 'I'm sorry.'

He nodded and said, 'Okay. Let's just drop it, all right?'

I nodded, pretending to be placated, and a few minutes later we made love and I convinced myself that everything would be fine. We were just going through a rough patch, a few growing pains, and I needed to be patient, ride the wave, take the bad with the good. I told myself that love is sometimes a war of attrition, and that through sheer force of will, I could fix our problems, love him enough for both of us.

But days later, we got into our final fight, which was dramatic only as far as the calendar; it was the New Year's Eve of the new millennium.

'New Year's is amateur night,' Leo had been insisting for weeks, every time I begged him to come to the party I had promised Margot I'd attend. 'You know I hate those scenes. And this Y2K hype is unbearable. It's just another year.'

'Please come,' I said. 'It's important to Margot.'

'Then let Margot party it up.'

'It's important to *me*.'

'Well, it's important to *me* to stay home,' he said.

I negotiated, pleaded. 'Just come for a little while. An hour or two. Then we'll go home.'

'We'll see,' he finally conceded — an answer that almost always means no.

But that night, I clung to the faith that he'd surprise me and show up. I imagined the gauzy, backlit scene. Our eyes locking and the crowd parting as he found my lips, right at midnight. Just like in *When Harry Met Sally*. I spent the whole night watching the clock and the door, and feeling generally heartsick, but ever hopeful. Until eleven fifty-nine came, and I stood in a corner alone, listening to Prince's pulsing remix of '1999' and then the final, stomach-turning, ten-second countdown. A drunk, giddy Margot found me minutes later, hugging me hard, gushing about how much she loved me and how much we had to look forward to. But then she returned to her own date, and I went home alone, sleeping with the phone next to my pillow, waiting, even praying.

But Leo never called that night. Nor did he call the next morning. Around noon, when I couldn't stand it another second, I took the subway to his apartment. He was home, reading the paper and watching MTV.

'You never came,' I said, pathetically stating the obvious.

'Sorry,' he said, sounding not at all sorry. 'I meant to. I fell asleep around ten-thirty.'

'I was all alone at midnight,' I said, pitifully, self-righteously.

'So was I,' he laughed.

'It's not funny,' I said, now more angry than hurt.

'Look. I never promised you I'd come,' he said, agitated.

I quickly backed down, resting my head on his shoulder as we watched a bowl game on television, then made Greek omelets — Leo's specialty — followed by sex on the couch. But some time afterward, when he stood abruptly and told me he had to go work on a story, I got

77

upset all over again.

'It's New Year's Day,' I whined, detesting the sound of my own voice.

'I still have deadlines,' he said flatly.

I looked at him, my head spinning with bitter resentment and desperate grief, and then opened my mouth and uttered those infamous words.

'This isn't working,' I said, believing in my heart that I was only testing the waters, pushing the limits, trying another tactic to reel him back in. 'I think we should break up.'

I expected resistance, a fight, at least a robust discussion. But instead, Leo quickly agreed that I was right. He said so tenderly, almost lovingly, which made me feel worse than an angry response would have. He put his arms around me, his relief almost palpable.

I had no choice but to play along. After all, it had been my suggestion in the first place.

''Bye, Leo,' I said, sounding way braver than I felt.

'Good-bye, Ellen,' he said, at least feigning sadness.

I hesitated, but knew there was no turning back. So I left his place, in shock and denial, springing for a cab home instead of taking the subway.

When I got back to my apartment, Margot was in the family room, reading a magazine. 'Are you okay?' she said.

I told her I didn't know.

'What happened?'

'We broke up.'

I considered saying more, confiding all the

gory details, but could feel myself shutting down, becoming defensive and closed.

'I'm sorry,' she said. 'Do you want to talk about it?'

I shook my head and said, 'I don't know . . . It's really . . . complicated.'

And it *felt* complicated in the way that all breakups feel complicated when you're embroiled in them. While in cruel actuality, most are really quite simple. And it goes something like this: one person falls out of love — or simply realizes that he was never really in love in the first place, wishing he could take back those words, that promise from the heart. Looking back, I can see that that was likely the case with Leo and me — the simplest explanation is often the right one, my mother used to tell me. But at the time, I didn't believe that could be the case.

Instead, I hoped for what all girls hope for in my situation: that he'd change his mind, come to his senses, realize what he had in me, discover that I couldn't be replaced. I kept thinking, even saying aloud to Margot and my sister, 'Nobody will love him like I love him,' which I now realize is far from a selling point to a man. To anyone.

Even worse, I kept replaying in my head that dreadful saying that starts, 'If you love something, set it free.' I pictured the laminated poster-size version of it that my sister hung in her bedroom after a particularly scarring high school breakup. The words were written in purple, sympathy card-style script, complete with a soaring eagle and mountaintop view. I remember thinking that no eagle in the world is going to willingly fly back to captivity.

'Damn straight, he was never yours,' I always wanted to tell Suzanne.

But now. Now *Leo* was that eagle. And I was certain that he would be the one exception to the rule. The one bird who would return.

So I stoically waited, desperately clinging to the notion that ours was only a trial separation. And, incredibly enough, my feelings became even *more* intense post-breakup. If I was obsessed with Leo when I was with him, I was drowning in him afterward. He occupied every minute of my day as I became a cliché of the broken-hearted woman. I tortured myself with his old answering machine messages and sad, bitter songs like Sinead O'Connor's 'The Last Day of Our Acquaintance.' I wallowed in bed and burst into tears at the most random, inopportune moments. I wrote and revised long letters to him that I knew I would never send. I completely neglected my personal appearance (unless you count candlelit pity parties in the bathtub) and vacillated between eating nothing and gorging on ice cream, Doritos, and the *ultimate* cliché, Twinkies.

I couldn't even escape Leo during sleep. For the first time in my life, I remembered vivid details of my dreams, dreams that were *always* about him, us. Sometimes they were bad dreams of near-misses and poor communication and his cold, slow withdrawal. But sometimes they were amazing dreams — Leo and I wiling away the hours in smoky cafés or making hard, sweaty love in his bed — and in some ways, those happy dreams were more agonizing than the bad. I'd awaken, and for a few, fleeting seconds, I'd actually believe that we were back together again. That the breakup was the dream and that I had only to open my eyes and find him right there beside me. Instead, grim reality would set in again. Leo was moving on to a new life without me, and I was alone.

After weeks, nearly *months* of this sort of melodrama, Margot intervened. It was a Saturday, early evening, and she had just failed in about her sixth straight weekend attempt to get me to go out with her. She emerged from her bedroom, looking radiant in a funky, indigo sweater, hip-hugging jeans, and pointy-toed, black boots. She had curled her usually stick-straight hair and applied a shimmering, perfumed powder along her collarbone.

'You look awesome,' I told her. 'Where are you going?'

'Out with the girls,' she said. 'Sure you don't want to come?'

'I'm sure,' I said. '*Pretty in Pink* is on tonight.'

She crossed her arms and pursed her lips. 'I don't know what you're so mopey about. You were never really in love with him,' she finally said, as matter-of-factly as if she were stating that the capital of Pennsylvania is Harrisburg.

I gave her a look like she was crazy. Of course I was in love with Leo. Wasn't my profound grief *proof* of a grand love?

She continued, 'You were only in lust. The two are often confused.'

'It was *love*,' I said, thinking that the lust was

81

only one component of our love. 'I *still* love him. I will *always* love him.'

'No,' she said. 'You were only in love with the *idea* of love. And now you are in love with the *idea* of a broken heart . . . You're acting like an angst-ridden adolescent.'

It was the ultimate slam to a woman in her twenties.

'You're wrong,' I said, gripping my icy tub of pralines 'n' cream.

She sighed and gave me a maternal stare. 'Haven't you ever heard that true love is supposed to make you a better person? Uplift you?'

'I *was* a better person with Leo,' I said, excavating a praline. 'He *did* uplift me.'

She shook her head and started to preach, her Southern accent kicking in more, the way it always does when she's adamant about something. 'Actually you *sucked* when you were with Leo . . . He made you needy, spineless, insecure, and one-dimensional. It was like I didn't even *know* you anymore. You weren't the same person with him. I think the whole relationship was . . . unhealthy.'

'You were just jealous,' I said softly, thinking that I wasn't sure if I meant she was jealous she didn't have a Leo — or was jealous that he had replaced her as the most important person in my life. Both theories seemed plausible despite the fact that she, as always, had a boyfriend of her own.

'*Jealous.* I don't *think* so, Ellen.' She sounded so convincing, so borderline amused with the mere thought of envying what I had with Leo, that I felt my face growing hot as I retreated on this point and just said again, 'He did *too* make me better.'

It was the closest we had ever come to anything resembling a fight, and despite my rising fury, I was also nervous, unable to look her in the eye.

'Oh yeah?' she said. 'Well, if that's true, Ellen, then show me *one* good photo you took when you were with him. Show me how he inspired you. Prove me wrong.'

I put down my ice cream, right onto her April issue of *Town & Country*, and marched over to my roll-top desk in the corner of our living room. I pulled open a drawer, grabbed a manila envelope filled with photographs, and dramatically fanned them onto our coffee table.

She picked them up, flipping through them with the same detached expression with which one shuffles a deck of cards during rounds of mindless solitaire.

'Ellen,' she finally said. 'These pictures . . . They just aren't . . . that good.'

'What do you mean they aren't that good?' I said, looking over her shoulder as she examined the photos of Leo. Leo laughing. Leo looking contemplative. Leo asleep on a Sunday morning, curled up next to his dog, Jasper. I felt a pang of longing for the surly boxer I never liked much to begin with.

'Okay,' she finally said, stopping at one of Leo that I took the summer before. He was wearing shorts and a T-shirt that says 'Atari' and is reclined on a bench in Central Park, staring directly into the camera, directly at *me*. Only his eyes are smiling.

'Take this one, for example,' she said. 'The lighting is good. Nice composition, I guess, but it's . . . just sort of boring. He's good-looking and all, but so what? There's nothing else going on here but a reasonably cute guy on a bench . . . It's . . . *he's* trying *way* too hard.'

I gasped, at least on the inside. This insult was, perhaps, even *worse* than likening me to a lovesick teenager. '*Trying* too hard?' I said, now full-fledged pissed.

'I'm not saying *you're* trying too hard,' she said. 'But *he* definitely is. Just look at his expression . . . He's affected, smug, self-aware. He knows he's being photographed. He knows he's being worshipped. He's all, 'Look at my sultry stare.' Seriously, Ellen. I *hate* this photo. Every single shot you took in the year before Leo is more interesting than this one.'

She tossed the photograph back onto the coffee table, and it landed face up. I looked at it, and could almost, *almost* see what she was saying. I felt a stab of something close to shame, similar to the way I felt when I went back and read my cringe-worthy junior-high haikus about the summer surf at the Jersey Shore. Haikus I once proudly submitted to a literary magazine, feeling genuinely stunned when the rejections came in the mail.

Margot and I stared at each other for what felt like a long time. It was probably the most powerful, honest moment of our friendship, and in that moment, I both loved and despised her. She finally broke our silence.

'I know it hurts, Ellen . . . But it's time to move on,' she said, briskly straightening the pile of photographs and returning them to the envelope. Apparently Leo was no longer worth the energy it took for her to rip his face in two.

'How am I supposed to do that?' I said softly back. It wasn't a rhetorical question — I really *wanted* to know the mechanics of exactly what I was to do next.

She thought for a second and then gave me instructions. 'Go ahead and sit around in your sweats with Molly Ringwald tonight. Then tomorrow, get up and take a long shower. Blow out your hair, put on some makeup. Then get your camera out and get back to it . . . He's not coming back. So do *your* thing . . . It's time.'

I looked at her, knowing she was right. Knowing that once again, I was at a crossroads in my life, and once again, I needed to take Margot's advice and turn to photography.

So the very next day I bought a new camera — the best one I could afford on my meager credit — and enrolled in a comprehensive course at the New York Institute of Photography. Over the next year, I learned the ins and outs of the equipment, everything from lenses and filters to flash, tungsten, and strobe lights. I studied in exhaustive detail aperture, shutter speed, and exposure as well as film and ISO parameters, white balance and histograms. I learned theories of composition, color, patterns, and framing, as well as 'the rule of thirds' (something I think I knew instinctively) and how to use lines for more powerful images. I had already learned a ton about printing, but I was able to practice my technique on much more sophisticated machines. I took a course in portraiture, studying lighting and positioning. I studied product photography, food photography, architectural photography, landscape photography, even sports photography. I delved into digital photography, mastering Adobe Photoshop and the language of megapixels and chip size (which was cutting edge stuff at the time). I even took a class in the business and marketing side of photography.

With every fresh week, every new technique I learned, every photo I snapped, I felt a little more healed. Part of it was just the passage of time, an essential ingredient of any emotional recovery. Part of it, though, was that one passion was slowly replacing another. And although one broken heart doesn't make me an expert in the subject, I believe you need *both* things — time *and* an emotional replacement — to fully mend one.

Then, about nine months post-Leo, I finally felt ready — technically *and* emotionally — to show my portfolio and apply for a real assistant's job. Through a friend of a friend, I heard that a commercial photographer named Frank Brightman was looking for a second assistant. Frank did mostly fashion photography and advertising, but also some occasional editorial work. He had a distinct cinematic style that evoked realism — a look that I both admired and could imagine someday emulating, with my own twist, of course.

Before I could talk myself out of it, I called Frank about the opening, and he invited me to interview at his small Chelsea studio. Right away, Frank both impressed me and put me at ease. He had beautiful silver hair, impeccable clothing, and a soft-spoken kindness. There was also something subtly effeminate about his mannerisms that made me think he was gay — which at that point in my life, hailing from a blue-collar town and a conservative Southern school, still felt like a sophisticated novelty to me.

I watched Frank sip his cappuccino as he reviewed my amateur portfolio housed in a faux-leather album. He flipped the pages as he murmured approval. Then he closed the book, looked me in the eye, and said although he could see that I had promise, he wasn't going to sugarcoat it — he already had a first assistant, and mostly just needed a lackey. Someone to pay the bills, go on coffee runs, and stand around a lot. 'Decidedly unglamorous work,' he finished.

'I can do that,' I said earnestly. 'I was a waitress. I'm great at standing. I'm great at taking orders.'

Frank remained stone-faced as he told me that he had just gone through four second assistants. He said they all had better credentials than I, but had been lazy and unreliable, every one of them. Then he paused and said he could tell that I was different.

'You have a sincerity about you,' he said. 'And I like that you're from Pittsburgh. That's a good, honest place, Pittsburgh.'

I thanked him, flashing him an ever-eager-to-please smile.

Frank smiled back and said, 'The job is yours. Just show up every day, on time, and we'll get along fine.'

So I did just that. I showed up every day for the next two years. I willingly and gladly took orders from Frank and his first assistant, a quirky, older woman named Marguerite. Frank and Marguerite were the creative geniuses while I quietly handled all of the background details. I secured certificates of insurance for larger shoots — and sometimes even hired police. I handled the rental equipment and set up lights and strobes under Frank's detailed specs, beginning many days' work at dawn. I loaded film (by the end of my tenure, Frank said he had never seen someone load so quickly, which felt like the highest of praise) and took literally thousands of lighting meter reads. In short, I learned the ins and outs of commercial photography while I became more and more confident that I would someday strike out on my own.

And that's where I was when Andy came to me.

They say timing is everything, and when I look back, I am a big believer in this theory. If Andy had asked me out any sooner, I might have viewed the invite as a pity maneuver, something Margot had put him up to. I would have said no, flat out, and because Andy isn't the most aggressive guy, that likely would have been that. And, more important, I wouldn't have had time to squeeze in my incidental, insignificant, but still very important rebound guys, most of whom lasted only one or two dates.

But if he had made his first move any later, I might have become cynical — a difficult feat for a woman pre-thirty, but one that I felt grimly capable of. Or I might have begun to seriously date someone else — maybe someone like Leo since they say you usually date the same type, again and again. Or I might have become *too* absorbed in work.

Instead, I was optimistic, content, self-sufficient, and as settled as you can really be when you're young, single, and living in a big city. I still dwelled on Leo (and 'what went wrong') much more than I cared to admit to anyone — even myself, and the thought of him could still stop me in my tracks, send a ripple through my heart, fix a knot in my chest. But I had learned to manage those emotions, compartmentalize them. The worst of the pain had receded with time, as it always does, for everyone. I mostly saw Leo for what he was — a past love who was never coming back, and I saw myself as a wiser, more complete woman for having lost him. In other words, I was ripe for a new relationship, a better man.

I was ready for Andy.

8

I will never forget the moment when I knew that Andy was interested in me as more than just his sister's best friend, or even, for that matter, *his* friend. Interestingly, it didn't happen in New York, even though Margot and I saw Andy on a fairly regular basis, usually out at the bars for a few drinks, our group of friends mixing well with his.

Rather, I was in Atlanta, home with Margot and Andy for Thanksgiving, the three of us flying in the night before. It was well after we had finished the feast that Margot's mother, Stella, had prepared single-handedly (the Grahams' longtime housekeeper, Gloria, had been given the week off), and the worst of the dishes had been cleared and loaded into the dishwasher. Andy and I were alone in the kitchen after I had volunteered to wash the crystal and silver (and nobody objected, which made me feel even more welcomed), and Andy had quickly offered to dry — which I thought was particularly nice in a traditional family where the men seemed to have a complete pass on any domestic duties.

Meanwhile, Margot, her parents, and her brother James had all retired to the 'TV den' and were watching *The Shawshank Redemption*. Incidentally, there were about three other rooms that could be called dens, but instead were called the game room, library, and family room. The entire house was grand and sprawling and filled with fine antiques, Oriental rugs, oil paintings, and other valuable heirlooms collected by way of exotic travels and deceased relatives. Yet despite how formal the house was, every room managed to feel cozy, which I attributed to the warm, soft lighting and the plethora of comfortable chairs to curl up in. Stella did not believe in a lot of things — store-bought salad dressings, regifting, hyphenated last names, for example — and a big one was uncomfortable seating. 'Nothing ruins a dinner party faster than hard chairs,' she offhandedly told me once. When she offered gems like this, I always had the feeling I should jot them down in a notebook somewhere to consult for future reference.

But in a house full of beautiful, comfortable rooms, the kitchen was probably my favorite. I loved the caramel-colored walls, the slate countertops, and the heavy copper pots and pans hanging from hooks over the island. I was enchanted by the picture window overlooking the back terrace and the stone fireplace beside which everyone congregated. It was just the sort of spacious, bright kitchen that you see in the movies. A kitchen featuring a large happy family with a strong yet traditional mother at the helm; a handsome, doting father; a gracious, well-groomed daughter; and a couple of good-natured sons who pop in to dip wooden ladles into simmering pots on the oversized Viking stove and praise their dear mom's — or dear housekeeper's — cooking. Everything about that kitchen was perfect — just like the family in it.

That is what I remember thinking as I plunged my hands into hot, soapy water and fished out two silver teaspoons. I was thinking how lucky I was to be here — that this was *exactly* how Thanksgiving was supposed to feel — except, perhaps, for the near sixty-degree weather.

My own family had disappointed me that year — which was not uncommon since my mother's death. My father tried for a few years to continue our traditions, but Sharon changed all of that — not in an ill-intentioned sort of way, but simply because she had her own children and her own way of doing things. That year, she and my father had gone to Cleveland to visit Sharon's son, Josh, and his new wife, Leslie, who was a former cheerleader from Ohio State, a fact that Sharon seemed exceedingly and disproportionately proud of. This left Suzanne and me to fend for ourselves, and although I was dubious about two single sisters creating a satisfying Thanksgiving, a holiday revolving around food, when neither of us was adept in the kitchen, I was willing to give it a go. Suzanne, however, was not. She made it clear to me that she wasn't going 'to do the holidays this year.' I wasn't sure exactly what that meant, but I had grown accustomed to her moods and knew that forcing a traditional Thanksgiving upon her was unwise. So I was beyond grateful when Margot invited me home with her.

I told Andy some of this now, as he asked about my family, careful not to sound bitter and betray my father and sister. Or worse, sound like Margot's pitiful, matchstick friend.

Andy, who had just strapped on a frilly blue apron, more for the comedic effect than any utilitarian purpose, listened intently and then said, 'Well, I'm very glad you're here. The more the merrier, I always say.'

I smiled, thinking that a lot of people use that expression, but the Grahams truly *believed* it, and so far today, at least a half-dozen friends had dropped by to say hello, including Margot's high school boyfriend, Ty, who had brought over two-dozen famed, pastel thumbprint cookies from Henri's, a long-standing Atlanta bakery. Margot denied it, but Ty was clearly still in love with her — or at least he was still smitten with her family. I could see how it could happen.

'You know,' I said to Andy, 'most families aren't like this.'

'Like what?'

'Functioning,' I said. '*Happy.*'

'We fooled you,' Andy said. 'It's all a façade.'

For a second, I was worried, nearly disillusioned. Was there a dark family secret I didn't know about? Abuse of some kind? White-collar crime? Or worse, a final-word, no-hope diagnosis, like the one that changed everything for my family? I glanced at Andy and saw his jovial expression, feeling awash with relief. My vision of the Grahams as, against all odds, well off *and* well adjusted was safely intact.

'Nah. We are pretty functioning . . . Except for James,' he said, referring to his younger brother, the lovable screw-up of the family who at the time was living in the guest house in the backyard, hence earning the nickname Kato

Kaelin. James had just lost *another* job — he had more 'God-awful bosses' than anyone I had ever known — and had recently totaled at least his third fancy, free car. Yet even James's antics seemed to add only good flavor, the rest of the family simply shaking their head in fond disbelief.

Andy and I were quiet for a few minutes, our elbows occasionally knocking together as we worked, until he said, out of the blue, 'So you ever hear from that guy you used to go out with? Leo, is it?'

My heart jumped. I had just thought of Leo earlier that morning, wondering if he was with his own family in Queens, or whether he was taking a break from the holidays, Suzanne style. I could see him pulling a similar stunt, particularly if he was on a tight deadline. Still, thinking about him was one thing, speaking of him was another. I took a breath, choosing my words carefully. I had the sense that I was going on record, and although I wanted to be accurate, I also wanted to come across as strong. 'No,' I finally said. 'It was a clean break.'

This was a bit of an exaggeration, given my grieving period, but I reasoned that it *was* clean on Leo's end. Besides, if you never contact someone even *once* after your final breakup, isn't it, by definition, clean? No matter what you feel like on the inside? I thought about the one occasion that I almost called Leo. It was right after September Eleventh. At most a week had passed, but the country — and certainly the city — was still in that awful haze of grief and fear. I

94

knew that Leo's offices and home were nowhere near the World Trade Center, and that he seldom had an occasion to visit New York's financial district. But still. There were so many crazy stories that day — stories about people being in places where they normally weren't — that I started to imagine the worst. Besides, I reasoned to Margot, I was getting lots of calls from old friends, even minor acquaintances, who were checking on me. Wasn't it the compassionate, decent thing to do? After all, I might have had bitter feelings toward Leo, but I wanted him to be *alive*. My rationalizing got nowhere with Margot who convinced me that I couldn't, under any circumstances, contact Leo, and she did so with one simple, irrefutable argument: 'He's not calling to check on you, is he?'

I added a bit more detergent to the running water, the scent of lemon filling the air, as Andy nodded and said, 'Clean breaks are always good.'

I murmured my agreement. 'Yeah. I never really understood those people who are all buddy-buddy with their exes.'

'I know,' Andy said. 'Someone's still holding a flame.'

'Like Ty,' I said, laughing.

'*Ex*-actly,' Andy said. 'I mean, c'mon, man, let the dream die already.'

I laughed, thinking that I had certainly let the dream die with Leo, not that I had much of a choice in the matter.

'So,' Andy came right out and asked next, 'are you seeing anyone now?'

I shook my head. 'No. Not really. Occasional

dates here and there — mostly compliments of Margot. I think she's set me up with every straight, single man in the fashion industry . . . But nothing serious . . . What about you?'

I asked the question even though I basically knew his status — he was single again after a short stint with an off-Broadway actress named Felicia. Margot didn't know many details, only that they had broken up, and that she was pretty sure it was mostly Andy's doing. Apparently Felicia was too high maintenance — a drama queen even off-stage.

Andy confirmed with a chipper, 'Single,' as I handed him a crystal goblet.

He shot me a sideways smile that made me suddenly wonder if he was doing more than making small talk and helping with the dishes. Could Margot's brother actually be *interested* in me? *Not possible*, was my first instinct. It didn't matter that Andy was approachable, friendly, and somewhat goofy; he was still Margot's very cute, very successful, *older* brother, which made him feel, somehow, out of my league, or at the very least, off-limits. So I pushed any romantic thoughts of Andy out of my mind as we continued our rhythm of washing and rinsing and drying. Then suddenly, we were finished. And surprisingly, I was sorry we were.

'That about does it,' Andy said, drying his hands, untying the apron, and folding it neatly on the counter. I pulled the stopper out of the sink and watched the water drain, slowly at first but then in a loud *whoosh*. I dried my hands and wiped down the counter with a monogrammed

G hand towel. I had the sense that I was stalling, but stalling for *what*, exactly, I wasn't sure.

That's when Andy looked at me and said, 'So. Ellen?'

Feeling somewhat nervous, I avoided his gaze and replied, 'Yeah?'

Andy cleared his throat while he fiddled with a box of matchsticks on the counter and then said, 'When we get back to the city . . . what do you say we go out? Grab some dinner or something . . . Just the two of us?'

There was no mistaking it — Andy was asking me out. My mind raced, thinking about the implications of going out with my best friend's brother. Wasn't it a risky proposition? What if we got serious and things ended badly? Would Margot take sides? Would our friendship survive? Or at the very least, would it be too awkward for me to ever return home with her? And so it occurred to me, in that second, to say no or to make up an excuse of some sort and avoid any potential conflict of interest. There were thousands of eligible men in Manhattan; why go down this road?

Instead, I looked into his blue eyes, icy in color, but warmer than any brown eyes I had ever known, and said coyly, carefully, 'I think that plan has some potential.'

Andy crossed his arms, leaned back against the island, and smiled. I smiled back at him. Then, just as we heard Margot making her way into the kitchen, he gave me a mischievous wink and whispered, 'And just think. If all goes well . . . you've already met the family.'

For the rest of the weekend, my excitement grew as Andy and I exchanged many knowing glances, particularly the following evening when Stella probed into her two sons' dating status.

'Isn't there *anyone* special?' she asked as we played Scrabble at the leather table in the game room.

James laughed and said, 'Yeah, Mom. There are *lots* of special girls . . . If you get my drift.'

'James,' Stella said, shaking her always professionally coiffed golden head, and feigning exasperation for her middle child, as she spelled out the word *gnomes* with her remaining letters.

'Good one, Mom,' Andy said adoringly. And then to me, 'Do you know that Mom never loses this game?'

I smile, noting how Southerners drop the word *my* when talking about their parents. 'I've heard that,' I said, feeling both impressed and slightly intimidated by the Graham matriarch. In fact, winning board games was only one of the many things I'd heard about Stella over the years that contributed to her beloved, almost cult-like, status in her family. Smart, stunning, strong Stella. Charming and charmed, she certainly wasn't going to die of cancer — I was sure of it — but rather asleep in her own bed, at the ripe old age of ninety-four, with a smile on her face, and that perfect head resting on her silk pillowcase.

'That's 'cause she cheats,' James said in his slow, deep drawl, an accent so much thicker than rest of the clan's — which I chalked up to his general slothfulness that permeated even his speech. He winked at me and said, 'You gotta keep your eye on her real good, Ellen. She's a slippery one.'

We all laughed at the preposterous image of the ever-proper Stella Graham cheating, while she shook her head again, her long neck looking particularly graceful. Then she crossed her arms across her gray couture dress, the heavy gold charms on her bracelet sliding toward her elbow.

'What about you, Andrew?' Stella asked.

I felt my face grow warm as I fixed my gaze on her Eiffel Tower charm, undoubtedly a gift from Margot's father, who I call Mr. Graham to this day, the only one not playing tonight. Instead he was reading *The Wall Street Journal* by the fire and occasionally consulting the dictionary and playing arbitrator of controversial words.

'What *about* me?' Andy said, evading his mother's question while looking simultaneously amused.

'He dumped Felicia,' Margot offered up. 'Didn't I tell you that?'

Stella nodded, but kept her eyes on Andy. 'Any chance of reconciling with Lucy? Such a sweet, pretty girl,' she said wistfully. 'I loved Lucy.'

James cracked up and then imitated Ricky Ricardo, '*Luuuuu-uuu-cy! I'm home!*'

We all laughed again, while Andy shot me a fleeting, eyebrows raised, insider's look. 'Nah. I'm over Lucy,' he said, his bare big toe finding my stocking-covered one under the table. 'But I do have a date lined up next week.'

'Really?' Margot and Stella said at once.

'Yup,' Andy said.

'Potential?' Margot asked.

Andy nodded as Mr. Graham looked up from the newspaper with minor curiosity. Margot once told me that her father's only wish was that Andy someday move back to Atlanta and take over his law practice — and viewed his marrying a Yankee as the only significant roadblock to his dream.

Sure enough, Mr. Graham peered over the paper and said, 'Is she from the South, by chance?'

'No,' Andy said. 'But I think you'd all really like her.'

I smiled, blushed, and looked down at my letters, taking it as a good sign that I had an *F*, *A*, *T*, and *E* on my rack.

★ ★ ★

So that's how Andy and I got our start. Which is why visiting Margot's family (whom I now refer to as *Andy's* family, having made the switch somewhere between our first date and marriage) always feels like a bit of a sentimental journey for me, like reading an old love letter or returning to the site of an early-relationship date. And I am thinking of all of this now, about a week after Margot's big baby news, as Andy and I fly to Atlanta for a weekend visit.

It is a smooth flight and there is not a cloud in the cobalt blue February sky, but I am still a bit on edge. I am a nervous flyer, perhaps inheriting the skittishness from my mother who refused to do so altogether. Not that my parents could ever afford to fly anywhere, a fact that pains me as I

100

watch my father and Sharon jet off to Florida every winter, where they embark on their gaudy Caribbean cruises. I want my father to be happy, but sometimes it doesn't seem fair that Sharon gets to enjoy the fruits of my father's retirement — and the fact that I have long since learned that life's not fair doesn't really ease the blow.

In any event, the flight attendant now makes a chipper announcement that we are nearing Hartsfield-Jackson Airport and that we should return our seats and tray tables to their upright position. Andy follows instructions and repositions his *USA Today* crossword to his lap. He taps his paper with his pen and says, 'I need a four-letter word for summit?'

'Apex,' I say.

Andy shakes his head. 'Doesn't fit.'

I try again. 'Acme?'

He nods. 'Thanks,' he says, looking proud of my crossword prowess. He is the lawyer, but I am the wordsmith. Like his mother, I now routinely kick his ass in Scrabble and Boggle — and really all board games. Which is fine by Andy — he has almost no competitive instinct.

As the plane softly swerves, I grip my armrest with one hand, Andy's leg with my other. I close my eyes, thinking again of that moment in the kitchen so many years ago. It might not be as titillating as striking a love connection with a dark stranger while sequestered on a murder trial, but in some ways it was even *better*. It had substance. A sweet, solid core. A foundation of friendship and family — the simple things that *really* mattered, things that lasted. Andy wasn't about mystery because I already knew him by the time he asked me out. Maybe I didn't know him *well*, and the knowledge I did have was mostly filtered through Margot — but I still knew him in some fundamental, important way. I knew where he came from. I knew who he loved and who loved him back. I knew that he was a good brother and son. I knew that he was a funny, kind, athletic boy. The sort of boy who helps with the dishes after Thanksgiving dinner, ulterior motive or not.

So when Andy and I went on our first date a few days later, we were much farther along than your average couple out on a first date. We were at least in fourth-date terrain, able to skip the autobiographical, get-to-know-you fare and just relax, have a good time. There was no pretense, positioning, or posturing, which I had grown accustomed to at the end of my relationship with Leo — and on so many bad first dates beyond. Everything felt easy and straightforward, balanced and healthy. I never had to wonder what Andy was thinking, or how he felt, because he was an open book, and so consistently happy. Moreover, he was concerned with making *me* happy. He was a polite, respectful Southern gentleman, a romantic and a pleaser at heart.

Somewhere deep down, I think I knew from the start that our relationship lacked a certain intensity, but not in a way where I felt something was missing. To the contrary, it felt like a huge relief never to fret — sort of like your first day of feeling healthy after a vicious case of the flu. The mere absence of feeling miserable was euphoric. This, I thought to myself as Andy and I gradually grew closer, was the way things were supposed to be. This was how love was *supposed* to feel. More important, I believed that it was the only kind of love that wouldn't burn out. Andy had staying power. Together, we had the potential to last forever.

I feel the plane begin to make its final descent as Andy folds his newspaper, stuffs it into the duffel bag at his feet, and squeezes my hand. 'You doing okay?'

'Yes,' I say, thinking that's the thing about Andy — I'm always at *least* okay when I'm with him.

Moments later we land safely in Atlanta, pulling into our gate several minutes ahead of schedule. Andy stands to retrieve our coats from the overhead bin while I turn on my phone to see if Margot has called. Our plan as of last night was to meet outside at Delta arrivals at nine-thirty sharp, but Margot often runs late or changes plans midstream. Sure enough, there is a blinking mailbox icon on my phone. One new message. I hit play, quickly realizing with both excitement and dread that the message is *not* from Margot. The message is from Leo. Leo, who, two weeks after our meeting, is apparently making good on his promise of a renewed friendship.

Flustered, I glance at Andy who is oblivious. I could easily listen to the whole message without his knowledge, and a guilty part of me is dying to hear what Leo has to say. Instead, I let him get no farther than, 'Hey, Ellen. Leo here,' before shutting off my phone and silencing him. I will not allow him to say more than that in Andy's hometown. In Andy's presence, *period*.

9

Andy and I make our way to baggage claim, and then outside to arrivals in record time. 'Like poetry in motion,' he says, proud of his ability to travel efficiently, just as we spot Webb and Margot's silver Mercedes SUV.

To our amusement, Margot appears to be in a clash of wills with a husky policewoman perched on a bicycle seat that looks way too small for her mammoth hips. She is undoubtedly telling Webb and Margot that there is no curbside waiting allowed. I can see through the half-open car window that, although Margot is wearing her sugar-wouldn't-melt-in-my-mouth expression, she is fully entrenched, determined not to back down and lose her spot. Her charm, however, does not seem to be doing the trick on the officer. Sporting a mullet and lug-soled, black motorcycle boots, she blows her whistle and then bellows, 'Loading and unloading only, lady! Move it *now!*'

'My *good*-ness,' Margot says, pressing her hand to her chest, before looking up, seeing us, and announcing, 'Why look here! My family has arrived. We're *loading* now!'

I smile, thinking that Margot has prevailed again, ever elegantly.

The officer turns and glowers at us, vigorously pedaling on to her next victim. Meanwhile, Margot bounds out of the car. She is wearing a

105

long, belted, camel-colored cashmere sweater, dark jeans tucked into chocolate suede boots, and oversized sunglasses (a look she stuck to even in the late nineties when small frames were the rage). She looks every bit the fashion plate she was in New York, maybe more so.

'We're so glad you're here!' she squeals, gathering Andy and me in a joint, but still dainty hug. Even though I knew she couldn't yet be showing, her petite frame and sprightly movements belie pregnancy. Only her chest gives her secret away; her C cups seem to be tipping over into the D range. I smile, thinking that it's the sort of thing you'd only notice on a best friend. I gesture toward them, and mouth, 'Nice.'

She laughs and says back, 'Yeah, they've already gotten a little bigger . . . But this is mostly just a quality push-up.'

Andy pretends to be embarrassed by our conversation as he tosses our oversized duffel bag into the back of the car. Seconds later, after a hearty greeting from Webb, we are exiting the airport and whizzing along the highway. Margot and I are in the backseat, all of us talking excitedly about the baby and their back-wing addition where the baby's room will be.

'Our contractors are as slow as molasses,' Margot says. 'I told them they'd *better* be finished by the time this baby arrives.'

'No way they'll finish by then, hon. Not with their hourly coffee breaks,' Webb says, running his hand back and forth over his chiseled jaw. I notice that he is also wearing a camel-colored sweater, and I wonder if he and Margot

106

purposely matched. It is the sort of thing they've been known to do, the most egregious example being their his-and-hers orange driving mocca-sins.

Webb glances over his shoulder before switching lanes to pass a slow-moving Volks-wagen and says, 'So did Margot tell y'all about our leather floors in the basement?'

'No,' I say, looking at Margot and wondering how that one fell through the cracks in our daily chats.

She nods and gestures toward Webb as if to say, 'His idea, not mine,' but I can tell she's proud of her husband's lofty sense of aesthetics.

'Leather floors?' Andy whistles. 'Holy smokes.'

'Yeah. Those bad boys are decadent,' Webb says. 'Wait 'til you try 'em out.'

'Won't they get all scuffed?' I say, realizing that I often sound overly practical, even pedestrian, around Webb.

'A little scuffing adds character,' Webb says. 'Besides, they'll mostly get barefoot traffic.'

Margot explains, 'We saw them at a spa in Big Sur and couldn't resist them . . . It's where I'll do my yoga and meditating.'

Naturally, I think fondly, but say, 'You're taking up yoga?'

Margot has never been very into workouts, and when she did go to the gym in New York, she was more a reclined-bike-with-*People*-magazine-in-hand sort of girl.

'Since the baby,' she says, rubbing her nonexistent tummy. 'I'm trying to become more . . . *centered*.'

I nod, thinking that the shift seemed to happen even before the baby news, around the time she moved from New York. It's not surprising — even leaving the city for a weekend has a calming effect on me. And although Atlanta is a major city by any measure, it feels so open, relaxed, and downright *lush* in contrast to New York. Even the downtown area, which we are passing now, looks like a very manageable Fisher Price-sized town after growing accustomed to New York's skyline.

Minutes later, we arrive in the heart of Buckhead, the affluent section of North Atlanta where Andy and Margot grew up. After first hearing the odd-sounding name *Buckhead* (apparently derived from a long-expired tavern that displayed a large buck's head), I conjured quaint, rustic images, but the area actually has a very cosmopolitan edge. Its shopping district comprises two high-end malls where Margot gets her Gucci and Jimmy Choo fix, as well as luxury hotels, condos, art galleries, nightclubs, and even five-star restaurants, hence earning the monikers Silk Stocking District and the Beverly Hills of the South.

But the real essence of Buckhead comes in the residential areas, along the winding, tree-lined streets, dotted with graceful Georgian mansions and stately neoclassical homes like the one Margot and Andy grew up in. Others, like Webb and Margot's 1930s painted brick house, are slightly more modest, but still utterly charming.

As we pull into their cobblestone driveway lined with white camellias, I feel the urge to use the words *lovely* or *delightful* — which aren't normally in my vocabulary.

Webb opens my car door, and I thank him and announce that I'm in the mood for sweet tea already. Sweetened iced tea is one of the things I love about the South, right up there with homemade biscuits and cheese grits. Andy and I simply don't understand why the beverage, present in virtually every home and restaurant in the South, including most fast-food chains, hasn't made inroads north of the Mason-Dixon Line.

Margot laughs. 'Well, you're in luck,' she says. 'I made up a batch this morning.'

Undoubtedly, she made more than just tea as Margot is a fabulous hostess, just like her mother. Sure enough, we walk into what could be a spread in *Southern Living*. In Margot's words, the style of their home is 'transitional with a Deco twist.' I'm not sure what that means exactly, but I love that it's beautiful without being at all predictable or overly traditional. The floor plan is open, her kitchen and living area spilling together with an array of seating areas. Her dominant color scheme is chocolate brown and pale sage, and silken fabrics softly drape the windows, creating a feminine, almost dreamy effect. Clearly Webb lets Margot call the shots when it comes to matters of décor because it's certainly not what you'd expect of a strapping sports agent. To this point, his framed, autographed jerseys and pennants, omnipresent in his bachelor pad in Manhattan, are now relegated to the basement and his manly, dark-wood-paneled office.

Andy points to the cream-colored couch in the living room adorned with a carefully arranged sage throw and coordinating pillows. 'Is that new?'

Margot nods. 'Uh-huh. Isn't it yummy?'

'Yeah,' Andy deadpans, and I can tell a joke is coming. 'Real yummy when the kid drops his SpaghettiOs all over it.'

'Or *her* SpaghettiOs,' Margot says as she leads us into the kitchen where she has prepared a brunch of fruit salad, spinach quiche, and cheese crêpes. 'I hope you're hungry.'

'Starving,' Andy says.

Margot suggests that we eat now as we have early dinner reservations at Bacchanalia, the Grahams' favorite restaurant in town.

'Mother and Daddy are joining us. I promised that we wouldn't monopolize you now that we live here.'

'Yeah. Andy and I were wondering about that. Does she mind that we're staying with you?' I ask.

'She understands,' Margot says, drizzling raspberry compote over her crêpes. 'But she also informed me, in no uncertain terms, that she expects that her son will continue to sleep under *her* roof when he's in Atlanta for the holidays.' Margot finishes the sentence in her mother's regal Charleston accent.

Andy rolls his eyes, and I smile, feeling grateful that although he is a dutiful son, he shows no signs of being an outright mama's boy. I don't think I could handle that routine. I went to a wedding recently where the mother of the groom had to be peeled off her son at the end of the reception as she sobbed, 'I don't want to lose you!' The whole scene bordered on unwholesome. Margot's theory on the topic is that when a woman has only sons, and no daughters, this dynamic is more likely to kick in. Perhaps because the mother hasn't had to share any of the limelight with another woman, perhaps because of that adage, 'A son is a son 'til he gets a wife, but a daughter is a daughter all her life.' She might be right about this because although Stella adores her sons, she focuses most of her time and energy on her daughter.

As I watch Margot maneuver around her kitchen, I ask if there's anything I can do to help. She shakes her head and pours tea from a big glass pitcher into three rock-cut glasses and Perrier into her own. Then she calls us to sit down, prompting Webb to say a quick blessing, a practice that seems more cultural than religious, as the two abandoned it, along with church attendance, while in New York.

As Webb finishes his short, formal prayer, and Margot smiles and says, 'Enjoy!' I have the fleeting sense that we have little in common other than our shared past. But within seconds, that feeling is gone, as Margot and I move rapid-fire from topic to topic, discussing and analyzing everything and everyone with what most, Webb and Andy included, would view as excruciating detail. More than anything, it is why Margot and I are such close friends — why we connected in the first place, despite being so

111

different. We simply love to talk to each other.

As such, we barely let the guys get a word in, covering New York and Atlanta gossip with equal scrutiny and fervor. We discuss our single New York friends who still get wasted every night and wonder why they can't meet a nice guy, and then the girls in her neighborhood who have full-time help so that they can play tennis, shop, and lunch every day.

'Who would you rather be?' I ask. 'If you had to pick.'

'Hmm,' Margot says. 'Not sure. Both extremes are sort of sad.'

'Do you ever miss working?' I ask her tentatively. Although I can't imagine giving up my career, I'm not yet a mother-to-be. That might change everything.

Margot shakes her head. 'I really thought I would . . . but I'm just so busy.'

'Playing tennis?' Andy deadpans.

Margot's mouth twitches ever so defensively. 'Some,' she says. 'But also decorating the house . . . getting ready for the baby . . . and doing all my charity work.'

'She bagged the Junior League, though,' Webb says, reaching for another helping of crêpes. 'It was too much to take. Even for her.'

'I didn't say the Junior League was too *much* to take,' Margot says. 'I simply said that the Atlanta League is *young*. I felt like the old mother hen around all those early-twenty-something girls, most of them fresh out of college and already married to their high school sweethearts.'

Webb's face lights up, as he says, 'Speaking of . . . Tell your brother and Ellen who you hired to do our landscaping.'

Margot says her husband's name in a playful reprimand, her fair skin turning azalea pink. I smile, ever amused at how easily she and Stella embarrass, even blushing on behalf of others, so great is their empathy. In fact, Stella can't even watch award shows — she is too nervous watching the acceptance speeches.

'C'mon,' Webb says, grinning. 'Go on and tell 'em, honey.'

Margot purses her lips as Andy clamors, 'Who?'

'Portera Brothers,' Webb finally says, which everyone in the room knows is the last name of Margot's high school boyfriend, Ty, the one who still drops by every Thanksgiving.

'*Portera* Brothers?' Andy says, smirking. 'As in Loverboy Ty? . . . Ty 'The Right Stuff' Portera?'

' 'The Right Stuff'?' Webb says.

'Margot didn't tell you about her little boyfriend's stirring Jordan Knight air-band performance in high school?' Andy says, standing, spinning, and singing, 'Oh! Oh! Girl! You know you got the right stuff!'

'Wait a sec, Margot. Your high school boyfriend lip-synced to the Backstreet Boys?' Webb says, giddy with his fresh ammunition.

'Get it straight, Webb. It was the New Kids on the Block,' Andy says. 'And I think the year before he did Menudo, didn't he, Margot?'

Margot slaps the table. 'No! He most certainly didn't do Menudo!'

I resist the temptation to point out that the only one at the table who can recite New Kids' lyrics is Andy.

'New Kids, huh? Well, I guess that helps ease the blow a little,' Webb says, chuckling. 'I mean, maybe the guy's gay now. Or in a boy band. Or, God forbid, *both*.'

I smile, although I mentally put this comment in the category of 'What makes Webb different from me' — I'm quite certain he has no gay friends.

Webb continues, 'Seriously. Can y'all believe Margot hired her ex?'

'No,' Andy says with exaggerated somberness. 'I really, *really* can't. Disgraceful.'

I know Andy and Webb are only joking, but my stomach still jumps thinking of the message waiting on my phone. The message I should have deleted. I look down at my plate, tapping a sprig of parsley with a tine on my fork.

'C'mon, Ellen!' Margot says, resting her elbows on the table, something she would never ordinarily do. 'Help me out here!'

I cast about for a second, trying to think of something helpful but noncommittal. I weakly offer, 'They're just friends.'

'Just friends, huh?' Webb says. 'The *ollllllle* 'just friends' routine.'

'Good Lord,' Margot says, standing to clear her plate and Andy's.

'The Good Lord isn't on your side any more than Ellen here,' Webb says. 'Neither of them approves of these sort of reindeer games.'

''*Reindeer* games'? Oh, grow up, Webb! . . . Ty

is so grandfathered in it's not funny,' Margot says, returning from the kitchen. 'We made the transition to friends a zillion years ago. When we were still in high school. And he's been doing Mother and Daddy's yard for over a year now!'

'And that makes it *better*? That he's doing *their* yard, too?' Webb says, shaking his head. He looks at me and says, 'Watch out. They're all disloyal. The pack of them.'

'Hey! Don't lump me in with my folks and sister,' Andy says. 'I wouldn't use the guy. Even if I had a yard.'

'Sorry, man,' Webb says. 'They're all disloyal *except* you. Even James.'

'James doesn't have a yard either,' Andy says.

'Yeah. But he plays golf with the guy. Disloyal bastard,' Webb says.

'It's not a question of loyalty to anyone,' Margot says. 'And besides, it's not like he'll be over here doing the planting himself. He has employees for that . . . His company does great landscaping at the right price. That's all there is to it, Webster Buffington, and you know it.'

'Yep,' Webb says. 'Keep telling yourself that and maybe you'll start to believe it.'

'Oh, puh-*lease*, you act like I just put my prom portrait on the mantel!'

'I'm sure that'll be next,' Webb says. He then turns to me and says, 'Ellen, you still talk to your prom date?'

I shake my head decisively.

'Does he . . . uh, clean your apartment or prepare your taxes or anything like that?' Webb presses.

'Nope,' I say.

'You talk to any exes, period?'

The follow-up is clearly for me, but I say nothing, dazed by the coincidence, and hoping that someone will jump in and save me. No such luck. The room falls silent. I look at Andy, as if the question were directed his way.

'What?' Andy says. 'Don't look at me. You know I'm not friends with any girls, let alone exes.'

'Lucy sent you a Christmas card a few years ago,' I say, feeling the familiar stab of faint jealousy thinking about sweet, hot, little Lucy.

'With a photo of her *kid* on it,' Andy says. 'That's hardly a come-hither invitation . . . Besides, I never sent *her* a Christmas card.'

'Yes, but you never sent them at all until we got married,' I say, standing to help Margot clear the table.

Andy shrugs. As a lawyer, he certainly knows an irrelevant tangent when he sees one. 'The point is — I don't talk to her. Period.'

'And I don't talk to my exes, *period*,' Webb says.

Andy looks at me expectantly.

'And I don't talk to my exes,' I echo shamefully. *Anymore.*

'Oh, get over yourselves,' Margot says, wiping crumbs from Webb's placemat into her open palm. She looks up and then around the table, adding, 'And, while you're at it, how about getting over your exes, too?'

★   ★   ★

116

That afternoon, Leo's message is far from my mind as Margot and I shop for gender-neutral newborn clothes at a boutique called Kangaroo Pouch, cooing over the exquisite, impossibly tiny items and finally selecting a white knit gown and matching receiving blanket for the baby's homecoming, along with a half-dozen fine-cotton onesies and an array of hand-embroidered booties, hats, and socks. I feel my nesting instinct kicking in, and for the first time, *really* wish I were pregnant, too. Of course I know that craving a baby while you shop for a layette for your best friend's firstborn is akin to wanting to get married while you watch her slip on a Vera Wang gown and twirl before a dressing-room mirror — and that there are plenty of not-so-fun-or-cute things that come with motherhood. Still, as we go on to cruise by a few houses for sale, 'just for fun,' I can't help thinking how nice it would be to relocate to Atlanta, live near Margot, and watch our children — cousins and best friends — grow up together in a happy, beautiful world filled with white camellias and sweet tea.

But by the time Margot and I are changing for dinner, thoughts of Leo have returned full-force, my cell phone burning a hole in my purse. So much so that I feel dangerously close to divulging everything to Margot. I remind myself that although she is my best friend, she is also Andy's sister. And, on top of that, she hated Leo. There is no way that that conversation would end well.

Instead I very casually resurrect the 'Can you

be friends with an ex?' debate, trying to feel my way through my emerging moral dilemma.

'So,' I say as I fasten the side zipper of my charcoal pencil skirt. 'Webb doesn't *really* care about Ty, does he?'

Margot laughs and waves her hand in the air. 'Of course not. Webb is the most secure man I know . . . and he's certainly not threatened by a nothing, high school crush.'

'Right,' I say, wondering if Andy would feel threatened by Leo — and more significantly, whether he *should*.

She holds up two options from her closet, a black jersey dress and a lavender crocheted jacket with a mandarin collar, and says, 'Which one?'

I hesitate, then point to the jacket and say, 'But let's suppose for a second that you hired Brad to do your landscaping.'

'Brad *Turner?*' she says, as if I could be speaking of a Brad other than the handsome, bespectacled bond trader whom she dated for nearly two years before meeting Webb.

'Yeah,' I say. 'The one and only.'

She squints and says, 'Okay. I got a visual . . . Brad in his power suits out there with his lawn mower.'

'Would Webb be pissed?'

'Maybe,' she says. 'But I'd never hire Brad. We don't even talk anymore.'

'Why not?' I ask, because, after all, that's the real crux of the issue. Why does one keep in touch with certain exes, and not others? Why is it okay to segue into a friendship with some? Is there a multipronged test or is it really more simple than that?

'Oh, I don't know,' Margot says, looking concerned. For one second I worry that she's on to me, but as she slips on a pair of black pants and patent, peep-toe heels, her expression becomes placid again. Leo is the last person on her mind. I only wish I could say the same. 'Why? Do you miss Brad or something?'

I smile and shrug and say, 'I dunno . . . I was just wondering what the golden rule is when it comes to exes . . . I just think it's an interesting topic.'

Margot pauses to consider this, and then proclaims very definitively, 'Okay. If you're totally over the guy, and he's *totally* over you, and you were never *that* serious to begin with, I see absolutely nothing wrong with an occasional, friendly hello. Or some innocent yard work. Assuming, of course, your current beau-slash-husband is not a complete psycho freak. Then again, if your current guy is a psycho freak, you have much bigger issues than who you should hire to do your lawn.'

'Right,' I say, feeling pleased with her summation and even more pleased with the loophole she unwittingly created for me. 'Well said.'

With that, I breezily tell Margot that I'm going to brush my teeth and put on my makeup, and seconds later, I am sequestered in the guest bathroom, the door locked and the water in the sink running full blast. I carefully avoid my own reflection in the mirror as I open my purse and pull out my cell phone.

After all, I say, repeating Margot's sound, careful reasoning, there is absolutely nothing in the world wrong with an occasional, friendly exchange when you're *totally* over someone.

10

Ellen. It's Leo. Look. I got a question for you. Call me when you can.

Leo's message, only four seconds and fifteen words long, still manages to intrigue me in a way I can only describe as highly confounding and even more annoying. After standing at the sink and staring into space for several minutes, I listen to it again, just to be sure I didn't miss anything. Of course I didn't, so I hit delete, saying aloud, *Don't hold your breath, buddy.*

If Leo thinks that he can let all of these years pass, then call just like old times with some purported *question*, and expect that I will just hop to it and fire off a call back with some great sense of urgency, well, he has another think coming. At best he is being presumptuous; at worst, downright manipulative.

I indignantly brush my teeth, then carefully apply a new, rose-toned lipstick to my full lower lip and thinner top one. I blot with a tissue, realize that I've removed too much, and reapply, finishing with a layer of clear gloss. I highlight my cheeks, forehead, and chin with a bronzer and line my eyelids with a dark charcoal pencil. A touch of mascara and some under-eye concealer, and I'm good to go. I meet my gaze in the mirror, smile slightly, and decide that I look pretty — although *anyone* would look pretty in Margot's soft bathroom lighting. Like her mother,

Margot doesn't believe in fluorescent lights.

I open the door adjoining the guest room, telling myself that checking my voicemail is one thing, calling Leo back is another. And I will *not* call him back anytime soon, if ever. I kneel in front of my duffel bag and rifle through it to find a small, snakeskin clutch that I remembered to pack at the last second. Stella gave it to me for Christmas last year, and I know it will please her greatly to see me using it. She is a thoughtful, generous gift giver, although I often read into her presents that she wishes I would be a certain way, a little more like her own daughter. In other words, the kind of girl who instinctively switches out handbags for the evening.

I transfer my lip gloss, a small mirror, and a pack of wintergreen Certs to the clutch. There is a little room left so I toss in my cell phone, just in case. In case of *what*, I'm not quite sure, but it's always best to be prepared. Then I slip on a pair of black kitten heels and head downstairs where Margot and the guys have gathered on barstools around the kitchen island and are feasting on wine, cheese, and stuffed olives. I survey Andy and Margot, standing side by side and laughing at Webb imitating one of his clients, and note that their resemblance is even more striking than usual. Beyond their heart-shaped faces and round, well-spaced blue eyes, they share the same happy aura — a certain authentic way of being.

Andy's face brightens even more as he looks over at me.

'Hey, honey,' he says, standing to kiss my cheek and then whispering in my ear, 'You smell nice.'

Incidentally, I am wearing a blueberry-vanilla body lotion, also compliments of Stella. 'Thanks, honey,' I whisper back, feeling a pang of guilt toward my husband *and* his mother.

I tell myself that I have done nothing wrong — this is all Leo's fault. He has painted me into a corner, created a layer of deceit between me and the people I love. Sure, it is a small secret in the scheme of things, but it is still a secret, and it will grow — *multiply* — if I return his call. So I simply won't do it. I won't call him back.

Yet as I pierce an olive with a toothpick and half-listen to another of Webb's client stories, this one about a Falcons football player who got caught trying to carry marijuana onto a plane, I feel myself caving ever so slightly. I reason that if I *don't* call Leo back, I might continue to wonder what he has to say, what he could *possibly* want to ask me. And the more I dwell on those possibilities, the more I will be filled with unease, and the more he, and the past he featured in, might undermine the present. Furthermore, not calling might look strategic, creating the impression that I care too much. And I don't care. *I do not.* So I'll just call him back, field his so-called question, and then inform him, in fifteen words or fewer of my own, that despite what I said in the diner, I have enough friends. I don't need to resurrect an old one — if, in fact, that's ever what we were. Then I will be done with him once and for all. I take a long sip of wine, and think that I can hardly wait to get back to New York and get the conversation over with.

And yet, despite my vow to rid Leo from my life come Monday morning, I can't manage to shake his hold on me this evening, even after I'm at Bacchanalia with the entire Graham family. I am so distracted, in fact, that Stella turns to me at one point, just after the third course of our tasting menu complete with wine pairings that Webb deems 'brilliant' and says, 'You're a bit fidgety tonight, dear. Is everything okay?'

Her tone and gaze are concerned, but I've seen her in action enough with her children — and husband, for that matter — to know that it is a veiled reprimand. In her words, 'being present' when you are with others is of the utmost importance — and too often in our culture of BlackBerrys and cell phones, people are disengaged and disconnected and distracted from their immediate surroundings. It is one of many things I admire about Stella — that despite her emphasis on appearances, she really does seem to understand what matters most.

'I'm sorry, Stella,' I say.

I feel guilty and embarrassed by her reproach, but her comment also has the odd ancillary effect of making me feel squarely in the family fold, like I am one of her *own* children. It is the way she has treated me for years, but even more so since Andy and I married. I think back to the Christmas after we got engaged, when she put her arms around me in a private moment and said, 'I'll never try to replace your mother, but know that you are like a second daughter to me.'

It was the perfect thing to say. Stella *always* knows the perfect thing to say — and more important, always *means* what she says.

She shakes her head now and smiles as if to absolve me, but I still go on to stammer an explanation. 'I'm just a bit tired. We had a pretty early start . . . and then . . . all of this wonderful food.'

'Of course, dear,' Stella says, adjusting the silk, patterned scarf tied effortlessly around her swanlike neck. She is never one to hold a grudge, big or small, the one quality she did not manage to convey to her daughter, who can impressively hold on to petty ill will for years, much to all of our amusement.

And, with this observation, I push Leo out of my head for the hundredth time today, focusing as hard as I can on our next topic, spearheaded by Mr. Graham — the renovated golf course at the club. But after about three minutes of talk of bogies and eagles and holes-in-one among the four men at the table, and apparent rapt interest by Margot and her mother, I start to lose it again and decide I can't wait another second. I must find out what Leo wants. Now.

My heart races as I excuse myself and make my way into the small upscale gift shop adjoining the restaurant where the ladies' room is positioned. With my clutch in sweaty hand, I am perfectly aghast at myself, as if I'm watching one of those idiotic women in a horror movie — the kind who, upon hearing a disturbing noise late at night, decides that rather than calling 911, it makes a lot of good sense to go tiptoeing barefooted in the heavily wooded backyard to investigate. After all, there might not be an axe murderer lurking, but there are certainly clear and present dangers here, too. Margot or Stella could, at any moment, catch me in the act. Or Andy could, for the first time ever, decide to skim my cell phone bill when it arrives at month's end and inquire who in Queens I felt the sudden need to contact right in the middle of our family dinner in Atlanta.

But, despite such obvious pitfalls, here I foolishly am, holed up in yet another bathroom, urgently debating whether to call Leo back or merely text him. In what feels like a moral victory, I decide to tap out a hurried message with two rapid, eager thumbs. 'Hi. Got your message. What's up?' I type, hitting send before I can change my mind or dwell on my word choice. I close my eyes and shake my head.

I feel simultaneously relieved and appalled at myself, the way an addict must feel after that first sip of vodka, emotions that are amplified a few seconds later when my phone vibrates and lights up with Leo's number. I pause just outside the restroom, pretending to admire a display of pottery for sale in the shop. Then I take a deep breath and answer hello.

'Hi!' Leo says. 'It's me. Just got your text.'

'Yeah,' I say, pacing and nervously glancing around. Now, in addition to the possibility of getting caught by Margot or her mother, I am exposed to any of the male members of my family who could be making a trip to the nearby men's room.

'How are you?' Leo says.

'I'm fine,' I say tersely. 'But I really can't talk

now . . . I'm at dinner . . . I just . . . I just wondered what you had to ask me?'

'Well,' Leo says, pausing, as if for dramatic effect. 'It's sort of a long story.'

I sigh, thinking that, of course, Mr. Cut-to-the-Chase suddenly has a long-winded proposition for me.

'Give me the short version,' I say, feeling desperate for some sort of clue. Is it as frivolous and contrived as a question about his camera? Or as serious as whether I am the culprit for an STD he picked up along the way? Or is it something in between?

Leo clears his throat. 'Well . . . it's about work,' he says. '*Your* work.'

I can't help smiling. He has seen my photos after all. I *knew* it.

'Yeah?' I say as breezily as possible while I tuck my clutch under my perspiring arm.

'Well . . . Like I said, it's sort of a long story, but . . . '

I walk up the few steps to the dining area, and cautiously peer around the corner into the dining area, seeing that my family is still safely seated. The coast is clear for a few more seconds, at least. I duck back to safety, making a 'get on with it' hand motion. 'Yes?'

Leo continues, 'I have a potential portrait gig for you . . . if you're interested . . . You do portraits, right?'

'Yeah, I do,' I say, my curiosity piqued ever so slightly. 'Who's the subject?'

I ask the question, but am fully prepared to turn him down. Say I have plenty of jobs lined up in the weeks ahead. That I have a booking agent now and don't really have to scrounge around for random work. That I've made it — maybe not in a *big* way — but in a big *enough* way. So thanks for thinking of me, but no thanks. *Oh, and one more thing, Leo? Yeah. Probably better not to call me anymore. No hard feelings, all right? Toodle-oo.*

I will say it all in a rush of adrenaline. I can taste the satisfaction already.

And that's when Leo clears his throat again and throws down a trump card. 'Drake Watters,' he says.

'*Drake Watters?*' I say, in stunned disbelief, hoping that he's referring to another Drake Watters — other than the ten-time Grammy-winning legend and recent nominee for the Nobel Peace Prize.

But, of course, there is only one Drake.

Sure enough, Leo says, 'Yup,' as I recall my high school days, how I sported a Drake concert T-shirt to school at *least* once a week, along with my pegged, intentionally ripped, acid-washed jeans and Tretorn sneakers covered with black-Sharpie peace signs. And although I haven't been a big fan of his since then, he certainly remains on my elite list of 'Icons I'd Kill to Photograph,' right up there with Madonna, Bill Clinton, Meryl Streep, Bruce Springsteen, Queen Elizabeth, Sting, and, although he's really not in the same league as the others and for perfectly shallow reasons, George Clooney.

'So what do you think?' Leo says with a hint of

128

flippant smugness. 'You interested?'

I softly kick a floorboard, thinking that I hate Leo for tempting me like this. I hate myself for folding. I almost even hate Drake.

'Yeah,' I say, feeling chagrinned, defeated.

'Great,' Leo says. 'So we'll talk about it more later?'

'Yeah,' I say again.

'Monday morning work for you?'

'Sure,' I say. 'I'll call you Monday.'

Then I hang up and head back to the table where I harbor a brand-new secret while feigning wild enthusiasm for my spiced cardamom flan with candied kumquats.

11

Monday morning comes in a hurry as is always the case when you're not quite sure how to play your hand. Since Saturday night, I have been all over the map with my Leo-Drake strategy — everywhere from never calling Leo back, to telling Andy *everything* and making him decide about the shoot, to meeting Leo face to face to hear all the exciting details of the biggest assignment of my life to date.

But now, as I pause at the door of our apartment after kissing Andy good-bye for the day, with Drake's mesmerizing voice in my head, singing 'Crossroads,' a song about the disastrous aftermath of one unfaithful evening, I know what I must do. I turn and run across the family room, sliding over to the window in my fluffy purple socks for a final glimpse of my husband descending the stairs of our building and striding along the sidewalk in his handsome three-quarter-length navy overcoat and cashmere, red-plaid scarf. As he disappears toward Park Avenue, I can make out his profile and see that he is cheerfully swinging his briefcase at his side. It is this fleeting visual that solidifies my final decision.

I walk slowly back to the kitchen and check the clock on the stove. Nine-forty-two — plenty late enough to phone anyone. But I stall anyway, deciding I need coffee first. Our coffee maker broke a few weeks ago, and we don't own a kettle, so I bring a mug of tap water to a boil in the microwave and rifle through the cabinet for a jar of instant coffee, the kind I watched my mother make every morning. I gaze back at the familiar gentleman on the Taster's Choice label, marveling that he used to seem so *old* to me. Now he seems on the young side — early forties at most. One of time's many sleights of hand.

I unscrew the cap and stir in two heaping teaspoons, watching the brown crystals dissolve. I take a sip and am overcome with a wave of my mother. It really is the little things, like instant coffee, that make me miss her the most. I consider calling Suzanne — who can sometimes ease these pangs by simple virtue of the fact that she is the only one in the world who knows how I feel. For although we had very different relationships with our mother — hers was often turbulent as she inherited my mother's stubborn gene — we are still sisters who prematurely lost our mother and *that* is a powerfully strong, permanent bond. I decide against calling her, though, because sometimes it works the other way, too, and I can end up feeling even sadder. I can't afford to go down that road right now.

Instead, I distract myself with the Style section of the *Times*, leisurely reading about the new leggings trend that Margot predicted last year, while I sip my stale-tasting coffee, wondering how my mother stood it for all those years. I then make the bed, finish unpacking our duffel bag, organize my sock drawer, then Andy's, brush my teeth, shower, and dress. Still not feeling quite ready, I alphabetize the novels on my bookshelf by author's last name, a project I've been meaning to undertake for ages. I run my fingers over the neatly aligned spines, feeling a rush of satisfaction, relishing the underlying order despite the chaos in my head.

At eleven-twenty-five, I finally bite the bullet and make the call. To my simultaneous relief *and* frustration, Leo doesn't answer, and I go straight to his voicemail. In a rush of adrenaline, I give the speech that I've pieced together over the past thirty-six hours, while at church and brunch with the Grahams, then afterward as we casually drove around Buckhead looking at more homes for sale, then on our uneventful flight home.

The gist of my spiel is that a) I'm impressed that he has a Drake Watters connection (why not throw him a harmless bone?), and b) very appreciative that he thought of me for the job, and c) would be positively thrilled to take the assignment, but d) don't feel 'entirely comfortable with the notion of a renewed friendship and think it's best if we not go there.' At the last second, I excise e) 'out of respect to my husband,' as I don't want Leo to think he is in the Brad 'You're so fine you bug my husband' Turner category, rather than the Ty 'You're so harmless that it's fine to yuck it up with you in my backyard' Portera category.

I hang up, feeling relieved, and for the first time since seeing Leo weeks ago, nearly lighthearted. The call might not be closure in the classic sense of the word, but it is still closure of *some* sort, and more important, it is closure on my terms. I called the final shot. Which is even more meaningful given that I had the perfect excuse — *Drake Watters* for goodness' sake — to meet Leo, jollily chat him up, and even segue into a more somber conversation about 'what really happened between us, anyway?' But I turned down the opportunity. Slammed the door on it, in fact. Not because I can't *handle* a friendship with Leo, but because I simply don't *want* one. End of story.

I imagine Leo listening to the message, wondering if he'll be crestfallen, a tad disappointed, or largely indifferent. No matter what, though, I know he'll be surprised that his power, once so all-encompassing, has dried up completely. He will surely take the hint — and his photo lead — elsewhere. And I will just have to live with the fact that I could have photographed Drake Watters. I smile to myself, feeling strong and happy and righteous, and then belt out the only uplifting line from 'Crossroads' in my dreadful, tone-deaf singing voice: *When the light breaks, baby, I'll be gone for good.*

Several unmemorable days later, after I've almost completely purged Leo from my system, I am working in my lab on the fifth floor of an industrial warehouse on Twenty-fourth and Tenth Avenue. Sharing the space, along with the rent, are Julian and Sabina, photographers who work as a team, and Oscar, a solo printer, paper conservationist, and fine-art publisher. The four of us have been together in the bare-bones workroom for over two years now, and as such, have become very close friends.

133

Sabina, a pale, wispy woman whose anemic looks don't match her brash personality, does most of the talking, rivaling only Oscar's BBC radio that he keeps at a frustrating volume, one that I can't quite hear and yet can't quite tune out. She is now regaling us with a story of her three-year-old triplets' latest stunt: flushing her husband's entire vintage cufflink collection down the toilet, causing a flood in her fourth-floor walk-up and extensive water damage to the apartment below. She laughs as she tells the gory details because in her words, 'What else can you do but laugh?' I happen to think she secretly delights in the tale, as she often accuses her husband of being materialistic and uptight. I enjoy Sabina's stories, particularly during mindless retouching projects, which I'm in the middle of now. Specifically, I'm removing a constellation of acne from the face of a skateboarding teen for a print ad for a small record label.

'What do you think, guys? Should I give this kid a slight chin implant?' I ask.

Oscar, a somber Brit with a streak of dry humor, barely glances up from one of his many small drawers filled with lead, antimony, and wooden typefaces. I know from standing over his shoulder when I arrived that he is working on an artist's book using Etrurian, his favorite Victorian font. I love watching Oscar work, perhaps because his craft is so different from mine, but more likely because of his graceful, almost old-fashioned manner.

'Leave the poor kid be,' he says as he dampens paper and then mutters something about 'digital-plastic-surgery malarkey.'

'Yeah, Ellen. Quit being so shallow, would ya?' Julian, who just returned from his umpteenth smoking break of the day, chimes in, as if he, himself, hasn't shaved down the thighs on many a size-zero woman.

I smile and say, 'I'll try.'

Of my three workspace colleagues, I probably like Julian the best of all — at the very least, we have the most in common. He is about my age, and is also married to a lawyer — a lively, cool girl named Hillary.

Sabina tells Julian to hush as she scurries toward me in tight blue jeans, ripped at the knee, her long, sixties-style hair swishing behind her. She apologizes in advance for the garlic on her breath, mumbling something about going overboard on an herbal supplement, and then peers down at the print in question.

'Great movement there,' she says, pointing to a blurred-out board in mid-air.

I consider movement my single greatest weakness as a photographer so I really appreciate this comment. 'Thanks,' I say. 'But what about his chin?'

She holds the print to the light and says, 'I see what you mean, but I almost think his chin makes him look more surly . . . Does surly work for the ad?'

I nod, 'Yeah. They're called Badass Records. So I think surly will do just fine.'

Sabina takes one last look and says, 'But I might make his nose a bit smaller. That's more distracting than his weak chin . . . Have you ever

135

noticed how often weak chins and big honkers go hand in hand? Why is that, anyway?'

My cell phone interrupts Sabina in mid-thought.

'One sec,' I say, expecting it to be Margot who has called twice in the last hour. Yet when I glance down, I see that it's Cynthia, my agent.

I answer, and as usual, she shouts into the phone. 'Sit down. You're not going to *believe* this one!'

Leo streaks across my mind, but I am still dumbfounded as I listen to her gush the rest of the news.

'*Platform* magazine called,' she says. 'And get this, girlfriend, they want *you* to shoot *Drake Watters* for their April cover story!'

'That's fantastic,' I say, feeling a mix of emotions wash over me. For starters, I simply can't believe Leo went ahead with his lead, although in hindsight, I can see clearly that I left a huge, rather *convenient* back door open for him to orchestrate everything through my agent. Still, I honestly didn't think he'd be so selfless. I thought — and perhaps even hoped — that the Drake bone was more of a power play, a design to lure me back in and force my hand in a borderline inappropriate friendship. Now I'm forced to see the gesture, if not Leo, in a new light. And of course, overshadowing all of this is the simple, giddy, unmitigated thrill of photo-graphing an icon.

'Fantastic?' Cynthia says. '*Fantastic* is an understatement.'

'*Incredibly* fantastic,' I say, now grinning.

Sabina, always nosy but never in an offensive way, whispers, 'What? *What?*'

I scribble the words *Platform* and *Drake Watters* on a notepad. Her eyes widen as she does a comical exotic dance around a pole connecting raw ceiling to cement floor and then rushes over to give Julian the news. He looks up and flips me off with a smile. We're not competitive, but definitely keep a friendly score. Before this, he and Sabina had the solid lead with a Katie Couric shoot for *Redbook* out in the Hamptons where Julian used to do all his work before he married Hillary and she lured him into the city full time.

'Did they say how they got my name?' I calmly ask Cynthia after she runs through a few details of the shoot — namely that it will take place in L.A.; the magazine will pay three thousand dollars, plus airfare, equipment rental, expenses, and a stay at the Beverly Wilshire.

'No,' she says. 'And who really cares? You should be celebrating right now, not asking questions!'

'Right,' I say, wanting so much to believe this very thing. After all, I think, as I thank her, hang up, and field a round of congratulations, there is principle, and then there is stubborn, prideful foolishness. *Malarkey,* as Oscar would say. And surely anyone, even Andy, would have to agree that Drake Watters isn't worth sacrificing for a bunch of ex-boyfriend malarkey.

12

About a week later, after much informal revelry, Andy and I are officially celebrating my upcoming Drake assignment at Bouley, one of our favorite restaurants in the city. Beyond the exquisite food and warm atmosphere, Bouley has sentimental meaning for us, as it is where we dined the night we first made love, which was, incidentally, exactly one month after our first date. The morning after, I teased Andy that it took Chef David Bouley's New French fare to inspire him to want to sleep with me.

'You're right,' he snapped back playfully. 'It was the venison. I will *never* forget that venison. Best I've ever had by a long shot.'

I laughed, knowing the truth — that the wait had everything to do with Andy's romantic, respectful ways. Aside from the high stakes of my friendship with Margot, Andy cared about me enough to want to do things *right* rather than rush into bed after one too many drinks, the methodology most men favored on the New York dating scene — or at least the two I had slept with after Leo. And although some might have criticized our first time as lacking spontaneity, I wouldn't have changed a thing about it. And still wouldn't.

Which makes it an even nicer surprise tonight when we are seated at the same intimate corner table in the vaulted dining room. I raise my eyebrows and say, 'Coincidence?'

Andy smirks with a shrug.

Clearly, this is no coincidence. I smile at my husband's unwavering thoughtfulness. Sometimes he really does seem too good to be true.

In the next few minutes, after an extensive review of the wine list and menu, we decide on our appetizers — the foie gras with a fricassee of cremini for me and the eggplant terrine for Andy — along with Bouley's best bottle of champagne. Andy stumbles over the pronunciation when ordering the latter, despite having taken at least ten years of French growing up. Our waiter murmurs his wholehearted approval, if not of Andy's clumsy accent, then at least of our selection.

Minutes later, after our champagne and appetizers arrive and Andy makes a toast to his 'beautiful, brilliant wife,' he launches right in with the nitty-gritty of the shoot. 'So what poses are you gonna put Drake in?' he begins.

I smile at the word *poses*, which hardly conjures a glossy, stylized magazine spread, but rather a Sears portrait sitting of the sort Suzanne and I endured growing up, complete with a white-picket fence, fake clouds in the background, and a nappy brown rug, rough against our elbows.

But I know what Andy's getting at — and the question, stated in a more technical way, has occurred to me dozens of times in the past few days. I tell him I've yet to talk to the art director or photo editor — so I'm not sure what they want, but that I have some definite ideas about

139

the feel of the shoot. 'I'm thinking moody. Almost somber,' I say. 'Especially in light of Drake's AIDS work.'

'Will you shoot him inside or out?' Andy asks.

'You know I prefer natural light. Either near a lot of windows or outside. Maybe overpowered,' I say.

'What's *overpowered*?' Andy asks, the way I frequently ask him what are probably basic procedural, legal questions.

'It's a technique where the subject is well-lit, usually in the middle of the day, but the background sort of fades to black,' I explain. 'It's a pretty common way to shoot outside. You'd know it if you saw it.'

Andy nods and says, 'Well, maybe the hotel has a terrace. That'd be cool. Or you could go out by the pool. Or, hell, *in* the pool! You know — tossing a beach ball around, that kind of thing.'

I laugh, picturing Drake in a Speedo and thinking that as excited as I am, Andy seems even *more* so. In part, I think it's because he's remained a much more loyal and ebullient Drake fan over the years. But mostly, I think it's just due to his star-struck tendencies, which are in marked and amusing (although Margot would say *mortifying*) contrast to the way most Manhattanites completely downplay celebrity sightings, almost as a badge of honor. Like the more blasé they are, the more they are making a statement that their own lives are *just* as fabulous, minus the hassle and tedium of fame, of course. But not Andy. I think of his wild enthusiasm when we spotted Spike Lee at an ATM on the West Side — and Kevin Bacon and Kyra Sedgwick running in the park ('two for the price of one!') — and Liv Tyler perusing stationery at Kate's Paperie — and the greatest score of all, Dustin Hoffman walking his black lab in East Hampton. After we passed the pair, Andy told me he had to use every bit of restraint not to burst out with that famous line from *The Graduate* — 'Just one word ... *plastics*!' — which cracked me up, but probably wouldn't have been quite as amusing to Dustin.

But Dustin Hoffman on the beach is one thing; Drake Watters at a photo shoot is quite another. So when Andy asks, only half in jest, if I'm going to get an autograph for him, I shake my head resolutely.

'Not a chance,' I say.

'C'mon,' he says, reaching across the table to steal another bite of my foie gras, which we both agree is the better selection by a very slim margin. 'Just have him write something short and sweet. Something like ... 'To Andy, my dear friend and great inspiration. Yours in melody, Drake Watters.' Or he can simply sign it 'Drake' ... Or even 'Mr. Watterstein.' It all works.'

I laugh, having forgotten from my *Teen Beat*-purchasing days that Drake's real last name is Watterstein. I think of how I used to pore over those juicy details — *Drake's real name! Rob Lowe's fave food! Ricky Schroder's love interest! River Phoenix's new puppy!*

Andy looks crestfallen — or at least pretends to be. 'You really won't hook me up? Seriously?'

'Seriously,' I say. 'I really, *really* will *not*.'

'Okay, *Annie*,' he says. 'Be that way.'

It is about the third time that he's jokingly, but with a note of admiration, referred to me as *Annie* or *Ms. Leibovitz*, and every time I feel like a bit of an imposter. A fraud for not telling him the full truth of how I got the job. Otherwise, though, the assignment has begun to lose its Leo connotation, and I've been able to largely convince myself that it really *was* my talent alone that scored me the job. After all, I reassure myself, Leo's true intentions (to assuage guilt over how he once treated me? pure benevolence? because he's seen my work and truly thinks I'm talented? to seduce me, at least mentally?) are really completely beside the point now. The job is mine, and it is a job I know I can do well. I refuse to be intimidated by Drake or *Platform*. And I refuse to feel indebted to Leo, if that is, in fact, his aim.

As I take my final bite, I appease my husband. 'Fine. Fine,' I say. 'I'll play the autograph thing by ear . . . If Drake and I hit it off, and the shoot goes well, I'll tell him that my dorky husband wants his autograph. Deal?'

'Deal,' Andy says happily, ignoring my 'dorky husband' comment as only a very secure man would. I smile, thinking that there are few things sexier than a man who doesn't take himself too seriously.

Our waiter stops by our table to expertly refill our champagne glasses, the bubbles reaching the highest point possible without spilling over. Andy gestures to our nearly empty bottle, asking

142

whether I'd like more. I nod, savoring the ease of marital, nonverbal communication and envisioning intoxicated, celebratory sex later this evening. Andy orders us another bottle, and we continue to talk about Drake and the shoot.

Then, sometime in the graceful interim between appetizers and our entrées, Andy's posture straightens and his expression becomes uncharacteristically grave.

'So,' he starts. 'I want to talk to you about something else.'

For one second, I panic, thinking that he saw my cell phone bill, or that he otherwise knows that I've been in touch with Leo.

'Yeah?' I say.

He fiddles with his napkin and gives me a slow, tentative smile, as I think that if he were the wife, and I the husband, I'd be certain that we were going to have a baby. That's how solemn, disquieted — and yet simultaneously *excited* — he looks.

'What?' I say, feeling grateful that *I'm* the one who gets to break that particular bit of news.

Andy leans across the table and says, 'I'm thinking about quitting my job.'

I give him an expectant look as this is hardly a newsflash. Andy has been talking about quitting since his very first day of work, which apparently is par for the course for large firm associates. 'What else is new?' I say.

'I mean *imminently*,' he says. 'I drafted a letter of resignation today, in fact.'

'Really?' I say. I've heard of this infamous letter many times before — but have never

143

known him to actually write it.

He nods, running his hand along his water glass before taking a long swallow. He dabs his napkin to his lips and says, 'I *really* want to quit.'

'To do what?' I say, wondering if Andy would ever follow his brother James's path — and do essentially nothing but sleep, play golf, and party.

'Besides mooch off my famous wife?' Andy asks, winking.

'Yeah,' I say, laughing. 'Besides that?'

'Well,' he says. 'I'd like to continue practicing law . . . but I'd like to do so in a smaller, more low-key . . . *family-oriented* setting.'

I think I know what he's getting at, but wait for him to spell it out for me.

'In Atlanta,' he finally says. 'With my dad.'

I take a sip of champagne, feeling my heart race with a range of unprocessed emotions as I say, 'You think you'd be happy doing that?'

'I think so,' he says. 'And my dad would be *thrilled*.'

'I know,' I say. 'He only mentioned it *five* times when we were in town.'

Andy looks into my eyes and says, 'But what about you? How would *you* feel about it?'

'About you working with your dad?' I ask. I know that I'm being obtuse, that he's asking about something much greater than his job, but I'm not sure why.

'No. About Atlanta,' Andy says, fidgeting with his knife. 'About living in Atlanta?'

Obviously Andy and I have talked about the move before, especially since Margot left the city. We even drove around and looked at houses on our last visit, but this time feels different. This time feels real, not theoretical — and in Andy's own words, *imminent*.

To confirm, I say, 'You mean moving there *soon*?'

Andy nods.

'Like this year? That soon?'

Andy nods again and then rushes into a nervous, heartfelt speech. 'The last thing I want to do is pressure you. If you want to stay in New York — or feel that it would hurt your career to leave — I can stay. I mean, it's not like I hate the city or feel desperate to move out or anything like that . . . But after that last visit to Atlanta . . . and looking at houses . . . and just thinking about our little niece on the way, and my folks getting older, and *everything*, really . . . I don't know — I just feel ready for a change. For an *easier* life. Or at least a different kind of life.'

I nod, my mind racing. None of what Andy is saying is out of left field, not only because we've discussed it all before but because we're at the age where lots of our friends are marrying, having babies, and making an exodus to the suburbs. But it still feels somehow astonishing to think about leaving the city in such immediate terms. My head fills with classic New York images — Central Park on a crisp fall day; ice skating at Rockefeller Plaza; sipping wine on an outdoor terrace in the dizzy height of summer — and I suddenly feel nostalgic for the past. I even feel nostalgic for tonight, for the meal Andy and I are having together, the very memory we are making now.

145

'Say something,' Andy says, pulling on his ear, something he only does when he's anxious — or when he *really* cares about something. There was definite ear pullage when he proposed, and it occurs to me that this moment isn't so different. He is asking me how I feel about a big change. A step that we'd be taking together. It is not the same commitment as marriage, but in many ways, it's an even bigger change.

I reach for Andy's hand, taking it in mine, wanting so much to please him, but also wanting to be completely honest with him. 'I think it could be really great,' I say, sounding less tentative than I feel — although the truth is, I'm not quite sure *how* I feel.

Andy nods and says, 'I know. And believe me, I'm not trying to put you on the spot. But . . . I did want to show you this.'

He lets go of my hand and reaches into the inner pocket of his sport coat, pulling out a folded piece of paper. 'Here ya go.'

I take the paper from him, unfold it, and gaze down at a large cedar and brick house with a covered front porch, similar to the home listings Margot has been e-mailing me since our last trip, always with subject lines like, 'Next-door neighbors!' or 'Perfect for you!'

But *this* house isn't from Margot passing the time at her computer during the day. *This* house comes from Andy over champagne at Bouley.

'Do you like it?' he asks hesitantly, although it is very, *very* clear what he wants my answer to be.

'Of *course*,' I say, skimming the details in the

written-up section below the photo — five bedrooms, four-and-a-half baths, fenced back-yard, heated pool, high ceilings, screened-in porch, finished daylight basement, three-car garage, butler's pantry, dumbwaiter servicing all three levels.

There is absolutely nothing *not* to like. It is a dream house in every way — like no house in my hometown or even anything I could have imagined as a child. Not even when my mother told me that she was certain that I would have a good life filled with beautiful things, beautiful people.

'I'm not worried about you, Ellie,' she had said, stroking my hair. 'Not at all.'

It was one week before she died, right after she returned from the hospital for the last time, and I remember listening to her soothing voice, picturing my own grown-up life with a husband, a house, and children — and wondering if any of that could ever erase the pain of losing my mother.

I look up from the flyer now and say, 'It's beautiful, Andy. *Really* beautiful.'

'And it's just as beautiful inside, too,' Andy says, talking rapidly. 'Margot said she's been inside . . . for some children's clothing trunk show or something. She said there's a huge workspace in the basement where you could set up shop. You wouldn't have to rent an office anymore. Just go right down the steps in your pajamas . . . And the best part is — it's, like, a hundred yards from Margot and Webb. How awesome would that be?'

I nod, taking it all in.

'It really *is* perfect,' Andy says. 'Perfect for *us*. Perfect for the family we want to have.'

I gaze back down at the house, noticing the price tag. 'Shit,' I say.

Money is something Andy and I don't talk about often — he and Margot have that in common — but whereas she seems oblivious to her family fortune, he sometimes seems sheepish about it, almost apologetic. As a result, he makes certain choices, like our small apartment, and I sometimes forget just how wealthy he is. 'You really are *rich*, huh?' I say, smiling.

Andy looks down and shakes his head. Then he looks back into my eyes and says earnestly, 'We're rich . . . In more ways than one.'

'I know,' I say, basking in the moment.

We stare at each other for what feels like a long time, until Andy breaks our silence. 'So . . . What do you think?'

I open my mouth, close it, then open it again.

'I love you, Andy,' I finally say, my head spinning from champagne and so much else. 'That's what I think.'

'I'll take it,' Andy says with a wink, just as our lobster arrives. 'It's no Drake autograph, but I'll take it.'

13

'I *knew* you'd get sucked in all the way,' my sister says a few days later after I call her and tell her about our potential — likely — move to Atlanta. Her tone is not quite critical, but one of definite forbearance. 'I just *knew* it.'

And I knew *this would be your reaction*, I think, but instead I say, 'I wouldn't call it 'sucked in.' For one, we haven't even made a final decision — '

Suzanne interrupts, 'Just promise you won't start talking in a Southern accent.'

'Atlantans don't have much of an accent,' I say. 'It's too transient . . . Andy barely has an accent.'

'And don't start using the word *y'all*,' she says somberly, as if asking for a pledge that I won't join a creepy religious sect and drink their Kool-Aid. 'You're a Yankee, and don't you forget it.'

'Okay. *If* we move — and that's still an *if* — I will safeguard against an accent, and I'll faithfully stand by 'you guys' instead of 'y'all.' I also vow never to drive a pickup truck, fly the Confederate flag, or distill whiskey in the backyard,' I say as I take a break from sorting dirty laundry into a pile of darks and lights and sit cross-legged on the bedroom floor.

Despite the consistent sense I get from Suzanne that she doesn't entirely approve of

149

Andy or Margot or their world, I am still smiling. I have great affection for my sister, and it feels good to finally hear her voice after weeks of playing phone tag. Since college, our communication has been sporadic, depending on our schedules, and more important, depending on Suzanne's mood. Sometimes she simply goes underground, and no amount of pestering will make her reemerge before she is good and ready.

As a result, I have learned to keep a list of topics to catch up on, which I pull out of my date planner now. I know I won't forget the big ticket items — like Atlanta or Drake — but I never want the trivial ones to fall through the cracks for fear that our conversations will lose their everyday, comfortable feel. I can't imagine it happening, and yet I know it does happen between sisters all the time, particularly when they don't live near one another or have a lot in common — or for that matter, a mother holding them together. Somehow I feel that if I catch her up on the mundane details in my life — whether it be the new under-eye cream I'm using, or the out-of-the-blue e-mail I received from a junior high acquaintance, or the random, funny memory I had of our parents taking us back-to-school shoe shopping one Labor Day — we will never be relegated to sisters-in-title only. We will always be more than two adult women who call and visit out of nothing but a thread of familial obligation.

So I tick through my list and then listen to her updates — which aren't really updates, just more of the status quo. Namely, Suzanne *still* hates her job as a US Airways flight attendant, and she *still* isn't engaged to her boyfriend, Vince. She's held both the job and Vince for nearly six years, each befitting her carefree lifestyle when she adopted them. But now, at thirty-six, she's tired of serving drinks in the air to rude people, and she's even more tired of serving drinks to Vince and his immature friends while they cheer on the Steelers, Pirates, and Penguins. She wants her life to change — or at least she wants Vince to change — but doesn't quite know how to make that happen.

She's also stubborn enough never to ask advice from her little sister. Not that I would know what to tell her anyway. Vince, a general contractor Suzanne met and exchanged numbers with during a highway traffic jam, is unreliable, won't commit, and once lived with a stripper named Honey. But he also happens to be warm, witty, and the absolute life of the party. And, most important, Suzanne truly loves him. So I have learned to just offer an empathetic ear — or laugh when it's appropriate, which I do right now as she details how Vince handed her an unwrapped ring box on Valentine's Day right after they had sex. Knowing Vince, I am pretty sure where the story is headed.

'Oh, no,' I groan, resuming my laundry sorting.

'Oh, *yes*,' Suzanne says. 'And I'm thinking, 'No *freaking* way. Tell me I haven't waited *six* years for a cheesy Valentine's Day proposal. In bed, no less. And, God, what if it's a heart-shaped ring?' . . . But at the same time,

151

I'm also thinking, 'Take what you can get, sister. Beggars can't be choosers.''

'So what was it?' I ask, in suspense.

'A garnet ring. My fucking *birthstone*.'

I burst out laughing — it's just so bad. And yet, a *little* bit sweet. 'Ahh,' I say. 'He tried.'

Suzanne ignores this comment and says, 'Who the *hell* over the age of ten cares about their birthstone? . . . Do you even know what yours is?'

'A tourmaline,' I say.

'Well, I'll be sure to tell Andy to get right on that. Get you that sweet pad in Atlanta, with a tourmaline to go.' Suzanne laughs her trademark airy laugh that almost sounds like she can't catch her breath, as I think that her sense of humor is what saves her life from being outright depressing. That and the fact that, despite her big, tough act, she has a very tender heart. She really could be bitter in the way that a lot of single women who are waiting in vain for a ring are bitter, but she's just *not*. And although I think she's sometimes jealous of my better fortune, easier road, she is also a great sister who genuinely wants the best for me.

So I know she will only be happy to hear about my Drake shoot — which I'm bursting to tell her about. Like Andy, Suzanne loves Drake, but less for his music than his political activism. Although my sister is not an outward hippie — she gave up weed and her Birkenstocks right after her Grateful Dead stage in college — she is very impassioned when it comes to her causes, particularly the environment and third-world poverty. And by impassioned, I don't mean that she simply talks the talk — Suzanne actually gets off her butt and *does* things that make a difference — which serves as an unusual contrast to the inertia that has always plagued her personal life. When we were in high school, for example, she could barely make it to class or maintain a C average, despite her genius IQ — fourteen points higher than mine — which we knew from snooping through our parents' files. Yet she *did* find the time and energy to found the school's Amnesty International chapter and circulate petitions urging the administration to put out recycling bins in the cafeteria — unprecedented stuff at the time, at least in our town.

And today, she always seems to be involved in some do-gooding mission or another — whether volunteering to plant trees in public parks and cemeteries, or firing off eloquent letters to her legislators, or even making a trek to New Orleans after Hurricane Katrina where she repaired homes with Habitat for Humanity. When Suzanne talks about her various projects, I find myself wishing that I were motivated to do more for the greater good; the extent of my activism is that I vote every November (which, incidentally, is slightly more than I can say for Andy, who only votes in presidential elections).

Sure enough, as I conclude my Drake tale — minus the parts about Leo — Suzanne says, 'Wow. You lucky bitch.'

'I know,' I say, feeling tempted to tell her the whole story, that luck really didn't play a part in this assignment. If I were going to confide in

153

anyone in the world, it would be Suzanne. Not only because of our blood loyalty — and the simple fact that she's *not* related to Andy — but because she was really the only person in my life who didn't seem to dislike Leo. They only met once, and neither was very chatty, but I could tell that they had an instant rapport and quiet respect for each other. I remember thinking that they actually had quite a few similarities — including their political views; their cynical habit of sneering at much in the mainstream; their acerbic wit; and their seemingly contradictory way of being both passionate and profoundly detached. Even when Leo broke my heart, and I was sure Suzanne would viciously turn on him, she was more philosophical than protective. She said everyone needs to get dumped once — that it's part of life — and that obviously things weren't meant to be. 'Better now than down the road with three kids,' she said — although I remember thinking I would have preferred the latter. I would have preferred to have something lasting with Leo, no matter what the accompanying pain.

In any event, I resist telling her about him now, thinking that Leo really is a moot point. Besides, I don't want this to unfairly color her views on my relationship with Andy, and I can just see it queuing up her depressing outlook of how nearly every marriage is tainted in some way. Either one or both parties settled, or someone is dissatisfied, or someone is cheating or at least considering it. I've heard it all before, many times, and it never helps to point out that our own parents seemed very happy together because she rebuffs that argument with either, 'How would we really know otherwise? We were kids,' or an even cheerier, 'Yeah, but so what? Mom died. Remember? What a fucking fairy tale.'

Margot, who is downright aghast by my sister's cynical tirades, maintains that it must be Suzanne's way of rationalizing her in-limbo, unmarried state. I can see some truth in this, but I also think there's a bit of the chicken-or-the-egg going on. In other words, if Suzanne were a bit more traditional and romantic or actually threw down an ultimatum like most girls in our hometown over the age of twenty-five, I truly think that Vince would change his tune pretty easily. He loves her too much to let her go. But with all of Suzanne's marriage bashing, Vince has a built-in excuse for putting off a wedding while remaining guilt-free. In fact, I think he gets way more pressure from their mutual friends and his family than he does from Suzanne — and it is usually she who will chime in with, 'No disrespect intended, Aunt Betty, but please mind your own business . . . And trust me, Vince isn't getting any milk for *free*.'

But, as it turns out, there is no opening to discuss the Leo angle because Suzanne blurts out, 'I'm coming with you,' in her authoritative, big-sister way.

'Are you serious?' I say.

'Yeah.'

'But you're not star-crazed,' I say, thinking that at least she *pretends* not to be, although I've

155

busted her with her share of tabloids over the years, including an occasional *National Enquirer*.

'I know. But Drake Watters isn't your typical star. He's . . . Drake. I'm coming.'

'Really?'

'Yeah. Why not?' she says. 'I've been meaning to come see you for months now — and it's no big deal for me to hop on a plane to L.A.'

'That's true,' I say, thinking that it is the best part about her job — and likely the reason she sticks with it. Suzanne can go just about anywhere, anytime she wants.

'I'll be your assistant . . . Hell, I'll work for free.'

'*Platform*'s providing a freelance assistant,' I say, reluctant to agree, although I'm not sure why.

'So I'll be the assistant to the assistant. I'll hold that big silver disk thingy for you like I did when you shot the Monongahela River that one ass-cold winter day. Remember that? Remember how I dropped my glove in the river and almost got frostbite?'

'I remember,' I say, thinking that Suzanne won't let you forget certain things. 'And do you also remember how I bought you a new pair of gloves the next day?'

'Yeah, yeah. I remember those cheapies,' she says.

I laugh and say, 'They were *not* cheapies.'

'Were too,' she says. 'So make it up to me and let me come to L.A.'

'Fine,' I say. 'But no autographs.'

'C'mon,' she says. 'I'm not that lame.'

'And no more griping about the gloves.'
'Deal,' she says solemnly. 'Never again.'

★ ★ ★

Over the next few days, while Andy is away on a document review in Toronto, I focus on my shoot, working out logistics and consulting several times with *Platform*'s photo editor and art director who inform me that the focus of the feature is on Drake's humanitarian work. As such, they want two to three 'somber, visually rich, environmental color portraits.'

'Do you know what situation you're after?' I ask the photo editor, feeling my first wave of nervousness.

'That's what we have you for,' she says. 'We saw your work on your Web site. Loved it. Such stark beauty. Just do your thing.'

I feel a boost of confidence and a little rush that I always feel when someone appreciates my work. I ask if there's any way I can set up at a restaurant I found on the Internet that is only a couple of miles away from the hotel. 'It's one of those classic, retro diners with black-and-white, hexagon-tiled floors and red booths,' I say, thinking that it's not unlike the booth I last saw Leo in. 'You know, the red will be sort of symbolic of his AIDS work . . . I think it could look really cool.'

'Brilliant,' she says. 'I'll just call Drake's publicist and get the OK.'

'Great,' I say, as if I've heard such words a thousand times before.

A few minutes later, she phones back and says, 'Send the exact address of the diner, and Drake and his people will be there at three o'clock, sharp. Only caveat is that he's on a really tight schedule. You'll have to work fast. You'll only have about twenty to thirty minutes. That work?'

'No problem. I'll get the shots,' I say, sounding like the consummate professional — way more confident than I actually am.

I hang up and call Suzanne, asking her if twenty minutes is still worth a transcontinental flight. She is undeterred.

'Twenty minutes with greatness is still twenty minutes with greatness. And certainly more greatness than I've seen in a *long* time,' she says.

'Good enough,' I say. 'Just don't let ole Vince hear you saying that.'

Suzanne laughs and says, 'Oh, Vince knows he's mediocre at best.'

'At least he knows his place,' I say.

'Yeah,' she says. ''Cause there are very few things worse than a man who doesn't know his place.'

I laugh, memorizing this gem from Suzanne, but not appreciating the full truth of it until I arrive in L.A. three days later.

14

It is five-thirty in the evening L.A. time, and I've only been in town for an hour, just long enough to check in at the Beverly Wilshire, dump my suitcase and camera bags in my room, and call Suzanne, whose flight got in earlier this afternoon. She informs me that she's window shopping on Rodeo Drive — 'totally in my element,' she adds sarcastically — but will be back soon. She says that she's already scoped out the hotel bar options, suggesting that we meet at the Blvd Lounge for a drink.

I say great idea, my flight-nerve pills weren't strong enough for the heartland storms we flew through, and I could really use a glass of wine. Suzanne laughs and calls me a big sissy before I hang up and change into what feels like an L.A. outfit — dark jeans, silver platforms that put me near the six-foot mark, and a simple but chic (for me) lime green silk tank. Unfortunately, I forgot to pack the strapless bra that I bought to go with it, but I figure I'm flat-chested enough to pull it off without looking cheap. Besides, I'm in California now, where anything goes. I freshen my makeup, smoking my eyes more than usual, and finish with a spritz of perfume on the back of my hands, a trick that Margot taught me in college, saying that anyone who talks with her hands as much as I do should reap the benefits of simultaneously releasing her scent.

Then I'm down the elevator and through the posh lobby, strolling so confidently that I'm very nearly strutting into the Blvd, an intimate, modern, and very elegant lounge decorated in rich shades of amber, chocolate, and gold. As I admire the illuminated onyx bar with a large backlit wine display of at least a thousand bottles, I also find myself admiring the strong profile of a man seated alongside it, alone, drink in hand. A man who looks an awful lot like Leo. I do a squinting double take, and discover, with both amazement and something akin to horror, that he doesn't simply *look* like Leo — he *is* Leo.

Leo once again. Leo three thousand miles from home.

I freeze, and for one second, I'm actually naïve or dimwitted enough to think that this is yet another coincidence. *Another* chance run-in. And, in that beat, my heart stops with the foolishly shameful notion, *My God, what if this is fate chasing me down all the way across the country?*

But as Leo glances over, spots me, and raises his drink in the air, cheekbone level, I realize what he's orchestrated. I realize that I've been set up.

I shift my weight from one heel to the other as he slowly lowers his drink — what appears to be a whiskey on the rocks, his signature drink — and gives me a small, knowing smile.

I do not smile back, but take the half-dozen steps toward him. I am no longer strutting, and a sudden chill down my spine has me wishing for a bra. Or better yet, a full-length coat.

'Hello, Leo,' I say.

'Ellen,' he says, nodding. 'Glad you could make it.'

It sounds like a line right out of an old Hollywood movie, but I am far from charmed, not even when he stands and motions toward the stool beside him.

You are no Cary Grant, I think, as I shake my head, refusing the seat. I am too stunned to be angry, but am feeling something stronger than mere indignation.

'You come all this way and won't have a seat?' he says.

Another line.

Leo was never one for lines in the past, and I'm almost disappointed that he's throwing them out now. I have no vested interest in the man he has become over the last decade, but in some odd way, I don't want my image of him tarnished by lines.

'No, thank you,' I say coolly. 'I'm meeting my sister here any minute.'

'Suzanne?' he says with a note of smugness.

I look at him, wondering whether he actually thinks that remembering her name is impressive. I am tempted to rattle off *Clara, Thomas, Joseph, Paul* — the names of his four siblings, in birth order, but would never give him the satisfaction of my recalling details about his family.

Instead I say, 'Yes. Suzanne. I only have one sister.'

'Right,' he says. 'Well, I'm glad she's coming. That's a nice bonus.'

'A nice *bonus?*' I say with what I hope is a nonplussed furrow of my brow. 'As in . . . two sisters for the price of one?'

He laughs. 'No. As in, I always liked Suzanne . . . the few times we hung out.'

'You met her *once.*'

'Right. And I liked her on that *one* occasion. Very much.'

'I'm sure she'll be so pleased to hear that,' I say flippantly. 'Now if you'll excuse me . . . '

Before he can protest, I walk to the end of the bar and make eye contact with the bartender, a gray-haired, ruddy-cheeked man who looks like he would be cast in the role of a bartender.

'What can I get for you?' he asks me, his scratchy baritone just as role worthy.

I forgo my wine in lieu of a vodka martini, straight up with extra olives, and then point to an uninhabited chartreuse couch in the far corner of the lounge. 'And . . . I'll be over there, please.'

'Very well,' the bartender says sympathetically, as if aware of the fact that I'd rather be anywhere in the world than in the company of the only man at his bar.

I turn and walk briskly to the couch, feeling Leo's eyes on me. I sit, cross my legs, and fix my gaze out the window onto Wilshire Boulevard, my mind racing. What is Leo doing here? Is he trying to tempt me? Taunt me? Torture me? What will Suzanne think when she bursts into the lounge at any moment? What would Andy say if he could see me now, braless in a swanky lounge, martini on the way, with my ex-lover just across the room?

162

My drink arrives one beat before Leo.

'Are you . . . upset?' he asks, standing over me.

'No. I'm not *upset*,' I say, barely looking up at him before taking something between a sip and a gulp of my martini. The vodka is strong but smooth, going down easily.

'Yes, you are,' Leo says, looking more amused than concerned. When I see the corners of his mouth turn up in a satisfied little smile, I lose it and snap, 'What is this exactly?'

'What is *what*?' Leo asks, remaining infuriatingly calm as he settles, uninvited and unwelcome, next to me on the couch.

'*This*,' I say, angrily gesturing in the space between us, unwittingly releasing my scent. 'What are you doing here, Leo?'

'I'm writing the story,' he says innocently. 'On Drake.'

I stare at him, speechless and stupefied. Remarkably, Leo's writing the feature had never *once* occurred to me. Had I conveniently blocked the possibility out? And, if so, why? Because I had a subconscious hope that Leo would be here? Or because I wanted to absolve myself of any guilt in taking a dream assignment? I have the sinking feeling that a good psychiatrist would be exploring both possibilities.

'Oh,' I say, dumbly, numbly.

'I thought you knew that,' he says — and I can tell he believes it.

I shake my head, feeling myself soften as I register that at least he has a legitimate reason to be here; it's not just a straight ambush. 'How would I know that?' I ask defensively, but also

163

slightly embarrassed by my outburst — and the brazen assumption that he was here to see me.

'How else would I have an in on the photography assignment?' he asks, driving home the point even more.

'I don't know . . . Some contact?'

'Like Drake?' he says, looking mildly amused.

'You . . . *know* Drake?'

'Yup,' he says, crossing his fingers. 'We're like this.'

'Oh,' I say, impressed in spite of myself.

'I'm kidding,' he says and goes on to explain how he was working as the UNICEF correspondent during last year's AIDS Walk in New York and met some of Drake's people there. 'So long story short, we ended up chatting over a few pints . . . and I basically talked myself into this feature which I, in turn, pitched to *Platform*. And voilà . . . the rest is history.'

I nod, feeling almost completely disarmed by his talk of charity and journalism — topics that hardly conjure sleazy attempts to canoodle with married ex-girlfriends in swanky L.A. bars.

'So anyway,' he continues, 'the day I got the green light from *Platform* was the very day I ran into you . . . so it seemed . . . I don't know . . . serendipitous . . . fitting that I try to hook you up on the photography side.'

'But we didn't talk about my work,' I say, essentially asking him if he went home and Googled me — or whether he has otherwise followed my career over the years.

He smiles sheepishly and confirms. 'I know what you've been up to.'

'Meaning?' I say. My tone is merely inquisitive — but the pressing nature of the follow-up goes beyond information gathering.

'Meaning you don't have to talk to someone to think about them . . . and check up on them now and again . . . '

I shiver, feeling goose bumps rising on my arms and my nipples pressing against my tank. 'Is it cold in here?' I say, nervously crossing my arms.

'I'm rather warm, actually,' Leo says, leaning toward me, close enough for me to smell his skin and the whiskey on his breath. 'Would you like my jacket?'

I glance at his espresso suede jacket — the kind that a reporter or cowboy would wear — and shake my head in a gentle refusal. 'No, thanks,' I say, my voice coming out in a near whisper — a whisper that serves as a stark contrast to Suzanne's sudden, rowdy hello above us.

I jump, feeling startled and very busted. Flustered, I stand to hug my sister while sputtering an explanation, 'I . . . uh . . . look who I ran into? . . . You remember Leo?'

'Sure,' Suzanne says cheerfully, unfazed. She slips one hand into the back pocket of her jeans and extends the other to Leo. 'Hi, there.'

He shakes her hand and says, 'Hi, Suzanne. Good to see you again.'

'You, too,' she says sincerely. 'It's been a long time.'

An awkward pause follows, in which we all stand inches apart in triangle formation until

165

Leo moves aside and says, 'Well. I'll let you two catch up . . . '

Suzanne smiles and plops down onto the couch as if to give us a few feet — and seconds — of privacy. I seize the chance, feeling utterly conflicted. I want Leo to go; I want him to stay.

I finally say, 'Thanks, Leo.'

I'm not sure exactly what I'm thanking him for. The assignment? His confession that he never stopped thinking of me altogether? His willingness to leave now?

'Sure,' he says as if acknowledging all of the above. He turns to go, but then stops and spins back around, staring intently into my eyes. 'Look, uhh . . . I'm gonna grab a bite to eat at this great Mexican dive tonight. Best guacamole I've ever had — and the margaritas aren't bad either . . . No pressure, but give me a call if you guys want to join me . . . '

'Okay,' I say.

'You can call my cell or my room.' He glances at his plastic card key and says, 'Room six-twelve.'

'Room six-twelve,' I echo, noting that it's exactly one floor above our Room 512. 'Got it.'

'And if I don't hear from you, I'll just see you tomorrow afternoon.'

'Okay,' I say.

'I understand that I'll be conducting my interview at a diner of your choosing?'

I nod, grateful that I know now, ahead of time, that Leo will be there. Leo and Drake in the same room.

'You always did like a good diner,' Leo says, winking and then turning to leave for good.

Suzanne's poker face dissolves into a full-on grin as Leo disappears around the corner. '*Jesus*, Ellen.'

'What?' I say, preparing myself for the inevitable onslaught.

She shakes her head and says, 'You could cut the sexual tension with a butter knife.'

'That's ridiculous,' I say.

'Room six-twelve. *Got it*,' she mimics in a high falsetto.

'I didn't say it like that. It's *not* like that, Suzanne. Honestly.'

'Okay. Then what *is* it like?'

'It's a long story,' I whimper.

'We have time.'

'Get a drink first,' I say, stalling.

'Already did. Stood at the bar watching you two fools as I ordered the *Pretty Woman* special . . . Did you know the movie was filmed here?'

'Really?' I say, hoping to divert the conversation to vintage Julia Roberts. 'I love that movie. Didn't we see it together?'

She shrugs. 'All I remember is that it glorified prostitution,' Suzanne says. 'So . . . back to your dreamy ex . . . '

'He's not dreamy.'

'He's hot and you know it,' she says. 'His eyes are *ridiculous*.'

I try to stifle a smile, but can't. They *are* ridiculous.

'Now, c'mon. Tell me what's going on, would ya?'

I sigh loudly, drop my head in my hands and say, 'Okay. But please don't judge.'

'When have I ever judged you?' she says.

'Are you serious?' I ask, looking at her through my fingers and laughing. 'When *haven't* you judged me?'

'True,' she says. 'But I promise not to judge *this* time.'

I sigh again and then launch into the whole story, beginning with that heart-thudding moment in the intersection. Suzanne doesn't interrupt once — except to order me another drink when a waitress stops by with a silver bowl of salty snacks. When I've finished, I ask if she thinks I'm a horrible person.

Suzanne pats my leg, the way she used to when we were little whenever I'd get carsick in the back of our mother's Buick station wagon. 'Not yet,' she says.

'Meaning what?'

'Meaning the night is but one-martini young . . . and we have a little situation developing.'

'Suzanne,' I say, horrified by her implication. 'I would *never* cheat on Andy. *Never.*'

'Ellen,' Suzanne says, raising her brows. 'Who said anything about cheating?'

★ ★ ★

Two hours, three drinks, and many conversations later, Suzanne and I are back in our room, drunk and happy. As we raid the minibar, laughing that when you're this hungry, six bucks for a bag of candy doesn't seem so outrageous, my mind drifts to Leo's guacamole.

'Should we call the front desk for a restaurant

suggestion?' I say. 'I could really go for Mexican . . . '

'What a coincidence,' Suzanne says, smirking as she lifts up the receiver. 'Or we could just call Room six-twelve . . . Or better yet head straight for his room.'

I shake my head and tell her meeting Leo for dinner is not an option.

'Are you *suuuure?*'

'Positive.'

''Cause I think it'd be fun.'

'Fun to watch me squirm?'

'No. Fun because I happen to enjoy Leo's company.'

I can't tell whether she's kidding, testing me, or simply holding to her promise not to judge, but I snatch the phone — and the bag of peanut M&M's from her.

'C'mon,' she presses. 'Don't you want to know what Leo's been up to all these years?'

'I know what he's been up to. He's still reporting and writing,' I say, kicking off my shoes and sliding my feet into a pair of white terry-cloth slippers with the hotel's insignia. I pop a handful of candy into my mouth and add, 'That's how I got here, remember?'

'Yes, but beyond his work . . . You know nothing about his personal life, do you? You don't even known if he's married?'

'He's not married.'

'Are you sure?'

'He's not wearing a ring.'

'Means nothing. Plenty of married men don't wear rings.'

169

'Appalling,' I mutter.

'It doesn't necessarily mean they are players,' Suzanne says, taking the polar opposite stance of her usual rants on ringless, philandering pilots and leering businessmen populating her first-class cabins. 'Not wearing a ring can just be . . . sort of old school. Dad never wore his wedding ring — and I think it's safe to say that he wasn't on the prowl.'

'Can you really be old school if you're under forty?'

'Sure you can. It's the whole old-soul thing . . . and I think Leo is an old soul,' she says, almost admiringly, as it occurs to me that calling someone an 'old soul' is almost always a compliment.

I look at her. 'And you're basing that on *what* exactly?'

'I don't know. It just seems like . . . he's not caught up in materialism and all the other superficial trappings of our generation.'

'Suzanne! Where are you getting this crap? You've spent about four hours with him, total!'

'He does noble work,' she says, likely referring to his coverage of the AIDS Walk.

'Just because he cares about AIDS victims doesn't make him an old-soul saint,' I scoff — and yet I have to secretly admit that she is tapping into one of the things I once loved about Leo. Unlike so many guys, particularly guys I've met in New York, Leo was never a social climber or follower. He didn't consult *New York* magazine or *Zagat*'s to select our restaurants and bars. He didn't sport the omnipresent black

170

Gucci loafers. He never dropped references to great literary works he'd just read or artsy films he'd just seen or small indie bands that he had 'discovered.' He never aspired to settle down in a big house in the suburbs with a pretty wife and a couple of kids. And he always preferred travel and experience to fancy possessions. Bottom line, Leo wasn't about checking off boxes or trying to impress or *ever* striving to be someone or something he wasn't.

I say some of this to Suzanne now, mostly just musing aloud, but then silently comparing Leo to Andy. Andy who owns several pairs of Gucci loafers; Andy who frequently peruses the popular press for our restaurant selections; Andy who is anxious to exit the *best* city in the world so that we can live in a big house in Atlanta. And while my unaffected husband could never be accused of playing that pretentious urban game of name checking the hippest indie bands or art-house films or literary novel du jour, I had to concede that he at least *appeared* to have a more status-bound lifestyle than my ex.

A wave of guilt overcomes me as I shift in the other direction, feeling fiercely defensive of my husband. So what if he has an appreciation for the finer things in life, including the occasional brand-name good? So what if he wants a comfortable home and easy life for his family? It's not as though he makes choices to keep up with the Joneses or mindlessly follow the pack. He just happens to be a mainstream guy, adhering unapologetically to his own preferences — which makes him his own man every bit as much as Leo is his own man.

Moreover, why do I feel the need to make comparisons between Andy and Leo at all when there really is no connection between the two? I hesitate and then pose this question to Suzanne, fully expecting her to take the diplomatic high ground, say that I *shouldn't* compare them. That Leo has absolutely nothing to do with Andy and vice versa.

Instead she says, 'First of all, it's impossible not to compare. When you go down a fork in a road, it's impossible not to think about that other path. Wonder what your life could have been like . . . '

'I guess so,' I say, thinking that the Leo path was never really an option. I tried to take it, and it turned out to be a cold, dark dead end.

Suzanne runs her hands through her long, curly hair and continues, 'Second of all, Leo and Andy *are* connected, by simple virtue of the fact that you love — or once loved — them both.'

I give her a disconcerted look. 'How do you figure?'

'Because,' she says, 'no matter how much or how little two people you love have in common . . . or whether they overlap or have a decade between them . . . or whether they hate each other's guts or know absolutely nothing about one another . . . they're still linked in some strange way. They're still stuck in the same fraternity, just as you're in a sorority with everyone Andy has ever loved. There's just an unspoken kinship there, like it or not.'

As I contemplate this theory, she goes on to

172

tell me how she ran into Vince's stripper ex-girlfriend at a bowling alley recently and, although they only vaguely know each other and share just a few, attenuated acquaintances (which is almost impossible to avoid altogether when you're both from Pittsburgh), they still ended up having a long conversation while watching Vince score his first and only three-hundred-point perfect game.

'And it was really weird,' Suzanne says, 'because we didn't really talk about Vince — aside from his ungainly form and crazy Brooklyn-side approach — but it's as if she totally knows what I'm enduring . . . What it feels like to love Vince, in spite of all his bullshit . . . And even though you're my sister and I've told you so much more about my relationship than I'd *ever* confess to her, in some ways, she *still* knows more than you could *ever* know.'

'Even if she no longer cares about him?' I clarify.

'Well, based on the adoring look on her face when Vince was carrying on all over the place, high-fiving everyone he could find, that is certainly dubious,' Suzanne says. 'But yes. Even if.'

I put my head down on a pillow, feeling my buzz recede, replaced by fatigue and even greater hunger. I ask Suzanne if she wouldn't rather stay in and order room service, but then remember that her life is largely about flying to cities and never leaving the airport hotels, so I tell her that I could be motivated to go out, too.

'Nah. Fuck it,' Suzanne says. 'I didn't come here for the nightlife.'

173

'Aww,' I say, laughing and planting a big kiss on her cheek. 'You came here for your sister, didn't you!'

'Get off me!' she says.

'C'mon,' I say, kissing her cheek again, and then her forehead, basking in joking moments like these as the only chance I have to kiss Suzanne. Like our father, she is uncomfortable with most physical affection whereas I inherited my mother's cuddly gene. 'You adore your little sister. That's why you're here! Admit it!'

'Nope,' she says. 'I came here for two reasons . . . '

'Oh yeah?' I say. 'For Drake and what else?'

'To baby-sit your cheatin' ass,' she says, chucking a pillow at my head. 'That's what else.'

She is clearly joking, but it is still the last bit of incentive I need to change into my nightgown, select a club sandwich from the room-service menu, and call my husband.

'Hey, honey,' Andy says. 'You guys having a good time?'

'Very,' I say, thinking how nice — and somehow cozy — his voice is.

He asks me what I'm doing and I tell him that we're just staying in and talking.

'So you're not picking up any guys?' he says.

'C'mon,' I say, feeling a pang of guilt as I recall the smell of liquor on Leo's breath and the lingering look he gave me before he left the bar. I picture him now, sipping a margarita somewhere nearby.

'That's my girl,' Andy says, yawning. 'Love you.'

I smile and tell Andy I love him, too.

'Enough to get me that autograph?'

'Not that much,' I say. And then think — *But definitely enough to forgo that guacamole and the man who will later fall asleep in Room 612.*

15

Sometime in the middle of the night I am awakened by the sound of my own voice and a dream of Leo so graphic that I feel flustered — nearly embarrassed — a tough feat when you're lying alone in the dark. As I listen to Suzanne softly snoring in her bed, I catch my breath and slowly play back all the vivid details — the silhouette of his broad shoulders flexing over me; his hands between my legs; his mouth on my neck; and that first slow stroke inside me.

I bite down hard on my lip, alert and tingling with the knowledge that he is just one floor above me in a bed just like this one, perhaps dreaming of the very same thing, maybe even wide awake and wishing it were happening. Just as I am.

It would be so easy, I think. All I would have to do is reach over for the phone, call Room 612 and whisper: *Can I come see you?*

And he would say, *Yes, baby. Come now.*

I know he would tell me to come. I know because of this assignment tomorrow — the very fact that we are both here in L.A. staying at the same hotel. I know because of that unmistakable look he gave me in the bar, a look that even Suzanne couldn't miss. But most of all, I know because of how good we once felt together. Despite how much I try to deny it and ignore it or focus only on the way things ended, I know what was there. He must remember it, too.

I close my eyes, my heart racing with something close to fear, as I picture getting out of bed, silently stealing through the halls, finding Leo's door and knocking once, just as he knocked on my hotel door during our jury duty so long ago. I can clearly see Leo waiting for me on the other side, unshaven and sleepy-eyed, leading me to his bed, slowly undressing me.

Once under the covers, there would be no discussion of why we broke up or the past eight years or anything or *anyone* else. There would be no words at all. Just the sounds of us breathing, kissing, fucking.

I tell myself that it wouldn't really count. Not when I'm this far from home. Not in the very middle of the night. I tell myself that it would only be the blurry continuation of a dream too satisfying and too real to resist.

★ ★ ★

When I wake up again several hours later, sun is streaming through the window, and Suzanne is already shuffling around the room, tidying her belongings and mine as she watches the muted television.

'Holy eastern exposure,' I groan.

'I know,' she says, looking up from her bag of toiletries. 'We forgot to shut the blinds.'

'We forgot to take Advil, too,' I say, squinting from the throbbing sensation in my left temple and dose of guilt and regret that is evocative of the walk of shame in college — the morning after alcohol and loud music and the veil of nighttime induced you to kiss someone you might not have otherwise even talked to. I reassure myself that this is not the same thing at all. *Nothing* happened last night. I had a dream. That is all. Dreams sometimes — *often* — mean absolutely nothing. Once, when I was in the adolescent throes of braces-tightening torture, I had an appallingly provocative dream about my orthodontist, a balding, nondescript soccer dad of a guy, who was the father of a classmate to boot. And I can guarantee that I didn't want Dr. Popovich on *any*, even subconscious, level.

Yet, deep down, I know that *this* dream didn't come from nowhere. And more significantly, I know that the problem isn't the dream per se. It was the way I felt afterward, once awake. It is the way I still feel now.

I sit up and stretch, feeling better just getting out of a horizontal position. Then, once out of bed altogether, I shift into professional, efficient mode, even adopting a crisp, businesslike tone with Suzanne. I cannot afford to indulge in ridiculous, misguided fantasies when I have a huge, career-defining shoot in front of me. In my great mentor Frank's words, *It's show time.*

But hours later, after I've completed a thorough battery check and equipment inventory, reviewed my notes, phoned my freelance assistant to confirm our schedule, and triple-checked with the manager of the diner that she is indeed closing for two hours as per Drake's camp's request, I am in the shower, under very hot water, still brooding over Leo. Wishing I had packed cuter clothes for the shoot. Contemplating just how

178

awful I would feel if I had called him last night. Wondering whether it just might have been worth it — and then berating myself for even thinking such a terrible thing.

At some point, Suzanne interrupts my thoughts, shouting through a thick cloud of steam, 'Are you alive in there?'

'Yeah,' I say tersely, remembering how, as a teenager, she'd often pick the lock with a bobby pin and barge right into the bathroom during my only alone time in our cramped ranch.

'Are you nervous or just really dirty?' she asks me now, as she wipes down the mirror with a towel and sets about brushing her teeth.

I turn the water off and wring out my hair, as I admit that, yes, I am nervous. But I do not confess that the real reason for my nerves has very little to do with photographing Drake.

★ ★ ★

It is surreal, the sight of them together, talking earnestly over a burger (Leo's) and a Greek salad (Drake's). For a moment, I lose myself, taking in all the details. I observe that their hair is the same dark brown hue, but while Drake is sporting a five o'clock shadow and longish, slightly greasy hair, Leo is clean-shaven, nearly conservative in comparison. Both are wearing plain black T-shirts, but Leo's appears to be a Gap staple, and Drake's is more trendy and form fitting (and likely five times more expensive). He has also heavily accessorized the look with a silver hoop earring, several rings, and his trademark amber-colored glasses.

More than their dress or appearance, though, I am riveted by the placid, relaxed mood of their table. To Leo's credit, Drake looks unguarded, even engrossed by questions he's undoubtedly answered a thousand times, and Leo looks to be at complete, sexy ease. I note that he has ditched what used to be his standard yellow pad in favor of a small silver tape recorder which he has set up discretely beside the salt-and-pepper kiosk. In fact, but for the recorder and the sheer knowledge that Drake is *Drake*, there would be no way to discern that an interview is in the works. Even the grungy-but-still-ultra-fashionable posse whom I presume to be Drake's entourage is keeping a respectful distance near the counter, further kudos to Leo; I've seen public relations types swarm around celebrities far less famous with interviewers far more accredited, playing watchdog against inane or inappropriate questions. Clearly the pack has determined that Leo is a solid guy — or at least a solid journalist.

'Damn,' Suzanne whispers as she stares. 'What a *strong* face he has.'

I nod, even though I know we are not looking at the same man, basking for one final second in Leo.

Then I say, 'Okay. Let's get to work,' and begin unloading my equipment, surveying various backgrounds, and searching for the source of the best natural light. 'Try to act like an assistant, would ya?'

'Right-o,' she says, as the manager of the diner, a squat woman named Rosa whose

180

current giddiness belies her deep frown lines, asks if she can get us anything for at least the third time since ushering us into her diner. I have the sense that today is a highlight of her career, something we have in common — although only one of us has an 8 × 10 glossy shot of Drake and black Sharpie ready to go.

I tell Rosa no thank you, and she presses with, 'Not even a water or coffee?'

I am too jittery for caffeine, so accept her offer of water while Suzanne pipes up with an unabashed request for a strawberry milkshake.

'Super. We're famous for our milkshakes,' Rosa says proudly and scurries to put in the order.

I give my sister a disapproving, but mildly amused, look.

She shrugs. 'What can I tell ya? I work best with a sugar buzz. Don't you want to get the best out of your people?'

I roll my eyes, relieved to discover that my real assistant, a fresh-faced youth named Justin, has arrived with some larger lights and other rental equipment too cumbersome to fly with. After introducing ourselves and briefly chatting, I point out the shots that I think are best, then ask for his input, which seems to please him. His delight, in turn, makes me feel like the old pro and gives me a needed boost of confidence. Justin agrees with my assessment on background and lighting, adds one idea of his own, and the two of us get down to the nitty-gritty of setting up, taking light-meter reads, and snapping a couple of test sets. Meanwhile, Suzanne makes a feeble showing of helpfulness while doing her best to eavesdrop on the interview.

As we move about the small diner, I can't help overhearing an occasional question from Leo, and a few inspiring snippets from Drake until finally, Justin and I are ready to go. I glance at my watch, discovering that we are ahead of schedule, and feel relaxed for the first time all day — maybe even all week.

Until I hear Leo say my name, that is, and I turn around to find him and Drake watching me expectantly.

'C'mere,' Leo beckons as if we're the oldest of pals, and he has just run into the third friend in our once inseparable triumvirate.

My heart skips a beat — for so many reasons. Or at least two.

'Holy shit. He's looking *right* at you,' Suzanne mumbles behind her milkshake. And then — 'Whatever you do, don't trip over those cords.'

I take a deep breath, give myself a final little pep talk and, feeling grateful that I don't work in heels, stroll over to the table where several of Drake's staffers are now hovering.

Leo looks past them, as if they're invisible, and says to me, 'Hey, Ellen.'

'Hi, Leo,' I say.

'Have a seat,' he says, as I think *déjà vu*. Although upon further thought, the exchange actually *is* the same as yesterday's — which means it's not déjà vu. *Enough mental rambling*, I think as I take Leo's side of the booth. He moves over, but only barely, so that we are close enough to hold hands if we were so inclined.

'Ellen, this is Drake Watters. Drake, meet my good friend Ellen,' Leo says in what is another surreal moment. I simply can't believe that I'm being introduced to Drake — and that *Leo* is making the introduction.

I instinctively start to extend my hand, but then remember what Frank once told me about how germ phobic many A-listers are, so I give Drake a respectful nod instead.

'Hello, Drake,' I say, my heart racing.

'Very nice to meet you, Ellen,' he says in his lyrical South African accent. He looks every bit as cool as I thought he would, yet at the same time, there is something surprisingly unflashy, even understated, about him.

'Nice to meet you, too,' I say, stopping with that, as I recall another bit of advice from Frank: that a death knell for a photographer is to bore a celebrity subject with obsequious chatter. Not that anything springs to mind anyway, except for: *I was, like, totally deflowered to that one song of yours.* Although true, I know I would never in a million years utter such a ridiculous thing, yet I still feel mildly concerned that I might — the verbal equivalent of fearing that you will, for no reason at all, hurl yourself off a balcony at the mall.

At this point, one handler type rubs his palms together indicating that there will be no further small talk. 'You're Ellen Dempsey?' he says, also in a South African accent, but a clunkier one than Drake's.

'Yes,' I say, fleetingly wishing that I changed

my professional name when Andy and I married.

'You have fifteen minutes to shoot,' another handler instructs me, somewhat condescendingly.

'No problem,' I say, then turn my gaze back to Drake. 'Shall we get started?'

'Sure,' he says, nodding just as a rock star should — all loosey-goosey, cool. 'Where do you want me?'

I point to a booth behind ours, switching into auto-pilot. There is no time left for jitters. 'Right over there,' I instruct him. 'Just slide in toward the window, please. And could you take your cup of tea with you? I'd like it in the foreground.'

'Great,' Drake says, winking. 'I wasn't done with it, anyway.'

As he slides out of the booth, I catch Leo giving me a look that can only be described as fond. I flash him a small, sincere — nearly fond — smile in return.

'Break a leg,' he whispers, looking up at me.

I pause, getting sucked into his eyes. Then, against my better judgment, I say, 'Wait for me?'

Leo smiles. 'Was planning on it. You can't shake me that easily.'

I smile again as it suddenly occurs to me that I will not be able to hide Leo's connection to the story forever. Andy and Margot will see his byline. Everyone will. Our names will be printed together, along with Drake's, all on the very same page. But as I pick up my camera, I tell myself that this day might just be worth a little bit of trouble.

★ ★ ★

The next fifteen minutes are a high-adrenaline blur of snapping ninety-four photos while giving Drake a steady stream of monotone instruction: *Sit here, stand there, a little to the left, chin up a bit, small smile, no smile, half-smile, hand on your mug, hand on the table, hands on your lap, look out the window, look over my shoulder, look right at me.* Then: *Okay. That's it. Thank you, Drake.*

And I'm done. Blissfully done. And the best, most euphoric part is that I know I have my one, great shot. I *always* know when I have my shot — and today I am even more certain than usual. Drake, with just the right amount of natural light behind him, creating almost a soft halo effect; red booth contrasting with black shirt and white mug; strong lines of the table, window, and Drake's own bone structure. Perfection.

'Thank you, Ellen Dempsey,' Drake says, smiling. 'That was painless.'

I smile — no, *beam* — back at him, memorizing the way he makes my most ordinary name sound like a line of a poem, one of his songs. I am on an absolute physical, emotional high.

Then, after Drake is whisked off by his people, and Justin has packed up our equipment, and Rosa has prominently displayed her signed headshot next to the cash register, and Suzanne has hunkered down at the counter to sample a chocolate malt, I am finally alone with Leo in the back of the diner, leaning against a wall, looking into his eyes, once again.

16

'So? How do you feel?' Leo asks me, holding my gaze like a magnetic field.

His open-ended question makes me feel lightheaded, and I can't help wondering if he's being intentionally vague.

'About the shoot?' I say.

'Sure,' he says attentively. 'About the shoot. About anything.'

I look up at him, feeling tempted to confess that I'm positively exhilarated. That I've never had such a thrilling hour of work — and rarely felt the sort of pure chemical attraction that I am experiencing now. That I know I told him that I didn't want to be friends, but can't stand the thought of shutting down that possibility completely. That although I'm happily married, I feel a strange bond to him and don't want this to be *it* between us, forever.

But of course I say none of this, for more reasons than one. Instead, I give him a blasé smile and say that I'm pretty sure I got some decent shots. 'So don't worry . . . my photos won't water down your interview too much.'

He laughs and says, 'Good. 'Cause I've been really concerned about that. Ever since I called your agent I've been thinking, 'Shit. She's gonna ruin my piece.''

I smile, a little too flirtatiously, and he smiles back in the same vein. After a highly charged ten seconds pass, I ask if he got some good stuff.

Leo nods, patting the tape recorder in his back pocket. 'Yeah. I wasn't sure what to expect ... I'd heard that he was a pretty nice guy — friendly, open, personable ... but you just don't know what mood you'll walk into ... I guess you know how that is, right?'

I nod. 'Resistant subjects are never a good time ... although surly and moody can sometimes photograph better than you'd think.'

Leo takes one step toward me. 'I guess it's all about chemistry,' he says suggestively.

'Yeah,' I say feeling a ridiculous smile spread across my face. 'Chemistry is important.'

Another bloated moment passes before Leo asks, so casually and breezily that it becomes pointed, what I'm doing later. It is a question I've considered a dozen times today, wishing that we had one more night at the Beverly Wilshire, while simultaneously feeling relieved that I have an e-ticket to save me from myself.

'I'm headed back to New York,' I say.

'Oh,' he says as something around his eyes falls just a bit. 'What time's your flight?'

'I'm on the nine-thirty red-eye,' I say.

'Oh. That's too bad,' he says, glancing at his watch.

I make a noncommittal sound, calculating the time I have left in L.A. Searching for a plausible way to spend some of it with Leo, rather than my sister, who is still making herself scarce at the counter.

'So I can't convince you to stick around for another night?' Leo says.

187

I hesitate, casting about for a solution. A way to stay in town while keeping things above board. But then I conjure Andy's smile, his dimples, his clear blue eyes, and have no choice but to say, 'No . . . I really need to get back.'

There simply is no way to tread these dangerous waters.

'I understand,' Leo says quickly, seeming to read between the lines. He glances down to adjust the strap on his kelly green messenger bag — a brighter color than I'd expect of Leo — as I find myself wondering whether it was a gift; how beautiful the woman who gave it to him is; whether they're still together.

He looks up and winks playfully. 'That's cool,' he says. 'We'll just hang out the next time we're in L.A. doing a feature on Drake.'

'Right,' I say, struggling to outdo his sarcasm with a bold line of my own. 'We'll hang out the next time you dump me, then run into me years later, then reel me back in with an assignment of a lifetime . . . '

Leo looks startled. 'What are you talking about?'

'Which part is unclear?' I say, smiling to soften my somewhat confrontational question.

'I didn't *dump* you,' he says.

I roll my eyes, then laugh. 'Right.'

He looks hurt — or at least taken aback. 'It wasn't like *that*.'

I study his face, surmising that he must be trying to spare my pride by pretending that ours was a mutual split. But there is no trace of strategy, no trace of anything other than genuine surprise at my 'version' of our history.

'What *was* it like then?' I ask him.

'We just . . . I don't know . . . I know I was an ass — and took myself too seriously . . . I remember New Year's Eve . . . but I can't really remember *why* we broke up . . . It almost seems that we broke up over *nothing* really.'

'Over *nothing*?' I say, feeling something close to desperation as Suzanne suddenly rounds the corner.

She must catch my expression, because she says, 'Oh, sorry,' and halts abruptly.

I force a smile and say, 'No. You're fine. We were just chatting . . . about . . . Drake.'

Suzanne gives me a look like she doesn't believe me, but plays along. 'What did you guys think of him? Was he as down-to-earth as he seems?'

'Definitely,' Leo says. 'Very real.'

'Very,' I echo brightly as my insides churn.

'What was the best part of the interview?' Suzanne asks Leo. 'Or do I have to wait to buy the magazine?'

Leo pretends to consider this, but then says he trusts her and will give her the inside scoop, launching into some specifics about Drake's work on third-world debt relief and all his criticisms of our current administration, none of which I can focus on. Instead, I fight the wistful welling in my chest, and decide to rip off the Band-Aid during the next lull in conversation.

When it finally comes, I say as decisively as possible, 'Well. We better get going.'

Leo nods, his expression becoming familiarly

impassive. 'Right,' he says.

'So thanks again for everything,' I say.

'Thank *you*,' he says, withdrawing further. 'I can't wait to see your photos.'

'And I can't wait to read your piece. I know it's going to be great,' I say, feeling all the exhilaration from a few minutes before drain from my body. *Highs and lows*, I think. It always was about highs and lows with Leo.

Suzanne pretends to study a framed playbill hanging on the wall beyond us, as if to give us one last sliver of privacy while Leo nods another thank-you. For a moment, it seems as if he might give me a final hug, albeit a formal one. But he doesn't. He just tells us to have a good trip.

But all I hear is, *Have a good life*.

★ ★ ★

Once back in a cab, en route to the hotel, Suzanne's eyebrows knit into an empathetic frown. 'You look sad,' she says softly. 'Are you sad?'

I can't muster the energy to lie so I nod and tell her yes — although in truth, downright disconsolate is closer to the mark.

'I don't know *why*,' I say. 'It's all just . . . so weird . . . Seeing him again . . . '

Suzanne takes my hand and says, 'That's normal.'

'Is it, though?' I say. 'Because it doesn't *feel* very normal. And I certainly don't think Andy would call this normal.'

Suzanne looks out her window as she poses

the ultimate question. 'Do you still have feelings for him, or do you think it's just nostalgia?'

'I think it's a bit more than nostalgia,' I admit.

Suzanne says, 'I figured as much,' and then, almost as an afterthought, adds, 'But if it helps, I totally get what you see in him. Dark, sexy, smart . . .'

A wry laugh escapes my lips. 'That actually doesn't help. At *all*,' I say. 'Thanks anyway.'

'Sorry,' she says.

'And you know what else doesn't help?' I say as our cab pulls into the hotel driveway and several bellmen swarm around the car.

Suzanne looks at me, waiting for me to continue.

'Leo telling me he can't, for the *life* of him, recall why we broke up.'

'Fuck,' she says, her eyes widening. 'He said that?'

'Pretty much,' I say.

'That's something.'

I nod as I pay our driver. 'Yeah . . . You think he's messing with my head?'

Suzanne pauses and then says, 'Why would he do that?'

'I don't know,' I say as we make our way through the revolving doors and into the lobby to collect our stored luggage. 'Maybe to make me feel better about the past? Or maybe he's just . . . on some kind of a power trip?'

'I don't know him well enough,' she says. 'What do *you* think?'

I shrug and then say I really don't think so — on either front. It's not Leo's style to

191

gratuitously make someone feel better. Yet I don't think he's a manipulative game player either.

As we settle into two hard, high-back chairs in the lobby, Suzanne looks contemplative. 'Well,' she finally says, 'In all likelihood, he meant just what he said: that he really can't remember why — *how* — it ended. And maybe he also meant that he wishes things had gone down differently.'

I run my hands through my hair and exhale wearily. 'You think that's a possibility?'

Suzanne nods. 'Sure. And isn't that satisfying?' she asks. 'Sort of what every girl dreams of when she's dumped. That the guy will someday feel regret and come back and tell her all about it . . . And the beauty of it is . . . *you* have no regrets whatsoever.'

I look at her.

'Right?' she says, the question drenched in meaning. A one-word test of my choices. Of Andy. Of everything in my life.

'Right,' I say emphatically. 'Absolutely no regrets.'

'Well then,' Suzanne says with her usual conviction. 'There you have it.'

★   ★   ★

Three hours later, after Suzanne and I have shared a quick fast-food dinner at the airport and said our good-byes at the American security line, I am boarding my flight with a distinct ache in my chest and a nagging sense of unfinished business. As I settle into my window seat in the next-to-last row of coach, vaguely listening to

192

the flight attendant drone about limited overhead-bin space, I revisit the events of the day, specifically the very abrupt ending to my final encounter with Leo. In hindsight, I wish that I had just told Suzanne that I needed a little more time with him. It would have been undeniably awkward to make the request, but one hour — even thirty minutes — is really all it would have taken to ease the anticlimactic conclusion to such an emotional shoot, and wrap up the unsettling conversation about our breakup.

Despite the fact that I have no regrets about how things turned out in my life, I still can't help wanting to understand my intense relationship with Leo, as well as that turbulent time between adolescence and adulthood when everything feels raw and invigorating and scary — and why those feelings are all coming back to me now.

I quickly try to call Andy to let him know that we are taking off on time, but there is no answer. I leave a message, telling him that the shoot went well, and that I love him and will see him first thing in the morning. Then I turn my attention to the stream of passengers filing down the aisle, and say a prayer that the middle seat beside me will stay vacant, or, at the very least, that it will be filled by a tidy, quiet seatmate. But one beat later, a large, sloppy man with the distinct aroma of booze and cigarettes is bearing down on me with a bulging canvas tote, a Burger King to-go bag, and a Mountain Dew bottle filled with a questionable amber liquid.

'Helloo there!' he bellows. 'Looks like I'm next to ya!'

In addition to his boozy aroma and carry-on beverage, his bloodshot eyes and excessive volume make it pretty clear that he's already drunk — or very close to the mark. I envision a long night of cocktails, with some occasional spillage, accompanied by profuse apologies, inappropriate attempts to clean me up, and clumsy conversation starters. My only shot at peace is to shut him down quickly and nip all interaction in the bud. So I say nothing in response, just force the tiniest of polite smiles while he collapses into his seat and immediately stoops down to remove his filthy tennis shoes and stained tube socks, his beefy arms and chapped elbows invading every inch of my personal space.

'Eh, boy! These dogs are barkin',' he announces, once his sweaty feet are freed. He then offers me a fry. 'Want one?'

I suppress a gag, tell him no thanks, and promptly slip my inflight headphones on, turning my body toward the window. Then I jack up the volume on the classical music channel, close my eyes, and try to think about anything other than Leo. About fifteen minutes of jostling later, I feel the plane begin to move down the runway, picking up speed before tilting sickeningly backward. As we become airborne, I give my armrest a death grip, irrationally bracing myself while fighting images of flames and mangled steel. *We are not going to crash*, I think. Fate is not so cruel as to have me spend my last moments with the man next to me. But when I finally open my eyes, my seatmate — and his

Burger King feast — are nowhere to be found.

And, in his grubby place, as if by magic, is none other than Leo.

He gives me a sideways smile and says, 'I got on your flight.'

'I see that,' I say, trying to suppress my own smile, but quickly losing the battle.

'And then I — uh — switched seats,' he says.

'I see that, too,' I say, now full-on grinning. 'Pretty tricky, aren't you?'

'Tricky?' Leo says. 'I rescued you from that clown . . . who is now wasted — and barefoot — in business class. I'd tag it chivalrous — not tricky.'

'You gave up a *business-class* seat?' I say, feeling flattered and strangely empowered as I process all the logistical effort that went into this moment.

'Yeah. How about that? For a middle seat in the very back of the plane.'

'Well. You *are* chivalrous,' I say.

'Well? How about a thank-you?'

'Thank you,' I say, as it begins to sink in that I will be spending the next five hours trapped in close, dark quarters with Leo. My heart skips a beat.

'You're very welcome,' he says, reclining his seat ever so slightly and then flipping his tray table up and down with what I detect is some nervousness of his own.

We make fleeting eye contact, a tough thing to do when you're side by side in coach, before I smile, shake my head, and shift my gaze back toward the window.

The flight attendant makes an announcement that the seatbelt sign is still illuminated, and the captain will inform us when it is safe to move about the cabin. *Perfect*, I think. Absolutely trapped by no doing of my own.

A few minutes of charged silence pass as I close my eyes, thinking that miraculously, I'm no longer worried about flying.

'So,' Leo finally says as I open my eyes and the plane begins to steady in the California night sky. 'Where were we, anyway?'

17

I can't remember how I answer that first question of Leo's; only that we successfully dance around any discussion of our relationship, or how exactly it ended, or really anything of a personal nature, for a very long stretch of the flight. Instead we stick to safe harbors like movies and music, travel and work. It is the sort of conversation you have when you first meet someone you would like to know better — or an acquaintance you haven't seen in a long time. We stay on the surface of things, yet there is an underlying ease, too, a natural flow of questions and answers, marked by stretches of comfortable silence. They are so comfortable, in fact, that we are eventually lulled back into intimate terrain.

It happens innocently enough, as I finish telling him about a recent shoot I did in the Adirondacks. 'There's just something about photographing a small town, the locals,' I say, 'people who are tied so inextricably to their geography . . . It's so satisfying . . . '

My voice trails off as I feel Leo's gaze. When I turn toward him, he says, 'You really love your work, don't you?' His tone is so admiring that it makes my heart flutter.

'Yeah,' I say softly. 'I do.'

'I could see that today . . . I loved watching you work.'

I smile, resisting the urge to tell him that I

loved watching him during his interview, too. Instead, I let him continue.

'It's funny,' he says, almost as if he's thinking aloud. 'In some ways you seem like the same Ellen I once knew, but in other ways . . . you seem so . . . *different* . . . '

I wonder what exactly he's basing this assessment on, as our cumulative exchanges since passing in the intersection can't exceed an hour. Then again, I find that my sense of Leo is shifting, too, and it occurs to me that not only are there two sides to every story, but that those versions can also evolve over time.

I watch Leo take a sip from his plastic cup of ginger ale on ice and suddenly see myself through his eyes. Then and now. Two very contrasting portraits with something of the same core. I glimpse my former self — the needy, lonely, motherless young girl, new to the big city, struggling to find her own identity, an identity apart from her suffocating hometown, her sheltered college experience, her shiny best friend.

I see myself falling in love for the first time, and how that all-consuming love — how *Leo* — seemed to be my answer. He was everything I wanted to be — passionate, soulful, strong — and being with him made me feel at least a byproduct of all those things. Yet the more I tried to entrench myself in that relationship, the more insecure I became. At the time, this all felt like Leo's fault, but looking back, I can see that I have to share the blame. At the very least, I can see why I became less attractive to him.

I think back to Leo's earlier comments today, about how he took himself too seriously. Maybe that was true, but I can also see that I didn't take myself seriously *enough*. And it was that lethal combination that made our breakup virtually inevitable.

'Yeah. I like to think I've evolved a little,' I finally say, as more snapshots of our relationship return to me — things I had suppressed or simply forgotten. I recall, for example, how much Leo loved a good debate, and how his face would flicker with annoyance when I had no opinion. I remember his frustration at my lack of independence, his irritation at my tendency to settle or take the easy way out — whether in a job or mindset.

'We both had a lot of growing up to do . . . A lot of the world to see and figure out on our own,' Leo says, confirming that I'm not the only one thinking in terms of our relationship.

'So?' I say hesitantly. 'Have you figured things out?'

'A few things,' he says. 'But life's a long journey, ya know?'

I nod, thinking of my mother. *If you're lucky.*

Several minutes pass, as I realize that for the first time since meeting Leo at jury duty, I can no longer neatly categorize what he was during our time together. He was not the man of my dreams, the perfect guy I once put on a pedestal; nor was he the villain who Margot had done her best to demonize; nor really any guy on that particular continuum. He was just the wrong guy for me at the time. Nothing more, nothing less.

'You must be exhausted,' Leo says after a long

silent stretch. 'I'll let you get some sleep.'

'That's okay,' I say. 'Let's talk some more . . . '

I can hear the smile in Leo's voice as he replies. 'That's what you always used to say . . . '

A dozen things cross my mind in that instant — all inappropriate and half of which I nearly blurt out. Instead, I divert the conversation and ask the question I've been dying to ask since seeing him in the intersection. 'So. Are you with someone now?'

I keep my expression even while I brace myself for his answer, fearing a wave of jealousy that I desperately don't want to feel. But when he nods, I am only relieved, even as I envision a statuesque beauty with a foreign accent, a captivating wit, and an intriguing, irresistible mean streak. The sort of diva Nico sings about in the Velvet Underground's 'Femme Fatale.' I imagine that she has her pilot's license and can do tequila shots with the boys, yet also knits Leo sweaters and cooks with at least three different varieties of olive oil. She is lithe, long-limbed, and looks as good in an evening gown as she does in a white tank and a pair of Leo's boxers.

'That's great,' I say, a little too enthusiastically. 'Are you . . . is it . . . serious?'

'I guess so . . . We've been together a couple of years . . . ' he says. Then he surprises me by reaching into his back pocket for his wallet and pulling out a snapshot of her. Leo does not strike me as the type to have a photo of his girlfriend in his wallet, and certainly not the type to pass it around. But I am even more shocked when I turn on my overhead light and look down at a rather nondescript blonde, posing next to a man-sized cactus.

'What's her name?' I say, observing her hard, tanned arms, short pixie cut, and broad smile.

'Carol,' he says.

I repeat the name in my head, thinking that she looks *exactly* like a Carol. Wholesome, uncomplicated, kind.

'She's pretty,' I say, as I hand him back the photo. It seems like the right thing — really the *only* thing — to say.

Leo slides the photo back into his wallet and nods in such a way that tells me he agrees with my assessment, yet doesn't find her appearance terribly interesting or important.

Still, despite her ordinary looks, I feel an unexpected competitive pang I don't believe I would have felt if he had shown me the woman I was expecting. It is one thing to be defeated by an Angelina Jolie look-alike, another to lose to someone so squarely in my league. I remind myself that it's not a contest as I flip off my overhead light and ask, 'So where'd you and Carol meet?'

Leo clears his throat, as if contemplating a revision to the truth, but then says, 'It's actually not much of a story.'

This, of course, makes me happy.

'C'mon,' I press, rooting for a blind-date scenario — which I believe to be at the bottom of the romance totem pole.

'Okay,' he says. 'We met in a bar . . . on the most repugnant night of the year . . . at least in New York.'

'New Year's Eve?' I say, smiling, pretending not to feel any residual bitterness.

'Close,' Leo says, winking. 'St. Patrick's Day.'

I smile, thinking how I share his disdain for March seventeenth.

'C'mon. What's wrong with you? You don't love a good, raucous pub crawl?' I say. 'Whoopin' and hollerin' and sippin' green beer first thing in the morning?'

'Sure,' Leo says. 'About as much as I love all the Upper East Side frat boys puking all over the Six train.'

I laugh. 'What were *you* doing out on St. Patrick's Day, anyway?'

'I know. Shocking huh? . . . I'm still not going to win any popularity contests, but I guess I'm not quite as antisocial as I used to be . . . I think some Irish buddy must have twisted my arm that night . . . '

I resist the temptation to say, *More than I could do*, and instead ask, 'And Carol? Is she Irish?'

It is a stupid, throwaway question, but it allows me to stay on track with the subject of Leo's love life.

'Something like that. English, Scottish, Irish. Whatever.' Then he adds, somewhat randomly, 'She's from Vermont.'

I force a pleasant smile as I cringe a bit on the inside, picturing Carol, swinging open her family's barn door on a crisp autumn day, proudly demonstrating how to milk a cow to her boyfriend from the big city . . . the two of them laughing uncontrollably when he can't seem to

202

get the maneuver down . . . milk squirting into his face before he topples off the painted wooden stool into a bed of hay . . . she falling on top of him, sliding off her overalls . . .

I block out the image and allow myself one final inroad into Carol. 'What does she do?' I say. 'For a living?'

'She's a scientist,' he says. 'A medical researcher at Columbia . . . She studies cardiac arrhythmia.'

'Wow,' I say, impressed in the way I think all right-brained people feel about left-brained people — and vice versa.

'Yeah,' Leo says. 'She's a smart one.'

I look at him, waiting for more, but it is clear that he is finished talking about Carol. Instead he crosses his legs and says with what seems to be a purposefully breezy air, 'Your turn. Tell me about Andy.'

It is a hard question to answer, even when you're not talking to an ex, so I smile and say, 'I know you're a reporter — and love those open-ended questions — but can you be more specific? What do you want to know?'

Leo says. 'Okay. You want specific . . . Let's see . . . Does he like board games?'

I laugh, remembering how Leo would never play board games with me. 'Yeah,' I say.

'Ahh. Very good for you,' Leo says.

I smile, nod and say, 'Anything else?'

'Hmm . . . Does he skip breakfast — or believe that it's the most important meal of the day?'

'The latter.'

Leo nods as if taking mental notes. 'Does he believe in God?'

203

'Yeah,' I say. 'And Jesus, too.'

'Very well . . . And . . . does he . . . strike up conversations with people on planes?'

'Occasionally,' I say, smiling. 'But generally not ex-girlfriends. As far as I know . . .'

Leo gives me a sheepish glance, but doesn't take the bait. Instead he sighs loudly and then says, 'Okay . . . How about this one? . . . Does your husband seem genuinely surprised when he unscrews the cap on his Coke and discovers that, *lo and behold, holy shit,* he's 'Not a Winner This Time'?'

I laugh. 'That's so funny!' I say. 'Because *yes!* He *expects* to win . . . He's an eternal optimist.'

'So,' Leo says. 'Looks like you found yourself a solid, Checkers-playing, Cheerios-eating, God-fearing, glass-half-full kinda guy.'

I burst out laughing, but then worry that I've sold Andy short with Leo's round of Q&As — or, worse, somehow belittled who he is. So I end on a decidedly loyal note. 'Yeah. Andy is a great guy. A really good person . . . I'm very lucky.'

Leo turns in his seat and looks at me, his smile quickly fading. 'He's lucky, too.'

'Thank you,' I say, feeling myself blush.

'It's true,' he says. 'Ellen . . . I don't know how I let you get away . . .'

I give him a small smile, feeling very bashful as I marvel how such a simple statement can be so healing and thrilling and unsettling, all at once.

And it only gets worse — *and* better — when Leo reclines his seat and moves his arm onto the rest against mine so that our skin is touching from elbow to wrist. I close my eyes, inhale, and feel a rush of heat and energy that takes my breath away. It is the feeling of wanting something so much that it borders on an actual need, and the power and urgency of this need overwhelms me.

I command myself to move my arm, knowing how imperative it is that I do the right thing. I can hear the scream inside my head — *I am a newlywed, and I love my husband!* But it does no good. I literally cannot make myself retreat. I just can't. Instead I recline my seat to be flush with his and uncurl my fingers, desperately hoping that he'll find them. He does, tentatively at first, our pinkies barely touching, then overlapping slightly, then a bit more, and more still, as if there is a tide pulling him toward me, over me.

I wonder if he is still watching me through the shadows of the cabin, but I don't open my eyes to find out, hoping the dark will make me feel less culpable, make what I'm doing seem less real. Yet the effect is actually the opposite — it all feels *more* real, more intense, in the way that you can always focus more on one sense when others are shut off.

Time passes, but neither of us speaks, as Leo's hand completely covers mine. The weight and warmth of it is the same as it was at the diner, the day all of this began, but the gesture feels completely different. This contact is not incidental to a conversation. It *is* the conversation. It is also an invitation. An invitation I accept with a languid turn of my wrist until my palm is up, facing his, and we are officially holding hands. I tell myself that it is the most innocent of gestures. Grade-school crushes hold hands. Parents and children hold hands. *Friends* hold hands.

But not like this. *Never* like this.

I listen to the sound of Leo breathing, his face close to mine, as our fingers interlock, unlace, rearrange. And we fly east that way, eventually drifting off, suspended in the sky, in time, together.

★ ★ ★

The next parcel of time is hazy as I fall in and out of sleep. I vaguely hear the flight attendant's announcements, but don't awaken for good until we begin our final descent into JFK. Groggily, I look out the window at the lights of the city, then turn to find Leo still sleeping, still holding my hand. His neck is bent, his body curled slightly toward me, his face illuminated by the bright cabin lights. I frantically memorize the dark whiskers across his jaw; his slightly disheveled sideburns; the long, straight bridge of his nose; and his large, domed eyelids.

My stomach churns as it occurs to me that I feel almost exactly as I did the morning after we first made love. I had awakened before sunrise that day, too, and can distinctly recall being frozen next to him, watching him sleep, his bare chest rising and falling, as I thought to myself, *What next?*

I ask myself the same question now, but come up with a very different answer this time. There is nothing hopeful in this moment. This is not a beginning, but an end. It is almost time to let go of Leo's hand. It is almost time to say good-bye.

A few seconds later, we touch down with a hard jolt of speed. Leo's eyes blink open. He yawns, stretches in his seat, and gives me a slow, disoriented smile. 'Hello,' he says.

'Good morning,' I say softly. My throat is dry and tight, but I can't tell if it's more from thirst or some strain of sadness. I consider reaching down for the water bottle in my purse, but am not quite ready to break our contact — and certainly not for a little hydration.

'Is it morning already?' he says, glancing furtively out the window at the dark runway.

'Almost,' I say. 'It's six-thirty . . . We're ahead of schedule.'

'Shit,' he says, his face reflecting the sinking, conflicted way I feel.

'What?' I say, wanting him to verbalize it for us both, wanting him to tell me that he can't believe that we are back in New York and that it's time to get on with our day. Our separate lives.

He looks down at our clasped hands and says, 'You know what.'

I nod and follow his gaze to our crisscrossed thumbs. Then I squeeze his hand one final time before letting go.

For the next few minutes, we follow the herd, wearily gathering our belongings, putting on our jackets, and spilling off the plane into the gate area. We are both silent, not communicating at all until we exchange a glance outside the first set of restrooms — a glance that makes it clear that we intend to wait for each other.

And yet, several minutes later, after I've brushed my teeth and hair, I am still surprised when I round the corner and see him leaning against the gray wall, looking so ruggedly handsome that I catch my breath. He gives me a half smile, then very deliberately unwraps a stick of gum. He folds it into his mouth, chews, and extends the package toward me. 'Want one?'

'No, thanks,' I say.

He stows the package in his jacket pocket, then pushes himself off the wall with the weight of his shoulder. 'Ready?' he says.

I nod, and we are off again, headed toward baggage claim.

'Did you check anything?' he asks as we descend the escalator.

'Just my equipment. One bag . . . How about you?' I ask, knowing that the answer is no — Leo always traveled as lightly as possible.

'Nah,' he says. 'But . . . I'll wait with you.'

I do not object, and when we reach the claim area, I even find myself hoping that the baggage handlers have taken their sweet time this morning. But no such luck — I spot my black bag right away and have no choice but to lean down to retrieve it.

'I got it,' Leo says, gently brushing me aside and hoisting my bag from the belt with a small groan. For one guilty second, I pretend that this is really my life. Leo and I, reporter and photographer, traveling back to the city after yet another celebrity shoot together.

Leo balances his duffel bag over my suitcase

and asks, 'Did you order a car?'

I shake my head. 'No. I'm just taking a cab.'

'Same here,' Leo says. 'Wanna share?'

I say sure, knowing that we are only prolonging the inevitable.

Leo's face lights up in a way that I find both surprising and reassuring. 'Okay then,' he says briskly. 'Let's go.'

Outside, the early spring morning is cool and sharp. Soft pink light streaks a cloudless sky. There is no question that it is going to be a beautiful day. We walk along the curb to the cab stand and file into a short, swiftly moving line. A moment later, Leo is loading our luggage into the trunk of a taxi.

'Where to?' our cabbie asks once we've slid into the backseat.

Leo says, 'Two stops. The first will be in Astoria — Newton Avenue and Twenty-eighth . . . and the second stop? . . . ' He looks at me, his dark eyebrows raised, waiting for my address.

'Thirty-seventh and Third,' I say, as I picture the inside of my apartment at this very moment — the blinds drawn and everything quiet except for the muffled sounds of morning traffic gearing up; Andy, in a worn T-shirt and pajama bottoms, curled up asleep in our bed. Guilt slashes through my chest, but I tell myself that I will be home soon enough.

'Murray Hill, huh?' Leo asks approvingly. He was never a big fan of my old neighborhood.

'Yeah. We really like it,' I say. 'There's no scene . . . and it's very convenient, central . . . '

We, I think. *My husband and I.*

I can tell the pronoun registers with Leo, too, as there is the slightest adjustment in his expression as he nods, almost respectfully. Or perhaps he's just musing over the other half of his own *we* — Carol, who might even be on Newton Avenue right now, waiting for him in her prettiest nightgown. As we cruise along the Long Island Expressway, I realize that I have no idea whether they are living together or whether he sees marriage — with her or anyone — in his future.

I also realize that I never told Leo about my possible move to Atlanta. I would like to think this was simply an oversight, but deep down I know that it was an intentional omission, although I'm not sure why I held it back. Am I worried that Leo would view the move as the old wishy-washy Ellen trailing after her man? Or that he would discount me completely, on the basis of geography? Or is it because, on some level, I don't *want* to move, despite what I told Andy?

Once again, I tell myself there will be time for analysis later. Right now, I only want to relish the simple beauty of the moment I'm in — the sun rising on the horizon, the gentle hum of Egyptian music playing on the radio, the knowledge that Leo is beside me in the backseat as we finish the last leg of our journey.

A few minutes later, we exit at Astoria Boulevard, right under the Triborough Bridge and the elevated subway. I look up at the lattice of tracks and am overcome with memories, all the times I took the N train to this neighborhood. More memories flood back to me when we turn onto Leo's block and I see the familiar squat, brick row houses painted in shades of cream, red, and pink, with their trash cans and green awnings lined up in front. Leo points to his building, in the middle of the block, and says to our cabbie, 'Right there on the left, please . . . Next to the white pickup.'

Then, as the taxi slows to a stop, he looks back over at me, shakes his head and says pretty much exactly what I'm thinking. 'This is so fucking strange.'

'Tell me about it,' I say. 'I never thought I'd be back here.'

Leo chews his lower lip and then says, 'You know what I want to do right now?'

A few illicit images flash through my head as I nervously say, 'What?'

'Scoop you out of this car and take you inside with me,' Leo says, his voice so low that it's almost hypnotizing. 'Make us some eggs and bacon . . . brew up some coffee . . . Then sit on the couch and just . . . *look* at you . . . and *talk* to you all day . . . '

My heart races as I think of all the other things we did in his second-floor apartment, just a few steps from where I'm sitting now. All the things *besides* talking. I look into Leo's eyes, feeling weak and slightly nauseous as I frantically try to convince myself that going inside with him would be an okay thing to do. What if I only stay for a few minutes, for one quick cup of coffee? Andy isn't even awake yet. He wouldn't miss me for at least another hour or so. What would it really hurt?

211

I clear my throat, rake my knuckles against my thighs, and glance up at the meter, still ticking as we stall. I finally say, 'So that's what you want, huh? A bit more conversation over coffee?'

Leo gives me a long, grave look and then says, 'Okay. You're right. I'm sorry . . . ' Then he runs his hand through his hair, exhales, and pulls two twenties from his wallet.

I shake my head, a refusal. 'I got this, Leo.'

'No way,' Leo says. It is something Leo and Andy have in common, both steadfastly refusing to let a girl pay for anything. But Andy's way seems rooted in chivalry; Leo's, a matter of pride. He thrusts the bills at me again. 'C'mon.'

'That's way too much,' I say. 'The meter's only at fourteen now.'

'Just take it, Ellen,' he says. 'Please.'

Because I don't want our final exchange to be a skirmish over a few bucks of cab fare, I take his money and say, 'Fine. Thanks.'

He nods. 'My pleasure . . . The whole night has been . . . my pleasure.' His words are stiff, but his tone is anything but mechanical. He means it. He loved our time together as much as I did.

I catch the cabbie giving us a skeptical glance in the rearview mirror before stepping out of the car, around to the trunk, where he lights a cigarette and waits.

'Are we that obvious?' Leo says.

I laugh nervously. 'Guess so.'

'Okay,' Leo says. 'Where were we?'

'I forget,' I say, feeling dizzy and so very sad.

Leo looks up at the ceiling of the car and then

212

back at me. 'I think we just established that you coming inside is a bad idea, right?'

'I think so,' I say.

'Well, then,' Leo says, his eyes burning into mine. 'I guess this is it.'

'Right,' I say. 'This is it.'

He hesitates, and for a second, just like at the diner, I think he might hug me, or even kiss me. Instead, he just offers up a small, sad smile before turning to go. The cab door slams behind him, and I watch him swing his bag over his shoulder, cross the sidewalk toward his apartment, and take the stairs two at a time up to the front porch. He does not turn to wave good-bye, or even give the cab another look before opening the door and disappearing inside. My eyes sting with tears as we pull away from the curb, and I repeat those final words in my head, over and over. *This is it.*

18

Somewhere along my short journey from Queens to Manhattan, I go from feeling dejected and forlorn to merely wistful and nostalgic, which is at least a step in the right, repentant direction. But when I push open our apartment door and find Andy in his favorite green-plaid robe, carefully slathering butter on a toaster waffle, I feel nothing but pure, unadulterated, aching guilt. In some strange way, though, it is almost a relief to feel this bad — and proof that I haven't strayed too far. That at my core, I am still a decent wife.

'Hey, honey,' Andy says, dropping his knife onto the counter and wrapping his arms around me in a so-happy-to-see-me hug. I inhale his sweet boyish scent, so different from Leo's musky one.

'Hi, Andy,' I say, catching the formality of using his name, something couples almost never seem to do unless they are angry or calling one another from another room. Then I make it worse by asking, in a tone more accusatory than pleasantly surprised, what he's doing up so early. I just can't help thinking that this would be an easier, less abrupt transition if he were still asleep.

'I missed you,' he says, kissing my forehead. 'I don't sleep well without you . . . '

I smile and tell him I missed him, too, but the

sinking realization that this is nothing short of a lie — that I did not miss my husband at *all* — gives my guilt a tinge of panic. I reassure myself that that might have been the case even if I hadn't seen Leo. After all, it was a short, intense trip. I had serious work to do. I was spending quality time with my sister. I met and photographed *Drake Watters*, for goodness' sake. Under these circumstances, *not* pining away for your spouse seems fairly normal, even predictable. I reassure myself that the one left behind in the same, everyday surroundings always misses the other more. To this point, I *definitely* feel a bit lonely when Andy is away on business trips.

'You hungry?' Andy asks.

I nod, thinking that this, too, is predictable when you stay up all night and eat only a pack of peanuts.

'Here. Eat this,' he says, gesturing toward his waffle.

'No. That's yours,' I say adamantly. Because after all, it's one thing to hold an ex-boyfriend's hand during a romantic, middle of the night, transcontinental flight — it's another to steal an Eggo from your hungry husband.

'No, you take this one,' he says, drizzling syrup in a cursive *E* across the face of the waffle.

I think of how I took Leo's bills in the back of the cab, and decide that I can't very well accept his money and turn down this offer from Andy.

'Okay, thanks,' I say, selecting a fork from our utensil drawer, then leaning against the counter to take a bite.

Andy watches me chew. 'Is it good?' he asks

earnestly, as if he were a chef, and this a taste test for his latest culinary innovation. I relax and smile my first real, happy smile of the morning, thinking of how Andy can make the smallest domestic occurrence feel special, imbued with affection.

'*Superb*,' I finally say. 'Best toaster waffle I've ever had . . . '

He smiles proudly, then sets about making himself another and pouring two tall glasses of milk.

'Now, c'mon. Tell me about the shoot,' he says, gesturing toward our kitchen table.

I sit down and eat my waffle, telling him all about the trip but carefully stripping Leo from the experience. I talk about the hotel, my sister, the diner, how thrilling it was to meet Drake, how pleased I am with my photos.

'I can't wait to see your shots,' Andy says.

'I think you're going to love them,' I say.

Much more than the article.

'When can I see them?' he asks.

'Tonight,' I say, wondering if I can power through the day without a nap. 'I want to go in and work on them today . . . '

Andy rubs his hands together and says, 'Awesome . . . And my autograph? I'm sure you got my autograph?'

I make an apologetic face, thinking that if I had known Leo would appear on my flight, I definitely would have made the embarrassing request. Anything to mitigate the guilt I feel now.

'I'm sorry, honey,' I say sincerely. 'There just wasn't . . . an opportunity.'

He sighs melodramatically, then takes his last swallow of milk. A white mustache appears in the corners of his mouth, and remains there for a poignant second before he wipes it off with a paper towel. 'It's okay,' he says, winking. 'I won't question your loyalty *this* time.'

Although he is clearly being facetious, his words are like a dagger to my heart. There are no two ways about it — I suck. I am a bad, *bad* wife. Maybe not scarlet-letter bad, but certainly deserving-of-the-doghouse bad. For one second, I consider confessing everything, down to the final, unfaithful, wholly unnecessary detour to Astoria. But the opening quickly dissolves when Andy pushes his plate away, cracks his knuckles, and breaks into a grin that is giddy even by his standards. 'Okay . . . Wanna hear about *my* day yesterday?'

'Sure,' I say, picturing him at FAO Schwarz, playing hooky from work and sampling different toys like Tom Hanks did in the movie *Big*.

'I got a last-minute flight and went on a little day trip of my own,' he says.

My heart races. I know exactly what is coming and feel suddenly propelled into a state of high alert. 'You did?'

'Yup,' he says, as I hear a drumroll in my head. 'To Atlanta . . . To see our house.'

I look at him, feeling a forced smile stretch across my face, as I think, *Our house*.

Andy nods. 'It's awesome, Ellie. I *love* it. Margot loves it. My mom loves it. *You're* going to love it. It's seriously *perfect* . . . Even better in person.'

I muster enough breath to ask a question. 'Did you . . . *buy* it?'

I brace myself, almost wanting the answer to be yes so that I won't have to make a decision. And, more important, so that I can feel wronged. I picture my eyes welling with indignant tears as I softly rant, *You should have talked to me first! Who buys a house without consulting his wife?* Whether Andy ever knows it or not, the score will be even. One marital misstep for another.

But, of course, he shakes his head and says, 'No, I didn't *buy* it. I would never do that without talking to you first . . . Although,' he says excitedly, 'I do have an offer right here, ready to fax when — *if* — you say the word.' He pats a manila envelope on the table. 'I think it's going to go fast. It's way better than anything else we looked at . . . Charming, solid construction, all the bells and whistles. Totally perfect . . . and so freaking close to Margot . . . Do you want to fly down this week and see it? Maybe look around a bit more?'

He looks at me expectantly, innocently, as I think to myself, *You are so damn happy.* It feels like both praise and criticism. It is one of the things I dearly love about him, yet in this moment it is also what I wish I could change about him. Not to make him *unhappy*, of course, but to make him just a little less . . . *simple.* Doesn't he see this decision as at all nuanced? Doesn't he have any reservations about living so close to family? Working for his father? Leaving the city we love?

My heart suddenly floods with resentment,

and although I try to pin some of this on Andy's fervor, I know that my emotion is emanating from one source, one place, one internal conflict.

Leo.

As Andy awaits my response, I remind myself that no matter what the decision on this particular house, or whether we move to Atlanta at all, my life will go on without Leo in it. So I need to remove him from the equation and decide what is right for Andy and me.

But as I stare into my husband's eyes, the wall between the two worlds crumbles — the world on the plane last night and all that could have been, and my life with Andy, moving forward, in our home in Atlanta. A home with two, maybe three, cars in the garage. And a slobbering golden retriever chasing fuzzy yellow tennis balls across a lush, green lawn. And Margot, right down the street, ready to swap recipes and neighborhood gossip. And Andy heading out every morning to get the newspaper in his plaid flannel robe and old-man slippers. And chubby, chirpy, blue-eyed children with neon orange water wings splashing in their backyard pool. And me, standing at the kitchen window, peeling an apple as I wistfully recall my former life, the kind of jobs I used to get. The time I photographed Drake Watters out in L.A. The last morning I saw Leo.

I look down at the table, wondering how much time will pass before I no longer think of his touch on the plane. Before that final moment in the back of the cab is no longer burned in my mind like a haunting black-and-white still frame.

And the fear that it could be forever grips my heart and makes me open my mouth and say, *Let's do it.*

On the face of things, I am only giving my spouse permission to send a fax. I am only agreeing to a change of venue, the purchase of some real estate in Atlanta. But, deep down, it feels like much more. Deep down, I am also repenting. I am proving my love. I am renewing my vows. I am safeguarding my marriage. I am choosing Andy.

'You don't want to go down and see it for yourself?' he asks again, gently resting his fingertips in the crook of my elbow.

It is my final out, the last loophole. All I would have to do is go see the house and come up with something, *anything*, that doesn't feel quite right about it. A vibe I can't put my finger on. A particular, unpleasant feng shui that Andy, and two Southern women with an impeccable sense of aesthetics, somehow missed. I might appear irrational or ungrateful, but I could buy myself a little more time. Although time for what, I'm not quite sure. Time to keep checking voicemail in vain, hoping that he came up with 'one more thing' to tell me? Time to look for him in every intersection, every diner, every bar? Time to make the big mistake of jumping in a cab and returning to Newton Avenue? So I fight against what I want in this moment and instead nod and say, 'I trust your judgment.'

It is the truth, of course. I *do* trust Andy's judgment. At this point, I trust it even more than my own. But I also feel some other subtle emotions at work — unhealthy trace elements of passive-aggressiveness and a stoic resignation toward becoming a dutiful, traditional wife, and accepting a lopsided dynamic that has never existed, in any form, in our relationship.

These feelings will pass, I think. *This is a blip on the relationship radar screen. Just stay the course.*

'Are you sure, honey?' Andy asks softly.

My hand reflexively moves over my heart, and I say loudly and clearly, as if for a court reporter on permanent, irrefutable record, *Yes. Let's do it. I'm sure.*

19

Margot cries when we tell her that we're making an offer on the house, and my mother-in-law ups the ante even further by declaring that the news is the answer to her prayers. Now granted, Margot is an easy cry even when she's *not* pregnant, tearing up at long-distance commercials or a few bars of 'Pomp and Circumstance,' and Stella prays over a whole lot less than her beloved son returning home after so many years 'up North.' But still. There really is no turning back after those reactions — you just don't screw around with familial heartstrings.

So as spring comes to New York, my split-second, gut decision made over toaster waffles, no sleep, and a large dose of guilt takes on a crazy forward motion of its own.

Fortunately, once Andy gives jubilant notice at his law firm, he, too, seems to have at least ambivalent feelings about our impending move, although his focus is more on the big picture and has an almost merry abandon to it — sort of the same way that high school seniors barrel toward prom and graduation. He furiously makes plans with our closest friends, schedules final dinners at our favorite restaurants, and snaps up tickets to Broadway shows we've been meaning to see for ages. One Saturday morning, he even insists that we take a ferry out to the Statue of Liberty — a landmark I vowed to only ever admire from an airplane window, almost as a point of pride. Then, as we endure packs of tourists, misty rain, and a brutally monotone guide, Andy encourages me to snap photos of the view, so that we can display the prints in our new home. I humor him, but can't help thinking that a framed shot of New York Harbor, no matter how spectacular (if I do say so myself), isn't going to provide much solace when I'm missing the intangible energy of New York.

To this point, it's the little things that get to me the most as we wind down our affairs in the city and hurtle toward our June closing date. It's the rich fabric of my daily life — things that barely registered before but that now feel sentimental. It's my walk to work and the silent camaraderie of other commuters swelling in the crosswalks around me. It's Sabina and Julian's spirited banter in our workroom, and the pungent aroma of Oscar's printing press. It's our dry cleaner's deep frown lines as he determinedly knots the plastic around Andy's shirts and then tells us to have a nice day in his Turkish accent, and my Korean manicurist's chipper command to 'Pick polish,' even though she must know by now that I always bring my own. It's the sway of the subway careening efficiently along the tracks, and the satisfaction of flagging down a cab on a bustling weekend night in the Village. It's the burgers at P.J. Clarke's, the dim sum at Chinatown Brasserie, and the bagels at my corner bodega. It's knowing that when I walk out of our brownstone, I will see something new every single day. It's the diversity of choices and people, the raw urban beauty, the endless hum of possibility everywhere.

Underscoring all of this is Leo — his constant presence in my mind, along with the troubling realization that I deeply associate him with the city and vice versa. So much so, in fact, that leaving New York feels an awful lot like leaving him.

Not once do I contact him, though. Not even when I think of at least a half-dozen near-perfect, work-related excuses and just as many clever rationalizations about why a little more closure might be a good thing for everyone. Not even when the temptation is so strong that it actually frightens me — in the way that I imagine I would feel about cocaine if I ever tried it.

Rather, I steadfastly cling to the lofty notion of right versus wrong, black versus white, and one hundred percent loyalty to Andy. As the ultimate insurance policy, I make a point to keep him nearby whenever possible, which means pretty much all the time once he is freed from his firm. I encourage him to accompany me to work or my shoots, tag along with him to the gym, and plan all our meals together. I constantly initiate physical contact with him — both in our bedroom at night and in small ways out in public. I tell him often that I love him, but never in an automatic, rote way. Rather, I really think about the words, what they mean. Love as a verb. Love as a commitment.

All the while, I tell myself that I'm almost to the finish line. My emotions will soon run their course, and things will return to normal — or at least the way they were before that moment in the intersection. And, if that doesn't happen before we leave the city, it will most certainly happen in Atlanta, in a brand-new context, far from Leo.

But as the days pass, and our departure approaches, I find myself wondering what exactly normal ever was. Were things normal when Andy and I started to date? Were they normal by the time we got engaged or walked down the aisle? Was I ever truly over Leo? At one time I was sure that the answer was yes. But if seeing him again — and merely touching his hand — could peel back so many layers of my heart, then did I ever stop loving him the way you're *supposed* to stop loving everyone but the one you're with? If the answer is no, then will the lapse of time or a change of geography really fix the problem? And regardless of the answer, what does the mere *question* say about my relationship with Andy?

Making matters more upsetting is the strange, vague sense that this emotional terrain isn't completely foreign — that I experienced some of these same feelings a long time ago when my mother died. The parallels are by no means perfect as there is no tragic element in leaving New York or not talking to Leo. But, in some unsettling way that is difficult to precisely pinpoint, there is a distinct overlap.

So one late night when Andy is out with the guys, I cave and call my sister, hoping that I will find the right opening — and the right words

— to convey what I'm feeling without elevating Leo's importance or disrespecting our mother's memory.

Suzanne answers in a good mood — and tells me Vince is out with the guys, too, which in his case is par for the course. We make small talk for a few minutes, and then I indulge her complaints of the week, mostly Vince related, with a few colorful flight attendant tales in the mix. My favorite features a crazy old woman in first class who spilled Bloody Mary mix not once, not twice, but *three* times on the passenger beside her, and then became belligerent when Suzanne refused to serve her a fourth drink.

'Belligerent how?' I say, always enjoying — and marveling over — the in-flight drama.

'She called me a bitch. Good times, huh?'

I laugh and ask her what she did next, knowing full well that there will be some sort of retaliation involved.

'I had a few marshals meet her drunk ass at the gate.'

We both burst out laughing.

'She was right. You *are* a bitch,' I say.

'I know,' she says. 'It's my calling.'

We laugh again, and a beat later, Suzanne comes right out and asks me if I've heard from Leo.

I consider telling her about our flight, but decide that it is something I will forever keep private, sacred. Instead, I just say no, sighing so loudly that it invites a follow-up.

'Uh-oh,' she says. 'What's up?'

I cast about for a few seconds — and then

confess that ever since L.A. I continue to miss Leo in a way that hasn't really subsided at all. That something about my mood reminds me of 'that one winter' — which is the veiled way we often refer to Mom's death when we're not in the mood to fully revisit our grief.

'Whoa, Ell,' she says. 'Are you comparing *not* talking to Leo to Mom dying?'

I quickly and vehemently say no and then add, 'Maybe I'm just melancholy about leaving the city . . . all the changes.'

'So . . . what? You're comparing leaving New York to death?'

'No. Not that exactly either,' I say, realizing that I shouldn't have bothered to try to convey such a subtle feeling, even to my sister.

But in Suzanne fashion, she presses me to explain. I think for a second and then tell her that it's more the sense of impending finality, and that as much as I prepare myself for what is coming next, I really don't know what to expect. 'And there is this fear packed in the waiting period,' I say tentatively. 'Like with Mom . . . We knew for weeks that the end was really near. Nothing about her death was a surprise. And yet . . . it still *felt* like a surprise, didn't it?'

Suzanne whispers yes, and for a moment I know we are both silently remembering that day when the school guidance counselor appeared in our respective classrooms and then waited with us, outside by the flagpole and an exhaust-covered drift of snow, until our father arrived to pick us up, and take us home to her for the last time.

'And then after that,' I say, commanding myself not to cry or conjure any other visual specifics of that horrible day or the ones that followed. 'I just felt desperate to finish the school year, get in a new routine . . . a new place where I wasn't always reminded of Mom . . . '

'Yeah,' Suzanne says. 'Going away to camp that summer did sort of help.'

'Right,' I say, thinking that was part of my motivation to look at colleges far from Pittsburgh, in places Mom never visited or talked about, with people who didn't know that I was motherless. I clear my throat and continue, 'But at the same time, as much as I wanted to get away from the house and all of Mom's things and Dad's tears — and even *you* — I also felt scared that once I got away, or turned the calendar, or did anything at all differently than the way we did things with her, that we would be losing her all the faster. That we would almost be . . . erasing her.'

'I know exactly what you mean,' Suzanne says. '*Exactly* . . . But . . . Ellie . . . '

'What?' I ask softly, knowing that a difficult question is likely coming my way.

Sure enough, Suzanne says, 'Why don't you *want* to erase Leo?'

I think for a long minute, silence filling the airwaves. But as hard as I try, I can't come up with a good answer — or for that matter, any answer at all.

20

It is the first Saturday in June, and our final one in New York. A trio of thick-necked movers from Hoboken arrived this morning, and nine mad hours of packing later, our apartment is completely barren save for a few suitcases by the front door, some bits of duct tape stuck to the kitchen counters, and a hundred dust bunnies swirling along the hardwood floors. Andy and I are sweaty and exhausted, standing in what was once our family room while we listen to the hum of the window air-conditioning unit straining in the heat.

'I guess it's time to hit it,' Andy says, his voice echoing off the white walls that we never had time to paint a more interesting shade. He wipes his cheek on the sleeve of his old, stained T-shirt, one of about thirty he has designated for 'moving and painting,' even though I've teasingly pointed out that he can't possibly be in a situation where he's painting or moving for a solid month.

'Yeah. Let's go,' I say, my mind already shifting to the next step in our journey — our cab ride to our hotel where we will shower and change for our going-away party this evening. Andy's two closest friends from law school are hosting the event, although friends from all segments of our New York life will be in attendance. Even Margot and Webb are flying up for the festivities, only to return to Atlanta with us in the morning where they will become our official greeters. I clasp my hands together and force a peppy, 'Let's get the show on the road.'

Andy pauses and then says, 'Should we do something . . . ceremonious first?'

'Like what?' I ask.

'I don't know . . . Maybe take a picture?'

I shake my head, thinking that Andy should know me better by now; I might be a photographer, but I'm not really one to document symbolic moments like these — endings, beginnings, even holidays and special occasions. I much prefer to capture the random stuff in the middle — a fact that my friends and family seem to find puzzling — and sometimes frustrating.

'Nah,' I say. I shift my gaze out the window and follow a pigeon's trek on the cement terrace across the street from us.

After a long moment, Andy takes my hand and says, 'How're you doing?'

'Fine,' I say, which I'm relieved to realize is the truth. 'Just a little sad.'

He nods, as if to acknowledge that endings are almost always a little sad, even when there is something to look forward to on the other side. Then, without further fanfare, we turn and walk out of our first married home together.

★ ★ ★

A few minutes later our cab pulls up in front of the Gramercy Park Hotel, and I realize with a wave of remorse and panic that Andy and I have suddenly, *instantly* morphed into visitors — *tourists* — in a city where we once resided.

But as we enter the gorgeous, eclectic lobby filled with Moroccan tiles, handwoven rugs, Venetian-glass chandeliers, and sprawling works by Andy Warhol, Jean-Michel Basquiat, and Keith Haring, I reassure myself that there is a distinct upside to experiencing the city this way.

'Wow,' I say, admiring the huge stone-and-marble fireplace and a sawfish-snout lamp in front of it. 'This place is *very* cool.'

Andy smiles and says, 'Yup. Haute bohemian cool. Like my girl.'

I smile back at him as we stroll over to the front desk where a sultry brunette, whose name tag reads *Beata*, welcomes us in a thick eastern European accent.

Andy says hello, and the well-groomed, proper boy in him feels the need to explain our grubby appearance, so he mumbles apologetically, 'We just moved out of our apartment today.'

Beata nods her understanding and politely inquires, 'To where are you going next?'

I answer for us, saying *Atlanta, Georgia*, as grandly as possible, even adding a hand-in-the-air flourish, as if I'm revealing a well-kept North American secret, a jewel of a town she should be sure to visit if she hasn't already. I'm not sure exactly why I feel the need to hype Atlanta to a complete stranger — whether it's to make myself feel better, or to counteract the defensiveness I feel whenever I tell someone in the city where we're moving and inevitably get a pitying stare or a downright critical, 'Why *Atlanta?*'

Andy takes it a bit more personally — as I do when I hear anyone bad-mouth Pittsburgh — but I actually don't think this reaction is an affront to Atlanta as much as it is a function of the New York superiority complex, a smug sense that the rest of the world, or at least the rest of the country, is sterile and homogenous and somehow lacking in comparison. And, while I resent that attitude now, the uncomfortable truth is, I don't altogether disagree with the assessment, and know I've felt similarly when friends have left the city — whether for a job, or a relationship, or to have babies in the suburbs. *Better you than me*, I've thought, even though I might have been bitterly complaining about the city the moment before. After all, I think it's that intense edge that is the most compelling part about living in New York, and the very thing that I will miss most.

In any event, my preemptive, proud tone with Beata seems to do the trick, because she smiles, nods, and says, 'Oh, very beautiful,' as if I've just said *Paris, France*. She then checks us in and tells us a bit about the hotel, before handing Andy our room key and wishing us a wonderful stay.

We thank her, and as inconspicuously as possible, wander back through the lobby over to the adjoining Rose Bar, which is just as richly decorated as the lobby, complete with a red-velvet pool table and another looming Warhol. I feel my mind start to drift to Leo, and the last time I was in a trendy hotel bar, but push these thoughts away as Andy says with feigned formality, 'Care for an aperitif?'

I skim the cocktail menu and tell him the pineapple-and-cinnamon mojito looks interesting. He agrees and orders us two, to go, and a few minutes later, we are alone in our plush, jewel-toned room overlooking Gramercy Park, one of my favorite spots in the city, even though I've never been inside the locked gates — perhaps *because* I've never been inside.

'Gorgeous,' I say, sipping my mojito and taking in the view of the romantic, impeccably kept private park.

'I knew you always wanted to see inside,' he says, draping his arm around me. 'I thought it would be a nice way to say good-bye.'

'You always think of *everything*,' I say, feeling a wave of deep appreciation for my husband.

Andy gives me an 'aw, shucks' grin and takes a hearty gulp of his drink, before undressing down to his boxers and bursting into a stirring rendition of 'The Devil Went Down to Georgia.'

I laugh and shake my head. 'Get in the shower,' I say, vowing to be happy tonight. Even though I'm exhausted. Even though I hate being the center of attention. Even though I don't like good-byes. And even though a certain someone on Newton Avenue won't be in attendance and doesn't even have an inkling that I'm leaving.

★ ★ ★

One hour later our party at Blind Tiger, a microbrewery on Bleecker, is in full groove. The lights are dim, the music is just loud enough, and

I'm well into my fourth beer of the night. My current selection, the Lagunitas Hairy Eyeball, is my favorite so far, although that might be purely a function of my ever-growing buzz. One thing is for sure — I've put all my worries aside and am having an even better time than I vowed, in large part because everyone else seems to be having so much fun, which is never a given when diverse groups come together at one event. My photographer friends really have little in common with Andy's lawyer crowd or the Upper East Side fashion torchbearers whom Margot and I used to hang with when she lived in the city. To this point, Margot actually deserves much of the credit for bringing everyone together and making things feel cohesive, as she is the single greatest asset you can have at any party. She is outgoing, gracious, and inclusive, finding a way to bring even the most awkward, peripheral guest into the fold. I watch her now, working the room, virgin daiquiri in hand, looking stunning in a pink, empire-waist sundress and strappy, silver stilettos. At nearly six months pregnant, she has a small, round bump right in front, but hasn't gained an ounce anywhere else, and her hair, nails, and skin are even more amazing than usual. She says it's due to the prenatal vitamins, although I don't think the battery of expensive spa treatments she had today have hurt her cause. In short, she's the cutest pregnant woman I've ever seen, a sentiment I've heard at least five people echo tonight, including one woman from Andy's firm who is exactly as far along as Margot but looks like she's been blown up with helium everywhere — nose, ankles, even her earlobes.

'Get away from me,' the girl jokingly said to Margot. 'You make me look bad.'

'She makes everyone look bad — pregnant or not,' I said.

Margot modestly waved us off and told us not to be ridiculous, but deep down she must know it's true. Fortunately, though, she's also more charming than the rest of us, so nobody ever really holds her looks against her, including her ghastliest of pregnant peers.

We make eye contact now as she joins me, Julian, and Julian's wife, Hillary, at a cracked-wood table in the back of the bar, just in time to hear Hillary gush about how much she admires Andy's decision to drop the big-firm culture. It is a common theme of the night among the disgruntled-lawyer crowd, and for Andy's sake, it makes me feel better about our move.

'I've been meaning to quit for over seven years now,' Hillary says, laughing as she tugs on her long, blond ponytail. 'Never quite happens, though.'

Julian shakes his head and says, 'If I had a dollar for every time she said she was going to do it, we could *both* retire . . . But what does she do instead?'

'What?' Margot and I ask in unison.

Julian flicks his wife's shoulder and proudly says, 'She goes and makes partner.'

'No way! Why didn't you tell me that?' I say to Julian, hitting his arm.

'She just found out yesterday,' he says, as I

think about all the many tidbits of his life I'm going to miss now that we're no longer sharing a workspace. We have vowed to keep in touch — and I think we will e-mail and phone occasionally — but it won't be the same, and eventually, I fear that he, Sabina, and Oscar will all become holiday-card friends only. But I mentally put that on the list of things not to worry about tonight, and instead turn to Hillary and congratulate her. 'Andy says it's virtually impossible to make partner at a big firm.'

'Especially for a woman,' Margot says, nodding.

Hillary laughs and says, 'Well. I'm sure it'll be short-lived. At least I hope it will be . . . I'll hang in there only until he knocks me up . . . Then I'm going to take my maternity leave and run for the hills.'

I laugh and say, 'Sounds like a plan.'

'You think you'll have one soon?' Julian asks me.

It is a question Andy and I have gotten a lot since announcing our move, so I have my answer both prepared and well rehearsed. 'Not right away,' I say, smiling vaguely. 'Sometime soon, though . . . '

Hillary and Julian grin back at me, as everyone seems to like the 'soon' part of my response the best. Topping that list is Margot, who now nestles closer to me and links her arm through mine. I inhale her perfume as she explains that we want our kids to be close in age.

Hillary says, 'Oh, *definitely*. That's going to be so nice for you guys . . . I wish I had someone to go through the baby thing with, but I'm so far behind my other friends. They're already applying to preschools, in a whole different stage of life . . . You're *so* lucky to have each other and live so close to one another.'

Margot and I both murmur that we know, we are lucky, and for one satisfying moment, I feel the full weight and truth of it. Sure, the timing might not be ideal. I might not be quite ready to leave the city, and my children might be a few years behind Margot's, but those are minor details. The big picture is pretty darn *wonderful*. My relationship with Margot, my marriage to Andy, our house in Atlanta — all of it *is* wonderful.

And that is my final thought before my agent, Cynthia, bursts into the bar, scans the room, and makes a breathless beeline toward me. As a former plus-sized model and stage actress, Cynthia has a lush, larger-than-life quality and a slightly outlandish sense of style that causes people to stare and wonder if she's famous. In fact, she told me once that she frequently is mistaken for Geena Davis, and even occasionally signs fake autographs and fields questions about the filming of *Thelma and Louise* or *Beetlejuice*. I watch her pause to manhandle Andy with a double-cheek kiss and a tousle of his hair, before continuing her purposeful march toward me, my husband in tow.

'Just wait! Just wait until you see what I have,' I can hear her tell him from halfway across the room. One beat later, they are both beside me, and as I thank her for coming, I realize in an off-kilter, slow-motion panic, what she is about to unveil at our going-away party.

Sure enough, her full, magenta lips pucker dramatically as she pulls the oversized magazine from her fringed, white Balenciaga bag and then trills to her ever-growing audience, '*Platform* magazine! Hot off the presses!'

'I thought it wasn't coming out until later this month,' I say, feeling numb and exposed as I envision not my photos of Drake that I toiled over and perfected for so many hours, but the byline of the piece.

'Well, you're right, it doesn't hit the newsstands for another couple weeks,' Cynthia says. 'But I worked my magic and got an early copy for you . . . Thought it would be the perfect going-away present for you, pookie.' She bends down and taps my nose twice with her index finger.

'Oh, man. Awesome,' Andy says. He rubs his hands together eagerly and calls a few more of his friends, including Webb, over to the table.

'You've already seen the shots,' I tell Andy in a small, worried voice, as if there is anything I can do to stop Cynthia's attention-grabbing tide.

'Yes, but not on a big, glossy cover,' Andy says, standing behind me and massaging my shoulders.

Another full, torturous minute passes as Cynthia continues her suspense-building mission by pressing the cover against her substantial cleavage and delivering a Shakespearean monologue about how gifted I am, and how proud she is to represent me, and how I'm headed for true

238

greatness, no matter where I live.

Meanwhile, I fix my eyes on the back of the magazine, a black-and-white ad featuring Kate Moss, by far my favorite model, and someone I'd love to shoot. In the photo, her lips are slightly parted, her windswept hair partially covers her right eye, and her expression is serene but suggestive. As I stare into her smoky eyes, I have the sudden, ridiculously narcissistic sense that she is there on that page not to advertise David Yurman watches, but specifically to taunt me. *You should have told them sooner*, I hear her say in her English accent. *You've had weeks and weeks to tell them, but instead you wait for a packed house on your final night in New York. Nice job.*

'C'mon, Cynthia!' Andy shouts, interrupting my paranoid thoughts. 'Show us the darn magazine!'

Cynthia laughs and says, 'Okay! Okay!' Then she flips Kate around, thrusts the magazine high over her head, and slowly spins to reveal Drake, in all his glory. For a few seconds, as her small but rapt audience claps and whistles and cheers, I have a surreal sense of satisfaction that that is actually *my* cover. My shot of Drake Watters.

But my fear returns in full force when Cynthia hands the magazine off to Andy and says, 'Page seventy-eight, lambkin.'

I hold my breath and feel all my muscles tense as Andy takes a seat next to Julian and flips eagerly to the Drake story. Meanwhile, everyone gathers behind him, oohing and aahing over the photographs that I labored over and virtually memorized but can't bring myself to look at now. Instead, I focus on Andy's face, feeling a sense of profound relief when I determine that he is slightly more intoxicated than I am, and in no shape to be reading the article let alone focusing on any words on the page. Instead, he is all smiles, basking in the running commentary among my photographer friends who kindly praise the more artistic elements of my shots, while the rest of the crowd asks eager questions about what Drake was like in person, and Margot, in her typical nurturing fashion, instructs everyone to be careful not to wrinkle or spill anything on the pages. This chatter goes on for some time, as the magazine works its way around the table and ends up in front of Margot and me, on the last page of the article.

'This is amazing,' she whispers. 'I'm *so* proud of you.'

'Thanks,' I say, watching her slowly flip backward through the five-page spread until she returns to the beginning again.

'I think this one's my favorite,' Margot says, pointing to the very first shot of Drake, framed by Leo's text, with his name floating there at the top, centered on the page. Although my eyes are drawn right to it, the point size is actually not as big as I had feared, nor is it very dark or bold. So as Margot chatters about how hot Drake is, and how I so perfectly captured his essence, I conclude that I might just escape tonight unscathed. In fact, I might even get away with this *forever*. I feel a jolt of adrenaline — my sense of relief and triumph outweighing any shame that I know I should feel. It is the way I imagine a shoplifter must feel as she nods her placid good-bye to a store security guard, while feeling her stolen goods pressed into the lining of her pockets.

But one beat later, my fortune fades as I feel Margot freeze beside me and then recoil. I look at her, and she looks right back at me, and I can tell in an instant that she has seen Leo's name, registered the import of it, and knows. Obviously she can't know *exactly* what I've done or haven't done, but she is certain that I've been dishonest with her and more important, her brother. If it were anyone else, I'd brace myself for a wave of wrath, or at the very least, a string of questions or accusations. But I know Margot better than that. I know how restrained she is, how careful with her words, how non-confrontational. And beyond that, I know that she would never in a million years say anything to ruin this party, *any* party. Instead, she doles out a far-worse punishment. She becomes silent, her expression stony and stoic, as she closes the magazine and turns away from me for the rest of the night.

21

'Do you *really* think she's pissed at you for taking an assignment?' Suzanne asks the following morning when I call her from a gift shop at LaGuardia, give her a rundown of the night before, and solicit her advice about how to approach Margot when we meet her at our gate in a few minutes. 'Maybe you're just being paranoid?'

I nervously assess Andy's progress in line at an adjacent Starbucks and say, 'Yeah. Pretty sure. Except for a quick good-bye at the end of the night, she didn't speak to me again. Not once.'

Suzanne clears her throat and says, 'Is that all that unusual at a big party? Weren't a bunch of your friends around? Would you guys normally be connected at the hip all night?'

I hesitate, knowing that these questions are somewhat pointed — Suzanne's not-so-subtle way of criticizing what she believes is, and once even referred to as, my codependence with Margot. And, although I'd usually finesse the inquiry and defend the friendship, I don't have time now to take that detour. Instead I just reiterate, 'Look, Suzanne. She's definitely *not* happy about the whole thing . . . And to be fair — I can't really blame her. I'm married to her brother, remember? . . . Now any ideas about how to handle it?'

I hear the sound of running water and the

clatter of breakfast dishes — or in Suzanne's case, what could likely be the dinner dishes from last night. 'What should *you* do or what would *I* do if I were in your shoes?' she asks.

'I don't know. Either,' I say impatiently. 'And talk fast . . . Andy will be back any second.'

'Okay,' Suzanne says, turning off her faucet. 'Well, *I'd* go on the offensive and tell her to get a grip. Stop being so high and mighty.'

I smile, thinking, *Well, of course you would,* as she continues her rant. 'I mean, what's the big fucking deal? Your ex-boyfriend gave you the professional lead of a *lifetime* — the chance to photograph an A-list celebrity — and you appropriately and wisely seized that chance . . . for your *career,* not to rekindle a romance.'

When I don't respond, Suzanne prompts me. '*Right?*'

'Well, right,' I say. 'Of course.'

'Okay. So then you fly to L.A. and unbeknownst to you, Leo is there, too. Not something you planned, correct?'

'That's correct, too,' I say, perking up somewhat at this benign, yet so far completely accurate, version of events.

'Then, you decline Leo's invitation to dinner — really you diss him *completely* — and hang with me all night.'

I nod eagerly, thinking that I should have phoned Suzanne from the bar last night; I could have avoided quite a bit of internal strife with this pseudo-pep talk.

She continues, 'And at the actual shoot the following day, you spend about ten minutes with

243

him *total*, always conducting yourself in a completely professional manner. Right?'

Technically, all of this is true, too, but I hesitate, thinking of my lustful thoughts the night before the shoot; Leo's lingering look at the diner; and of course, that long, intimate, heart-pounding, hand-holding flight. Then I clear my throat and say with a little less conviction, 'Right.'

'And you haven't spoken to him since you got back to the city?'

'No,' I say, thinking this much is true — and a credit-worthy feat given the number of times I *wanted* to call him. 'I haven't.'

'So tell me?' Suzanne says. 'Where's the big affront to the Graham family?'

I pick up an 'I love New York' snow globe from a shelf crammed with plastic trinkets and gently shake it. As I watch the flakes fall onto the Empire State Building, I say, 'There isn't one, I guess.'

'Come to think of it,' Suzanne says, more riled by the second. 'Does Margot even *know* that you saw Leo at all?'

'Well . . . no,' I say. 'She probably just assumes that there had to be some contact . . . which, of course, there was.'

'*Professional* contact,' she says.

'Okay. I hear you,' I say. 'So . . . do you think I should just clear the air and tell her all of that?'

'Actually, no. I don't,' Suzanne says. 'Two can play her passive-aggressive game. I think you should just sit tight and wait for her to address it with you.'

'What if she doesn't?' I ask, thinking of Courtney Finnamore, one of Margot's closest friends from college whom she excommunicated when Courtney got wasted at a sorority formal and puked all over Margot's brand-new Saab. Although Courtney seemed appropriately contrite, she never offered to clean the car or pay for any damage. It wasn't the cost, Margot insisted, which I believed; it was the incredible thoughtlessness and boorishness of it all, as well as the assumption that because Margot has money, she wouldn't mind footing the cleaning bill. Margot just couldn't get past the incident, noticing more and more how cheap and selfish Courtney was. Yet, despite her strong feelings, she never confronted Courtney. Instead, she just quietly withdrew from the friendship — so quietly, in fact, that I don't think Courtney really noticed Margot's change of heart until Courtney got engaged and asked Margot to be a bridesmaid. After very brief consideration, Margot decided she just couldn't be that two-faced, so she politely declined the 'honor,' offering no explanation, no excuse, and no apology. Margot still attended the wedding, but obviously their friendship rapidly deteriorated after that, and today, the two don't talk at all — not even when they ran into each other at a sorority tailgate during homecoming weekend last fall.

Although I can't fathom such an estrangement ever happening between Margot and me, I still feel a surge of angst as I say to Suzanne, 'It's not really Margot's style to confront people.'

'You're not 'people.' You're her so-called *best*

245

friend. You're telling me that she won't address something like this with you?' Suzanne whistles for dramatic effect.

'I don't know. Maybe she will,' I say, bristling at her use of *so-called* as I try to backtrack with an example of Margot being direct with me. Ironically, my only example is Leo-related. 'She confronted me when Leo and I broke up and I turned into a sappy loser — '

Suzanne adamantly interrupts, 'You weren't a sappy loser. You were heartbroken. There's a difference.'

This sentiment of course, disarms me, as no one wants to believe they were ever sappy — or a loser — and certainly not a *sappy* loser, but at this point, I really *am* out of time as Andy is headed my way with our lattes. 'Here he comes,' I say. 'Give me the bottom line.'

'The bottom line is that this is between *you* and *Andy* . . . not you and your sister-in-law, BFFs or otherwise,' she says, spitting out *BFFs* sarcastically. 'But if you feel you must clear the air, then do so . . . '

'Okay,' I say.

'Whatever you do, though, *don't* be a scared rabbit. And *do not* grovel or cower . . . Got it?'

'Got it,' I say as I take my coffee from Andy and flash him a grateful smile. I don't remember ever needing caffeine this urgently.

''Cause Ellie?' Suzanne says fervently.

'Yeah?'

'If you grovel and cower . . . you're setting a mighty bad precedent for yourself down in Dixie.'

Suzanne's advice rings in my ears as Andy and I buy the snow globe on a final, sentimental whim, and round the corner toward our gate.

Don't grovel and cower, I think, wondering if that's the sort of demeanor I adopted last night. I know I didn't grovel as there was no verbal exchange, but did I cower? Was I avoiding Margot as much, or perhaps more, than she was avoiding me? If so, maybe I made things worse, elevating her minor worry into full-blown suspicion. And, although I'm certain she saw Leo's name, maybe I also exaggerated her reaction in my head, allowing my own plagued conscience, the intense emotions of our move, and at least one drink too many to distort reality. Maybe everything will look and feel different this morning. It was something that my mother used to say all the time, and as we approach Margot and Webb already settled in at the gate, I cross my fingers that today is no exception to her rule.

I take a deep breath and belt out a preemptive, enthusiastic hello, hoping that I don't sound as stilted as I feel.

As always, Webb stands and kisses my cheek, 'Mornin', darlin'!'

Margot, who is impeccably dressed in a navy sweater set, crisp white pants, and cherry red flats that match her lipstick, looks up from a Nicholas Sparks novel and smiles. 'Hey! Good morning! How was the rest of your night?'

Her blue eyes move from me to Andy, then back to me, as I detect nothing in her face or tone or demeanor to suggest that she is angry or upset. On the contrary, she seems like her usual warm, chummy self.

I feel myself relax ever so slightly as I take the seat next to her and offer up a safe answer. 'It was fun,' I say breezily.

'A little *too* much fun,' Andy says, flanking me on the other side and tossing our carry-on bags at his feet. 'I probably shouldn't have done that last shot at two in the morning.'

Margot creases a tiny dog ear in a page of her book, closes it, and slides it into her large black bag. 'What time did you get back to your hotel?' she asks us.

Andy and I look at each other and shrug.

'Three, maybe?' I say, almost completely at ease now.

'Something like that,' Andy says, rubbing his temples.

Margot grimaces empathetically. 'I have to say . . . that's one of the best parts about being pregnant. Hangover free for nine months.'

'Baby, you've been hangover free for nine *years*,' Webb says.

I laugh, thinking that he's probably right about that. In fact, I can count on one hand the number of times Margot lost control in college or in our twenties. And by 'lost control' I don't mean dancing topless at a party — I mean, taking out a pair of perfectly good contact lenses and flicking them into a bush on the way home from a party, or polishing off a whole bag of barbecue potato chips.

A few moments of casual, idle chatter later,

Webb says he's going to go pick up a paper before we board. Andy offers to go with him, and Margot and I are suddenly alone, in what feels to be some kind of moment of truth.

Sure enough, it is.

'Okay, Ellie,' she says urgently. 'I've been *dying* to talk to you.'

You could have fooled me, I think, as I give her a sideways glance and decide that her expression is more curious than accusatory.

'I know,' I say hesitantly.

'Leo?' she says, her eyes wide, unblinking.

My stomach jumps a little hearing his name aloud, and I suddenly wish he had a more common name, like Scott or Mark. A name diluted by other casual acquaintances and associations. But in my life, there is only *one* Leo.

'I know,' I say again, stalling as I take a long sip of coffee. 'I should have mentioned it sooner . . . I was going to . . . but the move . . . your baby . . . There've been so many distractions . . . '

I realize that I'm stammering, and that Suzanne likely would categorize my end of the conversation as something approaching scared-rabbit groveling, so I gather myself and try another angle. 'But it's really not the way it seems . . . I . . . I just ran into him on the street one day, and we caught up very quickly . . . Then, a short time later, he called my agent and gave me the Drake lead. And that was it, really . . . '

It is enough of the truth that I don't feel

249

altogether bad by editing the story — omitting that I saw him in L.A. — and afterward on our flight home.

Margot looks visibly relieved. 'I *knew* it had to be something like that,' she says. 'I just . . . I guess I thought you would have told me about it?' She adds the last part gingerly, conveying disappointment more than judgment.

'I really meant to . . . and I was going to before the magazine came out,' I say, unsure of whether this is the truth, but giving myself a generous benefit of the doubt. 'I'm sorry.'

I think of Suzanne again, but tell myself that a simple *I'm sorry* is a far cry from groveling.

'You don't have to be sorry,' Margot says quickly. 'It's okay.'

A few seconds of easy silence pass between us, and just as I think I might be off the hook completely, she twists her diamond stud a full turn in her ear and asks point-blank, 'Does Andy know?'

For some reason, it is a question I hadn't anticipated, and one that magnifies my residual guilt *and* hangover. I shake my head, feeling fairly certain that this is *not* the answer she was hoping for.

Sure enough, she gives me a piteous look and says, 'Are you going to tell him?'

'I . . . I guess I should?' I say, my voice rising in a question.

Margot runs her hands over her belly. 'I don't know,' she says pensively. 'Maybe not.'

'Really?' I say.

'Maybe not,' she says again more resolutely.

'Don't you think he'll notice . . . the byline?' I ask as it occurs to me that we haven't engaged in this sort of relationship strategy and analysis in years. Then again, we haven't needed to. Other than a few silly arguments that arose during our wedding planning (in which Margot sided with me), Andy and I have never really been at odds — at least not in such a way that would have necessitated girl-friend collusion or intervention.

'Probably not,' Margot says. 'He's a guy . . . And does he even know Leo's last name?'

I tell her I'm not sure. He once did, I think, but perhaps he has forgotten.

'And really,' she says, recrossing her legs at the ankle, 'what does it matter anyway?'

I look at her, ninety percent thrilled by the direction she's headed in, and ten percent worried that it might be some kind of a trap set by one loyal sibling for another.

Blood is thicker than water, I can hear Suzanne saying as I nod noncommittally and wait for Margot to finish her thought.

'It's not like Leo was some big love of your life or anything,' she finally says.

When I don't respond immediately, she raises her well-arched eyebrows even higher, obviously looking for confirmation and reassurance.

So I say as decisively as I can, 'No, he wasn't.'

This time, I *know* I'm lying, but what choice do I have?

'He was just . . . some guy from a long time ago,' Margot says, her voice trailing off.

'Right,' I say, cringing as I think of that flight together.

Margot smiles.

I make myself smile back at her.

Then, just as the gate attendant announces the start of boarding and our husbands rejoin us with a stash of newspapers, magazines, and bottled water, she leans in and whispers confidingly, 'So what do you say we just go ahead and keep this one to ourselves?'

I nod, picturing the two of us literally sweeping debris under an expansive Oriental rug as we hum along to the *Golden Girls* theme song, one of our favorite shows to watch after class in college.

'All's well that ends well,' Margot says, words that, oddly enough, both soothe me and fill me with a sense of foreboding. Words that echo in my head as the four of us gather our belongings and saunter down the Jetway toward my new life, a fresh start, and something that feels a little bit like redemption.

22

For the next few weeks, as Andy and I settle into our new home, I do my best to stay on the road to redemption. I wake up every morning and give myself rousing pep talks, repeating chipper clichés out loud in the shower — things like, *Home is where the heart is*, and *Happiness is a state of mind*. I tell Andy and Margot and Stella, and even strangers, like the clerk at Whole Foods and a woman behind me in line at the DMV, that I am happy here, that I do not miss New York. I tell myself that if I can only will these things to be true, my record will be expunged, my slate cleaned, and Leo forgotten for good.

But despite my best, most pure-intentioned efforts, it doesn't quite work out that way. Instead, as I go through all the moving-in motions — whether it's arranging our framed photographs on the built-in bookcases flanking our stone fireplace, or perusing the aisles of Target for Rubbermaid storage containers, or poring over drapery fabric samples with Margot's interior designer, or planting white caladiums in big bronze pots on our front porch — I feel out of sorts and out of place.

Worse, I have the nagging, sinking feeling that I was more myself on that red-eye flight than I have been in a long time — and that I've made a mistake in leaving New York. A big mistake. The kind of mistake that brews resentment and

253

dangerous fissures. The kind of mistake that makes your heart ache. The kind of mistake that makes you long for another choice, the past, someone else.

Meanwhile, Andy's contentment, bordering on outright glee, makes me feel that much more alienated. Not so much because misery loves company — although there is an element of that — but because his happiness means that our move is permanent, and I will be stuck in this world forever. *His* world. A life sentence of sitting in traffic and having to drive everywhere, even to grab a cup of coffee or a quick manicure. Of sterile strip malls and no late-night dinner delivery options. Of mindlessly accumulating shiny, unnecessary possessions to fill the empty spaces in our sprawling home. Of falling asleep listening to absolute unsettling silence rather than the satisfying hum and pulse of a city. Of still, sweltering summers with Andy off playing golf and tennis every weekend and no chance of a white Christmas. Of saccharine-sweet, blond, blue-eyed, Lilly Pulitzer-wearing, Bunco-playing neighbors with whom I have virtually nothing in common.

Then, one morning in August, just after Andy leaves for work, I find myself standing in the middle of the kitchen, holding his cereal bowl which he carelessly left on the table, and I realize that it's not such a subtle feeling anymore. It's full-blown suffocation. I practically run to the sink, toss his bowl into it, and phone Suzanne in a panic.

'I hate it here,' I tell her, fighting back tears.

Just saying the words aloud seems to solidify my stance and make my feelings both official and entrenched.

Suzanne makes a reassuring sound and then offers, 'Moving is always tough. Didn't you hate New York at first?'

'No,' I say, standing over the sink and almost basking in feeling like a downtrodden, taken-for-granted housewife. 'New York was an adjustment. I was overwhelmed at first . . . But I never *hated* it. Not like this.'

'What's the problem?' she asks, and for a second, I think she's being sincere — until she adds, 'Is it the doting husband? The huge house? The pool? Your new Audi? Or wait — it's *gotta* be the sleeping in late and not having to get up and go to work, right?'

'Hey, wait a second,' I say, feeling spoiled and ungrateful, like a celebrity whining about her lack of privacy, insisting that her life is *soo* hard. Still, I continue, believing that my feelings are legitimate. 'It's driving me crazy that my agent hasn't called with anything and I spend my days snapping shots of magnolia trees in our backyard, or of Andy puttering around the house with his toolbox, pretending to be handy . . . or of the kids on the corner selling lemonade until their nanny glares at me like I'm some kind of child molester . . . I *want* to work — '

'But you don't *have* to work,' Suzanne says, cutting me off. 'There's a difference. Trust me.'

'I know. I *know* I'm lucky. I know I should be thrilled — or at least *comforted* by all of . . . *this*,' I say, glancing around my spacious

255

kitchen — with its marble counters, gleaming Viking stove, and wide-planked, cedar floors. 'But I just don't feel right here . . . It's hard to explain.'

'Try,' she says.

My head fills with a litany of my usual complaints before I settle on a trivial but somehow symbolic anecdote from the night before. I tell her how the little girl next door came over peddling Girl Scout cookies and how irritated I was as I watched Andy labor over the order form as if it were the decision of a lifetime. I imitate him, exaggerating his accent — 'Should we get three boxes of Tagalongs and two Thin Mints or two Tagalongs and three Thin Mints?'

'It *is* a pretty big decision,' Suzanne deadpans.

I ignore her and say, 'And then Andy and the little girl's mother made twenty minutes of small talk about their two degrees of separation — which, apparently, is a *lot* in this town — and all their mutual acquaintances from Westminster — '

'The one in London?' she asks.

'No. More important than that little ole abbey in England. This Westminster is the most elite private school in Atlanta . . . in all of the Southeast, my dear.'

Suzanne snickers, and it occurs to me that although she wants me to be happy, on some level she must be relishing this. After all, she told me so, right from the start. *You're an outsider. You're not one of them. You will never really belong.*

'And then,' I say, 'when I think it's finally over,

and we can go back to our mindless, numbing television watching — which by the way, feels like all we ever do anymore — the mother prompts her daughter to thank 'Mr. and Mrs. Graham' and for one disorienting second, I look over my shoulder for Andy's parents. Until I realize that *I'm* Missus Graham.'

'You don't want to be Missus Graham?' Suzanne asks pointedly.

I sigh. 'I don't want the highlight of my day to be about Thin Mints.'

'Thin Mints are pretty damn good,' Suzanne says. 'Particularly if you put them in the freezer.'

'C'mon,' I say.

'Sorry,' she says. 'Go on.'

'I don't know. I just feel so . . . trapped . . . isolated.'

'What about Margot?' Suzanne asks.

I consider this question, feeling torn between a sense of underlying loyalty to my friend and what feels to be the sad truth of the matter — that, despite the fact that I talk to Margot several times a day, I have a slight feeling of estrangement lately, a feeling that began with her reproachful stare down at our going-away party — and has lingered despite our conversation the next day at the airport.

At the time I was grateful for her exoneration, her keeping me in the fold despite my transgression. But now I have the disturbing, chafing sense that she actually believes I owe her and Andy and the entire family so much. That I'm *so* lucky to be down here, in the thick of the Graham dynasty, and that I can't possibly miss

New York, and that I'm not entitled to have any feelings about anything or anyone if it in any way deviates from their vision, their notion of proper decorum and good values.

What appeals to you the most is the very thing that will drive you crazy, I think — and it's really true. I used to love how picture-perfect the Grahams' world was. I admired their wealth, their success, their closeness — how even rebellious James (who finally moved out of his parents' guest house) manages to show up in church most Sunday mornings, albeit with bloodshot eyes and a distinct aroma of cigarette smoke on his wrinkled khakis. I loved that they all consult with one another before doing things, are fiercely proud of their family name and traditions, and that they all put Stella on a pedestal. I loved that nobody had died or divorced or even disappointed.

But now. Now I feel trapped. By them. By all of it.

For a second, I consider admitting this to Suzanne, but I know that if I do, it will be game over. I'll never be able to take it back or soften it, and someday, when the storm has passed, my sister might even throw it back in my face. She's been known to do that.

So I just say, 'Margot's fine. We still talk all the time . . . But we're just not on the same page . . . She's so all-consumed with the pregnancy thing — which is understandable, I guess . . . '

'You think you'll get on the same page soon?' she asks, obviously inquiring about our plans to start a family.

'Probably. I might as well pop out a few kids. We're already all hunkered down as if we have them. I was just thinking about that last night . . . How our friends in the city who have kids make parenthood seem so palatable. They seem completely unchanged — the same combination of immature yet cultured. Yuppie hipsters. The urban mainstream. Still going out to see good music and having brunch at cool restaurants.'

I sigh, thinking of Sabina, and how, instead of just taking her triplets to play dates and inane music classes, she also totes them to the MoMA or the CMJ Film Festival. And instead of dressing them in smocked bubbles, she puts them in plain black, organic cotton T-shirts and denim, creating mini-Sabinas, blurring generational lines.

'But here the converse seems true,' I say, getting all worked up. 'Everyone is a full-fledged *grown-up* even *before* they have kids. It's like the nineteen-fifties all over again when people turned into their parents at age twenty-one . . . And I feel us turning into that, Andy and I . . . There's no mystery left, no challenge, no passion, no edge. This is just . . . *it*, you know? This is our life from here on out. Only it's *Andy's* life. Not mine.'

'So he's glad you moved?' she asks. 'No buyer's remorse at all?'

'None. He's thrilled . . . He whistles even more than usual . . . He's a regular Andy Griffith. Whistling in the house. Whistling in the yard and garage. Whistling as he goes off to work with Daddy or off to play golf with all his good ole boy friends.'

'Good ole boys? I thought you said rednecks

don't live in Atlanta?'

'I'm not talking about good ole boy rednecks. I'm talking frat boy yucksters.'

Suzanne laughs as I rinse the few remaining Trix floating in a pool of Easter egg-pink milk down the drain, and although at one time I might have found Andy's breakfast of choice endearing, at this moment I only wonder what kind of grown, childless man eats pastel cereal with a cartoon bunny on the box.

'Have you told him how you feel?' my sister asks.

'No,' I say. 'There's no point.'

'No point in honesty?' she gently probes.

It is the sort of thing I have always told her when she and Vince are having problems. *Be open. Communicate your feelings. Talk it out.* It suddenly strikes me that not only are our roles reversed but that this advice is easier said than done. It only *feels* easy when your problems are relatively minor. And right now, my problems feel anything but minor.

'I don't want Andy to feel guilty,' I say — which is the complicated truth of the matter.

'Well, maybe he *should* feel guilty,' Suzanne says. 'He made you move.'

'He didn't *make* me do anything,' I say, feeling a pang of reassuring defensiveness for Andy. 'He offered me plenty of outs. I just didn't take them . . . I put up no resistance at all.'

'Well, that was stupid,' she says.

I turn away from the sink and, feeling like I'm about ten years old, say, '*You're* stupid.'

23

A few days later, Oprah is providing background noise while I succumb to my OCD, making slick white labels for our kitchen drawers. As I print out the word *spatulas*, I hear a knock at the side door and look up to see Margot through the paned glass.

Before I can so much as wave her in, Margot opens the door and says, 'Hey, hon. Only me!'

As I mute the TV and look up from my label maker, I am two parts grateful for the company, and one part annoyed by her come-right-in presumptuousness. And maybe just a bit sheepish for getting busted watching daytime television — something I *never* did in New York.

'Hey,' she says, giving me a weary smile. Wearing a fitted tank, black leggings, and flip-flops, she looks, for the first time, uncomfortably pregnant, almost unwieldy — at least by Margot's standards. Even her feet and ankles are beginning to swell. 'We still on for dinner tonight at my place?'

'Sure. I just tried to call you to confirm . . . Where have you been?' I say, recognizing that it's very unusual for me not to know Margot's exact whereabouts.

'Prenatal yoga,' she says, lowering herself to the couch with a groan. 'What have you been up to?'

I print a *slotted spoons* label and hold it up.

'Getting organized,' I say.

She distractedly nods her approval and then says, 'What about Josephine?'

I give her a puzzled look until I realize she's talking about baby names. *Again*. Lately, it seems to be all we discuss. Generally, I enjoy the name game, and certainly understand the importance of naming a child — sometimes it seems as if the name shapes the person — but I'm growing a bit weary of the topic. If Margot had at least found out the sex of her baby, it would cut our task in half.

'Josephine,' I say aloud. 'I like it . . . It's charming . . . offbeat . . . very cute.'

'Hazel?' she says.

'Hmm,' I say. 'A bit poserville. Besides . . . isn't it Julia Roberts's daughter's name? You don't want to be perceived as copying the stars, do you?'

'I guess not,' she says. 'How about Tiffany?'

I don't especially like the name, and it seems like a bit of an outlier on Margot's otherwise classic list, but I still tread carefully. Saying you dislike a friend's potential baby name is a dangerous proposition (like announcing you don't like her boyfriend — a sure guarantee that they'll marry).

'I'm not sure,' I say. 'It's pretty but seems a bit frou-frou . . . I thought you were going for a traditional, family name?'

'I am. Tiffany is Webb's cousin's name — the one who died of breast cancer . . . But Mom thinks it's sort of eighties, tacky . . . especially now that the brand has become so mass-marketed . . . '

'Well, I do know a few Tiffanys from Pittsburgh,' I say pointedly. 'So maybe she's right about it being down-market . . . '

Margot misses my subtle jab and merrily continues. 'It makes me think of *Breakfast at Tiffany's*, Audrey Hepburn . . . Hey! What about Audrey?'

'I like Audrey more than Tiffany . . . although it does rhyme with tawdry,' I say.

Margot laughs — she's a big fan of my playground-teasing litmus test. 'What little kid knows the word *tawdry*?'

'You never know,' I say. 'And if you stick with the family middle name Sims, her monogram will be ABS . . . and then she sure better have a flat stomach. Otherwise you set your daughter up for a lifetime of eating disorders . . . '

Margot laughs again, shaking her head. 'You're nuts.'

'What happened to Louisa?' I say.

For weeks, Louisa — another family name — was the front-runner for the girl's name. Margot even bought a swimsuit at a children's clothing trunk show and had it monogrammed with an *L* — just in *case* she has a girl. Which, by the way, is so clearly what Margot wants that I've begun to worry about the boy result. Just the night before, I told Andy that Margot was going to be like an actress nominated for an Oscar, waiting for the card to be read. Total suspense followed by elation if she wins — and having to pretend that she's just as thrilled if she doesn't.

Margot says, 'I love Louisa. I'm just not quite sold on it.'

'Well, you better hurry and get sold on

something,' I say. 'You only have four weeks.'

'I know,' she says. 'Which reminds me — we need to get cracking on that pregnant photo shoot . . . I'm getting my hair highlighted on Monday, and Webb says he can make it home early any night next week. So whenever you're free . . . '

'Right,' I say, remembering a conversation we had months ago in which she asked — and I agreed — to take, in her words, 'those artsy, black-and-white belly shots.' It seemed like a fine idea at the time but given my recent frame of mind, I'm just not that juiced to do it, particularly now that I know Webb is going to be in on the action. I picture him gazing at her lovingly, caressing her bare belly, and maybe even planting a kiss on her protruding navel. *Ugh.* How far I've fallen. If I'm not careful, I'll have gone from shooting for *Platform* magazine to wiping baby drool or jangling rattles in front of a cranky toddler.

So, with all this in mind, I say, 'Don't you think that's a bit . . . I don't know . . . *fromage?*'

Somehow calling her cheesy in French seems to dampen the mean-spiritedness of the question.

For an instant Margot looks hurt, but quickly regroups and says, quite emphatically, 'No. I like them . . . I mean, not to display in the foyer — but for our bedroom or to put in an album . . . Ginny and Craig had some taken like that, and they're *really* amazing.'

I refrain from telling her that I'd hardly aspire to be like Ginny and Craig, who top my list of Atlanta irritants.

Ginny is Margot's oldest, and until I dethroned her, best friend. I've heard the story of how they met at least a dozen times, most often from Ginny herself. In short, their mothers bonded in a neighborhood playgroup when their daughters were babies, but then dropped out of the group two weeks later, deciding none of the other mothers shared their sensibilities. (Specifically, one of the other moms served dried Cheerios for a morning snack, which might have been overlooked but for the fact that she also offered up some of the toasted treats to the fellow adults. In a plastic bowl, no less. At which point, Ginny inserts that always annoying and very insincere Southern expression, 'Bless her heart.' Translation: 'The poor *slob*.')

So naturally, their mothers seceded from the group to form their own, and the rest is history. From the looks of Margot's photo albums, the girls were virtually inseparable during their teenage years, whether cheerleading (Ginny, incidentally, always holding Margot's left heel in their pyramid, which I see as symbolic of their friendship), or lounging about their country club in matching yellow bikinis, or attending teas and cotillions and debutante balls. Always smiling broadly, always with sun-kissed tans, always surrounded by a posse of admiring, lesser beauties. A far cry from the few snapshots I have of me and Kimmy, my best friend from home, hanging out at the Ches-A-Rena roller rink, sporting feathered hair, fluorescent tank tops, and rows of nappy, frayed yarn bracelets.

In any event, just as Kimmy and I went our

separate ways after graduation (she went to beauty school and is now snipping the same overlayered do in her salon in Pittsburgh), so did Ginny and Margot. Granted their experiences were more similar, as Ginny attended the University of Georgia and also joined a sorority, but they were still different experiences with different people during an intense time of life — which will take the *B* out of BFF almost every time. To this point, Ginny stayed immersed with the same crowd from Atlanta (at least half of their high school went to UGA), and Margot branched out, doing her own thing at Wake Forest. And part of doing her own thing was bonding with me, a Yankee who didn't fit into (if not downright defied) the social order of Atlanta. In fact, looking back, I sometimes think that Margot's befriending me was a way of redefining herself, sort of like following a new, offbeat band. Not that I was alternative or anything, but a Catholic, brown-eyed brunette with a Pittsburgh dialect was definitely a change of pace given Margot's Southern, society upbringing. Frankly, I also think Margot liked that I was as smart, if not smarter than she, in contrast to Ginny who had passable book smarts, but no intellectual curiosity whatsoever. In fact, from overhearing snippets of their collegeera phone conversations, it seemed clear to me that Ginny had no interest in anything other than partying, clothing, and boys, and although Margot shared those interests, she had much more substance under the surface.

So it was pretty predictable that Ginny would

become jealous and competitive with me, particularly during those first few years of the gradual power shift. It was never anything overt, just a frostiness coupled with her pointed way of rehashing inside stories and private jokes in my presence. I might have been paranoid, but she seemed to go out of her way to discuss things that I couldn't relate to — such as their respective silver patterns (both girls' grandmothers selected their patterns at Buckhead's Beverly Bremer Silver Shop, upon their birth) or the latest gossip at the Piedmont Driving Club, or the ideal carat size for diamond-stud earrings (apparently anything less than one carat is too 'sweet sixteen' and anything more than two-and-a-half is 'so new money').

Over time, as their friendship became more rooted in the past and mine and Margot's became all about the present, first in college and then in New York, Ginny saw the writing on the wall. Then, when Andy and I got serious, and she realized that no matter how long she and Margot had known each other, I was going to be *family*, it became an absolute given that I would usurp her title and be named Margot's maid of honor — the unambiguous, grown-up equivalent of wearing best friend necklaces. And although Ginny played the gracious runner-up at all of Margot's engagement parties and bridesmaid luncheons, I had the distinct feeling that she thought Margot, and Andy for that matter, could have done better.

Yet all of this underlying girly drama wasn't anything I gave much thought to until after

267

Margot moved back to Atlanta. At first, even she seemed reluctant to entrench herself in the old scene. She was always loyal enough to Ginny — one of Margot's best traits — but would occasionally drop a casual remark about Ginny's narrow-mindedness, how she had no desire to vacation any place other than Sea Island, or that she never reads the newspaper, or how 'funny' it was that Ginny has never held a single job in her life. (And when I say never, I mean *never*. Not a lifeguarding job in high school nor a brief office job before getting married and instantly having — what else? — a boy, and then, two years later, a girl. She has never collected a single paycheck. And incidentally, to me, someone who has worked consistently since I was fifteen, this fact was beyond funny. It was more akin to knowing conjoined twins or a circus acrobat. Bizarre in the extreme and a bit sad, too.)

But since our arrival in Atlanta, Margot seems to no longer notice these things about Ginny and instead just embraces her as a trusty hometown sidekick making a best friend comeback. And although well-adjusted adults (as I like to consider myself) don't really do the straight-rank best friend thing, I still can't help feeling agitated by my blond former nemesis now that I'm catapulted into her stylized, homogenized Buckhead world.

So, when Margot's next words are, 'Oh, by the way, I invited Ginny and Craig over tonight, too. Hope that's okay?' I smile a big, fake smile and say, 'Sounds peachy.'

A fitting adjective for my new Georgian life.

* ★ ★

That night, I manage to run late getting ready for dinner, a curious phenomenon of having nothing pressing to do all day. As I wring out my wet hair and slather moisturizer onto my cheeks, I hear Andy run up the steps and call my name in an all's-right-in-the-world tone, and then add, 'Honey! I'm home!'

I think of that purported excerpt from a 1950s home economics textbook that routinely makes its way around the Internet, giving women *dos* and *don'ts* on being a good wife and specifically how we should greet our husbands after a hard day at the office. *Make the evening his . . . Put a ribbon in your hair and be fresh looking . . . Offer to take off his shoes . . . Talk in a soothing voice.*

I give Andy a kiss on the lips and then say primly, sarcastically, 'Good news, dear. Ginny and Craig will be joining us this evening.'

'Oh, come on,' he says, smiling. 'Be nice. They're not so bad.'

'Are too,' I say.

'Be nice,' he says again, as I try to recall if that was in the article. *Always be nice at the expense of the truth.*

'Okay,' I say. 'I'll be nice until the fifth time she calls something 'super cute.' After that, I get to be myself. Deal?'

Andy laughs as I continue, mimicking Ginny, 'This dress is *super cute*. That crib is *super cute*. Jessica Simpson and Nick Lachey were *soo super cute* together. I know it's a shame about the

269

Middle East turmoil and all, but that breakup is still, like, the saddest thing *ever*.'

Andy laughs again as I turn back toward my huge, walk-in closet, only about a third filled, and select a pair of jeans, leather flip-flops, and a vintage Orange Crush T-shirt.

'You think this is okay for dinner?' I say, slipping the shirt over my head and almost hoping that Andy will criticize my choice.

Instead, he kisses my nose and says, 'Sure. You look super cute.'

★   ★   ★

True to form, Ginny is dressed smartly in a crisp shift dress, strappy sandals, and pearls, and Margot is wearing an adorable pale blue maternity frock, also with pearls. (Granted Margot's are the whimsical, oversized costume variety tied in the back with a white grosgrain ribbon rather than the good strand her grandmother bequeathed her, but pearls they are.)

I shoot Andy a look that he misses as he bends down to pat Ginny's hairless Chinese crested puppy named Delores without whom she never leaves home (and, even worse, to whom she habitually applies sunscreen). I swear she prefers Delores to her children — or at least her son, who has such a raging case of ADD that Ginny brags about strategically giving him Benadryl before long car trips or dinners out.

'I feel so underdressed,' I say, handing Margot a bottle of wine that I grabbed from our wine cellar on our way out the door. I run my hands over my denim-clad hips and add, 'I thought you said casual?'

Ginny looks somewhat jubilant, oblivious to the fact that I secretly feel appropriate, even smug, in my jeans and T-shirt — and that I think she's the one who is overdressed. As she leans in to give me a demure collar bone-to-collar bone hug, Margot thanks me for the wine and says, 'I did. You look great.' Then, as she pours margaritas into oversized hand-blown glasses, she adds, 'God, I wish I had your height . . . Especially these days. Ginny, wouldn't you just kill for those legs?'

Ginny, who never made a postpartum comeback despite a personal trainer and a tummy tuck she doesn't know that I know she had, glances wistfully at my legs before murmuring noncommittally. Clearly, she prefers that her compliments to me be of the backhanded variety — such as the recent gem she doled out while we were selecting invitations for Margot's baby shower (an event I'm shamefully dreading) at Paces Papers. After laboring over our wording and the selection of pale pink, deckle-edged paper, charcoal ink, and an old-fashioned pram motif, I thought our task was finished. I picked up my purse, relieved to go, when Ginny touched my wrist, smiled condescendingly, and said, '*Font*, hon. We have to choose a *font*.'

'Oh, right,' I said, thinking of my old workroom in New York and how much I learned about typefaces from Oscar. Way more than

Ginny could have picked up from planning her wedding and a few showers and charity balls. But I still amused myself by throwing out, 'So I guess Times New Roman won't do this time?'

At which point Ginny did her best to convey horror to the cute redheaded girl helping us and then declared, 'Oh, Ellen. I *so* admire how laidback you are about these *details* . . . I *try* to be more that way, but just *can't*.'

Bless my heart.

So anyway, here I sit in Margot's family room in my Orange Crush T-shirt, the only bright color in a sea of preppy chic, summery pastels. And the only one who hasn't heard the summer's breaking news — that Cass Phillips discovered her husband, Morley, had purchased a three-thousand-dollar harp for his twenty-one-year-old lover who happens to be her best friend's goddaughter. Which, as you can imagine, has caused *quite* the stir at Cherokee, the country club to which all pertinent parties belong.

'A *harp*?' I say. 'Whatever happened to your standard negligee?'

Ginny shoots me a look as if I've totally missed the point of the story, and says, 'Oh, Ellen. She's a harpist.'

'Right,' I say, mumbling that I figured as much, but who the heck decides to pick up the harp, anyway?

Andy winks at me and says, 'Elizabeth Smart.'

As I recall the 'missing' posters of Elizabeth playing the harp, I smile at my husband's ability to conjure examples for just about anything, while Ginny ignores our exchange and informs me that she and Craig had a harpist at their rehearsal dinner, along with a string quartet.

'Elizabeth who?' Craig says, turning to Andy, as if trying to place the name in his tight little Buckhead context.

'You know,' I say. 'The Mormon girl who was kidnapped and then found a year later walking around Salt Lake City in a robe with her bearded captor.'

'Oh yeah. Her,' Craig says dismissively. As I watch him slice a big wedge of Brie and sandwich it between two crackers, it occurs to me that while he is like Webb in some ways — they are both ruddy, joke-telling, sports guys — he has none of Webb's affability or ability to put others at ease. Come to think of it, he never really acknowledges me much at all or even looks my way. He brushes a few crumbs from his seersucker shorts and says, 'I did hear the harpist was smokin' hot . . . '

'Craig!' Ginny whines her husband's name and looks aghast, as if she just caught him jerking off to a *Penthouse* magazine.

'Sorry, babe,' Craig says, kissing her in such a way that would suggest they've only just begun to date, when in fact, they've been together since virtually the first day of college.

Webb looks amused as he asks how Morley was busted.

Ginny explains that Cass found the charge on Morley's corporate Amex. 'She thought it looked suspicious and called the store . . . Then she put it together with his sudden interest in the symphony,' she says, her eyes bright with the scandalous details.

'Did he not think that, given his womanizing reputation, she was going to check his corporate Amex, too?' Margot says.

Craig winks and says, 'It's usually a safe harbor.'

Ginny whines her husband's name again, then gives him a playful shove. 'I'd leave you so fast,' she says.

Right, I think. She is *exactly* the sort of kept woman who'd put up with serial shenanigans. Anything to keep up their perfect appearances.

As the group continues to untangle the sordid harp saga, my mind drifts to Leo, and I consider for at least the hundredth time whether, in a technical, poll-one-hundred-people-in-Times-Square sort of way, I cheated on Andy that night on the plane. Always before, I wanted the answer to be no — both for Andy's sake and for mine. But on this night, I realize that a small part of me almost *wants* to fall in that dark category. Wants to have a secret that distances me from Ginny and this whole desperate-housewife world I have found myself in. I can just hear her gossiping with her Buckhead-Betty friends — 'I don't know *what* Margot sees in that tacky-font-selecting, T-shirt-wearing, unhighlighted Yankee.'

The rest of the night is uneventful — just lots of golf and business talk among the men and baby talk among the girls — until about halfway through dinner when Ginny sips from her wineglass, winces, and says, 'Margot, *darling*. What is this that we're drinking?'

'It's a merlot,' Margot says quickly, something in her voice tipping me off to trouble. I glance at the bottle and realize that it's the one I brought tonight — and upon further inspection, the very same one that my father and Sharon gave Andy and me after we moved into our New York apartment.

'Well, it tastes like *arse*,' Ginny says, as if she's British, a pet peeve of mine. (Just earlier tonight, she mentioned that she and Craig were planning a trip to *Meh-hee-co*.)

Margot flashes Ginny an insider's look of warning — a look that you'd think they would have perfected in high school — but Ginny either misses it or intentionally ignores it, continuing her banter. 'Where did you find it? Wal-Mart?'

Before Margot can offer a preemptive strike, Craig grabs the bottle from the table, scans the label, and scoffs, 'Pennsylvania. It's from Pennsylvania. Right. Everyone knows how world-renowned the vineyards are in Philadelphia.' He laughs, proud of his joke, proud to be showcasing his sophistication, his appreciation of all the finer things in life. 'You shouldn't have, really,' he adds, anticipating all of us to burst into fits of laughter.

Andy gives me a look that says, *Let it ride.* Like his sister and mother, he is one to avoid conflict of any kind, and deep down, I know that is exactly what I should do now. I am also fairly certain that no one meant to offend me — that Craig and Ginny likely didn't piece together that I brought the wine — and that it was only a good-natured ribbing between close friends. The sort of foot-in-the-mouth remarks that anyone can make.

But because they come from Ginny and Craig, and because I do not like Ginny and Craig and they do not like me, and because at this moment I want to be anywhere in the world but sitting at a table in my new town of Atlanta having dinner with Ginny and Craig, I pipe up with, 'Pittsburgh, actually.'

Craig looks at me, confused. 'Pittsburgh?' he says.

'Right. Pittsburgh . . . *not* Philadelphia,' I say, my face burning with indignation. 'It's *Pittsburgh's* finest merlot.'

Craig, who clearly has no clue where I'm from, and certainly has never bothered to ask, continues to look puzzled while I catch Webb and Margot exchange an uncomfortable glance.

'*I'm* from Pittsburgh,' I say, drolly, apologetically. 'I brought the bottle tonight.' I shift my gaze to Ginny and swirl my wine. 'Sorry that it's not up to snuff.'

Then, as Craig looks sheepish and Ginny stammers an awkward retraction and Margot laughs nervously and Webb changes the subject and Andy does absolutely *nothing*, I silently raise my glass and take a big gulp of cheap red wine.

24

On the short, muggy walk home that night, I wait for Andy to rush to my defense — or at least make cursory mention of the merlot episode. At which point, I plan to laugh it off, or perhaps chime in with a few choice comments about Ginny and Craig — her insipid chatter, his misplaced superiority, their relentless, almost comical, snobbishness.

But surprisingly and even more disappointingly, Andy doesn't say a word about them. In fact, he has so little to say that he comes across as uncharacteristically remote, almost aloof, and I start to feel he actually might be mad at *me* for causing a ruckus at Margot's so-called barbecue. As we near our driveway, I am tempted to come right out and ask the question, but refrain for fear that doing so would suggest guilt. And I don't feel that I've done anything wrong.

So instead I stubbornly avoid the subject altogether and keep things neutral, breezy. 'Those were some great filets, weren't they?' I say.

'Yeah. They were pretty tasty,' Andy says as he nods to a night jogger passing us in crazy, head-to-toe reflective clothing.

'No chance that guy's getting hit by anything,' I say, chuckling.

Andy ignores my half-hearted joke and continues in a serious voice. 'Margot's corn salad was really good, too.'

'Uh-huh. Yeah. I'll be sure to get her recipe,' I mumble, my tone coming off slightly more acerbic than I intended.

Andy shoots me a look that I can't read — some combination of doleful and defensive — before dropping my hand and reaching in his pocket for his keys. He fishes them out, then strides more quickly up the driveway to the front porch, where he unlocks the door and pauses to let me enter first. It is something he always does, but tonight the gesture registers as formal, almost tense.

'Why, thank you,' I say, feeling stranded in that frustrating no man's land of both wanting to fight and wanting to be close.

Andy won't give me either. Instead, he steps around me as if I were a pair of tennis shoes left on the stairs and heads straight up to our room.

I reluctantly follow him and watch him start to undress, desperately wanting to define what's in the air between us but unwilling to make the first move.

'You going to bed?' I say, glancing at the clock on our bedroom mantel.

'Yeah. I'm beat,' Andy says.

'It's only ten,' I say, feeling both angry and sad. 'Don't you want to watch TV?'

He shakes his head and says, 'It's been a long week.' Then he hesitates, as if he forgot what he was about to do, before reaching into his top dresser drawer to retrieve his best pair of fine, Egyptian-cotton pajamas. He pulls them out, and, looking surprised, says, 'Did you iron these?'

I nod, as if it were nothing, when in fact I felt like a martyr as I pressed them yesterday morning, with starch and all. *Spray, sigh, iron. Spray, sigh, iron.*

'You didn't have to do that,' he says, buttoning his shirt slowly, deliberately, while avoiding eye contact with me.

'I wanted to,' I lie, focusing on the curve of his slender neck as he looks down at the top button, thinking that I have nothing better to do in Atlanta.

'It wasn't necessary . . . I don't mind wrinkles.'

'In clothes or on my face?' I say wryly, hoping to break the ice — and *then* fight.

'Either,' Andy says, still stone-faced.

'Good,' I say flippantly. 'Because, you know, I'm not really the BOTOX type.'

Andy nods. 'Yeah. I know.'

'Ginny gets BOTOX,' I say, feeling slightly foolish by my overt, clumsy attempt to divert the conversation to what's *really* on my mind, and even more so when Andy refuses my bait.

'Really?' he says disinterestedly.

'Yeah. Every couple months,' I say, grasping at straws. As if the frequency of her cosmetic-surgery office visits will finally push him across some imaginary line and rally him to my cause.

'Well,' he says, shrugging. 'To each his own, I guess.'

I inhale, now ready to goad him into a proper argument. But before I can say anything, he turns and disappears into the bathroom, leaving me sitting on the foot of our bed as if *I'm* the bad guy.

To add insult to injury, Andy falls right to sleep that night — which is about the most galling thing you can do after a fight, or in our case, a standoff. No tossing or turning or stewing beside me in the dark. Just cold indifference as he kissed me goodnight, followed by an easy, deep slumber. Of course this has the infuriating effect of keeping me wide awake, replaying the evening, then the past few weeks, and the few months before that. After all, there is nothing like a little argument-induced insomnia to shift you into a state of frenzied hyper-analysis and fury.

So when the grandfather clock in our foyer (incidentally a house-warming gift from Stella which I'm none too fond of, for both its foreboding appearance and sound) strikes three, I am in such a bad mental place that I transfer to the couch downstairs where I begin to think of our engagement — the last time I can recall feeling defensive about my background.

To be fair (which I'm not in the mood to be), our wedding planning was mostly smooth sailing. In part, I credit myself for being a relatively laidback bride, as I really only cared about the photography, our vows, and for some odd reason, the cake (Suzanne believes this was simply my excuse to sample lots of baked goods). In part, I think things went well because Margot had just gone through it all, and Andy and I weren't afraid to shamelessly copy her, using the same church, country club, florist, and band. Largely, though, I think it went well because we only had *one* mother in the picture, and I was perfectly happy to let her run the show.

Suzanne didn't get it — didn't understand how I could so easily surrender to Stella's strong opinions and traditional taste.

'Pink roses aren't you,' she said, starting in on the Grahams one afternoon as we flipped through my CDs, looking for good firstdance song choices.

'I like pink roses just fine,' I said, shrugging.

'Please. Even so . . . what about everything else?' Suzanne said, looking agitated.

'Like what?' I said.

'Like everything . . . it's as if they expect you to become one of them,' she said, her voice rising.

'That's what a wedding is all about,' I said calmly. 'I'm *becoming* a Graham, so to speak.'

'But it's supposed to be two families coming together . . . and this wedding feels like it's more *theirs* than *yours*. It's almost as if they're . . . trying to take you over . . . phase out *your* family.'

'How do you figure?' I said.

'Let's see . . . You're on their turf, for one. Why the hell are you getting married in Atlanta anyway? Isn't the wedding supposed to be in the *bride's* hometown?'

'I guess so. Typically,' I said. 'But it just makes sense to have it in Atlanta since Stella's doing most of the work.'

'And writing all the checks,' Suzanne said, at which point I finally got defensive and said that she wasn't being fair.

Yet now, I wonder if finances weren't a factor, after all. I can say with unwavering certainty that I didn't marry Andy for his money, and that I wasn't, as Suzanne seemed to be implying, *bought*. But on some level I guess I *did* feel indebted to the Grahams and therefore complicit when it came to the details.

Beyond the money, there was something else at play, too — some dark thing I never wanted to look at too closely, until now, in the middle of the night, on the couch. It was a feeling of inadequacy — a worry that, on some level, maybe I wasn't good enough. Maybe I didn't quite measure up to Andy and his family. I was never ashamed of my hometown, my roots, or my family, but the more I became entrenched in the Graham family, the way they lived, and their traditions and customs, I couldn't help but start to see my own background in a new light. And it was this concern — perhaps only subconscious at the time — that gave me a tremendous sense of relief when Stella suggested that she plan our wedding in Atlanta.

At the time, I justified my feelings. I told myself that I had left Pittsburgh for a reason. I wanted a different kind of life for myself — not a *better* life — just a different one. And included in that was a different sort of wedding. I didn't want to get married at my drafty Catholic church, eat stuffed cabbage from tinfoil chafing dishes, and boogie down to the Chicken Dance at the VFW Hall. I didn't want to have wedding cake smashed in my face, a blue-lace garter removed by my groom's teeth, and my bouquet caught by a nine-year-old because virtually every other female guest is already married with kids. And I didn't want to get pelted with rice by my husband's friends — the few who had yet to pass out — then cruise off in a black stretch limo with empty Iron City cans tied to the back bumper all the way to the Days Inn where we'd spend the night before flying to Cancun for our package honeymoon. It's not that I turned up my nose to any of that — I just had a different concept of the 'dream wedding.'

Now I see that it wasn't only a question of what I wanted for myself — it was also what I feared the Grahams and their friends would think of me. I never tried to hide how I grew up, but I didn't want them observing too closely for fear that someone might come to that horrifying conclusion that I wasn't good enough for Andy. And it was this emotion, this *fear*, that crystallized and manifested itself in the purchase of my wedding gown.

It all started when Andy asked my father for my hand in marriage, actually flying to Pittsburgh so that he could take my dad to Bravo Franco, his favorite downtown restaurant, and ask for permission, face to face. The gesture won big points with my dad, who sounded so happy and proud when he told the story that for a long time I joked he was worried he could never marry me off (a joke I stopped telling once it became apparent that this might be Suzanne's fate). In any event, during the course of their lunch, after my dad gave his jubilant blessing, he became earnest as he told Andy about the wedding fund he and my mother had long ago set up for their girls — a savings of seven thousand dollars to be used any way we wished. In addition, he told Andy that he wanted to buy my gown, as it was something my mother had always talked of doing with her daughters, one of her symbolic big regrets during her final days.

So after Andy and I got engaged, he passed along these details to me, expressing his gratitude for my dad's generosity, telling me how much he really liked my old man, and how much he wished he could have taken my mother to lunch, too. Meanwhile, though, Andy and I both knew without saying it that seven thousand dollars would not make a dent in the cost of our lavish wedding — and that the Grahams were going to make up the rather significant shortfall. And I was okay with this. I was okay playing the role of gracious daughter-in-law, and I knew I wouldn't have to hurt my dad's feelings by telling him that his contribution would barely cover the cost of all those pink roses.

The problem was the dress. At some point, my dad insisted that he wanted me to send him the bill directly. This left me with two unpalatable choices — buy an inexpensive dress, or choose something my father could not afford. So with this conundrum in mind, off I went, uneasily dress shopping with Stella, Margot, and Suzanne, constantly trying to check the price tags and find something for less than five hundred dollars. Which simply doesn't exist in Manhattan, at least not at the couture Madison and Fifth Avenue stores where Margot had booked our appointments. Looking back, I know I could have confided all of this in Margot, and that she would have tailored our search accordingly, finding us a boutique in Brooklyn that fit my dad's budget.

Instead I had to go and fall in love with a ridiculously expensive Badgley Mischka gown at Bergdorf Goodman. It was the dream dress I didn't know I had to have until I saw it — a simple but lush ivory crêpe sheath gown with a beaded netting overlay. Stella and Margot clasped their hands and insisted that I just *had* to get it, and even Suzanne got a little weepy as I spun around on my toes in front of the three-way mirror.

When it came time to pay, Stella whipped out her Amex Black card, insisting that she really, *really* wanted to do this. I hesitated and then accepted her generous offer, shamelessly pushing aside my dad — and, even worse, my mother — and filling my head with rationalizations of every kind. *What he doesn't know won't hurt him. I won't have my mother at my wedding — at least I can have my dream dress. She'd want me to have this.*

The next day, after much thought and angst, I came up with the perfect strategy to cover my tracks and keep my dad's pride intact. I went back to Bergdorf, selected a five-hundred-dollar veil, and told the clerk that my father wanted to buy it and would be calling with his credit card details. I also hinted rather directly that I wanted him to think the charge covered my dress, too.

The clerk, a thin-lipped, fine-boned woman named Bonnie whose affected Upper East Side accent I will never forget, winked as if she understood, called me dear, and conspiratorially said she'd handle it, no problem whatsoever.

But of course ole Bonnie screwed everything up, sending my father the receipt *and* the veil. And although he never said a word about it, the look on his face when he handed me that veil in Atlanta said it all. I knew how much I had hurt his feelings, and we both knew why I had done it. It was the most ashamed I have been in my life.

I never told Andy the story — never told anyone the story — so great was my desire to forget it all. But I think those emotions resurfaced at Margot's dinner table tonight, and now again, in the middle of the night, as I am filled with shame all over again. Shame that makes me wish I could turn back time and wear a different dress on my wedding day. Wish I could take back that look on my father's face. Which obviously I can't do.

But I *can* stand up to the Ginnys of the world. And I can let her — and anyone else — know that I'm proud of where I come from, proud of who I am. And, by God, I can sleep on the couch in protest if my own husband doesn't get it.

25

The next morning I awaken to find Andy standing over me. He is already showered and dressed in a bright green polo, madras shorts, and a woven leather belt.

'Hi,' I say, clearing my throat and thinking that madras shorts look ridiculous on anyone over the age of five.

'Hey,' he says so curtly that I can tell sleep has not cured his problem. *Our* problem.

'Where are you off to?' I ask, noting his car keys in hand and his wallet bulging in his back pocket.

'Going to run some errands,' Andy says.

'Okay,' I say, feeling a resurgence of rage by his steadfast refusal to address last night, to ask what's wrong, ask why I'm sleeping on the couch, wonder or care if I am happy here in Atlanta.

He twirls his keys on his index finger — a habit that is starting to grate on my nerves — and says, 'So I'll see you later?'

'Yeah. Whatever,' I mutter.

I watch him take a few nonchalant steps toward the door before I snap. 'Hey!' I say, using the Northern definition of the word.

Andy turns, coolly gazing at me.

'What the hell's your problem?' I say, my voice rising.

'*My* problem?' Andy asks, an ironic smile tugging the corners of his mouth.

'Yeah. What's *your* problem,' I say, realizing that our arguing style is anything but sophisticated, probably because we don't do it enough. In fact, I can't recall a single fight of any consequence since we've been married. Something I used to wear as a badge of honor.

'*You're* the one sleeping on the couch,' Andy says, pacing in front of the fireplace, still playing with his keys. 'What's up with *that*? . . . We always said we would never do that . . . '

I whip the throw blanket off my legs, sit up, and finally come out with it. 'Why the hell didn't you defend me last night?'

Andy looks at me, as if carefully considering the question, and then says, 'Since when have you needed anyone to come to your rescue? . . . You seem to be perfectly self-contained these days.'

'What's that supposed to mean?' I snap back at him.

'You know what it means,' he says — which pisses me off even more.

Is he referring to the fact that I'm all alone here while he works and plays golf? Or that I have nothing in common with the women in my neighborhood? Or that we hardly ever make love anymore — and when we do, we barely talk afterward?

'I actually *don't* know what it means,' I sputter. 'But what I *do* know is that it would have been nice if my husband had something to say to that *bitch* and her dumbass, red-faced husband when she — '

'Give me a break. When she *what*?' Andy says.

288

'When she made a *joke* about wine?'

'Real funny joke,' I say.

'Oh, come *on*,' Andy says. 'She thought it was Margot's . . . Does that really make her a bitch?'

'She *is* a bitch. That just makes her a snob on top of it . . . A snob with absolutely *nothing* to back it up,' I say, thinking that *this* is the most offensive part of Ginny and Craig. Snobs are *always* offensive, but less so if they have some kind of game. But Ginny and Craig have *no* game — they are just insufferable bores whose self-identity is inextricably tied to *things*. To fancy cars and expensive wines, to staid pearls and seersucker shorts.

'So she's a snob,' Andy says, shrugging. 'You used to just laugh people like that off . . . And now . . . now you've got this huge fuck-you-Atlanta thing going on and you take everything so personally.'

'Last night *was* personal,' I say.

'Well, I'd argue that it wasn't,' he says, using his calm lawyerly tone. 'But let's say it was.'

'Yes. *Let's*,' I say, flashing a big, fake smile.

He ignores my sarcasm and continues, 'Was it really worth making my sister and Webb uncomfortable?'

My sister, I think. Andy never refers to Margot as his sister when he's talking to me, and I can't help thinking that this is very telling of his mindset. A mindset that is starting to mirror my own. *You versus them*, I can hear Suzanne saying. *You do not belong with them.*

'Well, apparently I thought it was,' I say, thinking that's the price of having such jackass friends.

'And apparently I thought it wasn't,' Andy says.

I look at him, feeling totally defeated and isolated, thinking that it's pretty impossible to argue with a controlled, holier-than-thou husband who has just told you, in so many words, that he prioritizes other people's feelings. Feelings other than mine, that is. So I say, 'Well, you're much better than I am. Clearly.'

'Oh, come *on*, Ellen. Get that chip off your shoulder, would you?'

It occurs to me that he's absolutely right — I do have a chip on my shoulder. A huge one. Yet this realization does nothing to soften my heart. If anything, it only makes me angrier — and more determined to stay that way.

'Just go run your errands,' I say, waving him toward the door. 'I'll just be here ironing all day.'

He rolls his eyes and sighs. 'Okay, Ellen. Be a martyr. Have it your way. I'll see ya later.' Then he turns and walks toward the door.

I make a face and hold up both middle fingers at his back, then listen to the garage door open and Andy's BMW start up and pull away, leaving me in deafening quiet. I sit for a few minutes, feeling sorry for myself, wondering how Andy and I got here, in both the state of Georgia and the strained emotional state of our marriage. A marriage that is not yet a year old. I think of how everyone says the first year is the hardest and wonder when — *if* — it will get easier. And, in those silent moments, I succumb to what I've been contemplating doing since we arrived in Atlanta.

I make my way upstairs to the office, dig to the

very bottom of my desk drawer, and excavate the forbidden *Platform* magazine that I have not cracked since our going-away party in New York. Not even when I spotted the magazine in the checkout line at Kroger or when Andy proudly showed his own purchased copy to his parents.

For several minutes, I stare at the cover photo of Drake. Then, something clicks inside me, and I take a deep breath, sit down, and flip to the story. My heart pounds when I see the bold byline, and the blocks of Leo's text, and my photos — photos that evoke all the emotions of that day — the stomach-churning anticipation, the desire. Foreign emotions these days.

I close my eyes, and when I open them, I start reading, hungrily devouring the story. When I get to the end, I read it twice more, slowly and methodically, as if searching for a secret, double meaning hidden in the paragraphs, sentences, words — which I manage to find, over and over, until my head spins, and all I want to do is talk to Leo.

So I keep on going.

I turn on the computer, and type out his e-mail address and a message to him:

Leo,

I just read your article. It is perfect. So satisfying. Thanks again for everything. Hope you're well.

Ellen

Then, before I can second-guess myself, I hit send. Just clicking the key wipes away all my frustration and resentment and angst. Somewhere deep down, I know I'm in the wrong. I know I'm rationalizing my actions, and worry I might even be manufacturing problems with Andy to get this result. I also know that I'm only inviting more trouble into my life. But for now, I feel good. *Really* good. Better than I've felt in a long, *long* time.

26

Exactly four minutes later, Leo's name appears in my inbox. I stare at the screen in amazement, as if I'm my grandmother marveling over technology — *How in the world did that get here?* — and for a second, regret what I've started. I actually consider deleting his e-mail, or at least getting up from the computer for a few hours to diffuse the knot in my chest.

But the temptation is too great. So, instead, I kick into rationalization overdrive and tell myself that I did not come to this point easily. I did *not* contact Leo on a whim. I did *not* write to him after a meaningless marital spat. It's taken weeks of loneliness and depression and frustration — bordering on desperation — to get here. It took my husband turning his back on me last night — and then again this morning. Besides, it's just an e-mail. What could it hurt?

So, I take a deep breath, and click open Leo's response, my heart pounding harder than ever as I read his message, all intimately lowercased:

thanks. i'm glad you liked it. that was a great day. leo ps what took you so long?

I feel flushed as I hurriedly type back:

To read your story or get in touch?

He answers me almost instantly:

both.

I feel my stress melt away as I smile, and then struggle to come up with something clever but truthful. A careful response that will keep the conversation rolling yet won't cross a line into flirtatious territory. I finally type:

Better late than never?

I hit send, then lean toward the computer, my fingers poised over the keyboard in the home position I learned in junior-high typing class, my whole body alert as I anticipate his response. A moment later it comes:

my point all along.

I tilt my head, mouth agape as I contemplate his precise meaning. I think of all those years that lapsed with no contact at all, and then the days since our flight. I think of how hard I tried, *still* try, to resist him — and our dangerous chemistry. I wonder what it all means — it has to mean *something*. And that *something* terrifies me and fills me with the deepest Catholic-schoolgirl guilt.

But then I picture Andy — tight-lipped at the table last night, then buttoning his starched pajamas before bed, then standing over the couch this morning with judgment all over his face. And, I envision him now, frolicking about town, waving *hey* to acquaintances and strangers alike, making small talk everywhere he goes. Small talk on the golf course, small talk in church, small talk at the gas station. Insouciant, jaunty, very *small* talk.

My breathing grows more rapid as I type:

I've missed talking.

I stare at the bold sentence, then delete it, watching the letters erase backward. Yet even when they're gone, I can still see them on my screen. Can still feel them etched across my heart. It is the truth, exactly what I feel, *exactly* what I want to say. I have missed talking to Leo. I have for years — and especially since our flight. So I retype them, then close my eyes and hit send, instantly feeling both queasy and relieved. When I open them, Leo has already responded:

i've missed you, too, ellen.

I gasp. There's something about him using my name. Something about his *too* — as if he knows, without my saying it, how much I've missed not only *talking* to him, but *him*. And there's something about how the words look on the screen — plain and bald and frank, like it's no big deal to say it, because it's the most obvious, undeniable thing in the world. Paralyzed, I consider my options while another e-mail lands in my inbox.

I click and read:

you still there?

I nod at the screen, picturing his face waiting expectantly for my responses, and thinking that Andy could return home, start a small fire in the kitchen, and then hover over my shoulder, and I'd probably stay fixed to this chair.

Yes.

I hit send, wait. He writes back:

good.

And then, seconds later, in a separate e-mail:

this might be easier on the phone . . . can I call you?

This, I think. What is *this*? *This* conversation? *This* confessional? *This* dance toward infidelity? I hesitate, knowing how much safer e-mail is and that agreeing to a phone call is another bridge crossed. But the part of me that wants to talk to him, wants to understand what we had together and why it ended, can't stop myself from typing:

Yes.

And so he does. I hear the muffled sound of my cell phone ringing merrily in my purse, thrown in my closet the night before, and rush to get it before it rolls to voicemail.

'Hi,' I say, trying to catch my breath and

sound casual, as if I'm not positively ecstatic to hear his voice again.

I can tell he's smiling when he says, 'Hi, Ellie.' My heart melts, and I grin back at him.

'So,' he says. 'You really *just* read my article?'

'Uh-huh,' I say, staring out the window to our driveway below.

'Didn't your agent give you the copy I sent?' he asks.

'Yes,' I say, feeling strangely contrite for appearing so indifferent to his story. He must know better, though. He must know how much that day meant to me — which was the real reason I waited so long to read his article. Still, I flounder for an excuse, saying, 'She did. I've just been . . . busy lately.'

'Oh, yeah?' he says. 'Working a lot?'

'Not exactly,' I say, as I hear Bob Dylan singing 'Tangled Up in Blue' in his background.

'Busy with what then?' he presses.

Busy making labels and watching Oprah *and ironing*, I think, but say, 'Well, I moved to Atlanta, for one.' I pause, awash with renewed guilt over my use of *I*. But I don't correct myself. After all, these days it feels like *I*.

Leo says, 'Atlanta, huh?'

'Yeah.'

'You liking that?'

'Not one bit!' I say with breezy, upbeat irony.

Leo laughs and says, 'Really? A buddy of mine lives in Atlanta — Decatur, I think? He says it's pretty cool there. Lots to do . . . good music, culture.'

'Not so much, really,' I say, thinking that I'm

probably not being fair to Atlanta. That it's probably just the Graham version of Atlanta I have a problem with. Which, of course, is a pretty major problem.

'What don't you like about it?' Leo asks.

I hesitate, thinking I should keep it vague, general, brief, but instead I detail all my misgivings about the so-called good life, tossing out words like *insular* and *pampered*, *social climbing* and *stifling*.

Leo whistles. 'Man,' he says. 'Don't hold back.'

I smile, realizing how much better I feel after my diatribe — and better still when Leo says, with a note of hopefulness, 'Can you move back to New York?'

I let out a nervous laugh and force myself to say my husband's name. 'I don't think Andy would appreciate that too much.'

Leo clears his throat. 'Right. I guess not . . . He's . . . from there, right?'

'Yeah,' I say, thinking, *He's quite the hometown hero.*

'So have you told him you think his city blows?' Leo asks. 'That living anywhere other than New York is like drinking warm soda that's lost its fizz?'

'Not exactly,' I say lightly, walking a tightrope of loyalty. I have always felt that griping about your spouse is, in some ways, *worse* than physical betrayal; I'd almost rather Andy kiss another girl than tell that same girl that I was, say, lousy in bed. So, despite our argument last night, I change my tone and try to be as fair as possible. 'He's really happy here . . . he's working with his dad now . . . you know, the whole family-business thing . . . and we already bought a house.'

'Lemme guess,' Leo says. 'A big-ass, phat house with all the trimmings?'

'Pretty much,' I say, feeling embarrassed by my riches — yet also the slightest bit defensive. After all, I agreed to them. I *chose* Andy. His family. This life.

'Hmm,' Leo says, as if contemplating all of this.

I continue, 'His family would die if we moved back.'

'So Margot's there, too?' Leo asks with a hint of disdain.

Feeling conflicted, I say, 'Yeah. She moved here about a year ago . . . and she's about to have a baby . . . So . . . it's . . . really too late to move back.'

Leo makes a sound — like he's laughing or exhaling hard.

'What?' I say.

'Nothing,' he says.

'Tell me,' I say softly.

'Well,' he says. 'Didn't we just say . . . that it's never too late?'

I feel my stomach drop, shake my head, and mouth *fuck*. I am fucked. And this feeling only intensifies when Leo says, 'Maybe you'd feel better if you came back for another shoot?'

'To New York?'

'Yeah,' he says.

'With you?' I ask hesitantly, hopefully.

'Yeah,' Leo says. 'With me.'

I inhale, rake my teeth across my lower lip, and say, 'I don't know if that's such a good idea . . . ' My voice trails off, leaving us in loaded, heart-thudding silence.

He asks why — although he *must* know why.

'Lemme see,' I say, putting up a shield of playful sarcasm. 'Let's see . . . Maybe because I'm married? . . . And you're my ex-boyfriend?' Then, despite my better judgment, I can't resist adding, 'My ex-boyfriend who disappeared into thin air years ago, never to be seen or heard from again, until he happened to run into me totally randomly one day?'

I wait for him to reply, nervous that I've said too much. After what feels like a long while, he says my name — *Ellie* — sounding exactly the way he used to, in the beginning.

'Yeah?' I whisper back.

'I have to ask you something . . . '

I freeze, anticipating his question as I say, 'What's that?'

He clears his throat and says, 'Did Margot ever tell you . . . that I came back?'

My mind spins in a hundred directions, wondering what he's talking about, fearing the worst — which is also the *best*.

'You came back?' I finally say, the import of his words making me dizzy. I turn away from the window. 'When did you *come back?*'

'About two years after,' Leo says.

'After what?' I say, already knowing the answer.

Sure enough, he says, 'Two years after we broke up — '

'When exactly?' I say, frantically piecing together the time frame — about a month after Andy and I started to date, possibly even the very day we first slept together — December twenty-ninth.

'Oh, I don't know. Sometime right after Christmas . . . '

I digest the crazy, unlikely chronology, and then ask, 'To our apartment?'

'Yeah. I was in your neighborhood . . . and just . . . came by to see you. She didn't tell you, did she?'

'No,' I say breathlessly. 'She didn't . . . She never told me that.'

'Yeah,' he says. 'I didn't think so.'

I pause, feeling giddy and weak and even more floored than I did that day in the intersection. 'What did you say to her? What did you want?'

'I don't remember . . . exactly,' Leo says.

'You don't remember what you wanted? Or what you said?'

'Oh, I remember what I wanted,' Leo says.

'And?'

'I wanted to tell you that . . . I was sorry . . . That I missed you . . . '

Nauseous and lightheaded, I close my eyes and say, 'Did you tell Margot that?'

'I didn't get the chance.'

'Why not? What happened? Tell me everything,' I demand.

'Well. She wouldn't buzz me up . . . she came down instead . . . We talked in your lobby . . . She made it pretty clear how she felt about me.'

'And how was that?' I say.

'That she hated me,' he says. 'Then she told me you were in a relationship . . . that you were very happy. She told me to leave you alone — that you wanted *nothing* to do with me. Something like that . . . '

I try to process his words as he continues, asking, 'So were you . . . in a relationship?'

'Starting one,' I say.

'With Andy?'

'Yeah.' I shake my head, anger welling up inside me. Anger left over from last night. Anger at the timing. Anger at myself for feeling so fragile, exposed. And most of all, anger toward Margot for not telling me such an important fact. Even after all these years.

'I can't believe she never said anything,' I say, tears stinging my eyes, wondering why he didn't call or e-mail. How could he have relied on Margot?

'Yeah,' he says. 'Although . . . I know it wouldn't have made a difference.'

Silence fills the airwaves once again, as I consider how to respond. I know what I *should* say. I should say that he's right — it wouldn't have made a difference. I should tell him that he was too late, and I would have made the same decision that Margot made for me. I should tell him that she was acting in my best interest. That Andy's *still* in my best interest.

But I can't make myself say any of this. I can't get over the feeling of being cheated. At the most, I was cheated out of the choice for a different life — a choice I had the right to make

302

and that nobody else should have made for me. At the very least, I was cheated out of the all-important closure — knowledge that would have made me feel better about the worst thing to ever happen to me short of my mother dying, as well as the chance to reconcile my feelings for Leo with the way things ended between us. Yes, we broke up. Yes, *Leo* did the breaking up. But he regretted it. He loved me enough to come back. I was worth coming back for. It might not have made a difference in my life, but it would have made a difference in my heart. I close my eyes, riding a wave of resentment and indignation and more anger still.

'Anyway,' Leo says, sounding slightly uneasy as he struggles to change the subject, return to the present.

'Anyway,' I echo.

Then, just as I hear the sound of the garage door opening and Andy returning from wherever he was, I cave to what I've wanted to do all along. 'So,' I say. 'Tell me about this assignment.'

'You're coming?' Leo asks, his voice brightening.

'Yeah,' I say. 'I'm coming.'

27

Over the next few minutes, I listen as Leo gives me a rundown of the assignment — a feature on Coney Island — praying that Andy doesn't burst in the room and catch me, breathless, cheeks ablaze. At some point, I will have to tell him that I'm going to New York — but I can't make this assignment about our fight. It's *not* about the fight.

'I'll just need a few general shots of the beach . . . the boardwalk . . . the rides . . . ' he says.

'Oh, sure,' I say distractedly. I am not ready to hang up — not by a long shot — but don't want to press my luck.

'Not quite as glamorous as the last shoot, huh?' Leo says, as if I'm doing this shoot for the glam factor.

'That's okay,' I say, flustered as I scramble for a few more details. 'What publication is it for?'

'*Time Out.*'

I nod and say, 'When do you need the shots?'

'In the next couple weeks. That doable?'

'Should be,' I say, trying to play it cool, pretend that I'm not reeling from my discovery that he came back. 'I want to hear more about it . . . but — '

'You gotta go?' Leo asks, sounding satisfyingly disappointed.

'Yeah,' I say — and then spell it out for him. 'Andy's home . . . '

'Gotcha,' Leo says in a way that seems to solidify our status as co-conspirators. Unlike the Drake shoot we are in this one together. From start to finish.

'So I'll get back to you . . . ' My voice trails off.

'When?' he says, and although his tone isn't eager, the question certainly is.

I smile in spite of myself, remembering how I used to try to pin him down in this same vein, always wanting to know when we'd next talk, next see each other. So I shoot back with one of his old-school, tongue-in-cheek answers. 'As soon as humanly possible,' I say, wondering whether he remembers his line — and if he uses it with what's-her-name.

Leo laughs, sounding *so* good. He remembers, all right. He remembers everything, just as I do.

'Great,' he says. 'I'll be waiting.'

'Okay,' I say, a shiver running down my spine as I think of how long I waited for him, how long it took for me to finally give up.

'So . . . 'Bye, Ellen,' Leo says, the smile back in his voice. ' 'Bye for now.'

' 'Bye, Leo,' I say, snapping my phone shut and taking a few deep breaths to compose myself. Then I erase the call log and head into the bathroom. *This is about work*, I think, as I look in the mirror. *This is about finding my own happiness.*

I brush my teeth, throw cold water on my face, and change into a fresh T-shirt and a pair of white shorts. Then I head downstairs, bracing myself to see Andy and realizing that although

I'm still holding on to residual anger from this morning, my conversation with Leo has dampened my rage, replacing it with measured excitement and guilt-induced tolerance. Andy could be in the backyard playing croquet with Ginny, and I honestly think I'd be unfazed. I might even serve them up mint juleps.

But instead of Ginny, I discover Stella with Andy; instead of croquet, I spot a row of glossy Neiman Marcus shopping bags perched on the kitchen counter. As Andy unravels white tissue paper from a large sterling-silver frame, he shoots me a look that is either apologetic or simply imploring me to keep our marital tension under wraps — perhaps both. I give him an appeasing, borderline patronizing, smile, and then launch into good-daughter-in-law auto-pilot.

'Hi, Stella,' I say brightly, standing a bit straighter to emulate her perfect posture — just as I often find myself enunciating and speaking more slowly around her, too.

'Hi, sweetheart!' she says, hugging me hello.

I inhale her signature summer fragrance — a mix of orange blossom and sandalwood — as she continues, 'I hope you don't mind . . . I did a little frame shopping for you.'

I glance down at the counter and see at least a dozen more sterling-silver frames of varying sizes, all embellished, all formal, and undoubtedly, all very expensive.

'They're beautiful . . . But you shouldn't have,' I say, wishing she hadn't. Because although these *are* beautiful, they are also so *not*

306

my style. Our plain black, wooden frames are my style.

'Oh, it was nothing,' Stella says as she slides open a heavily beaded frame and inserts a family portrait from her childhood, everyone dressed in fine white linen, grinning broadly from aboard a dinghy in Charleston. The ultimate casually elegant, WASPy, summer snapshot. She blows a speck of dust from the glass and removes a smudge from one corner with her thumb. 'Just a little housewarming gift.'

'You've given us so much already,' I say, thinking of the grandfather clock, the linen hand towels for our powder room, the hand-me-down yet still pristine Italian porch furniture, the oil painting of Andy as a child — all purported housewarming gifts, all things I couldn't refuse, and all in keeping with Stella's benevolent passive aggression. She is so kind, so thoughtful, so generous, that you feel you must do things her way. So you do.

She waves me off and says, 'It's really nothing.'

'Well then, thank you,' I say tersely, thinking that it was Margot who taught me, by example, the rule of protesting once or twice, but ultimately never refusing gifts or compliments.

'You're very welcome, darling,' Stella says, obliviously patting my hand. Her fingernails are red-lacquered perfection, matching her pleated skirt and Ferragamo clutch, and giving the hulking sapphire bauble on her right ring finger a patriotic flair.

'So. Ell,' Andy says, looking anxious. 'What do you say we use these frames for our wedding and honeymoon photos? The ones in the foyer?'

Stella beams, looking at me for my lady-of-the-house stamp of approval.

'Sure,' I say, smiling and thinking that would be a very fitting choice — given that the wedding was done Stella's way, too.

Andy gathers up several frames and motions toward the front of the house. 'C'mon . . . Let's check 'em out.'

Wink, wink. Nudge, nudge.

While Stella hums and begins to neatly fold the shopping bags, I roll my eyes and follow Andy to the foyer on our purported frame-reconnaissance mission.

'I'm so sorry,' he starts in a whisper, leaning on the high-gloss mahogany table (yet another 'gift' from his parents), where our wedding photos are displayed. His expression and body language are sincere, even earnest, but I can't help wondering how much of his readiness to repent is tied into his mother's presence in our home. How the Grahams seem to do *everything* with one another in mind. 'I'm *really* sorry,' he says.

'Me, too,' I say, feeling at war with myself as I avoid his gaze. Part of me desperately wants to make up with Andy and feel close to him again, but another part almost *wants* to keep things broken so I can justify what I'm doing. *Whatever* it is that I'm doing.

I cross my arms tightly across my chest as he continues, 'I should have said something last night . . . about the wine comment . . . '

I finally look into his eyes, feeling slightly

308

defeated that he *actually* seems to believe that our fight was about a lackluster vineyard near Pittsburgh. Surely he can tell there is more happening here — issues much larger than last night. Like whether I'm happy in Atlanta, if we're as compatible as we once thought, and why our fledgling marriage feels so strained.

'It's okay,' I say, wondering if I'd be so conciliatory if I hadn't just spoken to Leo. 'I probably overreacted.'

Andy nods, as if in agreement, which bolsters my dwindling indignation enough for me to add a petty footnote. 'But I really, *really* can't stand Ginny and Craig.'

Andy sighs. 'I know . . . But they're going to be pretty hard to avoid . . . '

'Can we at least try?' I say, nearly smiling for real this time, as I drop my arms to my sides.

Andy laughs quietly. 'Sure,' he says. 'We'll try.'

I smile back at him as he says, 'And the next fight — let's make up before we go to sleep. My folks have never gone to bed mad at each other — probably why they've lasted so long . . . '

Another smug notch for the perfect Grahams, I think, as I say, 'Well, technically, I went to the *couch* mad.'

He smiles. 'Right. Let's not do that either.'

'Okay,' I say with a shrug.

'So we're good?' Andy says, the worry lines gone from his forehead.

I feel a stab of resentment at how easily he thinks we can move on, gloss over our troubles, my feelings. 'Yeah,' I say reluctantly. 'We're fine.'

'Just fine?' Andy presses.

I look into his eyes, and briefly consider spelling everything out for him. Telling him that we're in the midst of a small crisis. Telling him *everything*. In my heart, I know that is the only way to fix everything, make us whole again. But because I'm not quite ready to be whole again, I halfheartedly smile and say, 'Somewhere between fine and good.'

'Well, I guess that's a start,' Andy says, leaning down to give me a hug. 'I love you so much,' he breathes into my neck.

I close my eyes, relax, and hug him back, trying to forget about our fight, and all my complaints about our life, and most of all, how Margot might have doctored my past, with good intentions or otherwise.

'I love you, too,' I tell my husband, feeling a wave of both affection and attraction — and then relief that I still feel this way about him.

But in the instant before we separate, right there by our wedding photos and with my eyes still closed, all I see is Leo, standing in my lobby all those years ago. And now, sitting in his apartment in Queens, listening to Bob Dylan, and waiting for me to call him back.

28

Despite the near-constant urge to do so, I manage to go the rest of the weekend without calling or e-mailing or texting Leo. Instead I do all the right things — all the things I'm *supposed* to do. I reframe our wedding photos. I write Stella a cheerful, almost-completely-sincere thank-you note. I go to church and brunch with the entire Graham clan. I take nearly one hundred quality black-and-white photos of Webb and Margot and her belly. All the while, I squelch any uprising of anger, reassuring myself that I'm not taking the assignment out of spite or revenge or to revisit the past. Rather, I'm going to New York for the work — and to spend a little time with Leo. I have a perfect *right* to work — and to be friends with Leo. And neither of these things should, in any way, detract from my marriage or my friendship with Margot or my life in Atlanta.

So, by Sunday evening, as I hunker down at the computer to buy a nonrefundable airline ticket to New York, I am fully convinced that my intentions, if not entirely pure, are pure *enough*. Yet when I find Andy in the family room watching golf on television and casually mention that I have a shoot on Coney Island for *Time Out*, my heart fills with familiar guilt.

'That's great,' Andy says, his eyes glued to Tiger Woods.

'Yeah . . . So I think I'll fly up the week after

next . . . do the shoot . . . then stay for a night . . . maybe catch up with a few friends,' I say as if I'm thinking aloud. My heart pounds with worried anticipation. I cross my fingers, hoping that Andy won't ask too many questions, and that I won't have to lie about how I got the assignment.

But when he only says, 'Cool,' rather than inquiring about any specifics, I can't help feeling somewhat slighted, if not downright neglected. After all, we *constantly* discuss his cases, as well as the interpersonal dynamic in his office — interactions with his father, the secretaries, and the other junior associates. He routinely practices his opening and closing arguments in front of me. And, last week, I went to watch the climax of testimony in an insurance-recovery case, getting gussied up and sitting in the front of the courtroom to silently cheer him on as he led the purportedly very injured plaintiff, sporting a full-body cast, down a path of lies before showing video footage of the guy playing Frisbee in Piedmont Park. Afterward, we laughed in the car, high-fiving each other and gleefully repeating, 'You can't handle the truth!' — our favorite line from *A Few Good Men.*

And yet — *this* is the best I can get when my work is involved? One word of generic praise. *Cool?*

'Yeah,' I say, picturing working alongside Leo. 'It should be good.'

'Sounds good,' Andy says, frowning as Tiger attempts a long putt. The ball heads straight for the hole, drops in, but then pops back out. Andy slams his fist on the coffee table and shouts, 'Dammit! How does that not go in?'

'So, what, he's like *one* shot behind now?' I say.

'Yeah. And he *really* needed that one.' Andy shakes his head and bends the rim down on his green Masters cap, which he superstitiously wears to bring good luck to his idol.

'Tiger always wins,' I say as the camera zooms in on his doting, gorgeous wife.

I find myself wondering just how solid *their* marriage is as Andy says, 'Not *always*.'

'Sure seems like it. Give someone else a chance,' I say, and although I'm somewhat annoyed with Andy, I'm also disgusted with myself for trying to drum up a debate about something as uncontroversial as the universally adored Tiger.

'Yeah,' Andy says, as if barely hearing me. 'I guess so.'

I turn my head to look at him, studying the faint, sexy hair growth along his jaw, his ears that seem to jut out a bit when he wears a cap, and the soothing blue of his eyes — a dead match for the azure stripes in his polo. I sidle closer to him on the couch, so there is no space between us and our thighs are touching. I rest my head on his chest and intertwine our arms. Then I close my eyes and tell myself to stop being so irritable. It's not fair to put Andy on trial — particularly when he has no clue he's being judged. Several minutes pass and we stay in that cozy position, as I listen to the lulling sound of the commentators and the occasional ripple of

313

applause from the otherwise respectfully silent crowd and tell myself, over and over, that I am happy.

But, a few minutes later, when something else goes awry for Tiger, and Andy is up like a shot, waving his arms and talking to the television, offering more support than he has given me in weeks — 'C'mon, buddy. You *never* miss these when they matter!' — I can't help feeling a fresh wave of indignation.

No wonder we're having trouble, I think, now putting an official label on what seemed to be only a one-sided undercurrent before. My husband shows more passion for golf — even golf on *television* — than he does for our relationship.

I watch him for a few more minutes, stoically observing the domestic scene that single-handedly assuages any guilt I have for going to New York. Then I stand, head upstairs, find my cell phone, and call Leo.

He answers on the fourth ring, sounding slightly out of breath, as if he ran to get the phone.

'Don't tell me you changed your mind,' he says before I can say hello.

I smile and say, 'No way.'

'So you're coming?'

'I'm coming.'

'For sure?'

'Yes,' I say. 'For sure.'

'When?'

'Next Monday.'

'Cool,' Leo says — the exact same way Andy

314

ended our conversation downstairs.

I stare up at the ceiling, wondering how the very same word can sound so different coming from Leo. How different *everything* feels with Leo.

★ ★ ★

The next morning, I catch Suzanne on her morning commute to the airport, and fill her in on the latest chapter in the seemingly neverending Leo saga. When I come to the part about Margot, she is predictably outraged.

'Who does she think she is?' Suzanne demands.

I knew my sister's focus would be on Margot, and I feel simultaneously riled and defensive as I say, 'I know. She should have told me . . . But I really do believe she had my best interest at heart.'

'She had her *brother's* best interest at heart,' Suzanne says, sounding disgusted. 'Not yours.'

'They're one and the same,' I say, thinking that in the best relationships, both interests are perfectly, inextricably aligned. And, despite our problems, I like to think that Andy and I still have such a bond.

'They're *never* one and the same,' Suzanne says adamantly.

As I reheat my coffee for the second time, I consider this statement, wondering who is right. Am I being too idealistic — or is Suzanne just bitter?

'Besides,' Suzanne says, 'who is she to play God like that?'

'I would hardly call it 'playing God,' ' I say. 'This isn't euthanasia . . . She simply spared me — '

Suzanne cuts me off and says, 'Spared you? From what?'

'Spared me from Leo,' I say. 'From myself.'

'So you would have picked Leo?' she asks with a note of jubilance.

I feel a pang of frustration, wishing she could be more unbiased in moments like these. Wishing she could be more like our mother, whose first instinct was always to see the good in people, look on the bright side. Then again, maybe our mother's death has made Suzanne the way she is — why she always seems to look for the worst and never really believes that things will turn out well. I push these thoughts aside, realizing how often my mother's death complicates things that really have very little to do with her. How much she colors everything, even in her absence. *Especially* in her absence.

'I like to think I would have told him the same thing,' I say, struggling to be honest with my sister — and myself. 'But I don't know . . . I also might have . . . revisited my feelings enough to screw things up with Andy. I could have made a horrible mistake.'

'Are you sure it would have been a mistake?' she asks.

'Yes,' I say, as I think of an ancient journal entry I recently read — an entry that I had logged around the time Andy and I started to date, right when Leo came back. I hesitate and then tell Suzanne about it. 'I was so happy to be

316

in a healthy, stable, *even* relationship.'

'You wrote that?' she asks. 'You used those words?'

'More or less,' I say.

'Healthy and stable, huh? . . . That sounds . . . *pleasant*,' Suzanne says, clearly implying that pleasant isn't something to strive for in the hierarchy of relationships. That passionate is better than pleasant, every time.

'Pleasant is underrated,' I say, thinking that half of America would kill for pleasant. These days, I'd take pleasant.

'If you say so,' Suzanne says.

I sigh, and say, 'It's better than what I had with Leo.'

'And what was that?' Suzanne says.

'Turmoil,' I say. 'Worry . . . Insecurity . . . Everything felt so different with Leo.'

'Different how?' she asks automatically, relentlessly.

I open the back door and settle down on the top step of our back deck with my cup of coffee, struggling to answer her question. But every time I try to put it in words, I feel as if I'm selling Andy short, somehow implying a dichotomy of passion versus platonic love. And it really isn't that way. In fact, just last night, Andy and I had sex — *great sex* — which I initiated, not from a sense of guilt or obligation, but because he looked so irresistible in his boxer briefs, stretched out in bed next to me. I kissed him along his golfer's tan line, admiring his rippled stomach that looks like it should belong on a teenager. Andy kissed me back as I thought of

317

how so many women complain that their husbands skip the foreplay — and how Andy never forgets to kiss me.

'Ellen?' Suzanne rasps into the phone.

'I'm here,' I say, glaring across our hazy backyard. It is not yet nine o'clock, but already approaching one hundred degrees. Too hot for coffee. I take one sip and pour the rest of the mug into a bed of mulch.

'Different how?' Suzanne asks again — although I have a feeling she knows *exactly* how it's different — that *all* women know the difference between the one you marry and the one that got away.

'It's like . . . the mountains and the beach,' I finally say, grasping at straws for some sort of adequate analogy.

'Who's the beach?' Suzanne asks as I hear an airport trolley beeping its way through the terminal followed by a blaring gatechange announcement.

I have a sudden pang, wishing I were at the airport about to fly somewhere. *Anywhere.* For the first time, I feel a bit envious of Suzanne's job — her physical freedom, her constant motion. Maybe that's the appeal to her, too — why she sticks with a job she often describes as waitressing without tips.

'Andy is,' I say, looking up at the scorched white sky. It's almost as if the relentless heat wave has blanched it, stripping the blue away, leaving a colorless expanse of nothing. 'Andy's a sunny day with calm, turquoise waters and a glass of wine.' I smile, feeling momentarily buoyed by the thought of us lounging on a beach somewhere. Maybe a good vacation is all we

318

need. Maybe I need to get on a plane *with* Andy — rather than flying away from him. But deep down, I know a romantic boondoggle would not fix our problem — and that I might be screwed no matter what.

'And Leo?' Suzanne says.

'Leo.' His name rolls off my tongue as my heart beats faster. 'Leo's an uphill hike in the mountains. In a cold drizzle. When you're a little disoriented and hungry and nightfall's approaching.'

Suzanne and I laugh together.

'No contest,' she says. 'The beach wins.'

'Every time,' I say, sighing.

'So what's the problem?'

'The problem is . . . I like it out there in the middle of the woods. I like the dark . . . the quiet. It's mysterious . . . thrilling. And the view at the top, overlooking the evergreens, down into the valley . . . '

'Kicks *ass*,' Suzanne says, finishing my sentence.

'Yeah,' I say, shaking my head as I picture Leo's strong forearms and bulky shoulders. The way he looks in a pair of worn Levi's, walking slightly in front of me, always in control. 'It *really* does.'

'Well, then,' my sister says. 'Go ahead and enjoy the view . . . '

'You think?' I say, waiting for her to prescribe exact parameters — tell me what I can and can't do.

Instead she only says, 'Just don't get too close to the edge.'

I let out a nervous laugh, feeling more anxious than amused.

'Or you just might jump,' she says.

*   *   *

And yet, in the days leading up to my trip, despite Suzanne's advice and my vigilance to keep Leo at arm's length, I find myself standing *way* too close to the edge and getting sucked back into his orbit. Our formal e-mail exchanges graduate to a flurry of familiar — even flirty — banter, that in turn gives way to a steady stream of longer and increasingly more intimate texts, e-mails, and even phone calls. Until I'm full-blown obsessing, just like old times, all the while trying to convince myself that I'm *not* obsessing. That it's *not* like old times.

Then, suddenly, it's the morning before my trip — which also happens to be the day of Margot's baby shower, an event I was already dreading on some level, at least to the extent that Ginny had hijacked the planning, making it a formal, ostentatious affair rather than good, close friends celebrating a beloved soon-to-be-born baby. But now, more than ever, I view the party as something to endure, get over with, so that I can escape to New York, pick up where Leo and I left off on our red-eye flight, and get down to the heart of the matter — whatever that is.

I stretch out under the covers, having just kissed Andy good-bye and wished him a good golf game, when my cell phone rings on high, vibrating its way to the edge of the nightstand. I reach for it, hoping that it's Leo, hungry for my morning fix of him. Sure enough, his name lights up my screen.

'Hello,' I answer groggily, happily, my heart beating faster as I anticipate his first words.

'Hi,' Leo says with sleep still in his voice, too. 'You alone?'

'Yeah,' I say, wondering for the hundredth time whether he's still with his girlfriend. Based on his occasional abrupt hang-ups, I have the sense that he is, and although the jealous, possessive part of me wants him to be single, in some ways, I like that he's in a relationship, too. Somehow, she makes the playing field more even, gives him something to lose, too.

'What're you doing?' he asks.

'Just lying here in bed,' I say. 'Thinking.'

'About what?'

I hesitate before offering what feels to be a confession. 'About tomorrow,' I say, brimming with simultaneous elation and fear. 'About you.'

'What a coincidence,' he says, and although his words are coy, he is speaking very plainly, directly. 'I can't wait to see you.'

'Me either,' I say, tingling everywhere as I picture the two of us together on Coney Island, walking along the water, snapping photos in the golden, romantic hour before sunset, laughing and talking and just *being* together.

'So what do you wanna do?' Leo asks, sounding as giddy as I feel.

'Right now?' I say.

He laughs his low breathy laugh. 'No. Not *now*. Tomorrow. After the shoot.'

'Oh, I don't care. What are you thinking?' I say, instantly regretting my response, worrying that I sound too much like my former wishy-washy self — always letting him make the decisions.

'Can I take you to dinner?' he asks.

'Sure,' I say, yearning for tomorrow to come as quickly as possible. 'That sounds *really* nice.'

'You sound nice,' Leo says. 'I like your voice all scratchy like that. Brings back memories . . . '

I smile, rolling away from Andy's side of the bed, his scent still lingering on the sheets. Then I close my eyes and listen to the thrilling, intimate silence. At least a minute ticks by like that — maybe even longer — as I drift back to our shared past. A time before Andy. A time when I could feel the way I'm feeling, with no remorse, no guilt. Nothing but pure, in-the-moment pleasure. Until I finally give in to the welling inside me, the physical longing that has been building for the longest time.

Afterward, I tell myself that he doesn't know what I've just done — and that he certainly wasn't doing the same. I tell myself that I had to get it out of my system, and that we will be all business in the morning — or at most, just close friends with an incidental romantic past. And most of all, I tell myself that no matter what happens, I love Andy. I will *always* love Andy.

29

A few hours later, Margot's baby shower has concluded, her scores of guests have departed, and I am wandering around Ginny's regal, tasseled living room (complete with oil paintings of her dogs, a tapestry of Craig's family coat of arms, and a baby grand piano that nobody in the house knows how to play — or, for that matter, is allowed to touch), stuffing stray bits of ribbon and wrapping paper into a white Hefty garbage bag and feeling generally conflicted. Par for the course these days, and especially now, on the eve of my trip.

On the one hand, I'm consumed with giddy thoughts of Leo, mentally repacking my suitcase, picturing the moment when I first see him, and the moment we say good-bye again. On the other hand, and completely in spite of myself, I've had a surprisingly decent time — bordering on actual *fun*, thanks in part to the heavy flow of mimosas. I still maintain that the Buckhead social scene is, at its macro level, superficial and shallow and dull in the extreme, but one-on-one, most of the women at the party were genuine — and more interesting than you'd think they'd be when you see them yapping on their cell phones in their Range Rovers with their designer kids in the backseat.

Moreover, as I sat beside Margot on the couch with the honored role of gift stenographer, I felt a sense of belonging, of pride to be a Graham. Andy's wife. Margot's sister-in-law. Stella's daughter-in-law.

At one moment in particular, my emotional dilemma crystallized when one of Stella's neighbors asked me where my parents live, and I had to make that split-second decision of whether to specify that while my dad still lives in my hometown, my mother passed away years ago. Meanwhile, Stella, the queen of fast-thinking tact, subtly reached over and squeezed my hand, responding in a way that seemed utterly natural and not as if she were answering for me.

'Ellen's father lives in Pittsburgh — in the very house she grew up in. She and Margot have that in common!' she said cheerfully, as the light from Ginny's crystal chandelier glinted off her diamond ring. I gave her a grateful look, relieved that I didn't have to sell my mother's memory short in order to avoid that uneasy moment when my audience looks teary — and I have to choose between feeling sad right along with them or, alternatively, alleviating the discomfort with a nonchalant, 'Oh, it's okay. It happened a long time ago.'

Because after all, although it did happen a long time ago, it will never *really* feel okay.

And now, as I wait for Andy to pick me up after his thirty-six holes of golf, I feel another unexpected stab of motherless grief as I sit with Margot, Ginny, and *their* two mothers, indulging in more champagne and the usual party post-mortem, covering everything including the best present (a bright green Bugaboo stroller given by Margot's tennis friends), the most shameful regift (a Red Envelope quilt that, unbeknownst to the giver, was embroidered with her daughter's name, *Ruby*), the best-dressed guest (wearing vintage Chanel), the worst-dressed invitee (donning a crocheted magenta halter with a black bra), and aghast speculation about who-in-the-world spilled merlot on Ginny's dining-room chair.

'If only I had turned my nanny cam on,' Ginny says, giggling and stumbling in her heels before plopping down on a leopard-print occasional chair.

I smile, thinking how much more tolerable — verging on *likable* — Ginny is when she's drunk and not constantly posturing, angling, and trying to prove how much closer she is to Margot than I am. She's still a bitch with an amazing sense of entitlement, but at least she's a *lighthearted* bitch with an amazing sense of entitlement.

'Do you *really* have one of those?' Stella asks, peering up at the ceiling.

'It's called a *hidden* camera for a reason,' I quip, playing with a strand of yellow raffia. My frugal side is tempted to cart the whole garbage bag home, as Margot unwrapped her gifts so delicately — but given my state of emotional turmoil, it doesn't seem to make much sense to worry about salvaging wrapping paper.

'Of *course* she has a nanny cam, Stell,' Ginny's mother, Pam, says, pointing to an artificial floral arrangement atop a built-in bookcase, in what feels to be a subtle form of worldly goods one-upmanship. 'And Margot should have one installed, too . . . particularly with a newborn and the influx of baby nurses and other help.'

I inwardly cringe at the oft-used term *help* — covering everything from gardeners to nannies to housekeepers to pool guys to even, in Pam's case, *drivers* (she hasn't been behind the wheel on a highway in twenty-two years — a bizarre point of pride for her). In fact, whether griping or bragging about their *help*, it has to be my least favorite topic in Margot's world — right up there with their children's private schools and black-tie galas (which are often galas *for* their children's private schools).

Stella continues, 'Have you ever caught anyone doing . . . anything?' Her eyes widen, as I note that my mother-in-law, otherwise so in charge and dynamic, seems to become somewhat passive around her brash, bossy best friend. I watch them together, fleetingly wondering whether I'm also a different version of myself around Margot.

Ginny shakes her head, plucking a whimsical lavender petit four from an heirloom silver tray that, I feel quite sure, her *help* polished this morning. 'Not so far . . . But you can *never* be too careful when it comes to your children.'

We all silently nod, as if pausing to observe the profound wisdom of this latest nugget from Ginny — nuggets she always delivers in a revelatory tone, as if she's the first to ever say or think such a thing. My favorite, that I heard her pipe up with as guests speculated that Margot must be having a boy because she's carrying so low, is: 'I'm so glad she and Webb are waiting to find out! It's the *only* surprise left in life.' Ahh, you're *so* original, Ginny! Never heard that one before. And, as an aside, although I have no real opinion on what seems to be a highly charged, value-laden decision, how do so many couples figure that *not* availing oneself of ultrasound technology qualifies as a *surprise*? Furthermore, what other surprises have gone by the wayside over the last few decades? People don't throw surprise parties anymore? No more unexpected flower deliveries or gifts? I don't get it.

I finish my glass of champagne, turn to Ginny, and announce, 'Well. I think I know who spilled the wine.'

'Who?' everyone says at once, even Margot, who can usually tell when I have a joke queued up.

'That ugly *slob* of a girl,' I say, suppressing a smirk.

'Who?' they all say again as Ginny starts to guess, actually tossing out names of less attractive guests.

I shake my head and then proudly announce, 'Lucy,' referring to *Andy's* Lucy. His high-school-turned-freshmen-year-in-college sweetheart who Margot added to the invite list after asking for my permission.

'If you're at all uncomfortable with it, I won't do it,' Margot said more than once, always going on to explain her various charity fundraiser and country club connections — along with the unfortunate, albeit attenuated, familial overlap

(Lucy is married to Webb's second cousin).

I repeatedly reassured Margot that it was no big deal at *all*, and that I was actually quite curious to meet Andy's first love — and that I'd rather have the meeting under controlled circumstances, i.e., with makeup on. But secretly, I think my real motivation had more to do with Leo. After all, Lucy coming to the shower would serve as another golden rationalization in my battery of internal excuses: *Margot's ex does her landscaping; Andy's ex comes to his sister's baby shower. So why can't I occasionally work with mine?*

In any event, I am clearly joking now, as Lucy's a *far* cry from ugly. Her Kewpie-doll features, ivory skin, and ringlet red hair put her squarely in the pretty category, and her body's probably the best I've ever seen in person — a cartoonish hourglass that would have looked even more outrageous had she been dressed less conservatively. Margot and Stella laugh appreciatively — while their petty counterparts exchange a satisfied, raised-brow look, their cat-fight radars delightfully sounding.

I roll my eyes and say, 'C'mon. I'm *kidding*. The girl is gorgeous.'

Ginny looks disappointed that there is no controversy while Pam throws back her head with an annoying laugh-track giggle and says, *way* too enthusiastically, 'Isn't she *precious*?'

'She is indeed,' I say magnanimously as I think back to my conversation with Lucy earlier that afternoon — how sweet, almost nervous, she seemed when she told me how wonderful it was to meet me. I told her it was great meeting her too, actually meaning it. Then, despite a disturbing image of her nineteen-year-old-self straddling my husband, I added, 'I've heard such nice things about you.'

Lucy, who very well could have been envisioning the same thing, blushed, smiled, and laughed. She then referred to Andy — and their time together — in exactly the right vein, acknowledging that he had been her boyfriend, but making it more about the era — and generic young love — than *their* relationship.

'I just hope he threw away those prom pictures. Hideous, big hair. What was I thinking? . . . Did you have big, eighties hair, Ellen?'

'Did I have big hair?' I said. 'I'm from Pittsburgh — where *Flashdance* was filmed. I had big hair *and* legwarmers.'

She laughed, as we gingerly segued to the present, discussing her five-year-old son, Liam, his mild autism, and how horseback riding, of all things, has so helped him. Then we covered our move to Atlanta and my work (I was surprised to discover that Margot had told Lucy — and a lot of guests, for that matter — about my Drake shoot). And that was pretty much that — we both moved on to different conversations. Yet throughout the shower, I caught her giving me at least a dozen sideways glances — glances that indicated to me that she still might have some lingering feelings for Andy. Which, of course, ushered in all sorts of mixed feelings — guilt and gratitude topping the list.

I feel this combination of emotions again now

as Stella looks at me and says so sincerely, 'Lucy is a pretty girl, but you're *far* prettier, Ellen.'

'And way smarter,' Margot says, adjusting the tie on her pale yellow wrap dress.

'Andy's so blessed to have you,' Stella adds.

As I open my mouth to thank them, Ginny interrupts what she must perceive to be a feel-good family moment and says, 'Where are those guys anyway? It's almost three . . . Craig promised he'd baby-sit this afternoon while I sleep off this champagne.'

I reach for my purse, thinking that when fathers spend time with their own children, it should not be called *baby-sitting*.

'Maybe Andy called,' I say, pulling out my cell at the very second that Leo's name lights up my screen. My stomach drops with excitement, and although I know I should put the phone right back in my bag, I stand and hear myself say, 'Excuse me for a sec. This is about my shoot tomorrow.'

Everyone nods their understanding as I scurry to the kitchen — already spotless thanks to Ginny's diligent caterers and invisible house-keeper — and answer a hushed hello.

'You still coming tomorrow?' Leo says.

'C'mon,' I whisper as I feel another jolt of adrenaline.

'Just checking,' he says.

A ripple of high-pitched laughter emanates from the living room, prompting Leo to ask, 'Where are you?'

'At a baby shower,' I murmur.

'Are you pregnant?' he deadpans.

'Yeah, right,' I say, feeling relieved that that's not a possibility — and then guilt for feeling such intense relief.

'So. About tomorrow. Do you wanna just come directly to my place? And we'll go from there?'

'Sure,' I whisper. 'That'll work.'

'Okay then . . . I guess I'll let you go,' Leo says, although I can tell he wants to keep talking.

'Okay,' I say, just as reluctantly.

'See you tomorrow, Ellen.'

'See you tomorrow, Leo,' I say, feeling flirty and fluttery as I snap my phone shut, turn around, and find Margot staring at me. My silly grin evaporates almost instantly.

'Who're you talking to?' she asks, her eyes blazing with bewildered accusation.

'It was about the shoot,' I say, floundering as I silently replay the conversation, wondering exactly what she heard.

She obviously heard me say Leo's name — as well as my tone of voice — because she says, 'How can you do this?'

'Do what?' I mumble, my face growing hot.

Margot's brow furrows and her lips become a thin line. 'You're going to New York to see him, aren't you?'

'I'm . . . going to New York for *work*,' I say — which clearly isn't a denial.

'For *work*? Really, Ellen?' she says, and I can't tell if she's more hurt or angry.

'Yes. It *is* for work,' I say, nodding adamantly, clinging to this last shred of truth. 'It's a *legitimate* photo shoot on Coney Island.'

'Yeah. I know, I know. Coney Island. Right,' she says, shaking her head, as I think back to the few questions she asked about the shoot — and the cursory answers I gave her before changing the subject to safer waters. 'But it's with *him*? You're going to see him, aren't you?'

I slowly nod, hoping for her mercy, some understanding — just as I've tried to give her, about her decision, years ago.

'Does Andy know?' she asks. It is the same question she posed in the airport; only this time, I can tell she is at her absolute tipping point.

I look at her, but say nothing — which is, of course, a resounding *no*.

'Why, Ellen? Why are you doing this?' she says.

'I . . . I have to,' I say apologetically but resolutely.

'You *have* to?' she says, perching one hand on her stomach as she slides her Lanvin ballet flats together. Even in a crisis, she looks graceful, poised.

'Margot,' I say. 'Please try to understand — '

'No. No, Ellen,' she says interrupting me. 'I *don't* understand . . . I don't understand why you'd do something so immature . . . and hurtful . . . and destructive . . . Taking the Drake assignment was one thing, but *this* . . . This is too much.'

'It's not like that,' I say, floundering.

'I heard you, Ellen. I heard your voice — the way you were talking to him . . . I can't believe this . . . You're ruining *everything*.'

And as she rests her other hand on her stomach, I know she means *everything*. Her

332

shower. The friendship. My marriage. Our family. *Everything*.

'I'm sorry,' I say.

And although I *am* sorry, I can feel my shame shifting into self-righteousness as it occurs to me that we might not be having this conversation had she been straight with me years ago. Had she remembered that we were friends *first* — before I was ever with Andy. My mind races as I consider whether to tell her that I know what she did — whether there is any downside. I allude to it, saying, 'I just need . . . to sort some things out that needed to be sorted out a long time ago . . . '

Clearly not getting the hint, she shakes her head and says, 'No. There's absolutely *no* excuse in the world for this — '

'Really?' I say, interrupting her. 'Well, what's *your* excuse, Margot?'

'Excuse for what?' She looks at me, confused, as I wonder if she forgot about his visit, or otherwise revised history, editing his return right out of her memory.

'For never telling me that he came back,' I say. My voice is calm, but my heart is pounding.

Margot blinks, looking momentarily startled before quickly gathering herself. 'You were with Andy,' she says. 'You were in a *relationship* with Andy.'

'So what?' I say.

'So *what?*' she says, horrified. 'So *what?*'

'I don't mean 'so what' that I was with Andy . . . I mean . . . what makes you think your telling me about Leo would have threatened anything?'

333

She crosses her arms and laughs. 'Well. I think we have our answer right here.'

I stare into her eyes, refusing to mix the two issues. 'You should have told me,' I say, spitting the words out. 'I had a *right* to know. I had a right to make that choice for myself . . . And if you thought my leaving Andy was even a *possibility* . . . well, all the more reason that you should have told me.'

Margot shakes her head, in perfect, outright denial, as I realize that I've never heard her say that she's sorry — or that she was wrong. About anything, to anyone. Ever.

'Well, Andy has a right to know *this*,' she says, ignoring my point altogether. 'He has a right to know what his wife is doing.'

Then she straightens her back, raises her chin, and says in a steely, cold, spitfire voice, 'And if you don't tell him, Ellen . . . then *I* will.'

30

A few seconds later, Craig, Webb, Andy, and James burst in from the side door, looking sweaty, sunned, and satisfied. I inhale sharply, struggling to regain my composure as I watch Margot do the same. For one beat, I worry that she might make an unprecedented scene and divulge everything right there on the spot. But, if nothing else, she would never embarrass her brother like that. Instead, she practically runs to Webb, resting her head on his chest as if seeking refuge in her own flawless relationship.

I watch the two of them together, marveling that I felt the same way about Andy — that he was my bedrock — only a few short months ago. Now I stand several paces away from him, feeling utterly alone, separate.

'Who won?' Margot asks as she casts Andy a furtive glance, seemingly hoping that he did. If his wife is going to betray him, at least he can have a good day on the golf course.

Sure enough, Andy flashes a cute, cocky smile, winks, and says, 'Who do you think won, Mags?'

'Dude is so lucky,' James says, as Ginny, Stella, and Pam join us in the kitchen, looking delighted to be back in the company of their men.

'Andy won!' Margot announces with artificial cheer as the guys regale us with their golf tales, including a guess-you-had-to-be-there moment when Craig, in a fit of frustration, whacked a magnolia tree with his brand-new driver. More than once. Everyone laughs, except for Margot and me, while Craig makes a proud point of telling us all just how expensive that driver was. Meanwhile, he retrieves four Heinekens from the refrigerator, opening them so rapid fire that he reminds me of a bartender during happy hour — a job I feel pretty sure he never held. He doles them out to Andy, Webb, and James, sucking his own down and, between gulps, wiping the bottle against his forehead.

'So how was the shower?' Andy asks, seemingly the only man in the room — including the father-to-be — who remembers that the real point of the day wasn't golf. I add a few points to his good husband tally, despite the fact that I know he shouldn't be under heightened scrutiny.

Margot cocks her head, smiles a subdued smile, and says, 'It was great.'

'It was so lovely,' Stella and Pam chime in, using the exact same inflection. They exchange a fond, girlfriendy look that makes me long for that dynamic with Margot — and worry that we might never get it back.

'Did you get some good loot?' James asks Margot, in a fake New York accent, rotating his visor a half-turn to achieve his favorite gangsta look.

Margot forces another smile and says yes, she received some gorgeous presents, while Ginny, unable to contain her glee, blurts, 'And Ellen got to meet Lucy!'

My stomach churns as I think of how much *more* gleeful Ginny will be when Margot

336

confides in her the full irony of the situation.

'Is that right?' Andy says, raising his eyebrows in an interested way that would, under any other circumstances, send me into a tailspin of jealousy and insecurity.

'So what'd you think?' James asks me with his trademark smirk, likely homing in on a golden opportunity to break his mother's prim protocol.

'She was very nice,' I say quietly, as James, true to form, mumbles something about her 'nice tubes.'

'James!' Stella gasps.

'You even know what tubes are, Mom?' James says, grinning.

'I have an idea,' Stella says, shaking her head.

Meanwhile, Andy pretends to ignore the sideshow, kindly doing his best to appear bored with the subject of Lucy — which only serves to bring Margot's outrage to a fresh boil.

'Well,' she finally says, clearly unable to stand being near me another second. 'I'm exhausted.' She looks up at Webb and says, 'We probably should go before my Braxton Hicks start up again . . . '

Webb massages her neck and says, 'Sure thing. Let's get you home, sweetie.'

'Yeah,' Andy says, yawning and then taking a long drink of beer. 'We better hit it, too. Ellen has a big day tomorrow. She's going to New York for a big shoot.'

'I've heard,' Margot says. Her expression is blank and her voice is drained of any emotion — but it is still perfectly obvious, at least to me, that she is upset about something more than potential contractions. I watch her, desperate to

337

make final eye contact, although I'm not sure what I wish to communicate. An appeal for mercy? A final explanation? An outright apology? When she finally glances over at me, I give her a plaintive look that covers all of the above. She shakes her head in refusal, looks down at Ginny's stone floor, and moves her lips almost imperceptibly, as if formulating what she's going to say to her brother in his hour of need.

★ ★ ★

That evening, after Andy and I return home, we are the portrait of a normal couple sharing a Sunday evening, at least on the surface. We make a chopped salad to go with our pepperoni pizza from Mellow Mushroom. We watch television, passing the remote control back and forth. I help him gather our garbage for pickup in the morning. He sits with me while I pay the bills. We get ready for bed together. Inside, though, I am a total wreck, replaying my conversation with Margot, jumping whenever the phone rings, and desperately trying to recruit the words — and the strength — to make my confession.

Then, finally, Andy and I are in bed with the lights off, and I know it is my absolute last chance to say something. *Anything.* Before Margot says it for me.

A hundred different openers flash through my mind as Andy leans over to kiss me goodnight. I kiss him back, lingering for a few seconds, longer than normal, feeling both nervous and profoundly sad.

'It was great meeting Lucy today,' I say when we finally separate, cringing at how lame I am for trying to drum up the can-you-be-friends-with-exes discussion.

'Yeah. She's a nice girl,' Andy says. He sighs and adds, 'Too bad she married an ass.'

'Her husband's an ass?'

'Yeah . . . Apparently he missed his own son's birth.'

'Well. I can see how that could happen. Did he have a good reason?' I say, hoping that my forgiving mood will be contagious.

'I know it *could* happen,' Andy says. 'If the baby came early or something . . . But he went on a business trip on his kid's due date . . . And then surprise, surprise, couldn't get back in time.'

'Who told you that?'

'Luce.'

In spite of everything, I flinch at the abbreviated pet form of her name. Andy must hear it, too, because he clears his throat quickly and corrects himself, saying, 'Lucy told me.'

'When?' I ask, shamelessly angling for shared culpability. 'I thought you guys didn't talk anymore?'

'We don't,' he quickly replies. 'She told me a long time ago.'

'Her son's five. We've been together longer than five years.'

'He's almost six,' Andy says, adjusting the covers around him.

'You have his birthday memorized?' I shoot back, only half kidding.

'Easy, Inspector Gadget,' Andy says, laughing.

'You know Lucy and I haven't talked in years. It was just one of those final, post-relationship talks where you check on each other and — '

'And confide how miserable your current relationship is? How your husband can't hold a candle to your first love?'

Andy laughs. 'No. She actually didn't seem to think that her husband missing the birth was that big of a deal. It was sort of an incidental part of her story . . . She was always one of those girls who seemed to care more about babies than husbands.'

'So did she call you? . . . Or did you call her?' I ask, feeling increasingly queasy.

'Jeez, Ell. I honestly don't remember . . . We didn't talk for long . . . I think we both wanted to make sure the other was okay . . . That there were no hard feelings.'

'And were there? Hard feelings?' I say, thinking that Leo and I never had such a conversation. We never had any closure, unless you count out red-eye flight — which obviously didn't do the trick.

'No,' he says, and then sits up and gently asks, 'Where are you going with this?'

'Nowhere,' I say. 'I'm just . . . I just want you to know that it'd be okay with me if you did talk to her . . . if you want to be friends with her.'

'C'mon, Ell. You know I have no desire to be friends with Lucy.'

'Why not?'

'I just don't,' he says. 'For one, I don't have any friends who are girls. And for another . . . I don't even *know* her anymore.'

I consider this statement, realizing that despite my bad breakup with Leo, and despite the fact that we didn't talk for years, I *never* had this feeling about him. I might not have known details of his day-to-day life, but I never felt like I stopped knowing *him*.

'That's sad,' I muse, although suddenly I'm not sure which scenario is sadder. Then, for the first time ever, I find myself wondering what it would be like if Andy and I ever went our separate ways — which breakup camp we'd fall into. I push the thought aside, telling myself it could never happen. Or could it?

'What's so sad about it?' Andy asks nonchalantly.

'Oh, I don't know . . . ' I say, my voice trailing off.

Andy rolls over to face me as my eyes make another incremental adjustment to the dark.

'What's on your mind, Ell?' he says. 'Are you upset about Lucy?'

'No,' I say quickly. 'Not at all. I *really* enjoyed meeting her.'

'All right,' he says. 'Good.'

I close my eyes, knowing I've come to my moment of truth. I clear my throat, lick my lips, and stall for a few final seconds.

'Andy,' I finally say, my voice starting to shake. 'I have to tell you something.'

'What?' he says softly.

I take a deep breath and exhale. 'It's about the shoot tomorrow.'

'What about it?' he asks, reaching out to touch my arm.

'The shoot . . . is with Leo,' I say, feeling both

341

relieved and nauseous.

'Leo?' he says. 'Your ex-boyfriend?'

I make myself say yes.

'What do you mean it's *with* Leo?' Andy says.

'He's writing the piece,' I say, delicately choosing my words. 'And I'm taking the photos.'

'Okay,' he says, switching on his bedside lamp and gazing directly into my eyes. He looks so calm and trusting that for the first time, I actually consider canceling my trip. 'But how? . . . How did this come about?'

'I ran into him in New York,' I say, knowing that I'm confessing way too little, way too late. 'And he offered me an assignment . . . '

'When?' Andy asks. He is clearly trying hard to give me the benefit of the doubt, but I can tell he's slipping into his deposing-attorney mode. 'When did you run into him?'

'A few months ago . . . It was no big deal . . . '

'Then why didn't you tell me?' he asks, a logical question and the clear crux of the matter. After all, it clearly *was* a big deal — and how all of this started back on that wintry day in the intersection when I returned home and decided to keep that very first secret from my husband. For a second, I wonder if I would go back and do things differently.

I hesitate and then say, 'I didn't want to upset you.'

This *is* the truth — the cowardly truth, but the truth nonetheless.

'Well, not telling me makes it a big deal,' Andy says, his eyes wide and wounded.

'I know,' I say. 'I'm sorry . . . But I . . . I really

want the work . . . this kind of work,' I say, struggling to put the best possible spin on things. In my heart, I truly believe that part of the reason I am going *is* for the work. That I need more in my life than simply sitting around a big, beautiful house and waiting for my husband to come home. That I want to be doing my own thing again. Feeling a small boost, and a measure of hope that he might actually understand, I add, 'I really miss it. I *really* miss New York.'

Andy pulls on his ear, his face clearing for a second as he says, 'We can go back and visit . . . Go to dinner and a show . . . '

'I don't miss it like that . . . I miss *working* in the city. Being a part of it . . . the energy.'

'So go work there,' he says.

'That's what I'm doing.'

'But why does it have to be with Leo? You suddenly can't work without Leo? You shoot Drake Watters for the cover of *Platform*, but now you need your ex-boyfriend to help you get work?' Andy asks, sounding so succinct in the trap he's just set for me that for a second, I think that he must have noticed Leo's byline after all. Or perhaps Margot already told him about that piece. Even Andy never gets this lucky on cross-examination.

'Well. Actually,' I say, glancing down at my day-old manicure before returning his probing gaze. 'He got me *that* assignment, too.'

'Wait. What?' Andy says, the first real traces of anger on his face as he begins to put it all together. 'What do you mean? How did he get you that shoot?'

I brace myself for the worst as I say, 'He wrote the article . . . He called my agent about that assignment.'

'Was he in L.A.?' Andy asks, his voice growing progressively louder, more distressed. 'Did you see him?'

I nod, struggling to mitigate my admission. 'But I swear I never knew he was going to be there . . . We didn't hang out . . . or go to dinner . . . or anything . . . I was with Suzanne the whole time. It was all . . . Strictly business.'

'And now?' he says, asking an open-ended question that fills me with trepidation.

'And now . . . we have another shoot,' I say.

'So what? Y'all are going to be some kind of team?' he asks as he bolts out of bed, crosses his arms, and glares at me.

'No,' I say, shaking my head. 'It's not like that.'

'So explain. What *is* it like?' he asks, his chest puffing with a surge of testosterone.

'We're friends,' I say. 'Who work together . . . occasionally. Twice. Not even occasionally.'

'Well, I don't know if I'm comfortable with that.'

'Why not?' I say, as if there is any doubt why not.

'Because . . . Because I've never heard one good thing about the guy . . . and now you want to rekindle a friendship with him?'

'Margot's not fair to him,' I say. 'She never has been.'

'You told me awful things about him, too.'

'I was hurt.'

'Yeah,' Andy says, rolling his eyes. 'By *him*.'

344

'He's a good person,' I say.

'He's a jerk.'

'He's not a jerk . . . And I care about him . . . He's . . . '

'What?'

'He's . . . *important* to me.'

'Well, that's just great, Ellen. That's great,' Andy says, his voice drenched in sarcasm. 'Your ex-boyfriend is important to you. Just what every husband wants to hear.'

'Lucy came to your sister's shower,' I say, circling back to my starting point. 'And Ty does your sister's yard.'

'Yeah,' he says, pacing at the foot of the bed. 'But she got that invite, and he does the yard, precisely *because* they're *not* important. They're just people from our past that we used to date. That's it . . . It doesn't seem that you can say the same about Leo.'

I can tell that he's asking a question, that he's desperate for me to jump in and change my answer — disclaim any feelings for Leo.

But I can't. I just can't lie to Andy on top of everything else.

So instead I say, 'Don't you trust me?' Asking the question makes me feel instantly better — makes me, somehow, trust myself.

'I always *have*,' Andy says, clearly implying that that's no longer the case.

'I'd never cheat on you,' I say, instantly regretting my verbal promise, knowing it should be an unspoken given. Something you don't *have* to say.

Sure enough, Andy says, 'Well, gee, Ellen.

That's really something. Thank you. We'll be sure to include that on your ballot for Wife of the Year.'

'Andy,' I plead.

'No. Seriously. Thank you. Thank you for promising not to cheat on me with your important ex-boyfriend for whom you care *so* deeply,' Andy says, as I realize I've never seen him so angry.

I take a deep breath, desperately shifting into last resort, offensive mode. 'Okay. I won't go. I'll cancel the trip and stay here and take some more snapshots of Margot's belly and . . . and lemonade stands while you . . . play golf all day.'

'What's that supposed to mean?' Andy says, squinting with confusion.

'It means your life is grand. And mine sucks.' I hate the bitter sound in my voice — and yet it captures *exactly* how I feel. I *am* bitter.

'Okay. So let me get this straight,' Andy shouts. 'You're flying up to New York to hang out with your ex-boyfriend because I like to golf? Are you trying to get back at me for golfing?'

'Stop oversimplifying everything,' I say, while I'm actually thinking, *Stop being so simple.*

'Well, you suddenly seem to be telling me that this is my fault.'

'It's not your fault, Andy . . . It's nobody's fault.'

'It's *somebody's* fault,' he says.

'I . . . I'm not happy here,' I say, my eyes filling. I hold them open, willing myself not to cry.

'Here? Here where?' Andy demands. 'In this

346

marriage? In Atlanta?'

'In Atlanta. In *your* hometown . . . I'm so tired of pretending . . . '

'Pretending what, exactly?' Andy says. 'Pretending that you want to be with me?'

'Pretending to be someone I'm not.'

'Who's asking you to do that?' he says, unfazed by my emotion — which has the odd effect of making my tears spill over. 'When have I ever asked you to be someone you're not?'

'I don't fit in here,' I say, wiping my face with the edge of our sheet. 'Can't you see that?'

'You act like I made you move here,' Andy says, his face twisted in frustration, 'when you told me it was what you wanted.'

'I wanted to make you happy.'

Andy laughs a sad, defeated laugh and shakes his head. 'Clearly. That's your mission in life, Ellen. To make *me* happy.'

'I'm sorry,' I say. 'But I have to do this.'

He watches my face, as if waiting for something more — a better explanation, a more thorough apology, reassurance that he is the only one for me. But when I can't find the right words — or *any* words — he looks down at the rug and says, 'Why do you *have* to do this?'

When he finally looks up at me, I say, 'I don't know.'

'You don't *know*?'

'I feel like I don't know anything anymore . . . '

'Well, Ellen,' he says, as he hurriedly puts on his jeans and shoes and scoops his keys and wallet off the nightstand. 'I guess that makes two of us.'

'Where are you going?' I ask through more tears.

'Out,' he says, running his hand through his hair as if to comb it. 'I'm certainly not gonna sleep here tonight and kiss you good-bye in the morning like some kind of stupid chump.'

I look at him, overcome with heartbreak and desperation as I babble, 'Andy . . . please try to understand. It's not you . . . It's me . . . I just . . . need to do this. Please.'

He ignores me and walks toward the door.

I get out of bed and follow him, my throat constricting as I say, 'Can't we talk about it more? . . . I thought we said we wouldn't go to bed mad?'

Andy turns and looks at me, then right through me. 'Yeah,' he says sadly. 'Well, we said a lot of things, Ellen . . . didn't we?'

31

In a moment more surreal than sad, I stand at our bedroom window, watching Andy back slowly and deliberately down the driveway, then use his turn signal as he makes his way onto the main drag of our neighborhood. I can almost hear the sound of it — *blinka, blinka, blinka* — in the quiet of his still new-smelling car, and persuade myself that a man who bothers with his turn signal isn't *that* angry. I'm not sure whether this is a comfort or convoluted evidence that we aren't meant to be together. That Suzanne's implication is right — we are short on passion, and merely have a caring, pleasant union that isn't even all that pleasant anymore.

I turn away from the window, telling myself that I'm not looking for proof of any kind, one way or the other. Maybe I'm in denial, but I just want to get on a plane in the morning, and go to New York, and do my job, and see Leo, and try to feel better about everything — the past, my marriage, my friendship with Margot, my work, myself. I'm not sure exactly how that's going to happen, but I know it won't happen if I stay here, in this house.

I switch Andy's lamp off again, and get back in bed, feeling as if I *should* cry, but realizing with a mix of fear and relief that all my emotions are dulled and watered-down versions of what I felt just minutes before when Andy was in the room with me. In fact, I'm so composed and detached that it's almost as if I'm watching the aftermath of another couple's big fight, merely waiting to find out what will happen next: *Will she stay or will she go?*

I close my eyes, exhausted and quite certain that I could fall asleep with just a little effort. But I don't let myself try; I have at least *some* right on my side, and sleeping might eviscerate it, turn me into the callous wife who gets a good night's rest while her devastated husband is driving in circles through the empty streets.

So instead of sleeping, I try Andy's cell, fully expecting to get his cheerful voicemail with that familiar, errant taxi honking in the background. *Don't ever change that outgoing message,* I recently told him, unsure whether I wished to preserve his happy voice or the New York background noise. In either case, he doesn't answer now — or any of the three times I hit redial. Clearly, Andy does not want to talk to me, and because I have no idea what to say to him, I don't leave a message. I decide against calling Margot's house, where I am pretty sure he'll end up eventually. Let them gang up on me. Let them invite Stella over, open a good bottle of wine, and simmer in their superiority. Let them do their thing while I do mine. I stare into the dark, feeling lonesome and yet so glad to be alone.

Some time later, I restlessly head downstairs where everything is dark and tidy, just the way Andy and I left it when we went to bed. I make a beeline for the liquor cabinet, where I pour vodka, straight up, into a small juice glass.

Drinking alone feels like a depressing cliché, and I desperately don't want to be a cliché. And yet, vodka is exactly what I want in this moment, and *what Ellen wants* feels like the emerging theme of the evening. Or so I'm sure my husband would say.

I stand in the middle of the kitchen, suddenly craving fresh air, too, so I head for the back door, noticing that Andy reset the security alarm as he departed; he might hate me, but he still wants me to be safe. At least that's something, I think, as I sit on the top step, which has become my favorite spot in Atlanta, sipping vodka and listening to crickets and thick, muggy silence.

Long after I've downed my drink, called Andy's cell one final time, gone back inside, relocked the back door, and placed my glass in the sink, I find his note. I don't know how I missed it before, as it is in the middle of the counter, written on a yellow Post-it note — the kind we usually reserve for notes of a very different kind. For 'I love you' and 'Have a nice day,' or 'Need razor refills.' My stomach drops as I hold the square pad up, under the stove light, reading Andy's block letters:

IF YOU GO, DON'T COME BACK.

I peel the note from the pad and consider *not* what I should do in the morning, but simply what to do with the note itself. Do I write a response on the blank lines underneath his instruction? Leave it on the counter in a crumpled ball? Toss it into the garbage? Press it into my journal as a sad memento of a sad time? None of the choices seem quite right — so I simply place it back on the pad, carefully aligning the edges to create the appearance that it was never disturbed, never read. I look at it one more time, feeling a sharp pang of remorse and regret that we have become the kind of couple who not only fights in the middle of the night but leaves ultimatums on Post-it notes in the kitchen.

We might even become the Buckhead couple that people talk about over a cocktail at the club. *Did you hear about Ellen and Andy? Did you hear what she did? How he laid down the law?*

I can just hear the Ginnys of the world: *And then what happened?*

She left.

Then he left her.

I stand at the counter for a long time, flashing back to the distant past and then the recent past, and a few snapshots in between, wondering if I believe Andy's words. I decide that I do. He might change his mind, but for right now, he means it.

And yet, instead of striking fear in my heart, or giving me pause of any kind, I feel all the more calm, resolute, indignant, as I head back upstairs and get back under the covers. How dare he draw a line in the sand? How dare he not even try to understand what I'm feeling? How dare he back me into a corner with his demands? I try to turn the tables, imagining Andy, homesick, wishing to reconnect with something or someone. And then I realize that that is why I moved to Atlanta. With him. For him. That is why I'm here now.

I fall asleep, dreaming random, banal vignettes about getting the easy chair in our bedroom slip-covered, and spilling sweet tea on my keyboard, and assembling a last-minute, makeshift gypsy costume for a neighborhood Halloween party. Dreams that, even under heavy scrutiny, make no sense at all given that I am at a crossroads, in a crisis.

When I wake up for good, it is four-fifty-nine, one minute before my alarm is set to go off. I arise, shower, dress, and go through all the matter-of-fact motions of a normal travel day. I gather my camera equipment, reorganize my suitcase, print my boarding pass, even check the weather in New York. Mid-sixties and scattered showers. Oddly enough, I can't conjure what mid-sixties feels like, perhaps because I've been hot for so long, so I focus on the rain, packing my umbrella and a black trench coat.

All the while, I think of Andy's note, telling myself I can always back out at the last minute. When the sun rises, I can decide to stay. I can ride the MARTA train to the airport, weave my way through security, meander the whole way to my gate, and still come home.

But deep down, I know that's not going to happen. I know that I will be long gone when Andy returns home to find his note, undisturbed on our marble counter.

★　★　★

Five blurry hours later, I find myself in the cab line at LaGuardia, the sounds, smells, sights all so achingly familiar. *Home*, I think. *I am home.* More than Pittsburgh, more than Atlanta, more than anywhere. This city, this very cab line, feels like coming home.

'Where are you headed?' a young girl behind me asks, interrupting my solitude. With ripped jeans, a ponytail, and an oversized backpack, she looks like a student. I imagine that she is near broke, and hoping to split cab fare into the city.

I clear my throat, realizing that I have not yet spoken today. 'Queens,' I say, hoping she's Manhattan bound. I am not in the mood for conversation, but don't have the heart to turn her down.

'Oh, drats,' she says. 'I was hoping we could share a cab . . . I was going to take the bus, but I'm kinda in a hurry.'

'Where are you going?' I ask, not because I really want to know, but because I can tell she's dying for me to ask. I bet a boy's involved. A boy is *always* involved.

Sure enough, she says, 'To see my boyfriend. He lives in Tribeca.'

She says *Tribeca* proudly, as if the word has only rolled off her tongue a few times before now. Perhaps she just learned that it stands for *Triangle Below Canal Street*. I remember when I learned that tidbit — just as I remember mispronouncing Houston Street, saying it like the city in Texas, and how Margot corrected me, admitting that she made the same mistake just the day before.

'Hmm,' I murmur. 'Great area.'

'Yuh,' she says, as I detect a Minnesotan or Canadian accent. 'He just found this *awesome* loft.' She flaunts the word *loft* as I'm sure he did to impress her. I wonder if she's seen this 'awesome' space yet, imagining it to be cramped and gray — yet *still* somehow wonderful.

I smile, nod. 'And where do *you* live?'

She pulls a wrinkled jean jacket out of her roller bag, as I think denim on denim — *not good*. She buttons it almost to the top, making the look even worse, and says, 'Toronto . . . My boyfriend's an artist.'

It is a glorious non sequitur once again proving her love, proving that everything comes back to him.

Dangerous, I think, but smile again and say, 'That's great,' wondering how they met, how long they've been together, whether she'll move to New York to be with him. How their story will end. *If* it will end.

The line snakes forward, bringing me inches closer to Leo.

'So . . . are you coming home?' she asks.

I give her a puzzled look until she clarifies, 'Do you live in Queens?'

'Oh . . . no,' I say. 'I'm meeting someone there . . . for work.'

'You're a photographer?' she asks.

For a second, I am amazed by her intuition, but then remember my bags, my equipment.

'I am,' I say, feeling more and more like myself by the minute.

I am a photographer. I am in New York. I am going to see Leo.

355

She smiles and says, 'That's cool.'

Suddenly reaching the front of the line, I tell my new, nameless friend good-bye.

'Good-bye,' she says, so happily. She waves — which is an odd gesture when you're standing so close to someone.

'Good luck,' I tell her.

She says thanks, but gives me an inquisitive look, likely wondering what luck has to do with anything. I want to tell her *a lot*. It has a lot to do with everything. Instead, I give her a smile, then turn to hand my bags to the cabbie.

'Where to?' he asks as we both climb in the car.

I give him the long ago memorized address, nervously checking my makeup in my compact mirror. I am wearing only mascara and lip gloss, and resist the temptation to add more, just as I made myself stick with a ponytail and a simple outfit of jeans, a white button-down shirt rolled at the sleeves, and black flats. This trip might be about more than work, but at least I have *dressed* the part.

I nervously pull my phone out of my bag just as Leo texts me: *You here yet?*

My heart pounds as I envision him freshly showered, checking his watch, waiting for me.

I send back: *In a cab. See you in a few.*

An instant later, he texts a lone smiley face, which puts me at ease, but also surprises me. Leo has never been an emoticon type of guy, unless you count his occasional colon-dash-slash face:-/ that he sometimes tacked onto the end of his e-mails, mocking my slightly asymmetrical lips — something Andy has never noticed, or, at least, has never pointed out.

I smile back at my phone, in spite of my mood — which isn't bad, but is by no means smiley. Then I slip my earphones on, turn on my iPod, and listen to Ryan Adams singing 'La Cienega Just Smiled,' one of my favorite songs that can make me feel either *really* happy or *really* sad, depending. Right now, I am both, and as I listen to the words, I marvel at how closely aligned the two emotions are.

I hold you close in the back of my mind,
Feels so good but, damn, it makes me hurt.

I jack up the volume as I hear my mother saying, 'You'll go deaf, Ellie.' Then I close my eyes, thinking of Leo, then Andy, then Leo again. *After all*, I think, *isn't it always about a boy?*

32

As we turn onto Newton Avenue, I can't decide whether it seems like only yesterday or a lifetime ago that I was last here, dropping Leo off after our return from California, sure that we had come to the end. I fleetingly revisit the emotions of that morning — how chokingly sad I was — wondering if I *truly* believed that I'd never see him again. I also wonder what, exactly, brought me back here, to this moment. Was it the move to Atlanta and all that came with it? My discovery about that distant December day when he tried to come back? Or was it simply Leo's inexplicable, inexorable pull on my heart? We stop at the curb in front of his place, and I pay my fare, hoping for some answers today. I need to find some answers.

'Receipt?' my cabbie asks as he pops the trunk and steps out of the cab.

'No, thanks,' I say, even though I know I should keep track of my expenses — that doing so would make my trip more of a legitimate business venture.

As I slide out of the taxi, I catch my first glimpse of Leo, leaning on the railing on his porch. He is barefoot, wearing jeans and a charcoal gray fleece, squinting up at the sky as if checking for rain. My heart skips a beat, but I calm myself by looking away, focusing only on the transaction of bags from the trunk to the sidewalk. I can't believe that I'm actually here, not even when I muster the courage to meet Leo's gaze. He raises one arm and smiles, looking perfectly at ease.

'Hi,' I say, my voice getting lost in a sudden gust of wind and the loud slam of the trunk. I hold my breath as my taxi vanishes from sight. My visit is now official.

Seconds later, Leo appears beside me.

'You made it,' he says, seemingly acknowledging that it took a lot more than merely getting on a plane to arrive here. *He is right about this*, I think, picturing the note on the counter, and Andy finding it still there this morning — and his wife gone.

'Yeah,' I say, feeling a wave of guilt. 'I made it.'

Leo looks down at my bags and says, 'Here. Let me get these for you.'

'Thanks,' I say and then fill the ensuing awkward silence with, 'Don't worry . . . I'm not staying here. I got a hotel.' Which, of course, makes everything all the more awkward.

'I wasn't worried about *that*,' Leo says, as if he *was* worried — but about something else altogether.

I watch him lift my suitcase with his right hand, despite the rolling option, while swinging my camera bag over his other shoulder. I suppress a feeling of longing as I follow Leo up the stairs to his front porch, then into his apartment where I inhale coffee and his familiar, old-house smell. I glance around his living room, overcome by an avalanche of memories, mostly good. Sensory overload, I think, feeling weak, nostalgic, twenty-three again.

'Well?' Leo says. 'What do you think?'

I'm not sure what he's asking so I keep it safe and focus on anything other than the past. 'You got new furniture,' I say admiringly.

'Yeah,' he says, pointing to a black-and-blue abstract painting and a cinnamon-colored, distressed-leather couch below it. 'I've made a few changes here and there . . . That okay with you?' He gives me a lighthearted look.

'Sure,' I say, trying to relax, trying not to look in the direction of his bedroom, trying not to remember quite so much. At least not all at once.

'Good,' he says, feigning relief. 'You get married and move to Georgia . . . I'm at least allowed to get a new couch.'

I smile. 'Well, I think you've done a bit more than that,' I say, referring to his work mostly, but also to Carol. I glance around again, looking for signs of cohabitation. There are none whatsoever. No feminine touches, no photos of Carol. No photos at all, in fact.

'Looking for something?' he asks teasingly, as if he knows exactly what I'm doing, thinking.

'Yeah,' I shoot back. 'What'd you do with my photo?'

He shakes his index finger at me, then takes two steps toward an old, banged-up hutch, pulls open a drawer and rifles through it. 'You mean . . . this one?' he says, holding up the front-toothless shot of me.

'Shut up,' I say, blushing.

He shrugs, looking both smug and sheepish.

'I can't believe you still have that,' I say, feeling way more delighted than I should.

'It's a good shot,' he says, as he props the photo up on a shelf, meant for china, but covered with newspapers. As before, everything about Leo's place is pared-down minimalism, except for all the paper. Books and newspapers and magazines and notepads are strewn and stacked literally everywhere — on the floor, coffee table, chairs, shelves.

'So,' he says, turning and heading for his kitchen, the only completely unchanged room in view, including a 1970s-green linoleum floor. 'Are you hungry? Can I make you something?'

'No, thanks,' I say, thinking that even if I were, I could never eat right now.

'Coffee?' he asks, as he refills his own mug. A *peach* mug. *A-ha*, I think. *Carol.*

'Sure,' I say. 'Just . . . half a cup.'

'Half a cup?' he says, pushing his sleeves up. 'Who are you? My grandma?'

'*Aw*,' I say fondly, remembering his feisty grandmother. I only met her once — at a birthday party for his nephew — but she was the kind of vivid, eccentric older woman who says exactly what's on her mind and can get away with it only because of her age.

'How *is* your grandma?' I ask, realizing we didn't talk much about our families on that red-eye flight.

'Still kicking . . . Still bowling, in fact,' he says, pulling a non-matching, white mug down for me. Something is written on the side of it, but I can't read it from where I'm standing.

361

'That's awesome,' I say. My mother flits into my head, as she always does when I hear about elderly relatives alive and well, but I refuse to let her fully form in my already crowded mind.

'So really?' Leo asks. 'Just half a cup, Gram?'

I smile and say, 'All right, fine. I'll have a full cup . . . I just think — '

'What?'

'That we should get going . . . '

'Are we in a hurry?'

'It might rain.'

'So?'

'I have to take photos,' I say emphatically.

'I know that,' he says just as emphatically.

'*Well*,' I say, as if I've already made my point and what's wrong with him for not grasping it.

'You can't shoot in the rain?'

'Of course I can.'

'Well?' he says, imitating my inflection.

We are now in full banter mode — which is a scary place when you are determined *not* to do something you might regret.

'I'm just saying . . . ' I say, my favorite junior-high retort, good for almost any uncomfortable situation.

'Well, *I'm* just saying that rainy Coney Island shots wouldn't be so bad . . . would they?'.

'Guess not,' I say, thinking that they might actually be better in the rain. That spending time with Leo might be *really* nice in the rain, too.

'So sit down,' Leo says, interrupting my meandering thoughts. He points to his couch, looks into my eyes, and says, 'Stay a while.'

I hold his gaze, both fearing and hoping what *a while* might bring. Then I turn to sit on the far end of the couch, propping my elbow on the armrest, waiting for my coffee, for him. I watch him fill my mug, saving only enough room for a dash of milk and two teaspoons of sugar. 'Light and sweet, right?' he asks.

'What makes you think I still like my coffee that way?' I say, giving him a coy smile.

'Oh, I *know*,' Leo says in a deadpan that still manages to come across as flirtatious.

'How do you know?' I ask, flirting right back.

'You had it that way at the diner,' he says, handing me my cup and sitting on just the right spot on the couch — close, but not too close. 'Back in January.'

'You noticed my coffee?' I say.

'I noticed *everything*,' he says.

'Like?' I press, that familiar Leo-induced, dizziness sweeping over me.

'Like . . . the blue sweater you were wearing . . . Like the way you cocked your head to the side when I walked in . . . Like your expression when you told me you were married — '

'And what was that?' I interrupt, wishing he'd stop using the word *married*.

'You know the expression.'

'Tell me.'

'The *I-hate-you* expression.'

'I never hated you.'

'Liar.'

'Okay,' I say. 'I kinda hated you.'

'I know you did.'

'And now?' I say, daring myself to look into his

brown eyes. 'Do I have the same look now?'

Leo squints, as if searching for an answer on my face. Then he says, 'Nope. It's gone. That look has been gone since . . . since our flight from L.A. when I saved you from that dirty old man.'

I laugh and pretend to shudder. 'He was gross.'

'Yes. He was. Thank goodness . . . Otherwise you might not have been so happy to see me.'

I shake my head, not in a contradictory way, but in a way that says, *No comment — at least none that I can share.*

'What?' he asks.

'Nothing,' I say. Ten minutes into my 'work' trip — and I am already drifting into decidedly dangerous territory.

'Tell me,' he says.

'You tell *me*,' I say, taking my first sip of coffee. It is a little too hot — but otherwise perfect.

'Well . . . Let's see . . . What can I tell you? . . . ' Leo looks up at the ceiling as I take in his clean shave, crisp sideburns, olive skin. 'I can tell you that I'm happy you came . . . I'm happy to see you . . . I'm *very* happy to see you.'

'I'm very happy to see you, too,' I say, overcome with sudden shyness.

'Well, good,' Leo says, nodding, sipping his coffee, then kicking his legs up onto the coffee table. 'We got that goin' for us, huh?'

'Yes,' I say as we both stare down at the floor. 'We do.'

Seconds later, our eyes lock again, our smiles

fade, and although I don't know how, I am quite sure his heart is pounding as hard as mine. I think of Andy, realizing that my guilt is starting to recede, which in turn fills me with fresh guilt, especially when Leo clears his throat and says my husband's name aloud.

'Does Andy know you're here?' he asks.

It is a simple question, but undercut with bold recognition that I might be here for a little more than a photo shoot.

'Yes,' I say, realizing that my answer clarifies nothing. My *yes* could mean that I view the trip as purely professional, therefore telling my husband only about the work. Or it could mean that I confessed *everything*. Or it could mean that I told him only enough to result in a big fight and a Post-it note ultimatum.

'And? . . . Was he okay with it?' Leo asks, looking concerned.

I look down at my coffee and shake my head, hoping that that says enough.

It must, because Leo simply says, 'I'm sorry.'

I nod my thanks, realizing that so much of our interaction is — and has always been — about subtext, what's happening beneath our surface.

'So . . . what about your girlfriend?' I ask, turning the tables.

He shakes his head, slices his hand through the air, and makes a clicking noise. 'That's done,' he says.

'You broke up?'

'Yup.' He nods.

'When?' I ask — but what I really want to know is, *Why? Who did it?*

'A few weeks ago,' he says vaguely.

'Do you . . . want to talk about it?'

'Do *you* want to talk about it?' he says.

'If you do,' I say tentatively.

Leo shrugs, and then starts speaking in choppy, matter-of-fact sentences. 'I told her I was talking to you again. She overreacted. I told her it wasn't like that. That you're married. She said what *is* it like, then? I said it wasn't anything, but she accused me of still having feelings for you.' He looks over at me, as I drop my gaze from his eyes to chin, then up to his lips.

'And?' I say.

'And.' Leo shrugs again. 'I couldn't tell her what she wanted to hear. So she took off.'

I imagine that stark, sickening conversation, my heart filling with empathy for a woman I've never met. 'You just . . . let her leave?' I say, in awe of his honesty — which can also come across as cruelty. One of the best — and worst — things about him.

Leo slowly nods. Then he puts his coffee down, shifts his body to face me, and says, 'Yeah. Well. The problem is . . . she was right. I *do* have feelings for you, Ellie.'

I swallow hard, my heart now in my throat, my ears, on the coffee table, as I replay his words and against my better judgment ask, 'What kind of feelings?'

'Feelings I should have sorted out a long time ago,' he says, meeting my eyes for a second and then staring across the room. 'Feelings that resurfaced when I saw you again . . . Feelings I shouldn't have for . . . a married woman.'

There it is again. *Married*.

I open my mouth, but can't find any words of my own. At least not words that I can say aloud.

'So,' Leo says, letting me off the hook. He rubs his hands together, then folds them, blowing across his knuckles before throwing out one of those profound, yet meaningless sentences he's so fond of. 'It is what it is.'

I nod my safe agreement.

'I mean . . . what're ya gonna do, right?' Leo asks.

It is a rhetorical question, but I answer it anyway, treading carefully. 'I don't know,' I say, shaking my head.

Leo gives me a raised-brow look, as if he understands exactly how I feel, *exactly* what I'm trying to say — and that, if nothing else, at least we're in this thing together.

33

An hour of safe conversation and two cups of coffee later, Leo and I are aboard a virtually empty N train, making our way to the southernmost tip of Brooklyn. We are pretending to be in work mode, but our undercurrent remains, and if anything, is growing stronger the more we *don't* talk about it.

As I count the number of stops on the subway map to Stillwell Avenue, estimating that we have at least an hour left on the train, Leo leans down to double knot the laces of his black tennis shoes. When he sits back up, he gives me an incredulous look and says, 'So really? You've *never* been to Coney Island?'

I shake my head. 'No . . . I feel like I have, though. I guess from movies and photographs.'

Leo nods and says, 'That's how I feel about a lot of places.'

'Like where?' I ask, ever curious about *all* of Leo's thoughts and feelings — no matter how trivial, how unrelated to us.

'Like . . . Stonehenge,' he says. 'I mean, who needs to go there once you've seen a few photos? Big rocks in an open field. I get it.'

I laugh at his random example, and then say, 'Tell me about your article. Did you write it yet?'

'Yeah. Mostly,' he says. 'Still needs to be fine-tuned.'

'What's it about, exactly?'

'Well . . . I guess you could say it's about the conflict between the old and new Coney Island. The inevitable changes on the horizon.'

I give him an inquisitive look, realizing that for someone who has tried to convince everyone, including myself, that this trip is about work, I know almost nothing about the piece I'm shooting for. Or about Coney Island, for that matter.

'What changes?' I ask.

Leo unzips his messenger bag and pulls a Coney Island flyer from it, pointing to an aerial photograph of the beach. 'In a nutshell, a major developer bought ten acres of the amusement district, and plans to give it a two-billion-dollar makeover — rezone it, put in high-rise hotels, condos, the whole nine yards . . . Some say it's exactly what Coney Island needs. You know, revitalize a neighborhood in decay . . . restore its old glory.'

'And others?'

'Others take a more nostalgic view. They worry that new construction will displace the locals, obscure the classic views, kill the mom-and-pop shops and rides, and basically undermine the kitschy, old-time character of the so-called Nickel Empire.'

'Nickel Empire?' I ask, as our train slows to a stop at Queensboro Plaza. The doors open, letting in a handful of passengers, all of whom glance our way, but choose another bench.

'Way back in the day, the subway ride to get to Coney Island was a nickel. The rides were a nickel. Nathan's hot dogs were a nickel

369

. . . Coney Island actually started out as a resort for the wealthy, but quickly evolved into a working-class playground, where you only needed a nickel to escape, let loose, forget your troubles,' Leo explains as we career forward, under the East River, toward Fiftyninth and Lex. 'And I think, in many ways, Coney Island still has that feel.'

'Did you interview a lot of people?' I ask.

He nods and says, 'Yeah. I spent a few days there, hanging out on the beach, wandering around Astroland, and all over Mermaid Avenue, talking to the locals . . . the 'old salts' as they call themselves. Heard so many great coming-of-age stories about the boardwalk, and all the old games and rides.' He smiles and says, '*Everyone* has a story about the Cyclone.'

'Is that the roller coaster?'

'Yeah.'

'Did you ride it?'

'Yeah . . . as a kid,' he says. 'And lemme tell you . . . that thing kicks your *ass*. Seventy-some years old, made of wood and it's no joke . . . I actually had a great conversation with the Cyclone manager — tattooed old guy who has run the ride for over thirty years but has *never* been on it.'

'Come on,' I say. 'Really?'

Leo nods.

'Is he afraid of heights?'

'Nah. Says he's climbed the thing plenty of times . . . he just has no desire to feel the plunge.'

I smile, thinking about how many times Leo

has given me that stomach-dropping feeling.

'So anyway . . . Coney Island's at a cross-roads,' Leo says, looking grave. 'The old versus the new.'

'And what camp are you in?' I ask. 'Old or new?'

Leo ponders my question for a few seconds and then gives me a knowing 'look I don't know. Change can be good . . . sometimes,' he says cryptically. 'But it's always tough to let go of the past.'

I'm not sure *exactly* what he means, but I still murmur my agreement as our subway car sways along the tracks, and we fall into another long stretch of very loud silence.

★   ★   ★

The afternoon is bleak and somehow seasonless when we emerge from underground, spilling onto Stillwell Avenue. Steel gray clouds hover low in the sky, promising a downfall soon. It is not exactly cold, but I still cinch the belt of my trench coat and cross my arms tight across my chest as I look around, memorizing my first glimpse of this famed sliver of New York. Of Americana. It is exactly how I pictured it would look during the off-season — dingy, faded, desolate — but still magical, *special*. The stuff of great photographs. The backdrop of indelible memories.

'So here we are,' Leo says, looking stoic.

'Yes,' I say.

'To the water first?' Leo asks.

I nod, as we stride, side by side, toward the boardwalk. Once there, we find a bench and sit, gazing toward the wide stretch of muted sand and dark, colorless surf. I shiver from the slight chill in the air, the stark view, and most of all, from Leo beside me.

'Beautiful,' I finally say, catching my breath.

Leo's face glows — as if he himself were an 'old salt' with his own tales to tell. I suddenly imagine him on this very beach as a child, in the height of summer, with his shovel and pail. Then again, as a teenager, sharing blue cotton candy with a pig-tailed girl, and carefully aiming a rifle with hopes of winning her a stuffed unicorn.

He cocks his head and says, 'Really?'

I nod and say, 'Yes. It has . . . so much character.'

'I'm glad you think so,' he says, running his hand through his hair. 'I'm *really* glad you think so.'

We stay that way for a long time — slightly reclined on our bench, taking in the scenery, watching the few souls out on such a questionable day — until at some point, I wordlessly pull my camera out of my bag, slide between the bars separating the boardwalk and sand, and head for the ocean. I snap a few dozen aimless mood shots, feeling myself relax, as I always do when I start to work. I photograph sky and sand and ocean. I photograph a middle-aged, long-haired woman in a brown tweed coat, deciding that she doesn't look quite shabby enough to be a bag lady, but is definitely down on her luck, sad about something. I turn and snap the storefronts along the boardwalk, most closed, some boarded up altogether, and a cluster of seagulls, circling a red-and-white-striped bag of popcorn, searching for remaining kernels. Then, on a final whim, I photograph Leo, still leaning back on our bench, his hands clasped behind his head, elbows out, watching and waiting.

He gives me a little wave and a twinkling, self-deprecating smile as I approach him. 'That last one's a keeper,' he says, as I recall my Central Park bench shots of him, how Margot had viewed them with disdain, calling him smug and affected. I think back to that day, realizing that she was wrong about that moment, captured on film. She was wrong about a lot.

I sling my camera over my shoulder and sit back down, letting out a sigh that sounds wearier than I intended.

Leo gives me a pretend-stern look as he elbows me and says, 'Remember what I told you, Dempsey? People come here to *forget* their troubles.'

Dempsey, I think, as my left thumb reaches over to stroke my wedding band. I force a smile, and say, 'Right,' as we watch the waves break, again and again. After a few minutes, I ask Leo if the tide's coming in or out.

'In,' he replies so quickly that I'm impressed, the same way I'm impressed when people — typically men — instinctively know that they are driving, say, northwest.

'How can you tell?' I ask, thinking that we haven't been watching long enough to observe a trend.

'No wet sand,' Leo says as thunder rumbles in the distance. 'If it were going out, there'd be a band of wet sand.'

'Oh. Sure,' I say, nodding. And then, 'You know what?'

'What?' Leo says, his face alert, expectant — as if he's ready for a big confession, or maybe something profound.

I smile and say, 'I'm *starving*.'

'Me, too,' he says, grinning. 'Wanna get a hot dog?'

'This *is* the birthplace of the hot dog, right?' I say, recalling a scrap of Coney Island history that I picked up somewhere. Perhaps from Leo himself, a long time ago.

'True,' Leo says, smiling.

We stand and slowly retrace our steps to the corner of Stillwell and Surf, the site of the original Nathan's, which according to Leo, was built in 1916. We duck inside, finding a longer line than you'd expect at nearly two o'clock in the off-season, even for the most famous hot dog stand in the world. I snap a few photos of the restaurant, the other customers, and the sweaty men behind the grill while Leo asks what I want.

'A hot dog,' I say, giving him a *no-duh* look.

'Can you be more specific?' Leo asks, his smile broadening. 'A chili dog? Plain? With relish? Fries?'

'Whatever you're having,' I say, waving the details off.

'Cheddar dogs, fries, root beer,' Leo says decisively.

'Perfect,' I say, remembering how much he loves root beer.

Moments later, after Leo has paid and I've gathered napkins, straws, and packets of mustard and ketchup, we select a table by the front window just as the rain starts to fall.

'Perfect timing,' Leo says.

I look across the table at him, while suddenly picturing Andy at his desk, in his jacket and tie. I marvel at the contrast between the two worlds — a hot dog stand in Brooklyn and a shiny law office in Buckhead. I marvel even more at the contrast between the two men — the way each makes me feel.

'Not really,' I say, holding his gaze. 'Pretty shitty timing actually.'

Leo looks up from his crinkle-cut fries, surprised. Then he picks one up, points at me with it, and says, 'You.'

'No. *You*,' I say.

'You,' he says again, firmly.

It is the way we used to talk — our between-the-lines language, seemingly nonsensical, but steeped in meaning. It is a way I've never talked to Andy — who is always so open, candid. I decide, for at least the hundredth time today, that one way isn't *better* than the other; they are just *different*.

Leo and I finish our lunch in virtual silence. Then, without hesitation, we head back outside into a light, steady rain, wandering up and down Surf, Neptune, and Mermaid Avenues. Leo holds my umbrella over me as I take endless photos. Photos of shut-down games and rides. Of the famed Cyclone and the impossibly large, iconic Wonder Wheel. Of a three-on-three pickup

375

basketball game. Of litter-strewn, barren lots. Of the people — a butcher, a tailor, a baker.

'Like a nursery rhyme,' I say.

'Yeah. If only we could find a candlestick maker,' he says.

I laugh, as I notice two teenaged girls checking the prices on a tattoo-parlor window.

'Ohh. I love the orchid,' one says. 'That's *so* cool lookin'.'

'Yeah . . . But I like the butterfly better,' the other says. 'On my shoulder? But in purple?'

I snap their picture, thinking, *Don't do it. You'll be sorry someday.*

★　★　★

It is dusk on Coney Island, and I am finally satisfied, at least as far as photos go. The rain has cleared, along with all the clouds, promising a crisp, breezy autumn night. Leo and I return to our bench, damp, tired, and chilled. As we sit even closer than before, he casually drapes his arm around my shoulders in a gesture that feels equal parts comfortable and romantic. I fight the urge to rest my head on his shoulder, and close my eyes, realizing that this would be so much easier if I could more neatly categorize my feelings. If Leo was all one thing, and Andy another altogether. But it's not that simple or clear-cut — and I wonder if it ever is when it comes to matters of the heart.

'What are you thinking?' Leo says, his warm breath on my hair.

I cave to the truth. 'I'm thinking about that

day in December . . . when you came back,' I say softly.

Leo breathes again, this time near my neck, sending a cascade of goose bumps down my arms and legs.

'I wish I had known,' I say.

'I wish you had, too,' Leo says. 'I wish I had known that it might have made a difference.'

'It *would* have made a difference,' I finally confirm, feeling a wave of wistfulness and bitterness, guilt and longing.

'It could *still* be different,' Leo says, his hand on my chin, moving it to look into my eyes.

'Leo . . . I'm married . . . ' I say, gently pulling away, thinking of Andy, our vows. How much I love him, even though I don't love everything about our life. Even though I am here right now.

Leo's hand drops. 'I know that, but . . . '

'But what?' I ask, exhausted from so much subtlety, the endless speculating, interpreting, wondering.

'But I can't help . . . wanting to be with you again,' he says.

'Now? Tonight?' I ask, bewildered.

'Yes. Tonight,' Leo says. 'And tomorrow . . . And the day after that . . . '

I smell his skin and say his name, unsure of whether I'm protesting or giving in.

He shakes his head, puts his finger to my lips, and whispers, 'I love you, Ellie.'

It is a statement, but sounds more like a promise, and as my heart explodes, I can't help myself from closing my eyes and saying it back.

34

The rest of the world falls away as Leo and I whisper in a corner of a packed subway, zigzagging underground from Brooklyn through Manhattan and back to Queens again. Our journey feels fleeting in the way that a return trip almost always seems faster than the outbound — and it is made even faster by fear and yearning.

I know that what I'm doing is wrong, weak, indefensible, but I still stay on course, fueling my indignation with a steady diet of grievances: Andy doesn't understand my feelings. Even worse, he doesn't even *try* to understand my feelings. *He* left *me* last night. He hasn't called today or softened his stance at all. He's the one who drew the line in the sand. He's the one who seems to care more about his family, hometown, job, and everything *he* wants than me. But perhaps most simply, underwriting everything else, he is not Leo. He's not the one who has, since the day I met him, been able to turn me inside out and upside down like no other — for better or worse.

So here we are. Picking up just where we left off on that flight, our fingers interlacing expectantly. I'm not sure what will unfold from here, but I do know I am going to be honest with myself, with Andy, and with Leo. I am going to follow my heart, wherever it leads. I owe it to myself. I owe it to everyone.

When we reach Leo's stop, we stand in tandem and walk onto the cement platform I remember well. My pulse races, yet I feel strangely at peace. The night is beautiful and clear — the kind where you could see a million stars if you were anywhere other than a city — and as we descend the stairs, more memories of nights just like this one return to me. I can tell Leo is thinking of the past, too, as he takes my hand and exits the station with sexy purpose. Neither of us speaks until we make the turn onto his block and he asks if I'm cold.

'No,' I say, realizing that I am shaking — but not from the cold.

Leo glances my way, then takes my hand, just as my cell phone rings, muffled in my trench coat pocket, for the first time all day. We both pretend we don't hear it, walking more hurriedly, almost as if our pace can make the ringing go away. It finally does, but a few steps later, starts again, somehow sounding louder, more urgent. I let go of his hand, reaching into my pocket for the phone, both hoping and fearing that it is Andy.

If you go, don't come back, I hear him saying. I hold my breath and see Suzanne's name illuminated on my screen, feeling awash with simultaneous relief and disappointment. Leo looks away, says nothing, as I decide not to answer, and instead slide the phone back in my pocket, keeping my hand there, too.

By now, we are only a few steps from his front stairs, and a sudden surge of adrenaline and guilt halts me in my tracks. Leo stops with me, looks into my eyes, and says, 'What?'

I shrug and give him a slight smile, as if I have no answer. But what I am thinking is this: that I wish I could freeze this moment, somehow delay my final decision, and just hang here in the balance between two places, two worlds, two loves.

We walk up the steps, and I stand beside Leo as he unlocks the door. Once inside, the familiar smell of the past bombards me again. My stomach is in knots. It might as well be the night of the jury verdict, that first night we were together — the dizzy anticipation is the same, even without the drinks. Anything, everything, could happen. Something is going to. I put my camera equipment and purse down on the foyer floor, as Leo does the same with his messenger bag. We wordlessly make our way over to his couch, but don't sit. Instead, Leo tosses his keys onto the coffee table and reaches over to flick on a small lamp with an opaque red shade resting on an end table. Leo squints at his watch and says, 'Our reservation's in twenty-five minutes.'

'Where?' I ask, although it doesn't really matter.

'A little Italian spot. Not too far from here,' he says tentatively, almost nervously. 'But we'd have to hurry to make it . . . or I could call and make it a little later?'

For some reason, his nerves calm me, and as I slip off my coat, draping it over an arm of the couch, I boldly say what I can tell he wants me to say, 'I don't want to go anywhere.'

He says, 'Me either,' and then extends his hand, palm up, asking for mine. I give it to him and then fall into him, my arms encircling his waist. His shoulders, chest, arms — *everything* feels so warm, solid, strong — even better than I remembered. I close my eyes as our embrace tightens and we slowly start to sway to imaginary music — a bluesy, plaintive ballad, the kind that can make you cry unexpectedly, even when you're not in the mood to cry.

He whispers my name. I whisper his back, my eyes welling.

Then he says, 'I've chased you in my dreams for a long time now, Ellie.' Just like that. From anyone else, the words would sound contrived. But from Leo, they are an honest line from our own epic ballad, written from the heart.

Is this really happening? I wonder and then ask the question aloud.

Leo nods, whispers, 'Yes.'

I think of Andy — of *course* I think of Andy — but I still raise my head slowly, just as I feel Leo's lowering. Our faces tilt and meet, softly colliding. We are cheek to cheek, then nose to cheek, then nose to nose. I hold perfectly still, listening to the sound of him breathing, both of us breathing together. An eternity seems to pass before his bottom lip grazes my top one, and we make a slight, final adjustment, our mouths now squarely touching, our lips parting. Then, as we do the unthinkable, the inevitable, my mind goes blank, and everything and *everyone* outside this tiny apartment in Queens melts away altogether. And it is just the two of us holding on to something I can't quite name.

Until my phone rings again.

The sound of it startles me as much as an actual voice in the room. *Andy's* voice. But when I reach down into my coat pocket, I see Suzanne's name again, and a text marked urgent. For some reason, I panic, imagining that something happened to our father, so perfectly visualizing the words: *Dad died.* Instead, I read her bigsister command: *Call me now.* I scroll down, expecting something more, but that is all there is.

'Everything okay?' Leo says, glancing down at my phone and then quickly looking away, as if he knows that whatever is on my phone can't be his business. Not yet anyway.

I flip it closed and stammer, 'I . . . I don't know.'

'Andy?' Leo says.

I flinch, feeling a stab of guilt as I say, 'No. It's my sister. I think . . . I think maybe I should give her a call . . . I'm sorry . . . '

'No problem,' Leo says, rubbing his jaw as he backs up two steps. 'I'll be . . . around.' He points toward his bedroom, and then turns and walks down the hall. I fight the urge to follow him, wanting so badly to sit on his bed, watch him watching me.

I take a few deep breaths and drop to the couch, speed-dialing Suzanne's number, thinking that the moment might be interrupted, but the mood is not broken.

My sister answers on the first ring and says what I know she will open with. 'Where are you?'

'I'm in New York,' I say, feeling evasive in a way I wouldn't have felt just moments before kissing Leo.

'Where?'

'Queens,' I say guiltily.

'Ellen. *Where* are you?' she demands.

'I'm at Leo's apartment . . . We just got back from the shoot . . . Remember? On Coney Island?' I say, wondering why I'm not more direct with my sister — someone who has always been on my side. Even before there was a side to be on.

'What's going on?' she says, now clearly agitated.

'Nothing,' I say, but my delivery suggests more, and she picks up on it instantly.

'Did you kiss him?' she says, sounding blunt even for Suzanne.

I hesitate, letting her intuit my silence. She does, and then says, 'Did you . . . *sleep* with him?'

'No,' I say, probably not sounding properly offended, perhaps because the thought has crossed my mind more than once in the past few hours, minutes, seconds.

'But you kissed him?' she says.

'Yes,' I say — and something about the aloud affirmation makes everything real. My feelings for Leo. My disloyalty to Andy. My marriage hanging in the balance.

'You need to leave there,' she says, her voice filled with angst and urgency. 'Leave there right now.'

'Suzanne . . . *no*,' I say.

She makes a clicking noise and then says, 'You're going to be sorry.'

'Maybe not.'

'You will, Ellen . . . God, I don't want you to be sorry. I don't want you to have regrets.'

I am thinking that the only thing I regret at this second is that I called my sister back — or that I had my phone on in the first place, but I say, 'Andy and I got in a huge fight last night. Everything's a mess.'

'Okay. I certainly know how that goes,' she says, at least feigning patience, 'but you're . . . making it so much worse.'

This, I can't deny. Instead, I resort to a junior-high justification. '*He* left *me*,' I say. 'Last night. He probably went to his sister's — '

Suzanne interrupts. 'No. He didn't go to his sister's. He went to a hotel . . . and called *your* sister.'

I blink, then stare at the red lamp shade until I see spots on the white wall above it. 'He called you?' I finally say.

She says yes, this morning from the Ritz, and then again, about thirty minutes ago. Her voice trails off, as I imagine the rest of her sentence — *while you were kissing Leo.*

'What did he say?' I ask, feeling torn, numb.

'He's upset, Ell. He's scared, and he wants to talk to you.' There is the smallest trace of condemnation in her voice, but mostly just worry — and a little sadness, too.

'No, he doesn't. He hasn't called me. Not once.'

'Well, he's hurt, Ell . . . He's really hurt . . . and worried.'

'He told you that?'

'Yeah. More or less.'

'What did you tell him?' I ask, unsure of what I want her answer to be.

'I told him not to worry . . . That you went to New York for work — *not* for Leo — and that he needed to trust you.'

I look down at my shoes, still damp from the rain, wondering if this same result would have happened if Andy hadn't left, hadn't left the note on the counter. Was it a foregone conclusion? Or not?

'Okay,' Suzanne says. 'I'm not saying Andy's perfect. Far from it. And you know how I feel about Margot's self-centered, controlling bullshit. And, Jesus, I still can't believe she didn't tell you about Leo trying to see you . . . *But* . . . '

'But what?' I ask.

'But they're your family. And you're lucky to have . . . a family.'

I think of our father, how reabsorbed he is in Sharon's life, children. Then I think of Vince — how he refuses to commit to my sister and what a frustrating place that must be. And, of course, I think of our mother. I *always* think of our mother.

'You're my family, too,' I say, feeling guilty in a way I hadn't anticipated.

'I know,' she says. 'And you're mine. But, c'mon, Ell. You know what I mean . . . They're a *real* Norman Rockwell family. And they include you in *everything*. They count you as one of their own. You *are* one of them.'

I close my eyes, thinking of Mr. Graham's

toast to me on our wedding day, saying words to that effect. How Stella treats me like a daughter, and Margot treats me like her sister — even *before* I married Andy.

'Do you really want to give all that up?' Suzanne says, her voice maternal, soft, careful. 'Do you want to give Andy up?'

'I don't know,' I say, the reality of the situation sinking in, becoming stark, scary. And yet — I don't want to make decisions based on fear.

A minute of silence passes and then Suzanne says, 'Can I ask you a question?'

'Of course,' I say.

Suzanne pauses and then says, 'Do you love him?'

I'm not sure who she means — Andy or Leo — but either way, I tell her yes, I do.

'Then don't do this,' she says, obviously talking about Andy.

'Suzanne,' I say, glancing down the hall toward Leo. 'It's not that simple.'

'Yes, it is,' she says, cutting me off. 'See, that's the thing, Ell. It really *is* that simple.'

35

I hang up with Suzanne and put my head in my hands, overwhelmed by the enormity of the situation. I am way too confused to describe what I'm feeling to myself, let alone to Leo, who has just returned to the living room and is now standing over me. One thing is for sure, though — no matter what rationalization I might try to conjure in the moments ahead, there is simply no way to recover from my wake-up, gut-checking conversation with Suzanne. No way to pick up where Leo and I left off. The mood is broken, not to be salvaged. Leo obviously senses this as he sits beside me, appearing uneasy on his own couch.

'Are you okay?' he says, his forehead lined with concern, his hand reaching out to lightly touch my knee where it rests for one second before returning to his own lap.

'I don't know,' I say, grappling with Suzanne's straightforward, yet somehow still enigmatic advice. 'I don't know what I'm *doing*.'

Leo exhales into his cupped hands. 'This is really tough . . . I'm sorry.'

I look at him, interpreting his *sorry*, processing that it is not a contrite, forgiveness-seeking apology, but the sympathetic sort of *sorry* offered at the feet of misfortune, divorce, death. In other words, he knows our situation is dire — but does not regret our kiss or his own feelings. I'm not yet sure if I feel the same. It's way too soon to tell.

I nod a thank you, or at least an acknowledgment, as it occurs to me that Suzanne never really addressed Leo, or my feelings for him. I wonder why, as I blurt out a question that suddenly seems utterly beside the point. 'Do you think we would have lasted?'

Leo looks puzzled and possibly wistful, perhaps noticing my use of *would* rather than *will*. 'What do you mean?' he asks.

'You know . . . If we had gotten back together . . . would we have *stayed* together?'

'Forever?' he says, his tone answering the question for me. He does not believe in forever. He never has.

But I *do* — at least in theory. 'Yeah. Forever,' I say, thinking about marriage and kids, all the things I *still* want.

'Who knows?' Leo says with a faraway, philosophical look.

I think of our breakup, and then his most recent breakup, wondering if the scenarios were at all similar. I pose the question as casually as I can under the circumstances. 'Why did you and Carol call it quits?'

'I told you this morning,' he says.

'Not really,' I say, feeling nauseous.

He throws up one hand as if at a total loss, and I recall how he pretended to be at a loss about our breakup, too, when the subject came up at the diner in L.A.

'There were a lot of reasons,' he says, as I watch him start to shut down. His eyelids become heavy, his expression vacant.

'Like?'

'Like . . . I don't know . . . she was a great girl . . . But she just . . . wasn't the one,' he says.

'How do you know she wasn't the one?' I press, searching for my own answers. Some secret, mysterious litmus test for true love. A definition of soul mates.

'I just know,' he says, reaching up to touch a sideburn. 'You always know.'

'Is that why we broke up, too?' I ask, hearing a needy note in my voice.

Leo sighs and says, 'C'mon, Ellen.' He sounds weary and vaguely annoyed in a way that ushers in vivid memories — *bad* memories — of the past.

But I stay on course. 'Tell me,' I say. 'I need to understand.'

'Okay. Look. We've already been over all of this . . . I think our breakup was about timing more than anything else. We were too young.'

'We weren't *that* young.'

'Young enough. I wasn't ready for . . . *this*,' he says, motioning in the space between us, finally admitting the obvious — that it was *him*, not me. He broke up with me.

I nod, as if I understand his assessment, even though I really don't. Yes, we were young, but in some ways, young love seems the most robust and idealistic, untarnished by everyday hardships. Leo threw in the towel *before* we were ever really tested. Maybe because he didn't *want* to be tested. Maybe because he assumed we would fail. Maybe because, at the time, he just didn't love me enough.

'Would staying with me have felt like . . . settling?' I ask.

The word *settling* echoes in my head, gnawing at my heart and filling me with trepidation. It is a word I've avoided for months, even in my own, private thoughts, but I suddenly can't avoid it any longer. In some ways, it feels like the scary heart of the matter — the fear that I settled when I said 'I do' to Andy. That I should have held out for this kind of love. That I should have believed that Leo would, someday, return to me.

'Hell, no,' Leo says, shaking his head with frustration. 'That wasn't it, and you know it.'

I start to pin him down further, but he offers and unprompted explanation. 'Look, Ellie. You *were* the one . . . You *are* the one . . . If such a thing exists . . . '

I look into his eyes, his pupils lost in the dark brown around them. My head spins as I glance away, refusing to get sucked back into his gaze when so much is at risk.

'Okay,' I say.

It is a wholly inadequate response, but the only one that feels safe in this emerging moment of truth.

'So . . . what do *you* think?' he says. 'What do *you* want?'

I close my eyes, feeling suspended in time and a little disoriented, the way you sometimes feel when you awaken in a strange place and momentarily forget where you are. Then I look at Leo again, and suddenly realize with shock and a dash of terror that this choice, taken away from me years ago, first by Leo, then by Margot, is now mine to make. Finally. I unwittingly imagine myself at a literal fork in the road, the kind that belongs in a spooky Disney animation. Two twisting, dirt paths. Two signs attached to gnarled trees, pointing in opposite directions. This way for Andy. That way for Leo.

I uncross my arms, letting them fall to my sides, my fingertips grazing the buttery soft leather of Leo's new couch. Then I silently replay Suzanne's parting words, wondering if my disillusioned, unlucky-in-love sister is onto something. It's not about what might have been. And it's not about whether I have genuine feelings for Leo now, underneath the layers of nostalgia, lust, unrequited love. It's really not about Leo at *all*.

It's about Andy, plainly, simply.

It's about whether I *truly* love my husband.

'I think I should go,' I say, the answer, always in my heart, finally crystallizing in my head, too.

Leo returns his hand to my leg, this time with slightly more weight. 'Ellen . . . don't . . . '

My mind races — as I hear only half of what he says next. Something about not wanting to lose me again. Something about how he knows that I'm married, but that we are too good together. He closes with, 'I miss *us*' — which is more powerful and compelling than merely missing *me* — especially because I feel the same way. I miss us, too. I always have, and probably always will. Overcome with grief and the sense of impending, final loss, I touch his hand. Sometimes there are no happy endings. No matter what, I'll be losing something, some*one*.

But maybe that's what it all comes down to. Love, *not* as a surge of passion, but as a choice to commit to something, someone, no matter what obstacles or temptations stand in the way. And maybe making that choice, again and again, day in and day out, year after year, says more about love than never having a choice to make at all.

I look into Leo's eyes, feeling heartbroken, but resolved, and somehow freed.

'I *have* to go,' I say, standing slowly, methodically gathering my things as if I'm moving in slow motion.

Leo stands along with me, reluctantly helping me into my coat and following me to his door, then onto his porch. As we head down the stairs, an errant cab appears in the distance, drifting toward us, down the otherwise desolate street. An omen to stay on course. I make my way onto the sidewalk, step off the curb, maneuver between two parked cars, and wave to the driver. Leo stands at a short distance, watching.

'Where are you going?' he asks. His voice is calm, but there is something frantic in his eyes. Something I've never seen before. A short time ago, I might have basked in it, feeling victorious, healed. Now it only makes me more sad.

'To my hotel,' I say, nodding at the driver as he puts my bags in the trunk.

'Will you call me when you get there?'

'Yes,' I say, wondering if I will keep this promise.

Leo walks toward me, puts his hand on my arm, and says my name in one final protest.

'I'm sorry,' I say, pulling away and sliding into

the backseat. I force a smile that feels brave, my vision starting to blur with tears that I frantically blink away. Then I close the cab door, holding my palm up to the window to say good-bye. Just like I did the morning after our red-eye flight.

Only this time, I don't cry, and I don't look back.

36

We cross the Queensboro Bridge in what feels like record time, moving against the heavy flow of commuters, racing toward the lights of Manhattan. Something about our speed, and my driver's haphazard lane changes, makes my departure from Leo's apartment feel like a very narrow escape. One swerve away from disaster.

As I sit in the middle of the backseat and stare through the partition out the front window, I struggle to digest the last twenty-four hours, and especially the past few minutes, feeling my first pang of remorse for crossing that black-and-white, physical line.

I can't believe I cheated on my husband — on *Andy*.

With a measure of self-serving irony, I reassure myself that perhaps I *needed* to kiss Leo to really let go of him — and dismiss the notion that staying in my marriage is *any* version of settling, or that I'm with Andy by default. After all, isn't settling about having no options at all? About taking something because it's better than nothing? I finally *had* a real choice. And I chose.

This epiphany is followed by another flash of insight, as I realize that for the longest time, I saw Andy as perfect, and our life together as perfect. And in some bizarre way, once Leo came back into my life, this yellow-brick road started to feel like settling. Settling for perfection, for all the things that you're *supposed* to want. A good family. A beautiful home. Wealth. It was almost as if I discounted my feelings, because surely I couldn't truly be in love with Andy, too, on top of all those check marks in his column. Subconsciously, I think I assumed that any feelings I had for dark, difficult, distant Leo *had* to be more legitimate. The stuff of sad love songs.

As we navigate our way through Upper East Side traffic, I remember how my mother once told me that it's just as easy to love a rich man as a poor one, one of her many bits of advice that seemed old-fashioned and inapplicable to me — and not only because I was still a kid. We were in the parking lot of the bank, and had just run into her high school boyfriend, a guy named Mike Callas who my mother had broken up with for my father after Mike left for college. Suzanne and I had looked at his yearbook photo plenty of times, deciding that despite dopey-looking ears, he was pretty cute with loads of dark, wavy hair. But upon our meeting, the hair was mostly gone, making his ears look even bigger, and he had faded into just another doughy, middle-aged man with nondescript features. Making matters worse, he had a smile too big to trust — although maybe I just assumed the last part because he drove off in a flashy Cadillac right after kissing my mother's hand and making her giggle. Still, I sensed no real nostalgia or misgivings from my mother — even after her rather unromantic advice — although perhaps I simply wasn't old enough to look for it.

But now I wonder what she was *really* thinking

at the time, how she truly felt about my father and Mike. Did she ever regret her choices? Were her decisions more clear-cut than mine — or are there always shades of gray when it comes to matters of the heart? I wish I could ask her, but suddenly *feel* her answer, just as I picture Andy in our kitchen with his loosened tie, disheveled suit. I envision him carefully reading the instructions on a box of frozen pizza, contemplating whether to microwave it or go the extra mile and preheat the oven, all the while doing his best to forget me and his note on the counter.

If you go, don't come back.

I realize with a stab of fear that just because I am making *my* choice, doesn't mean that Andy will make the same one. Especially if I tell him what I just did with Leo — which I see no real way around. Panic rises in me as I feel Andy slipping away from me. I suddenly want to see his face more than anything in the world — something that impending loss has a way of doing to you.

'Change of plans,' I say, leaning toward the front seat.

'Where to now?' my driver says.

My heart pounds as I blurt out the address of my old apartment. *Our* old apartment. I need to be there again. I need to remember how it was. How it can still be again, with a lot of work and a little luck.

My cabbie nods nonchalantly, turning down Second Avenue. Signs, lights, cabs, people blur by my window. I close my eyes. When I open them again, we are turning onto Thirty-seventh

Street. I take a deep breath and slowly exhale, feeling both relieved and remorseful as I pay my fare, step out of the cab, and gather my bags.

Alone on the sidewalk, I gaze up at our building and the black night enveloping it. Then I sit on the worn stone steps and find my phone in my pocket. Before I can change my mind, I dial Andy's cell, shocked when his hello comes back live.

'Hi,' I say, thinking that it feels like days — years — since we last talked.

I wait for him to speak, but when he doesn't, I say, 'Guess where I am?'

'Where?' he says, sounding remote, weary, and very wary. He is clearly in no mood for a guessing game. I can't blame him for that. I can't blame him for much.

'Our old apartment,' I say, shivering.

He doesn't ask why. Perhaps because he knows why. I know, too — even though I'm having trouble pinpointing it.

'Lights are on at our place,' I say, looking up at our living room windows and imagining the cozy, warm scene inside. It occurs to me that the new residents could be miserable, but somehow I doubt it.

'Oh, yeah?' Andy says distractedly.

'Yeah,' I say as I hear someone talking in the background. Maybe it's the television. Or maybe he's out, at a bar or restaurant, contemplating the singles scene. My mind races as I consider what to say next, but everything feels fragile and fraught with landmines, lies of omission, half-truths.

'Do you hate me?' I finally say, realizing that I had a similar exchange with Leo earlier, when he accused me of hating him when we broke up. I wonder why hate so often feels like a component of love — or at least a measuring stick for it. I hold my breath, awaiting his response.

He finally sighs and says, 'Ellen. You know I don't hate you.'

Not yet, I think, fearing that I'll never summon the courage to tell him what I did, but praying that I will someday have the opportunity to cross that bridge.

'I'm so sorry, Andy,' I say, apologizing for more than he yet knows.

He hesitates, as I wonder if he somehow, instinctively, knows what I did — and maybe even *why* I did it. There is a catch in his voice as he says, 'I'm sorry, too.'

Instead of feeling relief or gratitude, more guilt washes over me. Andy's certainly not faultless — no one *ever* is in a marriage — but in comparison to what I've just done, he has nothing to be sorry for. Not our move to Atlanta. Not siding with Ginny. Not all the golf. Not the disregard he seems to have for my career. Not even his threat last night — which suddenly seems entirely fair.

A bloated few seconds pass before he says, 'So I just got off the phone with Webb.'

Something tells me that he is not making small talk. 'Is Margot okay?' I ask.

'Yeah,' Andy says. 'But based on her intermittent groans, I'd say there's a baby on the way.'

My heart skips a beat and my throat tightens. 'She's in labor?'

'I think so,' Andy says. 'False alarm this afternoon. She went to the hospital, and they sent her home. But they're on their way back in now. Her contractions are about eight minutes apart . . . '

I look at my watch and cross my fingers that the baby comes tomorrow. Not on the day that I kissed Leo. It is a technicality, but at this point, I will take what I can get.

'So exciting,' I say. And I *am* excited — but wistful and sad, too, remembering how I once pictured this moment.

I suddenly realize that sometime over the last few hours, I have absolved Margot for what she did — and hope she will someday forgive me, too. I think of how life takes unexpected twists and turns, sometimes through sheer happenstance — like running into Leo on the street. Sometimes through calculated decisions — like Margot's. Or mine, tonight, when I left Leo. In the end, it can all be called fate, but to me, it is more a matter of faith.

'Are you going to the hospital?' I ask Andy.

'Not yet . . . ' he says, his voice trailing off.

'I wish I were with you,' I say, realizing with relief and gratitude and absolute joy that it is the truth. I wish I were with my *whole* family.

'In Atlanta or New York?' he asks somewhat wryly — enough for me to know that if he's not smiling, he very nearly is.

'Doesn't matter,' I say as a cab turns onto our old block and slows in front of me. I look up at

399

the sky, wishing I could see stars — or at least the moon — before returning my gaze to the taxi. Then, the door swings open, and Andy appears before me, wearing the exact suit and red tie I just imagined, along with his navy overcoat. For a few seconds, I am confused in that thrilling way I haven't felt since I was a child, back when I still believed in magic — and other things too good to be true. Then I see Andy's hesitant, hopeful smile — one that I will never forget — and I know that this is really happening. It is good *and* true.

'Hey, there,' he says, taking the few steps toward me.

'Hey, there,' I say, standing, returning his smile. 'What are you doing . . . here?'

'Finding you,' he says, looking up at me. He puts his hand on the railing, inches from mine.

'How . . . ?' I say, searching for the right question.

'I flew up this evening . . . I was already in a cab when you called . . . '

My mind clicks through the logistics as it sinks in that Andy got on a plane to see *me*, knowing that he could miss the birth of his sister's baby. Tears form again, but this time for very different reasons.

'I can't believe you're here,' I say.

'I can't believe I found you here.'

'I'm sorry,' I say again, now crying.

'Oh, honey. Don't,' he says tenderly. 'I shouldn't have changed our life and expected you to roll with everything . . . It wasn't fair.'

He takes one step up, so now we are a stair

400

apart, looking into each other's eyes, but not yet touching. 'I want you to be happy,' he whispers.

'I know,' I say, thinking of my work, New York, all the things I miss about our old life. 'But I shouldn't have left. Not like that.'

'Maybe you had to.'

'Maybe,' I say, thinking of my final embrace with Leo, that last kiss. How different this moment feels, for so many reasons. I tell myself that no two loves are identical — but that I don't have to compare anymore. 'I'm still sorry . . . '

'It doesn't matter now,' Andy says — and although I'm not sure exactly what he means, I also know *entirely* what he means.

'Tell me we're going to be okay,' I say, wiping away my tears as more stream down my cheeks.

'We're going to be *better* than okay,' he says, his eyes welling, too.

I collapse into him, remembering that night washing dishes in his parents' kitchen when I first wondered if I could actually fall in love with Margot's brother. I remember deciding that it was possible — that *anything* is possible — and then, sure enough, it happened. And right now, under the dark autumn sky, I remember exactly *why* it happened — if there ever really is a why when it comes to love.

'Let's go home,' I breathe into Andy's ear, hopeful that we can still get a flight back to Atlanta tonight.

'Are you sure?' he says, his voice low, familiar, sexy.

'Yes, I'm sure,' I say, thinking that for the first

time since I saw Leo in the intersection, maybe the first time *ever*, I am following my head *and* my heart. Both have led me here, to this decision, to this moment, to Andy. It is exactly where I belong and where I want to stay, forever.

One year and one day later . . .

It is Louisa's first birthday. I am boarding a plane at LaGuardia, bound for the elaborate party Margot is throwing for her daughter. I make the trip often, sometimes alone, sometimes with Andy, as we shuttle back and forth between our home in Buckhead and our one-bedroom apartment in the Village. Our living arrangement seems to puzzle many, particularly Stella, who just asked the other day how I decide what shoes to keep in which closet — or do I simply buy two pairs of everything? I smiled, thinking that I will never understand her obsession with shoes — just as she doesn't understand how Andy and I can be so happy with our messy compromise. It's not perfect, but it works for us, for now.

I still prefer the city — and feel most like myself there. I love working alongside Sabina, Julian, and Oscar in the old, drafty loft — and waiting for Andy or Suzanne to join me on the weekends. But I've begun to really appreciate Atlanta, too, tolerating the crowd I once disdained and making my own friends, independent of the Grahams. I've also discovered a surprising professional niche in our new town, doing child portraiture. It began with Louisa, quickly expanding to more. It's not glamorous work, but the quiet focus on family is satisfying, and I can almost envision a time when it might fulfill me completely.

Then again, maybe that will never happen. Maybe Andy and I will always have to work to find the right balance — within our family, our marriage, our lives. Yes, I am Andy's wife. And I'm a Graham. But I'm also Suzanne's sister, my mother's daughter, my own person.

As for Margot, things remained chilly between us for a long while, both of us stubbornly pretending that there was no rift — which only made the rift seem bigger, more insurmountable. Until finally one day, she came to me and asked if we could talk.

I nodded, watching her struggle for the right words as she swaddled a whimpering Louisa.

'Maybe I shouldn't have gotten involved the way I did,' she started nervously. 'I was just so scared, Ellen . . . and so surprised by . . . the disloyalty of it all.'

I felt a wave of guilt, remembering everything, knowing she was right — I *was* disloyal. But I still looked into her eyes and held my ground.

'I know how you must have felt,' I said, conjuring how I feel whenever Suzanne is hurt by Vince, by *anyone*. 'Andy's your brother . . . But what about our loyalty to each other? What about *our* friendship?'

She looked down, running her finger across Louisa's smooth, round cheek, as I found the courage to tell her the simple truth.

'I needed to go,' I said. 'I *had* to go.'

I waited for her to meet my gaze, and when she did, I could see in her eyes that something had clicked, and she finally understood that my feelings for Leo had nothing to do with her brother, nothing to do with our friendship.

She rocked the baby gently and said, 'I'm sorry, Ellen.'

I nodded as she continued. 'I'm sorry I didn't tell you he came back. I'm sorry I wasn't there for you . . . '

'I'm sorry, too,' I said. 'I really am.'

Then we both cried for a long time, right along with Louisa, until we finally had no choice but to laugh. It was a moment only best friends or sisters could share.

I close my eyes now, as the plane gathers speed on the runway, and we ascend into the sky. I no longer fear flying — at least not in the way I used to — but my heart still races, the old stirrings of anxiety commingling with memories of the past. It is the only time I really think of Leo anymore. Perhaps because of that red-eye flight we shared. Perhaps because I can practically look down and see his building from my window, the spot where I last saw him a year and a day ago.

I have not spoken to him in that long. Not to return his two calls. Not even when I sent him the photos from Coney Island, including the one I took of him on the beach. There were things I considered saying in an enclosed note. *Thank you . . . I'm sorry . . . I'll always love you.*

They were all true — and still are — but were better left unsaid, just as I decided never to confess to Andy how close I came to losing everything. Instead, I hold that day deep within myself, as a reminder that love is the sum of our choices, the strength of our commitments, the ties that bind us together.

We do hope that you have enjoyed reading this large print book.

Did you know that all of our titles are available for purchase?

We publish a wide range of high quality large print books including:
**Romances, Mysteries, Classics
General Fiction
Non Fiction and Westerns**

Special interest titles available in large print are:
**The Little Oxford Dictionary
Music Book
Song Book
Hymn Book
Service Book**

Also available from us courtesy of Oxford University Press:
**Young Readers' Dictionary
(large print edition)
Young Readers' Thesaurus
(large print edition)**

For further information or a free brochure, please contact us at:
**Ulverscroft Large Print Books Ltd.,
The Green, Bradgate Road, Anstey,
Leicester, LE7 7FU, England.
Tel:** (00 44) **0116 236 4325**
Fax: (00 44) **0116 234 0205**